MW00770842

Promise Me Sunshine

Promise Me Sunshine

A NOVEL

Cara Bastone

THE DIAL PRESS
NEW YORK

A Dial Press Trade Paperback Original

Copyright © 2025 by Cara Bastone
Dial Delights Extras copyright © 2025 by Penguin Random House LLC
Excerpt from *The Naked Eye* by Cara Bastone copyright © 2025
by Cara Bastone

Penguin Random House values and supports copyright. Copyright fuels creativity, encourages diverse voices, promotes free speech, and creates a vibrant culture. Thank you for buying an authorized edition of this book and for complying with copyright laws by not reproducing, scanning, or distributing any part of it in any form without permission. You are supporting writers and allowing Penguin Random House to continue to publish books for every reader. Please note that no part of this book may be used or reproduced in any manner for the purpose of training artificial intelligence technologies or systems.

All rights reserved.

Published in the United States by The Dial Press, an imprint of Random House, a division of Penguin Random House LLC, New York.

THE DIAL PRESS is a registered trademark and the colophon is a trademark of Penguin Random House LLC.

DIAL DELIGHTS and colophon are trademarks of Penguin Random House LLC.

This book contains an excerpt from the forthcoming book *The Naked Eye* by Cara Bastone. This excerpt has been set for this edition only and may not reflect the final content of the forthcoming edition.

Library of Congress Cataloging-in-Publication Data
Names: Bastone, Cara, author.
Title: Promise me sunshine: a novel / Cara Bastone.
Description: New York, NY: The Dial Press, 2025.
Identifiers: LCCN 2024015326 (print) | LCCN 2024015327 (ebook) |
ISBN 9780593595732 (trade paperback) | ISBN 9780593595749 (ebook) |
ISBN 9780593821497 (Ebook)
Subjects: LCGFT: Romance fiction. | Novels.
Classification: LCC PS3602.A84956 P76 2024 (print) | LCC PS3602.
A84956 (ebook) | DDC 813/.6—dc23/eng/20240404
LC record available at https://lccn.loc.gov/2024015326
LC ebook record available at https://lccn.loc.gov/2024015327

Printed in the United States of America on acid-free paper

randomhousebooks.com

2 4 6 8 9 7 5 3 1

Ornament by OneyWhyStudio/Adobe Stock

For anyone who has ever been a Miles for someone else.
I know it can sometimes feel thankless. So, thank you.
This book is a love letter to you.

And, of course, for Jon. Who carried me on his back.

PART ONE

After

Chapter One

This baby will not stop judging me.

The B train brakes and we all slide two inches to the side. Perched atop their mother's lap, the straps of a bright red sunhat pinned under chubby cheeks, somber, unblinking eyes, the baby studies me, trying to decide if I have a soul.

I stick my tongue out and make my ears dance.

No reaction.

I pull my cheeks out to the sides and do rabbit teeth.

Not even a blink.

Finally, as the train is pulling into my stop, in a last-minute bid to be judged human, I use my ponytail as a mustache.

And there. Finally. I get one radiant, two-toothed smile.

Thank goodness. I guess there is a soul in this scraped-out husk of mine after all. I wave goodbye and bound up, off the train, and head west. It's dog-breath hot out here and I can't believe I've mustered up the energy for this.

But the thing about losing the person you love the most on earth is—somehow—you still have to do mundane things like tie your shoes and make enough money to continue to exist in this punishing world. So, I plod on. Toward yet another short-term nannying gig. Just to keep the Froot Loops on the table. Even though I'd really rather crawl into that trash can over there and emerge in about a decade.

Oh, look. I'm here. It's a gigantic brick apartment building. The lobby is populated by a group of people who look so happy I wouldn't be surprised if their lives suddenly turned into a musical. They mob the doorman with luggage, so I go up on tiptoes and shout to him where I'm headed.

"Ah. They're expecting you," he calls to me in an Eastern European accent. "Eighteenth floor."

By the time the elevator dings, I'm in a better mood. One of my former babysitting families recommended me to Reese so that I can help out with her kid while she's out of town this weekend. Besides, here in the worst six months of my life, the only thing that's brought me even a hint of happiness has been hanging out with the kids I babysit. I'm between jobs right now, so this new family is likely going to be the only spot of light in my life for a bit.

I ring the doorbell and ten seconds later, perfection personified answers the door. She's got blond hair in a high ponytail and is decked out in head-to-toe Lululemon.

"Hi, I'm Reese." She holds out her hand and smiles so toothily that I find myself grinning back.

"Lenny. Nice to meet you."

"Thank you for agreeing on such short notice. My friend Harper usually helps out for stuff like this, but she's busy during the days this weekend. She's the one who will be staying overnight with Ainsley. Anyways, come in, please. Did you get my email?"

"I did," I assure her. It was literally six and a half pages single-spaced and filled with so much loving detail on how to care for her daughter that it teared me up. I come inside and kick off my shoes, straightening them when I realize that all the other shoes are in perfect pairs. We're in a roomy front hallway, painted a trendy mauve and lined with gigantic black-and-white photographs.

"So, Ainsley is back in the—" The doorbell rings again

right after Reese closes the door, and she frowns. She pulls the door back open and her shoulders cinch about two inches upward when she sees who it is. "What's up, Miles?"

There's a man standing in the crack of the door that Reese has just opened, and I get the feeling he might have wedged his foot in there so she can't close it.

He's not good-looking, really. Low-grade sexy. He's wearing a used-to-be-black hoodie stretched over two big shoulders and faded blue jeans. Viciously short dark hair and the kind of stubble you can't ever shave away. Judging by that promising scowl, he's the type who'd really enjoy partaking in a public bathroom tryst with a near stranger. I can already see it now. He and I will have a tumultuous two-year fuck-fest, defined by me perpetually being sent to voicemail. He'll stand me up on Thanksgiving, thereby dumping me. But then he'll realize horrifically, cataclysmically, that he's been in love with me this whole time. He'll come crawling back to me on all four appendages. I'll make him wait outside my door for a year before I let him back in. Eventually there'll be a ring with a black diamond so dark I can see his soul inside it. We'll get married on Halloween and his wedding present to me will be a sex toy. It sounds ecstatically fun.

It's probably apropos to mention that I instantaneously spin elaborate fantasies about almost every man I ever meet. Not to say that this guy isn't special; I have just fallen in love, after all.

He looks over Reese's shoulder and spots me, his gaze narrowing and his eyes taking me in from socks to eyebrows. I don't think I've passed the test because he leans forward and thus commences an aggressive (and nearly silent) whisper fight between the two of them and it's getting a little icy in here.

I occupy myself with the black-and-white prints for something to do. That's when I realize that what I'm looking at are actually gigantic photographs of someone very famous.

"Sorry about that," Reese chirps at my elbow, and I jolt. I hadn't heard her approach. She's got a plastic smile super-glued to her face and when I look back, the man is still standing in the now fully open door, glowering in our general direction.

"No problem," I say, and then jog one thumb toward the portraits. "Big Willie Nelson fan?"

"Hm? Oh! Ha. Willie's great. But that's my dad there next to him. They toured together for a while."

"Oh, wow!" I lean in and sure enough, there's another guy in all the pics, at the mic in some and jamming on a steel guitar in others.

"Carp Hollis," she says, supplying the name I clearly couldn't come up with. "Ever heard of him?"

"Your dad is Carp Hollis?" I don't know much about blue-grass or country, but even I know that he's kinda royalty.

"Yup. That's Dad." She looks affectionately at the pic-tures before her expression clouds. I instantly recognize that look, and my stomach drops to my toes. "He passed about a year and a half ago. This is his apartment. Ainsley and I are still getting used to it, to be honest . . . Why don't you come meet Ains."

She starts to usher me out of the hallway.

"Reese!" calls the man who is still standing in the open door.

She doesn't turn around. "Then stay if you want, Miles!"

I'm looking back and forth between them. "Um. I'm Lenny," I offer to him with a little wave of my hand. "Lenny Bellamy."

He's ignoring me, staring daggers into the back of Reese's head.

"That's Miles. Ainsley's uncle," Reese finally says into the silence. "He lives upstairs. He'll probably be around today, if that's okay with you."

"Oh, uh. Sure?" I don't usually enjoy babysitting with an audience, but he *is* my future husband after all, as prickly as he may be.

The apartment is gargantuan and curated and polished. Kitchen, living room, dining room, a handful of bedrooms and bathrooms, and then, finally, in what she refers to as the "drawing room," is a little somebody who is, in fact, drawing.

"Ains," Reese calls.

The little somebody doesn't stand, she just drops her colored pencil and pivots on her knees to face us. She's about seven years old, with dandelion levels of staticky hair. Tiny purple glasses magnify her eyeballs to twice their size and she's swimming in a very faded Madonna concert tee. "Is that a cat eating lasagna on your shirt?" she asks me.

"It's Garfield," I clarify.

"Who's that?"

"Oh, it's a good thing we're going to hang out all weekend because we've got a lot of ground to cover."

She nervously tugs the hem of her T-shirt. "Okay."

"I'm Lenny," I say, and I leave the adults behind to sit next to her. "What's your name?"

She frowns at me. "Mom didn't tell you?"

I smile. "She did, but people usually start getting to know each other by exchanging names."

"Oh. Yeah. I'm Ainsley." She makes a puke face.

"You don't like your name?"

"There are three other Ainsleys at my school. Different grades but . . ." She shrugs.

"Oh, really? Wow. Ainsley sounds like a unique name to me. If you could choose any other name, what would it be?"

She shrugs again, still nervous to meet me. "I don't know. Something cooler. Like . . . Blackbeard. Or Darth Vader."

I burst out laughing, and she tries to hide her pleased smile while she plays with the hem of her T-shirt.

I instantly like her, and I like her mom more by extension. This uptown address, Reese's perfect ponytail, head to toe in Lululemon, I would have put some serious money on Ainsley having been carefully manicured into a mini-Reese. I've seen it before. But Reese and Ainsley are a delightfully odd couple.

Reese is leaning in the doorway and smiling at us. "Listen, I'm going to get a little work done in my home office for a bit before I head out. Come get me if you need anything, Ains."

"'Kay."

Reese disappears with a wave and Ainsley does a double take at the doorway. "Oh. Hi, Miles."

"Hey. I'll be around too . . . if you need me."

Ainsley looks instantly confused. "Why would I need *you?*" she asks in that guileless yet utterly gutting way that children have.

For the length of a single camera flash Miles looks mortally wounded. But then his gaze hardens as it flicks over to me. "Just in case," he grumbles.

Miles disappears and Ainsley turns back to the hem of her shirt.

Well, ohhhhkay. Guess we've got some *family dynamics* to navigate here.

I spot some computer paper and help myself. Ainsley rolls a few colored pencils in my direction. Half an hour later—after her stomach starts making goblin noises—we're exploring the fridge and pantry, chatting about what we could make and laughing at how bad the fancy cheese in the cheese drawer smells.

Twice I think there's someone else standing there, but when I look up, we're alone. The third time, it's Reese in the doorway, smiling.

"I'm gonna head out in a minute," Reese says. "Do you wanna come help me pick my jewelry for the weekend, sweetie?"

Ainsley scampers after her mother and I'm left in the kitchen to make lunch. I put my hands on my hips and start a slow perusal of my options.

"How old are you?"

I jolt at the unexpected deep voice behind me. Miles is at the other end of the kitchen, leaning up against the counter.

"Twenty-eight. Are you staying for lunch?"

"I don't need you to feed me."

Good thing I'm not easily scared off. "Do you think Ainsley would want the white cheddar mac or the double-cheese stars and moons?"

"I think her mother would prefer she eats something that isn't pure chemicals."

I deftly ignore that, because Reese is presumably the person who bought the mac and cheese in the first place. I start searching through the cabinets for a pot. "How old are *you*?"

He frowns. "Got a lot of childcare experience?"

"Yes."

He's waiting for me to elaborate, but when I don't he crosses his arms over his chest. "What are you looking for?"

"A pot. There's a lot of real estate in this kitchen." I've opened six sets of doors and have yet to find the cookware.

He doesn't direct me toward it, which leads me to believe he either wants to make my life as hard as possible or he doesn't know his way around their kitchen.

Is *uncle* a euphemism? They don't seem to know each other very well. Or even *like* each other very well. Based on the way he's acting, I might have wondered if he was perhaps Ainsley's overprotective father, but Reese made it very clear when we spoke over the phone earlier in the week that she conceived Ainsley on her own and she's a single mother. Probably so I wouldn't put my foot in my mouth and ask Ainsley about her dad.

"Okey-doke," Reese says, reappearing with a rolling suitcase in one hand and Ainsley attached to the other. "I've gotta jet if I'm gonna make my flight." She bends and gives Ainsley a squeeze. "It's gonna be great. And it's only two nights. I'll see you after school on Monday."

Ainsley nods like they've already been over this. "I know."

"Okay. Well, Lenny, thank you. You're a lifesaver. Call me for *any* reason."

She gives Miles a nod and then heads to the front door. Ainsley trots after her and I migrate in that direction, wanting to give them some space for their goodbye but also wanting to be on hand.

Reese stops at the front door and slides her shoes on, saying something quietly to Ainsley.

"I *know*, Mom," Ainsley says, somewhat petulantly. "Just go already. You'll be late."

Reese gives her one last kiss on her staticky head and then the door clicks shut behind her.

Ainsley immediately power walks back in my direction, and even from here I can see that her eyes have gone watery and her chin is starting to quiver.

"What kind of movies do you like?" I ask her.

She skids to a stop. "I'm not allowed to watch movies during the day."

"Well, let's make an exception."

"Really?"

"Really."

"I like Indiana Jones."

I'm charmed. "Let's do it."

Ainsley happily eats two bowls of stars and moons while Indy punches his way through a crowd of fascists, and I consider that a win.

By the time we're done with lunch she doesn't seem so weepy anymore, but I want to keep her as distracted as possible, so we dig through the pantry and unearth a box of cake mix and frosting. We gleefully make a gigantic mess in the kitchen and I let her turn the vanilla frosting acid green with food coloring.

"You wanna know an old family tradition of mine?"

"Sure," she says, carefully mixing the frosting while her tongue is sticking out. She's wearing an apron fifty times too big and standing on one of the dining room chairs to reach the counter.

"When we make cupcakes, we always make one lucky one and hide it in with the rest."

"How do you make a lucky cupcake?"

"Well, first you fill the cups with batter, and then you pick one of them to be the lucky one. This one or this one?" I ask.

"That one." She points.

"Okay. And then you stick something unexpected into its batter."

"Like what?"

I open the fridge and consider my options. "Liiiike . . . ooh! Green olives. Or a little bit of lunch meat, maybe? How about—"

She bursts out laughing. "*Gross!*"

"Yes," I agree. "But so much fun. What should we choose?"

She scrambles down from the chair to come look. "How about those onions that Mom puts in fancy drinks?"

"Cocktail onions. PERFECT. I think you have a knack for this."

I open the jar for her and she pokes the onion so far into the cupcake she's got batter up to her third knuckle.

Her mom calls to check in while the cupcakes are baking and Ainsley starts to cry after they hang up. It seems like a good time to offer the little bit of videogame time she's allotted each day, and she jumps at the chance. By the time she's done zooming around the universe in a bright pink rocket ship, the cupcakes are cool enough to frost.

We each have a cupcake after dinner, and we decide we're both simultaneously relieved and disappointed to not get the lucky cupcake.

"It's getting late," Miles says from out of nowhere, and Ainsley and I both squeak and jump.

"Are you still here?!"

"It's her bedtime," he says, frowning and crossing his arms over his chest. I wouldn't say he's got a very gentle bedside manner, but I forgive him because he's wearing *that* sweatshirt and I'm in love and he's going to be my everything one day.

"Oh, you're right. Yeah. Things kind of got away from me."

"No kidding." He's frowning at the spilled batter on the counter, the dishes in the dripping sink, the opened packages of meat and cheese and bread I used to make sandwiches for dinner.

"I'll get to it," I say with a wave. I pull up Reese's email and refer to pages four and five. "Ainsley, shall we start the bedtime proceedings?"

She climbs down from the table and pads back toward her end of the apartment without a single complaint. Either she's tired or she doesn't know me well enough to argue yet.

She takes a shower and I help with the tricky buttons on her pajamas after she brushes her teeth. She E.T.'s herself into an impressively gigantic pile of stuffies and asks if she can read for a while before bed. I hand over her bedtime book, which is called *Squirrel Genius Mystery File #48*, and something tells me she's already read the other forty-seven.

"I'll be in the living room until Harper gets here to spend the night, but I'll see you bright and early, okay?"

She nods solemnly, already turning toward the wall with her book, and she just looks so tiny in her PJs. I let her have her privacy and gently click the door closed behind me.

The carpet in this place is a foot and a half thick so I pad soundlessly back toward the kitchen, freezing when I hear Miles hissing into his phone in the kitchen.

"Come on, Reese. She let Ainsley watch TV all day. They ate nothing but crap. Videogames for hours. The house is a total mess. Where did you even find this girl? . . . She looks like she's fresh off a week-and-a-half bender. Shouldn't we, I don't know, drug test her or something?"

And wow. Just like that. My love fantasy goes up in smoke.

What a total asshole.

I march into the kitchen and raise my eyebrows at him. He goes rigid, his eyes on mine, self-consciously running a hand over his hair. To my satisfaction he breaks eye contact first and leaves the room, finishing his phone call with Reese elsewhere.

In a flash I've got the kitchen polished to a high shine, so I gather my things and set up shop in the living room to wait for Harper.

I'm on the couch and digging through my backpack when:

"So—"

"Ah!" I jump at his sudden voice behind me. My backpack tumbles to the ground. "Quit doing that!"

"Sorry," he mumbles, and I can't tell which part he's apologizing for, but either way it's nowhere near enough. His eyes drop to my spilled backpack. My wallet and a book have skidded across the floor toward his feet. Our hands reach them at the same moment, but his freeze.

Grief and You, the title of the book blares up at us. *Life after the Death of a Loved One.*

I can feel his eyes flick from the book to my face and back.

I hate this book so much. If my mother hadn't given it to me at the funeral, inscribed with her sweet, perfect handwriting, I probably would have launched it into the Hudson River by now.

"So—" Oh, God. He's trying to talk again.

No. I've had enough for one night. I scramble the book into my bag.

"There are fresh-baked cupcakes in the kitchen," I offer sweetly, beating him to the punch and watching his face scrunch in confusion at my change in tone.

I turn away from him and flick on the TV. After a moment he seems to accept that there will be no more discussion from me and wordlessly heads back into the kitchen. I cross my fingers that he's selecting the cupcake at the top of the pyramid I engineered.

I strain toward the kitchen, turning the volume down just enough to hear him gag and cough. "What the fuck?" he mutters incredulously as he tosses the lucky cupcake in the trash.

I sigh with sweet, sweet satisfaction and settle back into the couch.

Two best friends sit facing one another on a twin bed. One of them will die too soon. The other one is me.

They are eating salt-and-vinegar potato chips and trying to figure out how life could possibly go on after unspeakable loss.

"Look . . . after this you're gonna have to come back to life at some point. You can't live dead, you know."

"Says who."

"Says me, your best friend."

"Fine then, Wise One. Lay it out for me. How. How am I supposed to come back to life after . . ."

"Oh, come on, complainer. Where's that happy-face T-shirt I bought you? You think that was ironic? No way. Life is for the living, yadda yadda."

"Easy for you to say, butthead. You're the one who won't have to go through all the after."

"OMG! I just came up with a brilliant idea for a T-shirt slogan. Ready?"

"Hit me."

"Life is what happens during the yadda yadda."

"We're going to be rich."

"Right?"

" . . . "

" . . . "

"You really have no idea how to live again on the other side of this? Like, seriously? No ideas?"

"Not one."

"Okay, fine. Here's what we'll do. We'll make it so easy. The easiest. We'll make it multiple choice."

"My life?"

"Yeah. We'll make a list. All you'll have to do is check the boxes. Pick task, perform task, reclaim your joie de vivre."

"A list for living again?"

"Bingo."

"Look, yes, you're my best friend. You obviously mean well. I know I'm not easy to be around sometimes. But . . . can we just not talk about this? Trying to imagine living again. Living without—Can we just not talk about this, please?"

"We're making the list. If you want to throw it in the garbage afterward, that's on you. Where's my pink pen?"

"I can't stop you, can I?"

"Item number one on the Live Again list: fall in love with a gorgeous man who is obsessed with you and is, like, a fireman or something."

"Wow, you even wrote the 'or something.'"

"There should be a little wiggle room to increase the odds of it actually happening."

"'Kay. Got it. Gorgeous man. Should be easy."

"Atta girl. Item number two: wear ridiculously ugly clothes and pretend that they're expensive ugly, not cheap ugly. Then eat amuse bouche and go underbid on outrageously priced art."

"Unless 'amuse bouche' is a fancy word for 'chili dog,' I don't want it."

"Fine, just the art, then."

"The Met?"

"Always . . . I bet your mom would let you wear your grandma's vintage fur coats."

"Fine! But I want one of those little Jackie O hats where the lace comes down over your eyes."

"Deal. Wear whatever you want, the Met is on the list as its own bullet point. Now for the next item—"

"Can there be no more items for now? It hurts to think about it."

"I feel I should warn you. It's probably never going to not hurt. Just thought you should know."

"I know."

"And that's why you need the list. When I'm not around you can use it to—"

"Let's watch Clueless and eat BLTs."

"You're a true queen of distraction. Okay, fine, but only because you know bacon is my weak spot—Hey . . . You're not throwing the list in the trash?"

"Well. You're going through all this trouble to make it. I figure the least I can do is keep it safe."

This is a love story, I swear.

This is what happens when you've promised someone you'll live again.

Chapter Two

Little-known fact: the Staten Island Ferry is the city's only twenty-four-hour bar. It goes back and forth all night and they never kick you off. Which is extremely useful whenever I can't face going home.

I didn't see Miles again before this Harper person came to relieve me. I had to be back at work in just six hours, and let's just say the commute all the way out to Brooklyn and back was the reason I chose to call the Staten Island Ferry my home for the night.

Let's ignore the fact that even in the best of circumstances I avoid my apartment at all costs. It's a mausoleum and the physics of time and space do not make sense in there. I can step into my apartment and three days will pass with nothing but a box of cereal to eat and nary a shower.

So these days I prefer to sleep anywhere but my own bed.

Which is why at twelve-forty-five at night I find myself washing my face in the ferry's bathroom and admitting that this Miles guy might be right about my appearance. I've got raccoon eyes and messy hair—far too long and scraggly—tied back haphazardly. My skin is dry, no makeup. My (once beloved) eyebrow piercing looks depressingly like a mistake in this lighting. My clothes are rumpled from the day and it's clear I've lost way too much weight way too fast.

Just because he's right about the way I look doesn't make him less of an asshole. Because he blamed it on alcoholism or a drug addiction, which is dickish to disparage in the first place. But what am I supposed to do, wear a sign? *Not strung out, just having a debilitating mental health crisis while navigating the most excruciating chapter of my life.*

That should go over well at the babysitting gigs.

All of the peppy laughter and encouraging creativity I dug up for Ainsley evaporates as I look at my dripping face in the mirror. All I've got left is the suffocating, impending fog of the night, trying desperately to find sleep that will definitely not come.

I find a secluded area and prop my backpack behind my head. Hey, who turned on the waterworks. All the tears I didn't cry in front of Ainsley start sliding down my face.

Maybe I sleep. Hard to tell, really, but at five-thirty A.M. a businesswoman in pumps clacks past and I jolt back to full consciousness. I'm a symphony of creaky joints and yawns as I head to the other side of the ferry to wait for dry land.

Disembarking in Manhattan, I start the ascent back to Reese and Ainsley's. When I make it to the Upper West Side, I reach into my pocket and search out the little laminated slip of paper I carry with me everywhere I go. The corners, once sharp, are softened with relentless worrying from my fingers. It reminds me that all I have to do is get my shit together long enough to hang out with this awesome kid. I can do that much.

Once I'm on their elevator, I slide my hand off the laminated paper. By the time I step onto their floor, I've fully gathered myself for work.

Of course Miles is the first person I see, waiting outside the door to their apartment for Harper to come let him in.

"Oh. Hi," I say.

He grunts and stares at the closed door.

He's clearly not going to provide any chitchat to fill the

silence. Because he's a ghoul. But in my former life, I was actually quite a lovely person and apparently old habits die hard even when macheted. "How was your night?" I hear myself ask.

He turns and glances at me from head to toe. I'm sure I look like a Monster Mash loyalist.

"Restful," he says, and I swear there's a world buried in that word.

"How lucky," I reply, and Harper swings the door open.

"Come in! Come in." She's bent over, one finger slid into the back of the high heel she's hopping her way into. She's wearing an Ally McBeal–style skirt suit and absolutely devouring the look. A year ago, in my former life, I'd probably have demanded she write down what kind of shampoo she uses. Her eyes catch on Miles. "Oh. Miles. Reese mentioned you'd probably be here."

Miles scratches the back of his head and slightly lifts his chin.

That's it. That's the whole greeting.

Harper's brow comes down, but she turns back to me, clearly inured to him. "Ainsley is already up, but she hasn't had breakfast yet. See you around nine tonight, Lenny?"

"Sure! Great. Have a good day at work." I flash her a double thumbs-up and she grins and flashes one back to me.

And then she's off toward the elevator and I just manage to shoulder my way into the front door an inch before Miles.

"So," he says behind me, but then Ainsley slides into the hallway in socks, *Risky Business* style. "Hey, Lenny, come see what I made."

I follow her into the living room and even though there's a cartoon playing on the TV, Ainsley's got her back to it. All the stuffies from her bed have been carted out and they're organized in a formation. I drop to my knees next to her to better observe. There's a tie-dye bear on a little pedestal of books, facing all the other stuffies, who have been carefully arranged to sit shoulder to shoulder in a big square.

"They're at a concert," Ainsley informs me solemnly.

Of course! I love it. "Ah," I reply, just as solemn. "But where are their tickets?"

"Oh! I didn't think of that . . ."

I quickly jump up and head out to the drawing room to grab supplies and come back with some paper, colored pencils, and scissors. "I'll be back to check your tickets in a few minutes, okay?" I'm addressing the stuffed-animal attendees with my hands on my hips. "Anyone who hasn't got a ticket is going to get the boot."

"What's 'the boot'?" Ainsley asks.

I choose a sacrifice. It's a stuffed hippo with little wire glasses sewn on. I toss him in the air and then kick him to the other side of the room. "That's the boot."

Ainsley bursts into laughter.

I go to collect the hippo. "Sorry, sir. Ma'am. Esteemed peer. You were just an example of what happens to free-loaders."

Ainsley scrambles to start making tickets.

"I'm gonna make some breakfast, okay?"

She nods, already engrossed in the task. "Egg over easy and lox on toast, please."

Her mother already informed me that Ainsley has this for breakfast every single morning, rain or shine. But even so, I'm thoroughly charmed. I can't name a single other seven-year-old who voluntarily opts for smoked fish and runny eggs.

I'm just entering back into the email her mom sent me, explaining exactly how to prepare said breakfast, when I hear Ainsley pipe up from the living room.

"Oh! Hi, Miles. You're here again?"

"I just . . . came over," he says in that low voice that's so hard to hear.

"Why?" she persists, and I choke back a laugh. Children have a way of identifying the heart of the matter and giving it a sunburn.

Yes, Miles. Why the hell are you here?

He clears his throat. "I just thought I'd . . . come hang out."

It's not an actual answer, but Ainsley seems to accept it because there are no more questions.

I'm not an over-easy-lox-on-toast girl myself, but I'm just so dang curious that I make two portions. I sprinkle the final flourish of capers and red onion and turn to set our breakfasts on the kitchen table. I startle when I see Miles lurking there, frowning down at the coffee maker. He squints, frowns more, and then accidentally presses two buttons at once. It makes a sad little beep.

I slide the food onto the table and set myself in front of the coffee maker with a sigh.

He steps back and looks past me, eyes narrowing in on the plates.

I almost justify myself: *Reese and I agreed that I can eat whatever I want while I'm here, okay? It's customary to feed your babysitter when she's working all day, okay?* But I choose to let him stew in his ridiculous judgments instead, getting the coffee percolating in less than forty seconds and then stepping back into the living room.

As soon as Ainsley spots me I put my hands on my hips and affect a hard-line expression. "I'm here to take some tickets."

There're scraps of paper strewn in a wide arc. She's on

her knees, bouncing on her butt she's so excited. "Check the tickets!"

At first I think she's just excited to show me the tickets she carefully cut out for each stuffie. But then I realize her excitement is actually because she's only distributed tickets to half the stuffies. She wants me to give the other half the boot. I gleefully roust the ticketless stuffies, kicking them across the room and making Ainsley scream with laughter. She does a few herself and then decides she's too hungry to go on. We leave the mess behind and head into the kitchen.

Miles is posted at the other end of the table with a frown and a cup of coffee. My stomach sinks. Apparently he intends to have a front-row seat to everything Ainsley and I do.

An idea occurs.

"Hey."

Ainsley turns to look at me as she gulps orange juice with two hands.

"Should we be super fancy today?" I ask her.

"What do you mean?"

"I'll show you after breakfast."

We finish eating (I have to choke mine down—not my choice of textures; good thing I only gave myself a quarter portion) and bring her stuffies back to her room in armfuls. I flip open the dress-up bin I'd noticed the day before. It's even better stocked than I'd hoped for.

"See, we have a lot of things to do today," I explain to her. "Museums. Lunch at the teahouse. A matinee show."

"Wait. Really?"

Reese left me a credit card and told me to show Ainsley a good time, so I'm taking her at her word. Besides, I have one very good reason to get us the heck out of the house today.

"Yes. But the problem is, these are very, very fancy locales. And we can't just wear jeans and T-shirts." I gesture to my sad apparel. (The same jeans from yesterday, a T-shirt boasting that I was a member of a walkathon in 2006, and a Big Bird sweatshirt tied around my waist.) "We need to dress the part." I gesture to her dress-up stuff and she gets a gleam in her eye.

"Let me change out of my pajamas!"

While she's doing that, I text Reese and explain my plan and get an immediate thumbs-up. I buy tickets for MoMA. The Met is probably a fancier profile, but I haven't been there since—no, not thinking about that right now.

I quickly make a lunch reservation for the teahouse. Last but not least, I try to figure out last-minute tickets to a Broadway show, but no dice. So I settle for a matinee movie.

Ainsley comes out of the bathroom in an oversized Billy Joel T-shirt and shorts.

I clap my hands together. "Let's get fancy."

Chapter Three

That's how I spend my day in a princess tiara and a tutu Velcroed over my jeans. I've got gobs of fake pearls around my neck and a plastic gem on every finger. To my delight, Ainsley opted for a top hat and waistcoat (both way too big for her) and also has enormous jewels on her hands. We swan around MOMA and practice saying things to one another like "Positively smashing, darling."

We watch a Pixar sequel and get hot dogs from a nearby stand for an afternoon snack.

Then, of course, we have to return to the land of Miles.

Ainsley is exhausted by the time we pile through the door, so I help her out of her dress-up stuff and she collapses on the couch for some videogame time while I make dinner.

Miles is reading the newspaper at the table, though now there's a can of Coke in place of a coffee cup in front of him. He surveys me when I come into the kitchen. "You went out in public like that?"

"Yes. Is that a problem for you?"

"No."

"Oh, it's such a crime to make a kid's day, huh?"

He blinks.

"Let's have pancakes from Stavros!" Ainsley calls down the hall.

"The diner on the corner?" I ask when she arrives in the kitchen.

I'm beat, but who could say no to a smile like that. So I divest myself of the fancy wear and am just tugging my sneakers back on when a large pair of feet materialize in my line of vision, sliding into a correspondingly large pair of sneakers. I blink up at Miles. "Are you joining us?"

"Miles tags along whenever Mom and I go to Stavros," Ainsley says, tugging at the tongue of her shoe.

My eyes cut back to his.

He shrugs. "I like pancakes."

So ten minutes later we file into a booth. I'm just perusing the menu when the waiter nearly ends my life. With his face. He must be one of the prettiest men I've ever seen in my life. Eyes, hair, lips, even his ears are good-looking.

I can already see it. On our first date we'll get drunk and wild and sober up over the Atlantic, on a last-minute red-eye to Madrid. Spain will suit us just fine, but after a few weeks we'll meander to Italy, where his family surely has a villa. I'll get fat and happy off olive bread and he'll paint me like one of his French girls. I can't wait to kiss this waiter's ChapStick right off.

He must see me giving him the eyes, because his instantly scream *Bedroom? Why not?* to me. I blush and play with the end of my ponytail. Miles orders pancakes and slaps the menu into the waiter's hand. Can't he see that I'm having a moment with the man who will surely be the great love affair of my life? Can't his dinner order wait a gosh-dang second?

Well, Ainsley's can't either because she's ordering us both a short stack. I add a cup of tea to my order and try to breathe through the sexiest eye contact of my life. The waiter speaks, his voice like slow-spilling caramel I'd lick off the floor if pressed.

Miles gets up to go to the bathroom and by the time he

gets back, our dinner's arrived. The three of us eat in silence, but it's more thoughtful than tense.

The bill comes and Miles hands his card up.

"Oh, you don't—" I start to say reflexively.

"I always do."

"He and Mom always have this argument too. But Miles always wins," Ainsley informs me as she licks the last of the syrup off her fork.

I shrug and concede. Miles pays quickly and jets out of the diner. Ainsley and I are standing up and shuffling out of the booth.

And then I look down at the receipt . . .

My mouth drops open.

I turn to stare at Miles through the window of the diner, but he's looking in the other direction.

He didn't. Tip. The waiter.

WTF? Who does that?

I'm so shocked it's all I can do to just scramble some cash out of my pocket, toss it on the table, and leave.

We walk back to the apartment in silence, but I can't help but glance at Miles a few times. His profile is resolute, dour, inscrutable.

I can't believe I ever had the hots for this man, no matter how briefly. Someone who doesn't tip waitstaff is . . . I mean, is there even a word bad enough for someone like that?

I put it to the side and focus on Ainsley for the rest of the night. We read a few chapters of her *Squirrel Genius* book together, and somehow in the last day she's made it all the way to #50 without me even noticing. She's asleep before I even turn out the light, and I congratulate myself on a job well done. Miles stays at the kitchen table until Harper arrives. She's baring her teeth at him in an attempt at politeness while I wave goodbye. I glance back to see Miles walk past Harper with barely a nod of acknowledgment. I'd put fifty bucks on her giving the door the finger the second she closes it. People do not like this guy.

He disappears up the stairs, the elevator doors close, and I collapse backward, burying my face in my hands. The performance is done for the day. I've done right by Ainsley, but now I'm dangerously depleted and can't stand the thought of going home.

I wave goodbye to the doorman and start trudging down the block. I get to Broadway but don't cross with the light. I am frozen, unsure of where to go. I reach into my pocket and involuntarily worry the edges of the laminated paper, always in safekeeping there. I can hear her voice in my head. I can hear the promises we made to one another. *Live again.*

But it's dark and lonely in this land with no sleep and barely enough air. There's no living here. There's barely surviving.

The crosswalk light changes again and then again.

A sparkle catches my eye and I notice the gem-studded backpack of the guy holding his bike's handlebars in front of me. The backpack is a constellation of twinkles in the city lights and—oh, shit—in the headlights of the car that screeches around the corner and nearly turns us into paninis.

I scream as the car skids so close that one tire clips the front wheel of the bike that Backpack Guy is holding on to. The bike rips from his hands, flattens, squeals, and drags against the blacktop.

There are more screams and I'm suddenly on my butt on the curb with an armful of backpack and guy. He scrambles to his feet and turns, helping me stand. He has medium-brown skin and a matching sparkly baseball cap holding his curly hair back from his face. His helmet that had been hanging on the handlebars of his bike spins on its back ten feet down the block. We stare into one another's eyes in shock.

"Roadkill," I say at the same time he asks, "Are you all right?"

"Yeah," he agrees.

"I think so," I say. "You?"

He pats himself down, then turns and sees the pretzeled mess of his bike. He groans, covering his face with his hands.

The front door of the car slams open and the driver unfolds himself. All six feet or so. He wrenches the bike out from under his car and wheels around, his narrowed eyes focusing on Backpack Guy. The driver bares his teeth and tosses the bike in our direction, the bell making a sad little cry when it smashes on the ground.

"What the hell were you doing standing in the street?" he shouts, his pasty face turning red as he stomps up to us.

I blink and process this absurdity, welcoming a familiar surge of liquid adrenaline. "Wait a second. Did you just *throw* that bike at us?" I ask, stepping around from behind Backpack Guy. "*After* almost hitting us with your *car*?"

His eyes focus on me. "Drivers can't see around the corner! What do you *expect* to have happen?"

"Silly me," I say, my voice rising to match his as I toe up with him. "I *expect* a driver to, I don't know, not take a corner at fifty miles an hour in the middle of Manhattan?"

"You totally fucked my bike," Backpack Guy groans from behind me, dropping to his knees next to it.

"You totally fucked your own bike, kid," the driver shouts.

I push up my sleeves. I'm wearing a sweatshirt with Big Bird on it and pink Converse, so he probably doesn't see this coming. I'm a foot away from him now, pointer finger at the ready. "You think you're going to blame him for getting hit by the car *you* were driving? Sir, how exactly do you think this works?"

He steps forward, his own pointer finger threatening to poke me between the eyes. "Somebody get this bitch out of my face."

I laugh and it sounds bone-chilling even to my own ears. "Oh, buddy. You think you can embarrass me by calling me a name? *Bitch*, I regularly weep in public. There is *nothing* you can do that'll scare me!"

I'm slapping his hand out of my area, stepping into his personal zone, about to do God knows what when suddenly there's a very broad, semifamiliar chest blocking my view.

"Uh," Miles says, looking down at me with a confused frown. He goes to nudge me toward the sidewalk but seems to think better of it and just makes a shooing motion instead. "Maybe let's . . ."

Maybe let's not accost a stranger in the street, I assume he means. Which, honestly, is pretty valid.

"Hey, asshole," the asshole pipes up from behind Miles.

"You talking to me, asshole?" I shout. There're a lot of assholes flying around. I try to dance around Miles but he gets in my way again. This time I'm barred by an uncrossable arm. I do what comes naturally and make it look like Miles is the only thing keeping me from permanently separating this guy from his toupee. "Because trust me, guy! You don't want it with us!"

I'm gesturing at Miles and he's looking down at me, seemingly extremely bemused to be lumped into an "us" with a woman attempting to pile-drive a gigantic stranger on the street. Miles is a conveniently large prop in my one-woman show right now.

I'm still flailing and Miles has me around the middle, gently but inexorably moving me farther from the driver.

"My friend is about two seconds from kicking your ass into next Tuesday!" I shout at the driver.

"No. I am not," Miles says point-blank, his eyebrows pulled down toward his nose.

"Well, could you at least do me a favor and pretend?" I hiss.

Miles sighs and then looks back over his shoulder, down at the man, and absolutely disintegrates him with a glare. "I mean," Miles says to him. "Do you *want* to fight?"

Which is, frankly, a brilliant question to ask someone who is pretending they want to fight.

Now that there's another glowering six-feet-plus person in the mix, the driver is holding his palms up. He takes the opportunity to slam back into his car and peel away.

"Hey!" Backpack Guy shouts. "You gotta pay for my bike, you dick—*damn it!*"

"I took a picture of his license plate," Miles tells him. And then he bends down, picks up the bike, and starts clearing us off the street.

"Here, I'll take it," Backpack Guy says dejectedly.

We all start walking down the block toward a bench, the bike dragging forlornly along with us.

Backpack Guy collapses onto the bench, but when I just stand next to it, Miles taps my shoulder and gestures for me to take a seat.

I scrunch up my face at him. "I'm fine now. You can"— I gesture at his jogging clothes—"carry on."

He obviously doesn't believe me. Hands on hips, frowny skepticism, et cetera.

"You're not going to run off and try to fight another potential WWE contestant?"

"No. I won't. But he had it coming." I plop onto the bench.

"He really did," Backpack Guy agrees with me. "It seemed like you wanted to light-saber his head off," he says.

"Good thing I left my light saber in my Elmo sweatshirt."

He cracks up. "He had no idea he messed with the head of the *Sesame Street* gang." This cracks me up too, but our laughing jostles the bike and one of the pedals clanks onto the sidewalk. "I built that bike myself," Backpack Guy groans. It was definitely once a thing of beauty.

"Next time I see that guy . . ." I trail off, because the adrenaline is waning and everything is starting to make less sense, including me.

"You'll what?" Backpack Guy prods.

"Honestly I have no idea," I say, so genuinely befuddled that he laughs and that makes me laugh and then the bench is shaking again as we descend into hysterics. "I'm Lenny, by the way." I hold out my hand and he takes it.

"Jericho."

Miles, who has not laughed, is standing in front of us with his arms crossed. He texts the photo of the license plate to Jericho and then there goes that sparkly backpack, the bike squeaking and groaning as he waves at me and Miles and makes his way into the night.

Speaking of disappearing into the night . . .

"Okay . . ." I say. "Well, thanks for the assist back there. Um. Bye."

I wave over my shoulder and start walking away from Miles because now that it's just the two of us, well, it's just the two of us and there's an awkwardness that I have zero ideas on how to ford.

"Wait. Hold on."

Miles catches up to me and I stop. He's glowering down at me and my face reflexively glares back.

"Yes?"

"Are you okay? From that fall? It looked like Jericho knocked you down really hard."

"Oh. I'm fine. It didn't hurt."

He tips back on his heels. "I thought I saw you hit your head."

"I didn't."

I'm walking again and, unfortunately, so is he.

He clears his throat. "You don't want to, ah, I don't know, swing past an urgent care?"

I look up at him incredulously but I don't slow down, desperate to get to the train stop just ahead. "Seriously, Miles. I'm fine." I take two steps down the stairs toward the train and turn to look back at him. "You can go jog, or whatever. Have a good night."

He eyes me for a second and then follows me down the stairs. "I . . . wasn't going for a jog."

I take stock of his running shoes, athletic shorts, sweat-wicking shirt, and yup, there is even a compression sleeve thingy over one calf. "Uh-huh. Sure. Then what were you doing?"

I swipe through the turnstile and talk to him, walking backward.

"I . . . was going to ride this train."

I stomp my foot as he swipes through as well. "I'm seriously fine! No concussion!"

"That's great."

The train comes squealing into the station and I jump on. Miles does too, crossing his arms and sitting opposite me.

I glance up at the train information sign and realize wryly that in my hurry to get away from Miles I've jumped on the 1 train. Which means that once again the universe is chewing me up and spitting me out at the Staten Island Ferry.

We ride in silence and at my stop I stand up and spear

him with my eyes. "Thank you and *good night.*" Before he can say anything else, I jump off the train and run above ground. The August night is dense with heat but as I get closer to the water, a loosely cool breeze beckons me to the ferry.

Well, it's a nice night to watch the Statue of Liberty pass twenty-two times in a row, I suppose.

I get settled in a seat away from the crowds and clutch my bag to my chest. To my utter shock, considering the altercation I've just had, sleep starts to descend. I nod off and then wake up back at Manhattan. I must have slept all the way through the Staten Island port and back. I nod a bit more while we head back to Staten Island. But then an interesting man catches my eye. He's got a leather jacket and velvet pants. He's leaning against the railing of the boat and tossing a baseball up and catching it. Tossing it and catching it. The fourth or fifth time, he fumbles it and it skips off his hands and over into the water. He and his friends burst out laughing. He's got a charming smile. I bet it'll look great on our Christmas card one day. We'll put our twin girls in matching velvet pants, just like those, and in fifteen years or so, he'll get down on one knee and ask me to renew our vows.

I close my eyes again when I feel the ferry leave the dock. A shadow darkens my eyelids as something blocks the overhead light.

"Why aren't you getting off the ferry?" a man's voice says from right in front of me.

"Oh, my *God!*" I jolt backward, scrambling my bag up to my chest. "*Miles?* You've gotta be kidding me."

I'm clutching my heart attack. He purses his lips but doesn't say anything.

"You scared the shit outta me!" I assert.

"Good," he says, and crosses his arms over his chest.

"What?"

"I said it's good that I scared the shit out of you."

"Why would that be a good thing?"

"Because it shows that you're at least partially sane if a man approaching you on the Staten Island Ferry in the middle of the night scares you. Now, why aren't you getting off?"

I scrunch up my face and take a page out of his book by simply not answering his question.

He makes a frustrated noise in the back of his throat, and after a moment he plunks into the seat beside me. "At first I thought you'd just fallen asleep and missed your port. But then I realized you were awake and riding back and forth."

I lift my pointer finger into the air. "Hold the phone. You thought I was asleep and missed my stop and you *didn't wake me up?*"

He shrugs. "You seemed tired. I wasn't going to let you miss it a second time. Tell me why you're riding back and forth."

I lay one cheek on top of my bag. "What do you even care?"

His eyes sweep across me and a change comes over his face. He's making an expression I haven't seen him make before. It almost makes him look like a human person with feelings and a backstory.

"Look . . . I know we're pretty much strangers . . . but I'm worried . . ."

About me? He doesn't elaborate.

I squeeze my eyes closed for a moment, cheek still on my bag.

I'm worried, he said.

Against my will I'm softening just a skosh.

"I really don't have a head injury."

"Okay, fine. Then why are you riding the ferry back and forth? You . . . you have a place to go, right?"

"I have an apartment in Brooklyn. I just . . . don't want to be there right now. Recently."

He's squinting at me, an incredulous expression on his face. "Let me get this straight. You have an apartment. But instead of going home, you're intentionally riding the ferry back and forth, making eyes at random men and planning to sleep on this bench?"

I sit up straight and gape at him. I feel like I've just been slapped across the punim. "How the heck do you know I do that?"

"Sleep on benches? You were counting sheep right here like two minutes ago."

"No, no. Making eyes at random men?"

His eyebrows flatten like the answer is obvious. "You have a very expressive face. You did it with me the first time we met."

I scoff. "*That* crush lasted all of twelve seconds."

"Next was the waiter at dinner. And then that dumbass who dropped his baseball overboard. Did I miss anybody?"

"Hey, you didn't tip that waiter, by the way. What a dick move."

"*He* was the dick."

"Why?" I cast back through my memory, trying to think of anything the waiter had done to deserve no tip.

Miles kicks at the back of one of his boots. "Doesn't matter. Not important. Just trust me, he didn't deserve a tip."

I glare at his profile, but he doesn't budge. Finally I sigh and settle back into the bench. There goes Lady Liberty again. "Why do you even care where I sleep? And why did you jump into that mess with that driver, while we're at it? Like you said, we're pretty much strangers."

"You're taking care of my niece. If you're caught up in

something . . . bad . . . or . . . look, I just want to make sure that Ainsley's safe when she's with you, okay?"

It's sweet. Sort of. But I can tell there's more he's not saying.

"I'm fine. I always make sure that Ainsley is safe and well taken care of. I hope you've been able to see that in all of your—honestly pretty relentless—observation of me at work."

He frowns and puts his elbows on his knees. He's either considering my words or he's coming up with another angle to argue with me.

"Hey," I say meaningfully. "We're almost back at Manhattan."

Now he's the one scoffing. "You honestly think I'm gonna leave you here on the ferry?"

"I'm twenty-eight years old, remember? I don't require a chaperone."

He crosses his arms again. "Fine. But if you keep looking at random men the way you first looked at me, one of them is going to decide that you'll look better as the upholstery for his couch pillows."

"Oh, my *God*!"

He ignores me. "So either you come back up to Reese's place and sleep on her couch—"

"No way! Harper would think I'm a total weirdo for that!"

He quirks his face. "What do you care? You don't even know Harper."

"Oh, come on." I wave my hand in the air. "I don't care if the people who know me think I'm a weirdo. They'd be right anyways. It's exactly the people who I *don't* know that I'm trying to keep the secret from. I'm not sleeping at Reese's."

"Fine. Fine. Whatever. Then option two. You can sleep on my couch."

I recoil. "Ew. Pass. You're a strange man."

He gestures around the ferry. "You are literally surrounded by strange men."

"Were there other options?"

He groans and drags a hand down his face. "Option three. We both stay on the ferry all night, get absolute shit sleep, and drag our asses back up to Ainsley in the morning."

"Well, option three is what I was gonna do anyways, so suit yourself, I guess."

I lean back and pretend to get comfortable as I feel the ferry slide into the port at Manhattan.

The passengers start to disembark. The horn blows. Miles is still sitting there. When I peek at him, he's staring at me but eye contact makes him quickly glance away. He frustratedly runs his hands over his short hair and then leans back with a sigh, crossing his arms.

I close my eyes.

"I saw the book," he says in a low voice.

My eyes pop back open and he's got dark eyes trained on my face. *Grief and You*. What an excruciatingly awful title. I can't look away.

"I've *read* that book," he continues, and my stomach drops out. Nobody reads that book for funsies. "I've been here . . . I mean, I *know* . . . Look, I've also yelled at a stranger or two in my time, okay?"

I don't say anything.

He holds my eye contact and then sighs. "If you want me to get off the ferry and leave you alone, I will."

I still don't say anything. The ferry pulls away from shore, headed back out onto open water. His eyes go closed again as he situates himself against the wall. It's a long time before I close mine.

Chapter Four

At five A.M. something warm and gentle touches my face. Wait, no, it's not gentle. It's Miles pressing two fingers into my forehead and foisting me off his shoulder.

"Can we please get off the ferry now?" he grumbles.

I blink fully awake and nod, nothing witty to say. Because what a terrible night's sleep. If he hadn't been here I probably would have stretched out with my bag as a pillow. Instead we sat up as straight as possible and nodded in and out for hours.

We drag ourselves onto land and eye the train distastefully. I get the feeling he's dreading more public transportation as much as I am.

"Coffee," I say, like a zombie, pointing at a little café that's just flicked on its lights.

"Coffee," he agrees. Zombie number two, I guess.

We're back out with our gallons of coffee clenched between our hands. It's August so it'll probably be hot again today, but right now it's predawn and chilly. It's so early that the sun is still a mere suggestion on the other side of the island, but this is New York, so there are already people lifting weights in the grass, yapping on cellphones, running the mile in under five minutes. I watch the world and attempt to think about nothing.

But his words come back to me. *I saw the book. I've read that book.* "So. Um."

He's staring at my profile, clearly waiting for me to say

more. When I can't come up with anything, he makes that same frustrated noise I'm starting to get acclimated to. "Look," he says. "It's clearly not my business. But . . . in terms of you taking care of Ainsley. Like I said, it's better for everyone if you're . . . not in a bad situation."

"You know today is my last day, right? It was just a weekend gig while Reese was out of town."

"Well, actually . . . I get the feeling that Reese might want to make it more permanent. Clearly you get along with Ainsley."

I squint up at him. "How would Reese even know that? She's barely seen me with her."

He shrugs and looks away. "Are you saying that you would turn it down if she asked you to stay on?"

"Are you saying that if I stayed on, you'd perform a personal background check on my life to make sure I was a good influence on Ainsley?"

He throws one hand up. "It wasn't a background check! You were yelling at strangers and sleeping in public! I just wanted to make sure . . . You said you didn't want to go home . . ." He tosses his empty coffee cup in the trash can and his hands are suddenly smashed into his pockets. "Is there a specific reason, or . . ."

When I look up at him again, I see it for a split second. Genuine concern.

I'm worried.

Ugh. It's my weak spot. I hate making other people worry about me. It's why I've avoided my parents. Because then they'd see how I'm actually doing and everything would get so much worse.

I sigh and toss my empty coffee cup away as well. It hits the rim of the trash can and ricochets. Miles lunges forward and snags it out of midair, dunking it for me.

"I'm not in a dangerous situation, I promise. It's safe," I reassure him. "Seriously. I just can't be there because—" My voice breaks and I clear my throat. "It's just so fucking *empty*."

"Oh." The sky is gray dawn now with a few splashes of orange. The Hudson is velvet-black and choppy, lapping up the light and tossing it back to us.

I mirror his pose and jam my own hands away. "Look, I'll spare you the suspense. It seems like you've probably guessed some version of this anyways . . . I used to live with my best friend in that apartment. And a couple months ago . . . she died." The words make my adrenaline start coursing through me. They don't feel real. I feel like I'm doing a play. A really shitty play. "And saying 'my friend died' doesn't convey what really—she was my sister. No. My A-team. My other half. And I'm so fucking stupid because I didn't realize she was my whole life until she was gone." The words are a waterfall and there's no stopping it. I can't look at him. "And I'm not . . . I'm not doing so well." A sob sneaks out. "And I can't be at home because all her stuff is in the same place it was since—"

I stop walking and sit on my heels with my knees pressed to my eyes. I tremble and attempt to squeeze myself down into nothing. When I crack my eyes I see the toes of two running shoes next to my sneakers. And then there's one knee on the ground. I feel my ponytail slide out from my face where it's gotten caught. He arranges it down my back.

"What was her name?" he asks quietly.

I roll my head to one side and look at the river. "Lou," I whisper. "Lou Merritt."

"Lenny and Lou," he muses. "Like two old men."

I laugh involuntarily. "She was the one who gave me that nickname. She said if she had an old man name, I had to have one too. My real name is Helen, believe it or not. But I've been Lenny since kindergarten, when we met."

I reach into my pocket and pull out a creased napkin, mopping at my face. I wish this napkin were the size of a Buick. I want to pull it over my entire body and sleep for a year. Right here in the middle of the park.

"What's that?" he asks. The laminated slip of paper rode along with the napkin and peeks up at us from between my fingers.

"Oh." I'm clutching it so hard I'm surprised it hasn't started smoldering. "It's something that Lou and I . . . I'm trying to follow it . . . But I haven't . . ." I give up on words and just hand it over to him. It's strange to see it in someone else's hand.

Live Again, he mouths as he reads the heading. Squinting, he surveys the bullet points and if he's judging them, it doesn't show on his face. But one of them makes him chuff a laugh.

"How many have you done?" he asks over the top of the list.

"None."

His eyebrows flick up.

It would be great if the tears corked themselves right about now. But I've been grieving long enough to know that that is definitely not how this works.

I put my head down and cry until my legs start to tingle from crouching and I get thirsty.

"We have to go soon or else we're going to be late for Ainsley," he says eventually.

I laugh involuntarily again. "Aren't you supposed to be murmuring meaningless platitudes to me?"

"Oh." He frowns and scratches at his knee. "Sorry."

But it's okay because he's inadvertently said the magic word. *Ainsley.* She's waiting uptown for me to take her to school and even if I can't take care of myself right now, I won't let Ainsley twist in the wind.

I stand up and scrub my face with my sleeve, heading back toward the café. Miles keeps pace and doesn't say anything when I wordlessly disappear into the bathroom and reemerge five minutes later with a washed face and a clean T-shirt and leggings on. He's got an egg sandwich in either hand and he wraps my fingers around one of them when I don't make a move to take mine.

"You look like you're about to dissolve," he informs me, demolishing half of his sandwich in one bite.

I eat as much of my sandwich as I can manage and move to toss the rest into the trash as we jog down the stairs to the train, but he rescues it at the last minute and polishes mine off as well.

We don't say anything as we sit next to each other on the ride uptown. At 42nd Street, he stands up to give his seat to a pregnant lady, and at Columbus Circle, I stand up to give mine to a woman with a cane. We stand shoulder to shoulder, swaying and listless until we make it to our stop.

When we're on the sidewalk in front of their building, Miles suddenly stops walking. "Lenny—"

I just shake my head and point upstairs. "Gonna be late."

I should probably be thanking him. For making sure I didn't get serial killed last night. Or for preventing me from giving a grown man a wedgie. Or for breakfast.

But the thing about thanking someone is that it requires acknowledgment that the situation is, in fact, real. And I just can't bring myself to do that.

"*C*heck pleassssse, baby!" Lou sings at the top of her lungs. "Because you're my checkmate, my checkmate girl!"

She's been obsessed with this song by the K-pop band 5Night for the last week and I've started hearing it in my nightmares. I love 5Night as much as Lou does. I mean, they have a no-skip discography as far as I'm concerned, but did I mention that it's been on repeat for a week?

"Lou!" I scream, slamming my bedroom door open when I hear her start the song over again. "If you don't shut this cursed song off . . . !"

"Make me!" she shouts defiantly, appearing in her own bedroom door, the two of us squaring off.

I lunge around her, faking her out as I make a break for her speaker. She gets me by the back of the sweatpants and attempts to wedgie me into submission. I kick her Bugs Bunny slippers out from under her, but unfortunately I also break her fall. She's got longer arms than I do, but I'm squirrelly. I'm out from her grasp and I fall triumphantly over her desk, her speaker clutched between my hands.

"Nooooooo," she cries from her bedroom floor. "Don't do it, Lenny."

My finger hovers over the power button. Peace is at my fingertips.

And then I impulsively smash the back button, starting the song from the beginning. She screams with victorious laughter and with a plunk I join her to sing on the floor.

Chapter Five

I take Ainsley to school and then that afternoon I meet her at the gate of the schoolyard with a hot pretzel and a bubble tea (her favorite snack, she informed me yesterday) and she's practically airborne as she skips her way home. Her mom is almost back.

I smile as I watch her. Obviously, being a mother must be desperately difficult, but to be on the receiving end of that kind of ebullient love probably makes it worth it.

We mess around at home for a few hours, working on a puzzle, then tossing a bunch of stuff into the instapot and hoping it creates something edible for dinner.

When we hear Reese's keys in the front door, Ainsley leaps down from the counter and sprints to the front hall. After a minute, Reese walks into the kitchen, holding Ainsley baby-monkey style, and it makes me grin. They look effervescent with joy to be reunited.

"Mom, I wanna watch a movie," Ainsley whines in a voice I haven't heard her use once all weekend.

"It's a weeknight, sweetie," Reese says firmly.

"But I want to!" Ainsley insists, immediately growing petulant.

"Ains—"

Tears burst out of the little girl and she squirms down from her mother's grasp and disappears down the hall toward her room.

"Sorry," Reese says, pinching at the space between her eyes.

"No apology necessary. It's understandable. She was an angel for me. Which means she saved up everything else for you."

"Exactly." Reese sighs. She's wearing a pantsuit and her hair down around her shoulders. For someone who just took a five-hour flight she looks impossibly fresh. I feel like a sewer creature in comparison. "Well, how was it?"

"A total dream. You've got a good one, Reese."

She smiles. "She's the best, isn't she? . . . I was really worried about her after my dad died. He was a father figure for her. But I think she's rebounding. So," she says, changing topics with a clap. "Tell me everything."

I fill her in on the weekend and then go say goodbye to Ainsley. She's not receptive to much, obviously on total overload, and I'm relieved. I don't think I could handle any more emotions right now. I hate that this is goodbye, but that's the way it is.

When I reemerge into the kitchen, Reese is standing there, biting her lip. "Are you sure you aren't looking for regular work? I just want to make it clear that the offer is out there."

"Thank you," I say quickly. "But I'm just here to help in a pinch. That's . . . that's what works for my life right now." I try not to burst into maniacal laugh-tears at the word *life*.

"Well," she says on a sigh. "If you ever change your mind, I can tell how much Ainsley liked you."

I shake her hand and gather my things. "Do you want me to lock up on my way out?"

"No, that's fine. I'm sure Miles will be down in a few minutes. Finding something to criticize." She collapses into one of the kitchen chairs. "If you can't save me from that, at least save me a trip to unlock the door."

I'm just closing their front door on my way out when suddenly I'm face-to-face with a crossed pair of arms.

"Hey," Miles says.

"Hey."

"Are you going home tonight?" he asks.

Men. You let them feed you one egg bagel and suddenly your whereabouts are their business. I'd like to tell him to mind his own, but then an image from this morning flashes in my mind: my ponytail being carefully extricated from the path of snot and tears. Sigh. He can be a real dick but I suppose he's not all bad. "Eventually. I have to shower at some point, ya know?"

"What does *eventually* mean?"

He's a quick one.

I shrug.

"The ferry, then?" he presses.

"No. Not on Mondays. There's this all-night dance party on the Lower East Side that they do every Monday night. I usually go there instead."

He crosses his arms over his chest. "You look like you need three days of sleep and an IV, but you're headed to an all-night dance party?"

"What can I say? I'm a dancing machine."

He takes a step toward the door but looks back at me.

He's pausing. I'm pausing. This is it for me and Miles. I can't bring myself to acknowledge anything that's passed these last few days. But we have to say something, right?

"Well," I say, holding out my hand for a shake. "We met."

He exhales quickly in what I think might be a laugh. "True."

We shake hands and he slides his hands into his pockets, catching my eye right as I'm about to turn away.

"Define all-night dance party."

"It's from seven to seven. People come straight from work and dance until dawn. It's a spiritual melee. You should come, seems right up your alley," I joke.

"Okay," he says with a shrug. "Let me just say hi to Reese and I'll be right back."

"Wait, I'm sorry." Words have stopped making sense to me. "What?"

"I haven't seen her in a few days. I just wanted to say hi." He points behind him to her apartment.

"Yeah. I got that part. I'm a little foggy on the part where you think you're coming with me?"

"Didn't you just invite me?"

"I mean, yes?" The word *yes* squeaks like a chipmunk has said it.

"Great. Give me two seconds."

DANCE LIKE NO ONE'S WATCHING, motivational kitschy kitchen signage insists worldwide.

Well, that's exactly what I'm doing right now (except for Miles side-eyeing me from a slight distance) and frankly I'm not sure what all the fuss is about.

I think I've passed social freedom and catapulted myself firmly into cry for help. Especially since in the last twenty minutes, twin rivers of tears have started coursing down my cheeks.

I dance harder.

Removing yet another grabby pair of hands from my hips, I rotate ten feet to the left, finding a clear spot among the mass of grooving humans.

You'd think dancing while crying and wearing a backpack would be enough to deter suitors, but I guess the people aren't picky tonight.

Usually this is kind of a family-friendly dance party. People come to shake the workday off or motivate themselves for tomorrow. But this seems to be an unusually horny night.

The music is grimier, the people are wearing fewer clothes, and the drinks are more plentiful.

Drinks! Maybe that'll help.

It won't. Obviously. But I'm exhausted and raw and nothing else is helping, so . . . I head to the bar area and peek around the crowd. Miraculously, some guy has just bought a round for everybody in earshot, and drinks in plastic cups are being distributed to the masses en masse. The guy in front of me hands me a cup of foamy something and I blink down at it.

Miles's hand comes from behind and plucks the drink away from me. "Do not drink this."

I'm not even surprised. Just annoyed.

"Did you come here with the *specific* intention to be a buzzkill?" I've got my hands on my hips and I'm hoping I look irritated enough to cow his audacity, but the fact that I'm crying probably dims the effect.

He hands the drink off to someone else. Since we got here he's been posted up in the corner, nursing a beer and occasionally raising his eyebrows at my dance moves.

The beat drops and I start dancing again, maintaining searing eye contact. "Why doesn't it surprise me that you don't dance?"

"Are we calling this dancing?"

I laugh and concede the point. I'm currently pretending to mow a lawn, so yeah, maybe dancing isn't quite the term.

"You, like, never dance?" I push.

"Not my thing."

"Says the man who voluntarily attended an all-night dance party."

"I . . . I came because I had something to talk to you about."

The bass makes the building rattle and I lean in. "What?"

He puts his hands in his pockets and his mouth at my ear. "Can we talk outside?"

I consider this, nod, and then follow him. Mostly for the same reason I gravitated toward alcohol. Nothing else is helping, so I might as well follow this man out into the night.

We get to the sidewalk, the noise blissfully dampens, and he turns to face me. He's looking a little . . . nervous? Uncertain? "I . . . wanted to ask you something . . ."

"Well?" I prompt after he pauses.

"How did you do all that? With Ainsley?"

"Do what?"

"Get her to laugh like that? And, I don't know, always figure out what she needs so fast? I've known her for almost two years and I've never . . ."

Two years? He hasn't known Ainsley her whole life? Did he marry into the family or something? I guess that partially explains Ainsley's indifference to him. Some of the awkwardness between him and Reese.

"Oh. Well . . . I'm good with kids." I wave my hand like it's nothing.

He gives me a narrowed look of appraisal. "Reese said that you turned down the job offer."

I rock on my heels. The music is beckoning me back inside. I'm going to scream if I have to think straight any longer. "Yeah."

"Why?" He must sense my desire to ditch him and get

back to the dance floor because he repositions himself between me and the door of the club.

"I don't do long-term gigs anymore. You know my . . . situation. Do you really think I'm fit to be permanently integrated into some kid's life right now? I'm a complete and utter mess. I can fake it for a couple days in a row, but regularly? No way."

He nods, apparently in total agreement with me. "What if . . . what if you came back for just a *little* bit longer?"

I frown, trying to figure out what he's getting at. That nervous look is back. "Spit it out, Miles. Whatever it is you're trying to say."

"I have a proposal for you."

I roll my hand in the air so fast I feel wind.

"Look," he says. "I'm not trying to convince you to be a full-time nanny for Ainsley. But . . . what would you think about coming back just long enough to teach me how to do what you do?"

"You want to be Ainsley's babysitter?"

"I want to be someone they can rely on. Who they like having around. And right now . . . I'm striking out on both counts. Neither of them really . . . like me. As you could probably tell. But they like *you*. So if you could just teach me some tricks and in exchange—"

"Tricks? Miles, it's my personality, not a magic show."

He's agitated. "Right, right. Of course. But there must be something you could, I don't know, coach me on? I just want to learn—"

"And what would be in that for me?"

"Ah." He's slowly shifting from agitated to wary. Backlit by the orange glow from the streetlight, his eyes are coal-black. "Look. You're clearly grieving right now."

I wince.

"Well," he continues. "I'm kind of a grief . . . expert, for lack of a better term. And I was thinking that in exchange for the babysitter lessons I could . . . help you get through this."

"How?"

"I understand what you're going through. Not the specifics, but the general idea. I *literally* know how to keep on living after . . ."

His eyes spark with pain and he cuts off.

It's this, more than anything, that makes me realize he might be on to something. Because if it were me, I wouldn't have been able to finish that sentence either.

"Have you talked to anyone about it?" he asks. "Your parents?"

I think of all the calls I've avoided from my mom, the texts unanswered.

"That's a nope."

"What about people you don't know? Doctors? Bartenders? Priests? Therapists? A grief counselor?"

I shake my head. I have to bully myself just to get the toothpaste on the toothbrush. Finding a grief counselor, making an appointment, clearing it with my insurance, hauling my ass to the appointment, and then talking about Lou to a stranger? Literally impossible.

"Well, then . . . you can talk to me. Anytime. That's what I'm offering."

"I don't think I need someone to talk to," I insist. "There's nothing to *say*. She's gone and I'm . . ."

"Then we don't have to talk. I'll just be your companion. I was thinking that it might be helpful . . . You might want someone . . . I could . . . you know . . . do your list with you. You haven't been able to cross anything off yet, right? I'll help. We can go through one by one. I'll be your list . . . buddy." He seems to be genuinely offering, but also he says the word *buddy* like someone else might say the word *vomit*.

We're interrupted when a couple stumbles out the door, sweaty and clasping hands, teetering and knocking sideways into Miles.

"Sorry, dude," the guy says over the girl's head.

Miles gives him a silent appraisal so slow, so diminishing that the guy can't help but shrink three inches.

"We *said* sorry," the girl snaps.

"Okay," Miles replies, completely flat. He turns to face me and boxes them out of his life forever.

For that, he gets four middle fingers spearing toward his back.

I snort.

"You know, you say you want me to talk to you about my feelings, but you're not the best at conversation, Miles." I make a meaningful nod toward the couple attempting to make out while they walk away.

He glances between them and me. "Was I rude?" He looks suddenly perplexed.

I almost laugh. "You really don't know what your face looks like, huh?"

He's glowering again. "I know I'm not good with people. I'm not . . . gentle. But I don't think you need someone gentle."

"Oh, is that right?" Now he knows what I need. How cute.

"Yeah, that's right. You need *strong*. You need someone who can stop you from fighting large men on the street. You need someone who can wade in and pull you out of the swamp if you need me to. And I can be that person." He's tapping on his own chest as he talks, and weirdly I can feel those taps echoing through my own rib cage. "I am not easy to shake off, Lenny. Look at Reese, she hasn't figured out how to. I'm stubborn. If you need to cross things off your list to survive, I'll do that. I can carry someone on my back if I have to." He takes a step forward and I stop breathing. He puts one palm on my shoulder and squeezes. A firm hold that reminds me I'm a citizen of Earth and belong right here, on the ground. "If we do this, I will *not* let you drown."

I gasp for air. He's winded me. The water rushes in. Is it silly that I didn't realize I was drowning until he told me he won't let it happen?

Apparently he *does* know what I need. How frustrating.

Overwhelmed, I crouch down again and tug at my hair and see spots and almost scream. He waits.

When I stand up again I can feel my bloodshot eyes, my sticking-up hair, my backpack falling off one shoulder. I gesture to it all. "You really think you can handle this? I'm not just gonna need a *tissue* every now and then. I need someone to, like, make me waffles and then not bat an eye when I punch those waffles in the face."

"Violence toward waffles. Got it."

"Seriously. You don't want this. I'll scar you."

"Oh, my God. Everybody thinks they're so unique. I'll be useful. I promise." He fixes my backpack strap. "I'm not scared of you."

"Look," I say. "Pretty much the *only* thing that's keeping me together right now is the fact that I haven't taken anybody else down in flames. It's *why* I'm only doing short-term gigs. It's why I'm avoiding my parents. So just, please, read the caution tape and save yourself."

He's giving me that narrowed look again. "Let me get an audition, then."

"Huh?"

"Let me see the list." He wags his hand at me until I dig it out of my pocket and hand it over. "Oh. This one." He snaps a finger against the list. "Easy. We'll do this one. Tonight. If you . . . enjoy my company, then you'll consider the deal. If you don't, we'll go our separate ways."

He's nothing if not persistent.

He's five strides down the sidewalk before he turns back. "Follow me," he says.

And for the second time that night, I do.

TEN MINUTES LATER we're still power walking toward some unknown destination and I'm flailing and sweating and out of breath.

Miles glances down at me. "Maybe we add a little cardio to the list."

"You can't add to the list!" I'm aghast. "It's *laminated*."

He grunts.

"Where are we going anyway?"

"You'll see."

I stop dead in my tracks and say the one thing that'll surely get him to stop walking, thus saving my life. "I can't take you up on your offer, you know."

He stops stock-still, three sidewalk squares away, hands in his pockets, framed under a streetlight. His bone structure is so strong the man is standing in a beam of light and he's still almost ninety percent shadow. "Why?"

I list on my fingers. "One. You called me emaciated, implied I have a drinking problem, and just generally made fun of the way I look. So yeah. Fuck you." He takes a step and eats up one of the sidewalk squares between us. "Two. You judged me for eating Reese's food while I worked a nonstop fourteen-hour shift, by the way. So yeah. Fuck you twice."

Another step, another sidewalk square disappears. "And three. Not tipping the waiter? Come on. That's, like, sociopathic."

The last sidewalk square disappears and he's looking directly down at me, the toes of his shoes a centimeter from mine. "I know what you're doing."

"What's that?"

"You're trying to buy yourself a little time for a breather."

I fake outrage. "These are legitimate gripes!"

"I tip waiters! I'm not a total dickhead, okay? He's the first waiter in my life who I didn't tip."

"So why didn't you?"

He does that sideways nod thing to get me to start walking alongside him again, and for some reason it works. This time he sets a more reasonable pace.

"On my way to the bathroom I heard him saying something really nasty and I didn't think he deserved a tip."

My spidey senses tingle. "Was it about me?"

He purses his lips, and that's all the confirmation I need.

"Well," I say. "It probably wasn't worse than calling me strung out, right?"

He winces. "Look. That was really bad. I'm sorry I said that. I . . . thought one thing and it was wrong. It's clear that you're going through a tough time, but I judged you before I could see it. Again. I'm very sorry."

I glare, but his apology has sucked all the venom from it. "You questioned my babysitting skills and told Reese to fire me."

"That was before I knew there was a method to your—" He cuts off, probably because it's a little too real to say the word *madness* to someone who puts cocktail onions in cupcakes. "Before I realized you had a method. I was shortsighted. And for the record I wasn't judging you for eating. I was worried that that was all you were going to eat. It wouldn't have been enough food for a hamster and you barely finished it."

I pull a face. "I've been having trouble with my appetite."

He nods. "That'll happen. Maybe this'll help."

We stop short in front of a hole-in-the-wall sandwich shop, and Miles goes inside to get our sandwiches. I sit on the bench outside and enjoy the sensation of *not* being in a hot, sweaty club.

A few minutes later he emerges with something called a Turkey Surprise and I get to experience a moment of nirvana.

"Holy guacamole," I groan after the first bite.

"Totally."

I've got half a sandwich hanging out of my mouth when he nudges me with his elbow.

"What?"

"Look up."

"Ah. Pigeon butts. Appetizing."

"Not at the pigeon butts. At the *sign*."

I can't read it from this angle, so I stand up, sandwich and all, and read out loud: "Cousin Sammy's Sammies, home of Omar's one and only Turkey Surprise."

My breath catches and my gaze drops to Miles. "Number seven," I whisper through bright pressure in my eyes.

I mean, I knew I was following him because he insisted he could cross one off, but I was not prepared for what it would feel like to actually do it.

"'Eat something famous you can only get in New York,'" Miles quotes from the list. "Not so hard, right?"

I look from him to the sign. I'm speechless.

He holds out his hand and I wordlessly hand him the turkey sandwich. He wraps the rest of it back up.

"It was so easy for you." I plunk back onto the bench beside him. "I think I must be bad at this," I murmur. "Like, maybe other people handle this better than I do."

He barks a sad laugh. "Lenny, not a soul on earth is good at this."

He takes a deep breath, then turns to look me in the eye. Smile lines, stubble, honest eyes, unswerving, unhidden face. Not friendly but not mean. "My mom and cousin were killed in a car accident about ten years ago. My life kind of . . . ended for a little while after that."

"Oh, my God. I'm so sorry." Sure, it's a platitude, but I've got two hands wrapped around his arm and I mean it from the bottom of my heart.

"Believe it or not, it gets easier to talk about after a while. A long while. But I've been there, Lenny. Right where you are. Where you lose control of your life and nothing makes sense anymore. When you can't remember how basic things function. Like when to eat or shower. Grief . . . it's not like any other emotion. It is utterly discombobulating. Among many other things."

"I'm *so* sorry," I repeat.

"Thanks. I'm still sorry about it too."

I study his profile. "I get . . . I get that you're wanting some guidance on how to be there for Ainsley. I understand you need my help with that. But honestly, why would you ever want to wade into all this with me? Especially if you have experience with it. Wouldn't you want to be as far away from it as possible?"

He considers this for a long time, chewing his sandwich and folding his legs in and out when pedestrians pass on the sidewalk in front of us. "Ainsley and Reese, they're my only family left. I'm not . . . well . . . you've seen it. I'm not always good with people. And you . . . even when you're like *this*, people like you. I need help." He shrugs. "Besides, look, seeing someone go through this . . . and not being able to help? It's awful. Not everyone will accept help when they're griev-ing. Some people just . . . go inward and bear it all alone."

I get the distinct feeling he's talking about someone in particular.

"We don't need to get into all of it," he continues. "But this has been a pretty useless couple of years for me. I mean me. *I'm* useless . . . Look, a project would be good for me."

I point to my heart. "Me being the project."

He shrugs. "And the list. *And* me. It's a really big project."

My phone buzzes and I see that it's a text from my mom. I quickly scan it. She wants to know how I am. But I ignore it and the two missed calls from her that came through while I was in the club, clearing away the notifications and black-ing my screen.

Miles looks from my phone to me. "You're really living out of that backpack? Never going home?"

I shrug. "Home is where the heart is. My heart died in a cancer ward six months ago."

I say it like it's just another thing to say, but Miles makes a sound in the back of his throat, like those words hurt him as much as they do me.

"I know what you mean about going back to your apart-ment . . ." he says in a low voice, and I turn to watch his profile. "We all lived together. Me and Anders and Mom. When they died, it pretty much meant losing my entire fam-ily at once. So yeah. I get it. It's awful to go back to the place where they just were but aren't anymore."

Images from my apartment crash over me. Lou burning Christmas cookies in our kitchen. Lou's coconut Suave shampoo in our bathroom. Lou's handknit sweaters drying in the sun after she washed them.

Being back in that apartment is like touching electricity.

"Miles, how does anyone do this?" I whisper, leaning forward and letting the tears pit-pat off my nose and onto my leggings.

"A very little at a time," he says, balling up his sandwich paper and giving me a squeeze on the shoulder. "And virtually none of it tonight. Tonight is all about finding you a place to sleep." He pauses. "And shower."

"I'll figure something out . . . It's fine."

"It's not. Look, I have an extra apartment; it's shitty but no one else is there right now. You can crash. At least for tonight."

He's already walking toward the train and I have to scramble to catch up. "Wait! What do you mean you have an extra apartment? Who can afford an extra apartment in New York City?"

He shrugs. "My current apartment was . . . a gift? It's hard to explain. I still pay rent on this other place just in case everything falls apart and I have to go back. I'm warning you. It's really tiny."

We take the train back uptown to a neighborhood about ten minutes' walk from Reese and Ainsley's place. The sun will be up in just a few hours. The building is a little brownstone with a beautiful front door and a crumbling cement porch.

"Third floor," he says, jingling keys in front of me. "Use whatever you want."

"Are you kidding me? I can't just go into some strange apartment that you claim is yours! I don't even know your last name!"

He sighs and digs in his pocket, coming up with his wallet, and then his license.

I eagerly study it, suddenly insatiably curious. "Hmmm. Brown eyes and six foot two, huh?"

He quirks his face at me. "Obviously?"

I survey his grumpy little picture, doing a double take at his last name. "Honey?" I ask, one eyebrow hiking up my forehead. "Such a sweet name for someone so . . . you."

"It's not pronounced like *honey*. It's *Ho-nee*. Rhymes with—"

"Baloney."

"I usually say *pony*, but sure. Whatever." He sighs, like he's tired, which he probably is. "Should we . . ." He holds out his phone to me and motions to trade numbers. I swipe it and call myself. "Okay." Now that he's said all he came to say he's suddenly looking awkward. He clears his throat. "Well. Go to bed."

He puts the keys in my hand and leaves while I laugh at being told to go to bed even though I'm pushing thirty. As I watch him go, one thought fills my head. *That man just crossed something off Lou's list for me.*

After he's gone I tiptoe up to the third floor.

Miles's apartment was almost certainly a closet in another life. It's mildly furnished, and clearly he never moved out completely. I reverently place the sandwich in the empty fridge.

A scalding hot shower with Ivory soap, a ridiculously oversized T-shirt I find in a dresser drawer, and clean cotton sheets on a twin-sized bed I simply cannot imagine Miles fitting in: it's all awfully close to wonderful.

I sleep for six deep hours, then three more fitful ones, and when I wake up at noon, I feel almost like a member of society.

I almost feel a little bit . . . good? I hate it.

I eat the other half of my sandwich as I take out my phone and compose a text.

Okay. You got yourself a deal.

Chapter Six

"Are you fantasizing about the one in the hat or the one in the glasses?" Miles asks me three hours later while we sit on a bench in Riverside Park.

"Huh?" I jolt upright. "Neither!" (Both.)

He gives me a look like *Come on*, but I definitely don't explain that Glasses was going to propose to me on a Jumbotron (I'd decline, most likely) and Hat doesn't believe in marriage but would eventually agree to a courthouse ceremony after he accidentally read a page from my diary and realized how important it was to me.

"All right," I say with a clap. "How is this going to work?"

"I mean . . . should we make a plan for how to get Ainsley to like me? . . . I guess you just start spending time with her and I tag along?"

I'm unimpressed. "I already reached out to Reese to get some regular hours with Ainsley. But don't you think she'll be weirded out if you're *always* tagging along? I mean, I kind of understood when I didn't know them at all and Reese was out of town, and not to be rude, but if she wanted you to be with her kid every day, wouldn't she have just asked you to do it instead of paying me?"

"Oh." He leans forward and rests his elbows on his knees, watching two novice rollerbladers hold hands and clop their way toward certain injury. "I didn't think of that. I guess . . . I'll have to ask her if it's okay."

"Definitely."

"Honestly, Ainsley will probably be the easier sell. She doesn't seem to care one way or the other if I'm around. Reese is the one I'm worried about."

"No way," I disagree. "You know what they say, hate is not the opposite of love. Indifference is."

"Oh, thanks," he says caustically. "Glad to know that Ainsley opposite-of-loves me."

"No!" I laugh because even though that's kind of exactly what I just said, it's not what I meant. "I meant that I think you're probably closer to connecting with Reese than you think. From the way I see it, you're probably like one great joke away from endearing yourself to her."

"It's just that . . . It's *really* not my skill set." He's scrubbing a hand over his buzzed hair. "Look, my mom, she just always kind of got me. So I just thought that it was easy. That if my intentions were generally good, people would get me. But obviously it doesn't work that way and, I guess, sometimes I bring out the worst in people. Without meaning to. So. Yeah."

I consider this. "Well, maybe we should give ourselves some homework. Yours is easy. Watch all the Indiana Jones movies and brush up on your Madonna discography. Endear yourself to Ainsley a little bit. It'll give you something to talk about. What's my homework? Find a priest and scare the pants off him with my bleak outlook on life? Wait, do priests even wear pants? Oh, my God, are they naked under their robes?"

He handles me like a pro by completely ignoring me. "If I just start bringing up Indiana Jones and Madonna she's going to see right through me. She's a smart kid. Trust me. I've tried to suck up to her before."

"True . . . okay, well, what are you *actually* interested in?" I turn to study him.

His brow furrows and his chin drops. A ladybug lands on his knee and he gently brushes it away. I grow more astonished as the seconds pass.

"You can't think of a single thing you're interested in?" I demand. "Well, what do you like to do around the city? Eat? Jog?"

He shrugs. "I've actually only been here for a little bit. I grew up upstate. Near the Adirondacks. I never thought I'd live in the city. I'd only been here twice before I moved here . . . still getting used to it. I guess? But I guess generally . . . I like nonfiction. Reading it, I mean. Let's see . . . I like watching *Jeopardy!* . . . I like dogs . . . I like music from the nineties . . . I'm not opposed to other music, I just don't spend a lot of time looking for new stuff."

"Cool! Okay . . . and for work?"

He sighs and crosses his arms. "I'm not going to even bother telling you about my job. You're going to think I'm lying."

I poke his thigh. "Midnight radio DJ?" I guess. "You play the oldies for star-crossed lovers? *This one's going out to Jan, Gary is sorry, come back to him?*"

"Yeah, that's me," he says flatly. "You got it in one."

"Ex-pilot? You lost your license because you banged a flight attendant in the cockpit while landing the plane? Just looking for a thrill wherever you could find one? Anything to feel alive?"

He makes a face that I'm almost positive is an attempt to keep himself from laughing.

I clap my hands. "Got it! Botanist. You've spent your career attempting to splice two different kinds of orchids together. When you finally achieve it, you'll name it after the girlfriend who dumped you in high school. When she finds out, she'll show up on your doorstep and reveal she never got over you. Aw, Miles, that's so sweet!"

This time he does laugh, scrubbing a hand over his face. I open my mouth to hazard another guess, but without even looking up he reaches over and stop-signs his hand two inches from my face. "I'm a bricklayer."

I blink, flutter my eyes as I try to assimilate this information. "Come again?"

"You heard me."

"Those *exist*? In the twenty-first century?"

"Someone has to lay the brick, Lenny."

"Well, shit," I say, leaning back on the bench and staring into nothing. "I guess so." After a minute I turn and eye him up. "Doesn't seem like you're . . . doing much bricklaying these days?"

"Yeah." He crosses his arms over his chest again. "My business was upstate, really. My neighbor taught me the trade. But then I . . . recently came into some money. New thing for me. So I moved here. To try to . . . you know . . . get to know Ainsley. It's not exactly going well. I'm bored out of my mind. I'm used to getting up at five and starting my day, working my ass off, and falling into bed after dinner. I miss it. Working. But what it would take to start a business in this city . . . maybe I'll just bleed my bank account dry and drag my ass back upstate in a couple years."

We sit side by side and chew on that.

"Maybe *Jeopardy!*"

"Hm?" he asks, pulling himself out of some reverie.

"I don't think there are gonna be many opportunities to teach Ainsley about bricklaying. So I guess let's try the *Jeopardy!* angle. I can see her being into it!"

"Lenny?"

I jolt and turn at the familiar voice calling my name from the cobblestone path in front of us.

"Lenny, that *is* you!"

"Marzia," I say weakly, standing up for a familiar hug that gets me poked in the chest, face, and back by her copious jewelry. "Hi."

"Honey, you've lost weight!" she crows, holding my hands out to the sides and surveying me closely.

It's true. And I look like a character from *Beetlejuice,* but I guess it's only the lbs she cares about.

"Your mother says you haven't been doing so well, but look at you . . ." She trails off suggestively, making wide eyes in Miles's direction. "Introduce me."

"Miles Honey, this is Marzia Marcutio, my family's long-time dental hygienist and . . . proxy family member?" How best to describe someone who has inserted herself into your family politics through sheer force of will? "Marzia, Miles is a friend. This isn't a date."

She nods knowingly, not believing me at all. "Well, it's good to see you out and about. The last time I saw you was at the funeral."

My stomach pulls tight like she's garroted it with fishing line.

"It was dreadful," she stage-whispers to Miles. "So young, of course, but we all saw it coming. Stage four doesn't leave much room for happy endings."

"Oh." Miles blinks at her and then slides his gaze over to me. He's probably trying to figure out if he's interpreting this correctly. If Marzia could possibly be this insensitive.

Trust me, she can.

"Ovarian cancer of all things!" she powers on. "And for such a pretty girl. Hysterectomy, you know, when she should have been out meeting a true love. What a shame she never met somebody. A waste. And then the cancer came *back*. I always wondered if it came back because of how much she celebrated after it was over the first time. You can't tempt fate like that! A hysterectomy something to celebrate? Well, it was dreadful, and this one here took it worst of all."

Even knowing Marzia, I'm still struck dumb. If she'd run me over with a taxicab I wouldn't be more stunned than I am right now. How could someone believe that about Lou? And how could she *say* all that? And to my face? Like Lou's entire journey is just a sad, gossipy story she gets to shill to whoever she happens to run into in the park? Like Lou got what was coming to her? I feel hot emotion creeping up from my extremities; when it meets in my chest, Marzia's gonna see me blow.

"Wow," Miles says, giving her the same face he gave the amorous dancers just last night. "Well, that was fucking rude."

"Hm?" Marzia blinks, certain she hasn't heard him correctly.

"I said you're being fucking rude."

Her mouth drops open.

My mouth drops open.

"Excuse me?"

I'm not sure if Marzia or I am more shocked. Someone telling her to her face that she's being fucking rude is enough to discombobulate my nervous system. My rage and pain just sort of scatter as he opens his mouth again.

"Lou's story clearly doesn't matter to you," he says slowly. "But to Lenny . . ." His hand clamps my shoulder. *I'm here*, it says. *So are you*, it says. "Like I said. Rude."

Marzia does a very good impression of an extremely flustered duck. "Lenny, honey. I didn't—I'm not sure. Well, your friend is—" She's oscillating between outrage and embarrassment. She's backing away from us, red in the face, sputtering. Giving up, she leaves without saying goodbye.

We sit back down on the bench and I study him. My heart doesn't feel like it's beating right. Probably all the adrenaline still pumping with nowhere to go. "You . . . stuck up for me."

He raises his eyebrows but looks a tiny bit embarrassed. "It seemed an obvious moment for me to hold up my end of the deal." One finger points at his own chest. "Grief wingman, you know."

I gag. "Worst kind to have. It's the only kind of wingman who doesn't try to get you laid."

He sucks air through his teeth and squints his eyes. "We're gonna have to cross that bridge eventually, you know. At least three items on your Live Again list are, ya know." He moves his hands in a few different configurations because he apparently can't say the words *sex positions* out loud.

"Those were *joke* additions," I insist. "Well, mostly."

We both laugh and then fall into silence. I kick his shoe with my shoe. "Thanks. For saying that to her. I was either going to politely defer to my elder and then hate myself forever or I was going to burst into flames and smite her entire bloodline."

"Happy to help."

It's just a thing people say, but I actually believe him.

"I'm sure she's calling up my mother to tell her the story right this very instant."

Miles grimaces. "Sorry."

"I'm not. If she tells it accurately, my mother will kick her ass for what she said." And then I grimace too. "Though she's not going to tell it accurately. Sorry. You're probably forever a villain in my family lore."

He shrugs. "Worth it." And then he glances at me. "You

mentioned you're not really talking to your parents right now?"

"I just don't want them to experience the trainwreck along with me. It's kind of a *Go on without me!* sort of thing."

He's quiet for a minute, absorbing that. "Did they know her well?"

"Lou? Gosh, yeah. I mean, she was my best friend since I was five years old."

"And you grew up here?"

"Brooklyn born and raised."

"College too?"

"Nah. Well, Lou did. She registered for Pratt, in the design school. But she dropped out after her first cancer diagnosis. Never actually attended. Another tragedy, as Marzia would say."

"But not you?"

"No. It probably makes me apathetic, but I really just never had the interest. I wasn't a good student."

"Lemme guess, you talked too much in class and distracted others?"

I laugh. "Oh, suddenly you're an expert, huh?" I stand and stretch. Those six hours of sleep last night were apparently less than a drop in the bucket because I'm suddenly overwhelmed with fatigue. I can feel it gumming up my cellular processes; my oxygen levels drop, my metabolism slows, and if Godzilla showed up right now, I'd roll facedown and let him stomp me.

He stands too; it's clear that parting is imminent. He hesitates and then offers me a hand. Like we're two golf associates who've just decided to commit tax fraud together.

"Oh, come on," I say again, batting his hand away and holding my arms out instead, for a hug. After all, he just took on the most gossipy dental hygienist in Brooklyn for me.

He stares down at me, nonplussed, but then he leans in.

It's a friendly hug, with our arms alternatingly linked, our ears pressed together, and for a moment he's stiff. His words come back to me. *They're my only family.* I wonder when was the last time he was hugged. Actually, come to think of it, when was the last time *I* was hugged? A moment passes, and the timing arrives when most people would stop hugging. But Miles has just loosened his tension by a shoelace and I can't let go now. Instead, I cinch up my arms and resituate my chin against his shoulder.

"I don't do anything halfway," I warn him.

"Okay," he says in a low voice.

When we come apart from the hug, his cheeks are slightly pink and he looks a little different to me than he did pre-hug. He's not quite the scowly asshole I'm used to. Now he's a scowly asshole who I've recently learned could really use a hug from time to time.

He clears his throat and reaches into his pocket to pull out two double-A batteries. "Do me a favor and change the batteries in the smoke detector at the apartment, yeah?"

"Oh. Sure."

"See you . . . tomorrow?"

"Yeah. There's no school. Private school teacher development day, their schedule is all screwy. Reese is working from home but she asked me to come by and hang out with Ainsley. I'll be there by ten A.M."

"Okay."

We say goodbye and I give him a wave as we walk our separate ways. I glance back and see that he's standing on the path, thirty feet back, hands in his pockets, eyes narrowed, studying me. I flash him a double thumbs-up and then shoo him away.

He laughs, shakes his head, and turns.

When I get back to the studio apartment, I change the batteries right away, so I don't forget. I'm confused, though, because the light is already blinking green even before I change them. I collapse onto the twin bed and pull my phone out.

Pretty slick, I text Miles.

A few minutes pass and then, *What?*

You assign me a fake chore just to make sure I go back to this apartment tonight?

Another few minutes pass. *So it worked?*

I will not dignify that with a response, I respond, and go take a shower. I scald myself and nearly weep, it feels so good. I make an honest attempt at combing my hair, but 2-in-1 was not designed for people who can tuck their hair into their waistbands. I give up.

I haven't bothered with any lights, so eventually darkness fills in all the cracks. I slide to my butt next to the bed and wipe the tears out of my eyes with my knees. The tears don't stop until I'm on my side, counting floorboards, until the light changes again and I'm hollow and ragged and the world that everyone else lives in is a funhouse.

The next day is here but I haven't done anything to say farewell to the last one. Time dogpiles me and I marvel at the fact that anyone, ever, has the strength to get up off the floor.

"I'm sorry," Lou says as I clear away the soup I just made for her that she couldn't make herself take even one bite of.

"Please don't apologize." I mean it with every fiber of my being.

"I have to apologize, Lenny," she replies, immediately humbling me beyond what I'd thought possible. Because, of course, she's the one who's sick, and that's her burden. I'm the one who's not sick and my burden is figuring out exactly how much I can carry for her. And her regret, sorrow, apologies, those are things I can carry for her.

"Cream of mushroom used to be my favorite," she laments emphatically behind two hands. Her fingers slide down and I spot her clear brown eyes. "No one tells you that cancer even steals all your favorites."

We wilt together, shoulder to shoulder, until suddenly I stiffen. "Cancer is such a loser! Quit bullying people. Get a hobby. Get a job, loser."

Lou laughs and my world rights itself. "Yeah! Totally. I bet cancer has a substack where it's always writing about how nice guys finish last."

"Cancer is probably convinced the female orgasm isn't real."

"Cancer probably pressures undergrads to drink shots of 151."

"Cancer probably got secret plastic surgery and then started selling diet pills on its Instagram page."

"*Cancer can blow me,*" Lou gripes.

"*Well.*" I consider this. "*Someone probably should. It's been a rough couple years.*"

"*It has,*" Lou agrees. "*It really has.*"

Chapter Seven

I'm convinced some people have all the luck because there's not really a better explanation for why I don't have any of it.

It probably seems like I'm making it up that I trip and fall in the crosswalk on my way to Reese and Ainsley's. But alas. I'm suddenly staring down at a square of concrete framed between my palms.

I dust the sting off my hands and hobble the rest of the way to the building. It's all so bleak. The apocalypse could be fun. At least it'd be socially acceptable to toss my hands in the air and run in a circle.

I dash into the building and hide from the world inside the elevator. The ding as I get to their floor is so artificially cheery it feels like satire.

"Try-hard," I accuse the elevator as I step off at Ainsley's floor. "You're probably faking it like all the rest of us."

I turn the corner in the hallway and there's a big scary man waiting for me outside Reese and Ainsley's apartment.

"Talking to yourself?" Miles asks dryly.

"Well, I have to. God's not picking up my calls ever since I tried to rope her into that MLM."

"I never have any idea what you're talking about."

"It's probably better that way."

He straightens up from where he was leaning against the wall and squints at me. "Hey, whoa. Hold on."

"What?"

"You look awful."

He's standing between me and the door, so I make an attempt to push past him. "Great. Thanks. You know, I was worried I was going to have a bad day, but with one simple sentence you've really turned things around for me."

I reach up to ring Reese's doorbell, but his fingers land firmly on my elbow. "Hold on," he says in a low voice.

But before he can say anything else, Reese's door flings open and there's Reese and Ainsley.

"Lenny! Hi!" Reese's eyes skate over and dim. "Miles."

He drops his head in an infinitesimal nod. I internally add greetings to the list of things Miles and I need to work on together.

"Headed out?" I ask them, confused.

"I was just texting you," Reese says, apology all over her face. "I'm such a dolt but I accidentally double-booked. Ainsley has a doctor's appointment in half an hour but I forgot when I asked you to come in. We're headed there right now."

"Is she okay?" Miles cuts in, glancing back and forth between them, and I make another internal note. Talk *to* Ainsley, not *about* her.

"Just a yearly physical," Ainsley answers for herself.

"Oh, okay," I say. "No problem. Do you need me to come in later?"

"Well . . ." Reese says with a grimace. "We usually go to this special restaurant that's down by her doctor's office. Let's just see each other tomorrow? You can pick her up from school for me? I'll compensate you for today, obviously. I'm so sorry to cancel like this." She's jamming on the call button for the elevator until the doors slide open. They're clearly very late.

"Good luck! I'll see you tomorrow." I wave at Ainsley. She waves back. I add another hand and wave both. She does both. I add a foot in the waving mix and, grinning, so does she. We both do identical hops, trying to wave the second foot as well, when the elevator doors slide closed and she disappears from view with a laugh.

"Well, I guess I'll—"

Then I'm being steered toward the stairs by my shoulders. But we're walking upward instead of downward.

"What are we doing?"

He points to an apartment door, the unit that's directly above Reese and Ainsley's. "My place."

He swings us through the door and I stand just across the threshold, blinking around at everything. "And why am I at your place?"

"Lenny, you're bleeding."

"Huh?" Oh. I guess I tore my pants when I fell. And skinned my knee like a five-year-old. I didn't even notice.

He makes it to the living room and turns to see that I'm still standing on his doormat.

"This is . . . not what I was expecting," I admit, peering around at his apartment.

He looks around, hands on his hips. "What were you expecting?"

"Bachelor pad? I guess? Huge TV playing sports commentators in perpetuity? Maybe some kind of tacky art made out of empty whiskey bottles? A framed hockey jersey?"

He laughs and shakes his head at me, so I kick off my sneakers and take a cautious step into his apartment. It's much smaller than Reese's. Just a central room that combines the living room and kitchen all in one. I can see a few closed doors around the edges that must be the bathroom and a bedroom or two. The walls are painted a rich blue. His furniture is all a matching set and looks squishy and warm. I can see from here that he has a full set of matching glasses on a shelf in the kitchen and, yup, that looks like matching multicolored plates and bowls as well.

An odd, disorienting feeling slips through me. This feels distinctly like . . . a family home. I realize I've been thinking of him as a bachelor, because he's got a real Lone Ranger thing going on. But . . .

"Are you married?"

He blinks at me. "What?"

"Kids?"

"Lenny, get in here and sit down."

I eye him up but follow directions, perching on the edge of his couch. And I mean the edge. I've got barely an eighth of a buttcheek on the cushion. My thighs are burning. "Well?"

He strides out of the room and comes back with a tiny white briefcase.

"No wife, no kids. Sit back." He's kneeling in front of me, glaring at my legs and opening the briefcase. I peer down into it. It's a mini pharmacy in there. Bandages, gauze, tubes of ointment, swabs, pills, tong thingies, you name it. He's a Florence Nightingale wannabe.

He moves the hole in my pants from one side to the other, trying to get to the scrape. Finally, with a sound of frustration in the back of his throat, he just reaches for my ankle and rolls my pants up, over my knee. I grimace down at my long-unshaven shins. "Sorry. Wasn't expecting company."

"Huh?"

I gesture to the leg hair.

He rolls his eyes. "Oh. Yeah. How dare you have leg hair."

I laugh for the shortest of seconds, but then he's disinfecting my knee and my time is better spent trying not to kick him right in the face for the searing pain he's inflicting on me. I'm wincing, sucking in breath, sliding down off the couch, and he's just rolling his eyes, the heartless lout. "Bear it if you can," he says tonelessly.

I'm in a puddle on the floor, but it doesn't seem to hinder his process. In less than a minute he's got me properly bandaged and my pant leg pulled back down. "Sorry about the pants. I don't think there's anything I can do about the rip."

"That's okay. I'll patch them later. Thanks for the bandage."

I lift two hands up to Miles, who is already standing. He grips me firmly and *bang* I'm on my feet. Just like that.

We're standing a foot apart and he closes a few inches of the distance, squinting into my face. Again I notice the fan of smile lines outside each of his eyes. They're not in service now, however. He's appraising me and frowning. "Did you sleep at *all* last night?"

I shoot him a little pouty grimace. "I slept like a baby. Twelve straight hours. They want me to star in a mattress commercial."

"Don't argue. It's obvious."

"Because I look so awful?"

"I mean, sorry to offend your vanity, but it's an objective fact."

This time I use my hands to squinch my face into a grotesque shape and waggle my tongue at him.

"Were you a good sleeper before Lou died?"

Hearing him say her name so easily is a guttural jolt. My hands drop to my sides.

"Yes."

"So why didn't you call me?"

"What do you mean?"

"If you couldn't sleep, or needed to talk, you should have called me. I shouldn't be finding out that you had a sleepless night because I happen to run into you when you drag your rotting carcass to work."

"What?" The rotting carcass comment is such a body slam I might not survive it. "Come on. I can't actually call you in the middle of the night!"

"Why?"

"Because it's the middle of the night!"

"So?"

"So, you should be sleeping."

"So should you."

We hold each other's glare until he drops his head and does the thing that people with buzzed hair get to do where they rub their palm all the way from the crown of their head to the back of their neck. "Lenny, I didn't suggest this because I thought it would be easy. I don't care if it's hard. Of *course* it's hard. But in order for me to be there for you, I need to actually *be* there. So what if I lose a couple hours of sleep."

"So . . . say I do call you. What would you even do?"

"Call and see."

I don't say anything and he sighs. "Just promise me that you'll try it once."

Well, I guess once can't hurt. "Okay, fine. It's your REM cycle, I guess."

There's a flash of triumph in his eyes and he stands up. "I'm heading to the grocery store. You stay here and sleep. I'll be back in an hour or so."

"Sleep here? Why?"

"You look like you can barely make it to the elevator on your own two feet. I have a perfectly good couch."

The thing is . . . the world is splashy Technicolor nonsense and I could really use a couple winks. But when I imagine dragging my—okay, okay—rotting carcass back to the studio apartment and collapsing into the twin bed, in theory it sounds luscious. But come on. It's the scene of the crime. The exact place I didn't sleep for a literal second last night. The blankets are on the floor, twisted, feverish, blighted. Who knows what happens there.

But here? Look, what a fluffy pillow. And I can see dust motes in a shaft of sunlight. There's a fan going in one of the rooms and it creates an oceanlike fog of sleepy sound.

Miles must take this for hesitation because he leans down, takes my backpack off, and sets it on the ground.

"Not to sound like a dick, but this is seriously for your own good." Then he plants his pointer finger smack-dab in the middle of my forehead and gently pushes me backward onto the couch.

Even if I hadn't given up Pilates after one horrific session, my core still wouldn't have been able to defeat basic physics. I collapse back into the couch cushions and decide not to fight the good fight. I curl onto my side, take a spare pillow, and squash it over my head. Blocking out him and the world. But mostly him.

I stay awake just long enough to hear the front door click closed and then I'm out.

WHEN I WAKE UP, the light has changed and one of my socks is halfway off my foot. I sit up so fast I scare the shit out of Miles, who is sitting at the kitchen table behind the couch, reading a newspaper.

"Holy shit!" He's got a hand over his heart as a page of the paper sifts to the floor. "You popped up like a mummy."

"What just happened," I grumble, rubbing my eyes and trying to make sense of my life.

"You just slept for five hours. You should see your hair right now. It's a real work of art." He's back to the paper.

"What am I smelling?"

"I made you lunch. Well, I guess it's more like dinner now. You want some?"

I stand up and groan. My muscles are aching, but not in a bad way. "Bathroom first."

"Through that door." He points without looking.

I head that way and actually laugh out loud when I see my hair. My bun has somehow migrated ninety degrees to one side and come halfway loose. The other side of my hair is floating in static. There are pillow lines on one cheek and my eyes are bloodshot and puffy.

I spend a few minutes unabashedly snooping around his bathroom. Hand towels that match his bath towels. No mildew in the shower. More 2-in-1 shampoo, which should be illegal, but his hair is a half inch long so I'll allow it. His toilet paper is upside down, though, feeding from the bottom side, so I take a quick second and flip it. There's a box of condoms in the medicine cabinet, which I nosily shake, trying to guess how many are in there. Other than that, nothing fun. I do, however, see a spare toothbrush. So I commandeer it and brush my teeth, tossing it in the cup next to his when I'm done. I wash my face and hands and slather some lotion on and that's pretty much that.

"What're we eating?" I ask when I reemerge, lifting the lid on a pot in the middle of the kitchen table. Steam billows out and a savory scent greets me.

"It's just chili. Sorry. I know it's still summer. But I wanted to make something that would stick to your bones."

I'm already spooning some into a bowl and don't bother accepting an apology I don't think is necessary. I'm suddenly famished.

We eat dinner together in silence, him still looking at the newspaper. I do the dishes, feeling energized by my nap and by the food. But as soon as I turn the sink off, I realize that the sun will set soon. There's a cold pit in my gut and tears spring to my eyes. I don't want to leave here, but I also don't want to stay.

This is the time of day when everything I've ignored for the last few hours starts knocking.

"Hey."

His eyes shoot up to mine. "Hm?"

"Let's do homework."

"HOMEWORK" MEANS THAT I drag him ten blocks south to a sporting goods store. It wasn't in our original plan but it's all in the name of Ainsley. I help him agonize over which baseball mitt to buy.

"Help" means that I fall in love with the sporting goods salesman (short king, full beard, looks like he'd know how to drive a Jeep down a mountainside) and Miles puts a hockey helmet over my head.

"So," I say as I watch him put a tiny baseball mitt on, like, one quarter of his hand and try to open and close it. "You're going with the *Come play a game of catch with the old man* angle, huh?"

He scratches at the back of his neck.

"It's a good idea!" I reassure him. "I just wondered why you chose baseball."

"I know it's cliché . . ."

"It's brilliant! But . . . what if you helped her get really good at a sport no one else is good at? Like . . . I dunno. That."

"Badminton? That would require me knowing literally anything about badminton."

"So, be bad at badminton with her. Learn it together!"

He considers the idea, then puts the baseball mitts back on the hooks and heads to the badminton area.

The salesman—aka love of my life—comes over to assist us and by the time we leave, Miles has a full bag of whoozits and whatsits and I've got hearts in my eyes.

"He was wearing a wedding ring," Miles says, looking down at me while we wait at the crosswalk.

"I *know*." I scowl back up at him. "Just let me fantasize from afar."

He glances back toward the store and then down at me again. "So . . . you never actually approach these guys? You just want to . . . daydream about them?"

"It's something to do." I nudge him to start walking once the light changes.

"Crossword puzzles. Push-ups. These are things to do."

"You've never fantasized about someone you've just met?"

His brow immediately, aggressively furrows and he's looking at me like *Exactly how much does this lady know about a man's mind?*

I burst out laughing. "I'm not talking about, like, *sex stuff.*"

He crushes down a laugh and shakes his head. "It's involuntary."

"I'm not judging you. It's clearly normal. Who would it hurt anyhow? You've got a face like a bulldog. Nobody would ever even know what you're thinking."

"Face like a bulldog . . ." he murmurs, but I plow on.

"I'm talking, like, you've never met someone and thought, wow, I bet she makes a great double fudge brownie? Wow, I'd like to eat one of those brownies after I get home from work. Wow, I bet she'd like to learn how to fish and one day we'll rent a cabin and fish and eat brownies and I'll give her my grandmother's engagement ring and someday we'll have twins?"

He's bemused. Possibly still digesting the bulldog comment. "No, Lenny," he says simply. "I've never done that."

I burst out laughing at his delivery. "Okay, fine. So, your fantasies are limited to, like, ooh, pretty lady, I'd like to give *her* the business."

"No." He starts walking in the other direction.

"What a stunner!" I throw my voice low and put on a wiseguy accent. "What I wouldn't give to teach her a thing or two."

"Oh, my God." Now he's turned and started walking in the other opposite direction.

I catch up to him quickly, an irreverent grin on my face that he deftly ignores. "So, have you always done this fantasy thing?" he asks.

"Maybe? I don't know. No." I shove my hands in my pockets while we walk, most of my mirth evaporating away. "Mostly just since Lou . . . Is it really that weird?"

"No." He turns to me, one hand on my shoulder, that familiar quick squeeze.

"It always comes back to her, doesn't it?" I laugh but there's no levity in it. "Everything reminds me of her. Like my hair earlier today. How ridiculous it was in the mirror. It would have made her laugh so hard. Not in a mean way! Just like . . . how to explain this?"

He slows to a stroll, puts his hands in his pockets.

"Lou had great hair," I try. "Long red hair that she could part down the middle. You know how hard it is to pull off a middle part? Really hard."

"I'll take your word for it."

"Well, she had the kind of hair that you could do anything to. It could hold curl, but it would also stay perfectly straight if you blow-dried it or flat-ironed it. It grew fast and she would try a million different hairstyles. It was always the first thing anyone ever commented on with Lou. Her hair."

He makes a little noise to show he's listening.

"She lost it twice. The first time when we were twenty, during her first round of chemo. I shaved my head to match hers. When her hair grew back in, it was a little different than before, but still beautiful." My voice cracks. "When she started to lose it again, four years ago . . . she didn't let me shave my head again. She said this time she wanted me to keep growing my hair, as long as I could possibly get it. So . . . here I am. Accidentally zipping my hair into my hoodies. And waking up with it looking like *that*."

"Wow. Lenny . . ." He pauses. "I'm sorry I was making fun of it this afternoon. I didn't realize . . ."

"No, no." I wave it away. "I know my hair looks ridiculous these days. I don't style it or take care of it. You didn't hurt my feelings."

"I am sorry, though. For making fun of the way you look."

"Oh, you mean that first day we met? You already apologized for that. And that was different than the jokes you made about my ridiculous hair. You weren't being *mean* about my hair. Besides . . . whenever my hair looks absurd, it makes me happy. I'm not explaining this right."

"Take your time."

"Lou and I used to call ourselves the Fuglies."

"I'm sorry, the *Fuglies*? As in . . ."

"Fucking ugly. Yeah. Exactly."

"Jesus."

"It sounds terrible, I know. But it was so great."

"You're not ugly."

"No, no. That's not the point! I mean, Lou and I were definitely ugly ducklings in our preteen years. And I have the pics to prove it."

"Can I see?" Miles asks, arching his eyebrows.

I laugh and then pull out my phone, texting him an album of Lou and me, post-Alanis, pre-Rihanna.

He takes a quick perusal and literally laughs out loud at some of them. I can't bear to check which ones brought him so much joy.

"The point wasn't ugliness," I try to explain. "The point was that when we were together, just the two of us, we didn't spend any time worrying about being pretty. It was that being ugly was okay, no big deal."

"Like a state-of-mind sort of thing."

"I guess? It was more about just letting ourselves relax. It's not that we were never interested in makeup or stylish clothes or whatever. It wasn't about rejecting any of that. It was more that . . . well, I guess my friendship with her was this safe zone . . . a sphere of fugly that other people's judgments just sort of bounced right off of."

"Ah. I get it. She wasn't just a pal. She was your comrade."

And I just break.

A torrent of tears burn their way out of me. I'm bent over and gasping for air and every muscle I have is bearing down, trying to squeeze this pain clear of me so that I can live. Because I won't survive if it stays. How could anyone endure this? How can I endure this?

Distantly, I'm aware of a group of people walking past us, probably staring at me. Miles takes a step to the side, shielding me from their view.

Comrade. "I never thought about it that way, but . . ." She was. It's the perfect word to describe her. She was the one at my side. Had my back. No words necessary. I had one person on this earth who would have died for me, and I would have died for her if possible. But it wasn't possible. There was nothing I could do.

"*There was nothing I could do.*" The words are broken, sliced, aching with fresh blood.

"You're doing it right now," Miles says quietly. "There's never anything we can do to keep someone alive, Lenny. There's no bargain you can make. It's an illusion. A terrible illusion. The only thing you ever could have done is what you're doing right now. Sending her off."

I keep crying. For a long, terrible time. Eventually we're walking again and then we're arriving at the studio apartment.

"Thanks," I manage, swollen eyes on the darkened sky. "Thanks for the nap and the food and the—" I gesture to . . . everything.

He nods and then, "You all right?"

"No. But . . ."

I have to be alone now and he seems to get it.

He follows me up the stoop stairs to the brownstone door, and when I drop the keys he scoops them up and unlocks the door for me. He turns my backpack strap right side out. I'm standing there watching him fix everything and tears are drop-drop-dropping off my nose. He's standing there watching me cry and then he lifts the hem of his T-shirt and quickly wipes the tears off my nose. New ones replace the old ones and he does it again.

"Call me," he says sternly.

I turn to leave and he puts one hand gently on my shoulder, pausing me.

"Lenny."

"I promise," I concede. "I'll call."

"**H**old still!"

I'm laughing and wiggling out from under Lou's eyeliner torture. But she's obsessed and I am her crash test dummy. The new 5Night music video is dropping in half an hour and she wants to re-create Min's eye makeup look from the promo pics so that we can enjoy the video release in style. She's already wearing Eunho's fake piercings in honor of our everlasting unrequited obsession with the group.

She's finally finished and I admire her talent in the mirror. I look like the sex kitten version of myself. But also a little bit like an alien. It works for me. "Can you re-create this look for my next date?"

She's touching up her lipstick. "Are you kidding me? I've been begging for that for years."

She moves on to adjusting the short black wig she's taken to wearing occasionally while her hair is still growing back in. She seems happy tonight.

I nervously pick up my phone. "Wanna . . . take a pic to show off our looks?"

For half a second, I see the no cross her face. She used to be the queen of the selfie, but this second bout with cancer has stolen another of her favorites. She never used to care about how she looks in pictures. But now everything is painful. And we haven't taken one together in over a year.

But this time her chin lifts. "It's their first comeback in a year and a half. We have to commemorate it."

Yes! "Plus we look amazing."

"Totally."

I pile onto her and she smashes our cheeks together and we take a gorgeously unattractive photo. The only thing that looks good is the painstakingly elegant makeup that Lou's done for us both.

She studies it for a second. "Should we upload it?"

My stomach flips. We used to upload pics of ourselves to our shared fan account all the time. I'm thrilled she wants to now.

"Yes."

"Hopefully 5Night will see it and they'll totally fall in love with us and DM us to be their new wives."

I laugh. "Yes. Hopefully."

Chapter Eight

"Sit down," I hiss to Miles as he jumps up from the playground bench for the ninetieth time. He stares down at me and then back at Ainsley, who is dangling one-handed from a monkey bar. He uses his baseball cap to scratch an itch on his head and then plunks stubbornly back down next to me.

"You honestly don't think that's dangerous?" he demands, jutting a thumb to where she's swinging like a wind chime.

"Of course it is! Playgrounds are state-sanctioned death traps. But I'm telling you, you do *not* want to be that guy." I use my chin to point toward a dad who is crouched down, arms out, at the heels of a toddler who is doing their royal best to escape his overbearing parenting.

"That guy looks like the only sane person here," Miles grumbles.

"Yeah, maybe, but it's no coincidence that his kid is clearly having the least fun."

Miles grumpily crosses his arms over his chest but seems to concede the point when Ainsley does one of those slow, over-the-arm somersaults that would literally tear an adult's rotator cuff. She releases from the bars, lands on two feet and two hands, and then jumps up, running off toward the mini climbing wall.

"Lesson number one to having a good relationship with a

kid," I tell him. "They're literally wired to have fun, so just get out of the way."

He raises an eyebrow. "Lesson number one isn't keep them safe?"

"Obviously. But you can't make it seem like that's what you're doing. If they think you're the safety patrol, they spend all their time trying to get farther and farther from you. If you're the fun patrol, they wanna be around you and then it's more likely that you'll be there when they actually need help."

He tips his head to one side. "I guess that makes sense. So, what's number two, then?"

"Don't treat her like you're scared of her. Like she's a baby tiger or something, and if you're not careful she'll scratch your face off."

"I don't do that!"

I stare at him, unblinking.

"Okay. Maybe I do that. But I just wouldn't know what to do if she ever had a meltdown."

"You've dealt with my meltdowns. You'd do better than you think."

"That's different."

"How?"

"It just is. Kids are scary. They're ruthless."

Ainsley comes running up to us. She runs like one of those giant blow-up dancing dolls outside car dealerships. All elbows and unexpected knees.

"Hit me!" she says, and opens her mouth like a baby bird. I take her water bottle and aggressively hydrate her. She laughs when some accidentally shoots into her hair. She turns and runs full speed back to the swings, which she lands on belly first, arms out, up up up halfway to the sky and back back back.

"Yes. Ruthless," I deadpan.

When it's time to go, I corral Ainsley, and Miles is right behind us. He's got a small Nancy Drew–style notebook and a little stub of a pencil. He's furiously writing something down, following in our wake.

Ainsley and I walk, holding hands and swinging our arms in wider and wider arcs until she almost falls down.

"Hey," I say. "What do you think your teacher's cooking for dinner tonight?"

She squints up at me. "Mr. Landry?"

"Yeah."

She looks into nothing, her hair sticking up every which way and her giant Prince concert tee falling off one shoulder. "Um . . . he told us once that lasagna is the food of the gods. So, probably lasagna."

I'm delighted with that answer. "Like Garfield!"

"That cat on your one shirt?"

"Yeah, he's obsessed with lasagna."

"Why are people obsessed with lasagna?" she asks. "I mean, it's all right, but . . ."

"Miles," I prompt. "What do you think?"

"Why people are obsessed with lasagna? I . . . I don't know."

And that's all he says.

Ainsley was staring up at him expectantly but then looks away, bored, kicking at a rock and nearly pulling my arm out of the socket when she trips for a second.

"People are obsessed with lasagna because cheese is actually three of the five food groups," I inform her sagely.

"That's not—" Miles tries to cut in, but I speak over him.

"What do you think Miles is going to have for dinner?" I ask her.

"Ummmm." She eyes him for a second. "Chicken noodle soup?"

"No way," I cut in. "He's a . . . protein shake, salad-hold-the-dressing type of guy."

"What?" He looks so incredulous that even Ainsley laughs.

"Okay, right. If I'm making a serious guess, I'd say that Miles could eat sandwiches every meal for the rest of his life and not get tired of it."

He looks like he's about to argue but then shrugs in concession.

And now I've made it to the real issue. "And your mom? What is she gonna have for dinner?"

The mirth leaves Ainsley's eyes. "I don't know. Sushi? That's what she gets sometimes with clients."

"Oh. She's not coming home for dinner again tonight?" Miles asks.

"No," Ainsley grumbles, looking down at her shoes. She drops my hand and fiddles with her backpack, her eyes still on the ground.

"That's like the fifth time this week," Miles observes (un)helpfully.

Ainsley is shrinking down into her thoughts, her shoulders caving in and her backpack suddenly looking huge on her back.

Miles jolts when he catches my eye. I probably look like I'm attempting to turn him into a mushroom with nothing but the power of my glare.

Ainsley takes my hand to cross the street, but once we make it to her block she runs ahead and disappears into the lobby.

"Well, that didn't go well," I inform Miles.

"Yeah. I gathered that. How'd I get it wrong?"

"I was trying to find a way to get *her* talking instead of hearing more adult opinions. Yes, we all know that Reese is gone a lot and it obviously bugs Ainsley, but what we don't know is how Ainsley actually feels about it all. If I want to know how *you* feel about it, I'll just ask you. But that's not how it works with Ains."

He's quiet. We make it to the lobby of the building and, as previously promised, she's waiting for us with the doorman, talking to him while he leans down to hear her. As soon as he sees us he stiffens and steps out to formally open the door.

His name is Emil. He's Ukrainian and a big soccer fan. I had to pry this information out of him. He's so painfully professional it borders on rude. I'm certain that on the inside he's a sugar cookie. Someday, after fifty years of marriage, we'll soak our feet side by side while we watch television and unwrap each other's Hershey's kisses.

"Really?" Miles says, studying my face as the three of us pile into the elevator to head up to the apartment. "He's like ten years old."

"He's twenty-two."

"Regardless, he's not old enough for you."

I shrug. "I've got time."

Miles laughs and drags a hand over his face.

When we arrive, Ainsley kicks off her shoes and scampers into the bowels of the apartment, away from the adults as fast as possible. Miles moves to go after her.

"Miles."

He turns.

"Let her do her own thing."

"You're not even going to check on her?" he asks. When I first met him, all I would have heard was judgment in that question. But now I can hear his earnest concern and confusion.

"Kids usually need some space after school. She'll come out when she's hungry."

He's posed, looking over his shoulder at me, and behind him Reese's gigantic black-and-white photographs loom. A face in the photo comes into focus next to his. Something big finally clicks.

"Come on," I say, leading him into the apartment. "Let's get her snack ready."

We head to the kitchen and I dig out some spinach artichoke dip and chips.

He dips a chip with an absurd amount of dip and hands it to me. "Eat."

I'm not hungry, but once a chip is dipped, what are you supposed to do?

"So," he says after a while, sitting back and dusting chip dust off his hands. "The whole what-are-they-eating-for-dinner thing, that was you backing into talking about Reese?"

I nod. "Sort of . . . I've noticed that kids rarely answer direct questions. *How do you feel about your mom's work schedule?* Those kinds of questions feel like a quiz. And she knows what she's supposed to say. *It's fine.* Canned answer, right? But if you can get a kid talking about their life in a different way then you'll usually get more insight into how they actually feel."

He nods. Thinks. Nods. Then pulls out that little Nancy Drew notebook and writes something down.

"This is good stuff. Gimme more," he says.

I press two fingers to each temple and close my eyes. "Condensing a lifetime of experience into a few simple sentences . . . Okay, well, kids are actually pretty easy. If you can figure out how to feed and water them in a calm place, they'll mostly be all right. Most meltdowns are because they're hungry or thirsty or tired or overstimulated. So if you can meet their immediate needs in a low-key way, everything will probably be all right."

"What about an emotional meltdown? Like when Ainsley misses Reese?"

"Well, a little comfort goes a long way. And then distract her. TV or a game or a book or an errand."

"So . . . that's why you set Ainsley up with TV right off the bat that very first day."

"Yup."

"I had thought you were being lazy."

"But . . ."

"You were actually strategizing."

"Like I said, I've been nannying for a long time."

"How long?"

"I babysat for my neighborhood since I was twelve, but I got my first real experience as an au pair in Spain when I was seventeen."

"How long were you there?"

"Three months. Right after graduation. But then Lou got sick and I came home. Nannying here paid well and for the most part I was able to mold a lot of my hours around Lou, to help take care of her. It worked for us."

"Did you mostly take long-term gigs at that point?"

"Yeah. My first family in the States was for four years. The second was for three and the last was for two. They're the ones who recommended me to Reese. I started doing short-term stuff when Lou really needed my time and energy, toward the end."

"And now you've just been floating from gig to gig like Mary Poppins."

"Ah, Mary Poppins, the OG commitment-phobe."

I clear my throat. "So . . ." I start. "As long as we're asking each other wildly personal questions . . ."

He hums to show he's listening, but he's still writing in his notebook.

"What was it like growing up with a famous dad?"

He abruptly stops writing but doesn't look up at me. For a long moment, I think maybe I got it wrong, or maybe I got it right, but he's not going to answer. But then he says, "It was . . . not fun."

"When she described you as Ainsley's uncle, I wasn't sure in which way she meant, but . . . You and Reese are brother and sister?"

He nods, eyes still cast down. "Half. Through our dad."

He tips his head toward yet another picture of Carp Hollis on the wall. I realize all at once that not only did Miles lose his mother and cousin ten years ago, he also lost his father a year and a half ago.

I study the photo and realize that it looks even more like Miles than the black-and-white ones in the entryway.

"I'm sorry," I say, reaching across the table to give his hand a quick squeeze. "I feel silly for not having noticed the resemblance before."

I pull my hand back and he flattens his own against the table. "Thanks. It's okay. We weren't close. Not until the last few months of his life, anyway."

"I can't believe I didn't put it together sooner."

He waves a hand. "Why would you? We don't even have the same last name."

"Honey was your mom's name?"

He nods, writes one last thing down, and then slides his notebook away.

"So," I say, tracing a flower in the place mat under my elbows. "You've only known Ainsley for two years. Does that mean you and Reese—"

"Hel-lo!" The front door slams and Reese is home.

Miles stands up and steps away from the chips and dip, like he doesn't want to get caught mooching off Reese.

Reese comes into the kitchen and shoots me a grin when she sees me sitting at the table. Her grin abruptly freezes when she spots Miles standing in the middle of the kitchen with his hands in his pockets.

"Oh. Hi."

It's distinctly awkward.

"You're home early," I say.

"Yes! I . . ." She glances at Miles. "Ainsley seemed really bummed when I told her I'd miss dinner. So . . ."

"I was just seeing Lenny and Ainsley for a little bit," Miles says. He clears his throat. "Is it okay with you if I . . . hang out with them a lot?"

OMG. He said he was going to ask her if it was okay, but *this* is what he meant? Just casual as hell and *in front of me*?

"Oh." She looks stymied. "I'll talk to Ainsley and Lenny about it, I guess."

Subtext: *without you here looming like Batman.*

He seems to glean at least that much and nods. "All right. Okay. Well, see you all later."

Miles leaves and Reese goes to check on Ainsley. I remember at the last second that I was supposed to get Ainsley's lunch for tomorrow all set before I leave. I'm just cutting the crust off a turkey sandwich when Reese comes back into the kitchen. She's changed out of her business suit and is wearing expensive yoga gear again. She snags the crusts I've just cut and eats them while leaning against the counter.

"So . . . this Miles thing."

"Yeah, sorry about that. I told him to clear it with you but I didn't think he'd do it . . . that way."

"*I'm* sorry . . . He must have totally ambushed you. And I'm sure you just want to do your job without him hanging around. Maybe I should have put my foot down that first day you came here, when he insisted on staying with you two . . . but I just couldn't argue with him about it anymore."

To my surprise, I feel a tiny prickle of annoyance at Reese. "It doesn't bother me."

Reese blinks. Her eyes narrow in confusion. "Oh. I mean . . . if it's okay with you . . ."

She lets it hang there and I know what she's really saying: *Why the hell would this be okay with you?*

"He wants to spend time with Ainsley," I attempt to explain. "And he knows that when you get home from work your time with her is really precious. He doesn't want to get in the way."

More blinking. "Well . . . okay. If it starts to bother you, just tell me."

I wave goodbye to Reese, shout down the hallway to Ainsley, and then head out, nearly tripping over something waiting for me in the hallway. It's a Tupperware with a sticky note stuck to the top. *Eat this*, it says.

What a poet.

Chapter Nine

ife is a sewer, I text him the next day. He said I should call, but . . . I'm working my way up to it.

Noted. He's such an empathetic texter.

I'm serious. Life is absolutely terrible.

You're just now noticing this? This is basic stuff. Life is pain. Duh.

There's a long pause while I ponder this and then, *Wait,* he texts. *What's going on?*

What?

Why are you texting me about life being a sewer. Something bad must be happening. Where are you.

Nowhere.

Lenny.

Oh, fine. I MIGHT be crying in a laundromat.

Why are you in a laundromat? I have laundry at my place.

I stare at my phone, turning this sentiment over in my mind when he texts again:

How much longer will you be there?

I'm packing it up now.

I'll meet you at the studio apartment. There's something I wanna do with you.

I hobble the three blocks and reflexively scowl when I see him haunting my doorstep. He hoists the laundry from my back and runs it upstairs.

When he comes back I've got my hands on my hips. "What, exactly, are we doing?"

"It'll be fun." He stops midway through jogging down the brownstone steps. "Actually, there's a good chance it'll be terrible."

"We need to work on your elevator pitch."

Thirty minutes later I find myself standing on a gigantic sailboat moored off the financial district at sunset, staring at a list of cocktails that have first, middle, and last names and cost more than my hourly babysitting rate.

It's one of the few bar/boats that dot the coastline of Manhattan, permanently moored and apparently lovely on a late-August night. I glance around at the beautiful people swilling drinks and flashing bone-white teeth in the candle-light. "I don't think we're supposed to wear ripped jeans and sneakers here."

"Yeah." He's frowning like everyone is stupid and he'd really prefer if this boat were sinking. "Well, let's get a drink."

He orders a beer from an unimpressed bartender with hair like the Fonz. And I order something called a Madam President Obama. It's the most delicious drink I've ever tasted, and I clutch it with two hands.

"So . . . why are we here?"

Miles takes a huge swig of his beer. "For that." He points at the prow of the ship. He sighs. "And that."

The second "that" is apparently my right leg. I frown in confusion.

"The list, Lenny," he prompts, nodding with his chin toward my front pocket.

"Oh! *Oh.* Oh no."

"Yup." He looks resigned as we weave our way through couples. "Let's do it."

I don't even have to pull the list out to reread the bullet point. Apparently, neither does he.

"So." He clears his throat as we approach the prow of the ship. "Number eight, was it? *Find a big boat and do the* Titanic *thing.*" He glances at me. "Which *Titanic* thing exactly?" He's leaning over the railing and eyeing the sunset-dyed water distastefully. "Should I be taking off my boots?"

I laugh. "No. It's the . . ." I hold out two arms and sway to show which part I'm talking about.

I expect him to look even more embarrassed about what we're about to do, but he only looks resolute. "Okay."

I ignore all the trendy people behind us, stepping up right where the two railings meet, and press my midsection there.

Oh, why not?

I throw my arms out and wait.

Nothing happens.

I turn around and glare. "Miles!" I hiss.

He sighs but steps forward, behind me; his clothes touch my clothes and his arms extend six inches beyond either of mine. We sway and I burst out laughing.

"Is this it?" he asks, understandably with a hint of incredulity. "There's no line or something we're supposed to say?"

"I . . . don't think they say anything at that part of the movie? I mean . . . we could sing the Celine Dion song?"

"Knock yourself out."

He's starting to step away so I reach back and grab his shirt, tugging him back into position.

"I know!" I assert. "Say *If you're a bird, I'm a bird.*"

"That's not even from the right movie!"

"Just say it!" I've started swimming my arms like I'm doing the breaststroke because they're running out of blood flow just hanging out in the air like that.

"Isn't that the girl's line?"

"You know *The Notebook* well enough to know who says which line?"

"I've had girlfriends, Lenny. Part of having a girlfriend is that she makes you watch *The Notebook*."

"Well, it's a classic and all your past girlfriends have wonderful taste. And since it was clearly so formative for you . . ."

"If you're a bird, I'm a bird," he grumbles, deadpan, presumably to get this all over with faster.

Still, I take the W and throw my head back on an overjoyed cackle. The crown of my head bumps into his collarbone and when I open my eyes, I can see up his nose, and that the center of the sky is just starting to turn the blueberry blue of twilight. Instead of panicked sadness, I simply feel that I might be briefly living inside a wonderful moment.

"Did we do it?" he asks, tipping his head down slightly, hands on his hips, waiting patiently for me to stop leaning on him.

I stand up straight and stomp a foot. "By God, I think we've done it!" I yank the list out of my pocket and draw a line through number eight with my finger. It's laminated so all line-crossing has to be imaginary.

That's two down. I'm feeling tingly and slightly unsettled. Am I living again, yet? Who can tell. Probably I won't know until every single thing is crossed off and Miles appears from behind a curtain with a flower sash. I feel slightly ill. Also I'm dying for a *Titanic* rewatch.

He takes another two inches of his beer down and then glances back at the people who are looking at us with mixtures of amusement and embarrassment. "I think it's time."

"Let's blow this popsicle stand," I agree.

We leave the second half of our drinks and wander through Lower Manhattan, vaguely toward the train.

"So," I say, hands in pockets. "You've had girlfriends."

He laughs. "You say that like it's weird."

"It is weird. But only in an existential way. Not because you're gross. I just mean, it's also weird that you were once in second grade or if you ever went to Disneyland, that would be weird. It's weird because you've got a whole life I don't know anything about."

"'Girlfriends' with an 's' might be pushing it. I've dated. And had one serious girlfriend."

"And?"

He frowns. "And?"

"Nothing more you wanna say about her?"

We pass a narrow alleyway and between the two buildings we get a glimpse of the half-red, rising moon. He eyes that instead of me. "Not really."

A world opens up between us. It's unexpected. Heart-break Miles. First Date Miles. First Kiss. I'm Sorry Flowers. Miles leaning over someone in bed to click the lamp off for the night.

"Huh."

"What?" he asks.

"I don't know. Just thinking about all the experiences other people have. Through all the, you know, *grief*, I've kinda forgotten that the entire world is filled with all these other realities . . . possibilities . . . that I've never even considered before." A man in SpongeBob pajama pants walks his pug past us and I wonder who he's going home to. "I think when you're depressed sometimes it's easy to think that everyone is depressed? But right this very second, there are billions of people having happy moments. I kind of forgot about those people. I thought I knew how everything worked. And that all of it was terrible."

He weighs his head from one side to the other. "Only some of it is terrible."

"That's a much better percentage than I was working with."

"Yeah," he says with a resolute nod. "It is."

Chapter Ten

"I'm home!" Reese calls from the front hall.

Ainsley doesn't react, because she's sitting at the kitchen table with her gigantic Princess Leia headphones on, presumably tearing her way through Sir Elton John's discography. She's got a gigantic nest of tiny rubber bands in front of her. When I was a kid we put those on our orthodontia, but these days kids apparently twist them into bracelets.

Miles, on the other hand, overreacts to Reese's arrival, going straight as an ironing board and immediately hiding away the Cheez-Its he's just been snacking on.

"Miles ate all your Cheez-Its," I say the second Reese enters the kitchen.

He turns and looks at me like he'd really enjoy punting me down a water slide if given the chance.

It's knee-jerk. She laughs at the expression on his face. "Yeah, that's okay," she says. "I can afford another box."

Would you look at that; perhaps for the first time ever, Reese and Miles have had a nonstiff greeting. He blinks at her as she crosses the room toward Ainsley.

"Ains. Ains!"

Ainsley jolts and one of the rubber bands slingshots off her finger.

"Ouch! Shit!" Reese bends forward into a crouch, her hands over one of her eyes. ·

"*Mom!* Oh, Mommy, I'm so sorry." Ainsley scrambles her headphones off and tumbles her chair in her hurry to get to Reese.

"It's okay. It's okay," Reese says, patting her daughter with one hand and covering her eye with the other. "I just . . . Let me just."

Miles is there in an instant. "Let me see."

"It's really okay," Reese insists, trying to get past Miles while Ainsley tugs on her pants leg.

"Mommy, I'm sorry," she says again, and then bursts into tears.

"Oh, Ains—"

"Seriously, Reese, just let me see." He puts a hand on her elbow as she's reaching down toward Ainsley, who is now fully wailing.

"It's okay, Miles. Ainsley, come up here, sweetie."

"You don't know if it's okay yet, just let me—"

"Miles! *Back off.* I'm fucking fine if I say I'm fucking fine, okay?"

We all freeze. There's a sobbing breath and it doesn't come from Ainsley.

"Just back off," she says again, her voice quaking. And then she turns, Ainsley in her arms, and leaves the kitchen.

Miles's back is to me, his hands on his hips and his head down. *Not everyone will accept help when they're grieving. Some people just . . . go inward and bear it all alone.* Those were his words when we sat outside the sandwich shop, when I asked him why it was so important to him to help me through this time.

I make it to his side. He looks down at me, so frustrated and hurt. Useless, is what he called himself.

He takes a deep breath.

"I've got stuff for pancakes. Come up when you're done here." He goes to leave, pauses in the hallway, and then makes his way out of the apartment.

A FEW HOURS LATER, I knock on his door upstairs. He opens up, looking a little wrecked.

"You okay?" I ask tentatively.

"Fine, fine. Sorry . . . you had to see that."

"You have nothing to be sorry for." I can't get the word *useless* out of my head. This ragged version of Miles is not what I'm used to. He needs a task. "Hey. I'm not really in the mood for pancakes. Plus. I'm . . . in the dumps." (I'm actually not, right now.) "Can you think of a way to cheer me up?"

He smirks, like he can see right through me, but he takes the bait. "Let's go for a walk."

He abruptly turns around and walks back into his apartment.

"Outside is the other way!" I lean into his apartment and call to him.

"Where's your Big Bird sweatshirt?" he asks, heading back my way. "You're always in T-shirts and it's getting chillier at night."

"I like my clothes!"

"Me too, but it's the beginning of fall." He's back at the door, a sweatshirt in hand. "You haven't been back to your apartment in Brooklyn to change out your summer clothes for fall clothes yet, have you?"

I sag down. "No." Now I *am* in the dumps.

"When's the last time you were back? I thought maybe because you always show up in different clothes . . ."

"I get new stuff from secondhand shops a lot. My ward-

robe is expanding. Soon it will consume your entire apartment. You'll have to dig me out with a snow shovel."

"Well, next time you're in a thrift store, buy some warmer
clothes. Put this on for now and there might be a couple
warmer things back at my place if you need them."

And then he is shoving a blue sweatshirt on over my
head. The hood is big enough to fall forward over my eyes
and when I thread my arms through the sleeves, there's eight
inches of fabric left before I make it to the wrist holes. It's
warm and soft and old and smells like laundry detergent.

"Why do you still keep clothes there?" I ask him.

He tilts his head toward the door and I follow him into
the hallway.

"In case Reese wants me out of this apartment. I mean . . .
technically it's mine. But if she asked me to leave, I'd go."

"Why would you leave the apartment if it's yours?" I ask.

He locks up and we're out on the street before he answers
my question. "Because that apartment used to be hers. Well,
sort of. I mean that she and Ainsley used to live there."

"Ohhhhhh." It's all coming together. "Did she leave most
of her stuff? Is that why everything matches and looks so
homey?"

He frowns at me. "Yes. I mean, I'm not a Neanderthal. I can
pick out matching furniture. But yeah. She left a lot of stuff
when they moved to the big apartment to be with our dad."

He takes a left outside the building and by now, I've
learned to follow without questions.

"So," I prompt him. "She moved out to live downstairs
with your dad and you moved into her old place?"

He sighs and I guess he gets tired of telling the story in
scraps. "About two years ago, Dad had a stroke. It was pretty
bad. He called me and asked if I'd come visit. He and I were . . .

sort of in contact before that. But he'd definitely never asked me for anything before. Or asked me to come to the city. So I showed up and . . . a lot of stuff happened all at once. But the most important part was that our dad needed help. And so did Reese and Ainsley. He'd been helping her raise Ainsley. But suddenly he was in rough shape and Reese went from having a co-parent to having to take care of both him and Ains. I stuck around and helped. First I lived in the studio apartment. But then I moved into the apartment above them. Then he had another stroke, a worse one, and he didn't make it. He'd owned both apartments and he left the upstairs one to me and the downstairs one to Reese and Ainsley."

His hands are in his jeans pockets, so I slide my arm through the loop of his arm and momentarily press my face to his shoulder as we walk. We're a tangle of sweatshirts. "That's what you meant when you said you unexpectedly came into money. That everything was so new for you. You're not used to any of it."

He kicks at an empty chip bag as we walk, and then thinks twice, picks it up, and tosses it in a trash can. "Honestly, I was shocked he called me to come be with him. We'd been in contact a *bit* since my mom died . . . he understood that I didn't really have anybody anymore. He started calling and checking on me. But I always knew there was a limit to what he could offer me . . ." He glances down at me, and the arm that I'm hugging goes tense. "Reese . . . didn't know about me. Not until I showed up at the door two years ago."

"Oh, *Miles.*" I give his arm a huge squeeze. So tight that it throws off our walking balance and we veer toward the street. He rights us and saves the day. "That must have been so terrible for both of you."

It's all starting to make sense, in an awful sort of way.

"Not as bad for me. I knew about her since . . . I don't

know. The beginning? He used to visit when I was a kid. But only when he was on tour. He was married to Reese's mom at the time. And his image was a family man, you know? So an extramarital kid definitely had to stay under wraps. Once when I was ten or so, he gave my mom and me tickets to one of his shows. Backstage passes. But after the show, when we went backstage, they told us the passes weren't good. I just thought it was because something was wrong with the actual passes. But when I was about twenty my mom explained that Reese and her mom had flown in and surprised him, so he'd told the bouncers backstage not to let us through."

"God." A huge feeling is rising in my gut.

"Mom didn't let him come visit me anymore after that. She . . . was the proudest mom of all time. She told me all the time how much she loved me and how proud of me she was. She never missed a basketball game. Saved for years to be able to buy me a used car for my sixteenth birthday. Taught me how to tie a tie and what to say to my first crush. She understood what it means to be someone's secret. It means that you're *not* their pride and joy. And she wanted me to feel that I was hers."

I tug him to a stop in the middle of the sidewalk and squeeze him around the middle. My cheek is pressed to his sternum and I do my best to melt my feelings out through my body and into his.

For someone so prickly, he sure is a good hugger. Firm arms and his hands spread wide.

"It was hard for Reese too, you know," he says. "That's why I give her a lot of slack to be so . . ."

"Much of a butthead to you?" I supply.

He laughs and his arms finally loosen. "Yes. Let's keep walking." We break apart and keep going. "Her dad had a stroke, her whole life was tumbling down, and then out of nowhere she had a brother. She . . . had a certain view of how her parents' marriage was. How her childhood was. And my existence kind of exploded all of it."

"Oh, man."

"We're here."

"Where? This bakery?"

"Have you ever been here before?" There's a slight sparkle in his eyes, and I'm not sure why.

I shake my head.

"I just found it recently," he says. It's a few blocks from Reese and Ainsley's but I've never thought to duck my head in before. As we stand outside in the grainy evening, the scent of lemon poppy seed mixes with warm vanilla and cinnamon, and it physically draws me toward the door.

We pause at the sign that says they close at seven.

"Dang. Five minutes late!"

But then the door swings open and a young man, maybe early twenties, sticks his head out the door. "Y'all can come in. Plenty left."

I double-take. So does the young man. Our mouths drop open in perfect unison.

"Jericho?"

"Lenny?"

Me and Sparkly Backpack Guy run into each other's arms like we've crossed oceans to get to each other.

"I'm so glad to see you!" he crows. "I regretted not getting your number that day." He turns back into the bakery. "Mom! This is the girl who defended my honor when the car smashed my bike!" And then back to me. "Come in! Come in. Everything's on the house."

I'm being tugged into the bakery and when I look back over my shoulder, Miles is grinning, hands in his pockets. That wily minx planned this.

"So you're Lenny!" Jericho's mother calls from behind the counter. They have the same coily black hair and big brown eyes. Hers have gone wide, taking me in. "Little miss, you are *way* too small to be picking fights with grown men in the street!"

I step up to the counter sheepishly. "Ah. Yes. Well, actually, I agree with you. It's not gonna happen again."

She narrows her eyes at me.

"Really! I swear. It's not something I would normally do."

"Huh." Jericho leans against the counter and eyes me. "Because it seemed to come very natural to you."

That makes me laugh but I shake my head. "No, I'm . . . a little off my rocker these days? I lost somebody very close to me this year. Not to explain away my momentary insanity . . ." No one quite knows what to say to that, so I put my grief wingman to good use. "But. Yeah. Don't worry about me. I've got Miles. He's making sure I keep things a little more . . . manageable." I put one hand on his back and shove him forward into the spotlight. It works.

She turns to Miles. "Oh, hello! You're becoming a regular."

He puts his hands in his pockets and ducks his head. "Yes, ma'am."

I double-glance up at him with wide eyes. Deferential Miles is really something to see.

"Let me guess," she says. "You want a loaf of the ten-seed bread, the cinnamon pistachio scones, and a lemon poppy seed muffin to go."

"Ohhhhh," I say, looking through the display case at what she's selecting. That's the exact bread and scones on hand in Reese and Ainsley's kitchen at all times. I guess because Miles provides them.

"You get these for Reese and Ainsley?"

He nods. "The muffin is just for me, though. I don't share."

Jericho's mom laughs. "That's my goal with my baked

goods. To make some of them so good you just have to share them and to make others *so* good you can't bear to share them."

Miles smiles at her. "The lemon poppy seed muffins remind me of my mom," he tells her. "They're just like she used to make."

"Is that right?" Her face has gone soft and sweet. She understands what he's saying.

"Yeah. Except hers were terrible."

This makes all of us laugh. "But she tried." Miles shrugs and then turns to me. "What are you going to choose?"

My mouth waters looking at all the baked goods, wide and sturdy, golden brown and friendly. "Hmm." I bend down and peruse. "To go healthy?" I point at a premade steel-cut oats cup. "Or indulgent?" I point at a Nutella croissant.

"We'll take both," Miles decides.

They pack up our order and Jericho comes around the counter to make sure to trade contact info with me.

We're grinning and waving goodbye and leaving the bakery with two hot chocolates and a paper bag that smells like heaven.

"You gotta lotta tricks up your sleeve," I say to Miles, back out on the sidewalk.

"I *thought* you'd enjoy that little surprise."

"Let's eat." I reach for the bag.

"Hold on," he says, swatting me away. "This trip wasn't just so you could see Jericho again. I want you to pay attention to this. It's important."

He pulls out the oatmeal cup and the croissant and puts one in each of my hands.

"Something good for you." He points at the oatmeal. "Something bad for you." He points at the croissant. "And a change of scenery." He points at the bakery.

"Huh?"

"It's hard-won wisdom. A formula I figured out in my dark days. One I still need sometimes. When everything is going dark and you can't understand why . . . when the grief catches up to you again . . . Or when your sister shouts at you and you feel like the world's biggest tool. Just remember. Something good for you, something bad for you, and a change of scenery. That's the winning formula."

I look at the food in my hands and up at him. "Just like that? It's magic?"

"No. Of course not. It doesn't actually fix anything. But it buys you a little time."

He takes the oatmeal back and shoves it into the bag.

I take a robust bite of croissant and cross my eyes with ecstasy. "Okay, I can see the wisdom here."

We start to walk and he eats his muffin, bumping our shoulders together. He uses his thumb to get some Nutella off the corner of my mouth and grunts when it tastes as good to him as it did to me. "Let me get a bite of that."

I offer him the croissant and he offers me the muffin and we eat each other's desserts for half a block.

"Something good for me, something bad for me, and a change of scenery," I muse.

"It really works. You gotta use it. Especially if you ever need me and I'm not there."

"Oh, come on, Miles. You'll always be there. You're Old Trusty."

"I hope so."

"I wish I could be yours. Or anybody's," I say with a sigh.

"You'll get there, Lenny. I promise."

Chapter Eleven

I'm not sleeping, I text a few nights later. *I'm only telling you because you said I had to. Don't call me. I'm serious.*

He calls me.

I reject the call and viciously text him.

I said don't call me!

Talk to me, he texts back.

I have nothing to say. I'm depressed and sleepless. You don't have to baby me.

I'm not babying you, he insists. *Talk to me.*

WHAT'S WRONG WITH ME? I text him a few days after that.

In what context?

I went to a noodle shop, couldn't decide what to order, so I left. Why can't I properly feed myself? It's annoying!

There's nothing wrong with you. You're getting used to a new reality. You don't know how to live right now. It'll all come back. You'll take care of yourself again someday.

The thing about bodies is that some of us, even when we don't know how to live, just keep right on living, no matter how poorly we feed and water ourselves. And then some of us, like Lou, don't get to keep on living. Our bodies just give way and the world rushes right past.

And I'm here, sitting on the curb in front of the noodle

shop, forehead pressed to my knees, dripping tears onto my jeans.

Time heals all wounds, they say. Well, I can picture myself in ten years. It's crystal clear. I'm still sitting on this curb, utterly disoriented that I'm the one still alive and she's still gone.

Where are you? he texts.

I lurch to my feet. The threat of him finding me to force-feed me noodles has me actioning.

Don't come find me! I text.

I'm going to parachute in from a chopper with a turkey sandwich.

Improbably, I laugh. *Turkey doesn't fly well. Maybe peanut butter is the wiser choice.*

Just go back to the apartment, he texts. *I'll order takeout for you.*

Wait! Don't! I'm too far away!

Where are you? he texts again. And then when I don't answer fast enough:

Lenny . . .

I have to 'fess up. *I accidentally fell asleep on the train. I made it out to Queens and got off to find something to eat. There. You're caught up now. Don't yell at me.*

Go home and eat.

An hour later I'm lying on the bed next to an unopened takeout bag.

I take a quick selfie doing a peace sign. He'll recognize the blue-and-gray bedspread under my head and know where I am.

I purposefully do not study exactly how terrible I look in this photo. Raccoon eyes and dry skin and drab brown hair pulled back into a tight ponytail because what else am I gonna do with this mess?

Now that he knows where I am, he's not texting back. My bad selfie sits like a punctuation mark at the end of our chat. I can't bear it.

Did this horrific picture of me scare you away? I ask after a while. *Come on. Pic for pic.*

Eat dinner, he texts back.

Boring. Send nudes.

There's soy sauce in the cabinet if you need it, he texts.

When I get back to my phone there's a text waiting for me from Miles. It's a very close-up picture of the pasta he's eating for dinner.

Not those kinds of noods! I text him.

SOMETIMES HE TEXTS me first.

For instance, tonight:

Are you doing something dumb right now.

No! I text back. *Yes. I'm about to fall asleep at a bar.* I stand up and drag my ass out onto the street. *Define dumb.*

Lenny. ISTG.

Look at you with your acronyms! You're so hip.

Go get in bed.

I suppose you're doing something totally normal and healthy right now?

None of your business.

Hey! If I have to report my comings and goings to you, then it should be mutual.

He texts me a picture of two big feet crossed on his coffee table and a Tom Cruise movie on a television screen in the background.

Oooh! Is that MI4? I'm coming over right now.

But he doesn't let me ogle Tom Cruise. Instead he rents a classic and, much to my grumbling, we cross number 6, *watch*

The Godfather *and finally understand what everyone is talking about,* off the list.

I fall asleep on his couch and when I wake up, I've been folded like a pie crust into blankets. There's a proper pillow under my head and a glass of water on the coffee table where his feet were last night. Dawn is clearing its throat outside. I fold everything neatly when I leave and head back into the world.

BUT MOST OF the time, I text him first.

I've been crying for almost three hours straight, I text him one night.

Good job. Get it all out.

He doesn't understand. My fingers shake as I type the next words. *I want to stop but I can't.*

Okay. Be there soon.

He must know how to teleport, because I swear I've barely received the text before he's knocking on the door to the studio apartment.

When I answer the door for him, he can't hide his wince.

Have you ever seen those big suspended slabs of cow that Rocky beats the shit out of? Pretty sure that's what my face looks like right now.

I drop to a squat and cover my expression with my hands.

"You need water," he decides, toeing his shoes off. His fingers touch the top of my head very lightly as he walks past. When he comes back with a tall glass of room-temperature tap water, he sits down right next to me and gently pushes my shoulder so that I land backward on my butt. The motion unfolds my pose and I reach for the water, finishing the glass in ten gulping seconds.

I breathe raggedly and can't catch air. A minute or so

passes and then Miles pushes his knee against mine. "What are you holding in?"

"What?"

"Look, with this kind of pain, you can't hold it in or hide it or swerve it. The *only* way out is through. So what is it?"

I make a choked sound and fold down over my gut. "I don't even know." I'm a sobbing mess. "Today was fine. Today was *fine*. Good even? This feels so random that it's hitting me like this right now. It's been months and I just don't understand why I'm not getting better. At all. I can't breathe. I can't live, Miles. I can't."

He takes my hand and uncurls my fingers. He presses hard on the muscle between my thumb and pointer. It's such acute pressure I gasp. When he releases the hold my chest expands by an inch. Air rushes in.

He does it to the other hand as well. "Look," he says low. "Consider it like you just had a heart transplant. When Lou died, your entire heart went with her. But you have to live, right? So now you've got this new heart. And you're getting used to it. No one would expect you to run up a hill right after a heart transplant. Go slow. Go easy on yourself."

I press my hands to my heart, one over the other. "I can't believe people survive this."

He nods. "Most of the time life is easy, but we think it's hard. Then something *actually* hard happens." His knee knocks mine again. "It's normal not to know how to get to the other side. You've never done it before."

"How did you do it?"

"I took it second by second. Sometime soon you'll be getting from minute to minute and then day by day. And so on. But . . . the point isn't trying to get where you're not. The point is just . . . enduring."

What an awful word. Like a curse. Next time I want to say *fuck you* to somebody I'll just shout *endure it* instead.

I curl to my side and before my head touches the hardwood there's a pillow being shoved under my ear. "I want to carry a framed eight-by-ten of her everywhere I go. If I'm with people who didn't know her," I continue, "I want to talk about her incessantly. If I'm with people who *did* know her, I can't figure out why they're *not* talking about her incessantly."

There's a beat of silence and then he says, "Then do it."

"Do what?"

"Talk about her incessantly. Let's say . . . two hours? That should be enough to get us started at least. If you need more time, we can add some. Tell me anything you want, in as much detail as you want. And you don't have to worry about pleasantries or asking about my life or checking to see if I'm bored. For two hours, I'll listen. No strings."

I peek up at him. "Seriously?"

He grabs another pillow and situates himself on his back, eyes up to the ceiling. "Shoot."

Now that I've been given permission to say anything I want about her, I have no idea where to start.

". . . Lou and I had our own world."

He laughs. "I can tell."

"How?"

He rolls his head to look at me. "It's written all over everything you do and say. Like a signature, or a fingerprint or something."

And so I tell him about our world together. Yankees games where we wore all the swag and ate all the hot dogs and scrambled for foul balls but chatted through the game and couldn't tell you the score if our lives depended on it. Getting accidentally sunburned at Coney Island once a summer no matter how vigilantly we tried to prevent it. Screaming with laughter in changing rooms at how absolutely terrible we looked in ill-fitting yet apparently fashionable outfits.

Dozens of inside jokes I attempt to explain: a jar of peanut butter left behind in the shower. Granny panties as a birthday gift. A box of condoms hidden in the tampon box.

It is mostly nonsense but he's laughing in most of the right places, a steady stream of tissues passed from the tissue box to my hand.

To my surprise, I don't make it to two hours. After about forty-five minutes my throat is dry and I'm not crying anymore. Words and panic are no longer taking turns slinging themselves at the fence lining the edges of my brain.

I roll to my side and study his profile. He's got a grizzly bear brow and a sharp line of a mouth. I like his nose. It's got a bump at the bridge. He reminds me of a gravel road. At night. With nothing but headlights to show you what comes next.

When he seems to realize that I've run out of steam, he stands and gets me another glass of water.

"Thank you," he says as I drink it down.

I blink up at him. "For what? I should be thanking *you*."

"For telling me about her. I know it's not easy to talk about her. Just like it's not easy to *not* talk about her. But you're trying. So, thanks."

He lies back down on his pillow and reaches one long arm up, over me, and drags a blanket off the bed. It's big enough to cover me completely and to cover one of his legs. That seems to work for him, though, because he crosses his arms over his chest, lets his head tip toward me, and closes his eyes.

"Miles," I whisper.

"Hm."

"..."

His eyes peek open at my pause.

I can see from his expression that there's nothing I actually need to say out loud right now. My eyelids get heavy and when I blink them back open, he's still gazing at me.

Chapter Twelve

A few days later, Ainsley and I take advantage of an early fall sunny day and go lie in Central Park together. A hundred feet past our feet there's a mossy, green pool teeming with turtles. A hundred heads past our heads there's a horde of shirtless middle-aged men galloping after a Frisbee and shouting things like, "You gotta lay out for that, Irv!"

"Hey, Ains."

"Yeah?" She rolls over and looks at me, Game Boy about two inches from her face.

I pillow my hands under one cheek. "Do you like Miles?"

"Sure." She shrugs. "He's my uncle."

"Do you . . . remember when he first came around?"

Ainsley sits up and picks at her shoelaces. "Yeah. It was right about the time that PopPop died." She tugs harder at her shoelaces. "He was kind of scary."

"Your pop-pop?"

"No," she laughs. "Miles was."

"Why?"

"He and Mom yelled at each other a lot. And . . . he doesn't laugh or smile much."

I nod. "I can understand why that would be scary. And he and your mom need to stop doing that, for sure. But, you know, none of that is because he's mad." She picks more at her shoelaces and I can tell she's listening intently. "He does that because he's nervous."

She doesn't say anything so I continue. "Sometimes when someone is nervous they can't really have fun or make jokes."

The Frisbee players break into a cacophonous argument that ends in raucous laughter, and Ainsley and I turn to watch the hubbub.

"He doesn't have to be nervous around me," Ainsley says almost absently. Now she's got hold of my shoelaces too. She's diligently tying us together.

"Let's teach Miles how to take care of kids."

"You and me?" she asks, looking at me suspiciously.

"Yeah."

"I don't think you can teach that to a grown-up." She rolls to her back and tosses a small handful of grass into the wind. It lands in a clump on my face.

"You definitely can!" I remove the clump of grass from my face and toss it onto hers.

She laughs and brushes it all away, spitting some out of her mouth. "What would I have to do?"

"Mmm. Hang out with him when you want to? Tell him if he's being weird or awkward?"

She pulls a face. "That's rude."

"Not to him. He'll appreciate the feedback."

"He had this badminton idea that seemed fun," she says with a shrug. "He brought a bunch of stuff over and put it in our closet. But then he never came to do it."

And then what? What is he waiting for?

The next day I sidle up while he's sorting Reese's recycling.

"Hey, what's the deal with the badminton thing?"

His brow furrows and the cans clank. "What do you mean? You were there at the store when we bought it all."

"No, I know that. I mean what's your plan for the whole thing?"

"Oh, nothing really. I showed her the stuff and said that I'm down if she ever wants. So . . ." He shrugs and starts breaking down a pizza box.

I take the pizza box and set it aside. "So, what?"

"So, the ball's in her court." He picks up another pizza box.

"The ball's in her court? She's seven." I take that pizza box as well.

His brow is even more furrowed. "I take it I did it wrong?"

Impossibly, there's now a third pizza box in his hands. I snatch that one too. "Good lord! How much pizza are they eating around here? No, you didn't do it wrong. Just go do it better. Dig up the badminton stuff and knock on her door and invite her to the courtyard to practice."

"Right now?"

"No time like the present. Carpe diem. Now or never. Et cetera, et cetera."

He's pausing, hands in his pockets.

"Go!" I command, and now I'm raising my arms like a mantis, ready to Karate Kid him into listening to me.

He's got two hands up in surrender and is backing away. "Okay, okay. But if she says no, it's your fault."

Three minutes later I watch both of them file past the kitchen toward the front door. Miles is clutching all the badminton crap in one hand and carrying a sweatshirt for Ainsley in the other. She's saying something to him and he doesn't even glance my way, he's listening so hard.

I can't decide which one of them is cuter.

I get some pasta on the stove and am just dressing a salad when the front door slams open. I hear some clomping, a paper bag tear, and a bunch of somethings tumble to the ground.

"Shit."

I find Reese squatting in a mini-mountain of produce.

"Bag broke," she says, squinting up at me from a three-point stance. I bend to help her clear them up and she starts listing to one side. Her forehead catches her slow-speed fall against the wall. She groans. I do believe this lovely lady is three sheets.

"I'll get this," I tell her.

"No, no. I got it." She insists on helping but I spend more time making sure she doesn't fall over than I do picking up produce.

Finally we're settled in the kitchen and I serve her a bowl of the pasta I just made. Normally she waits for Ainsley to eat, but tonight I think she might need something in her belly other than whatever has one of her high heels hanging off her big toe.

"Didn't mean to get so drunk," she says, eyes closed, her temple resting against one fist while she chews. "I was out with clients and they just . . . kept drinking."

"And then you went grocery shopping?"

She groans. "Who even knows what I bought. Where's Ains?"

"She's down in the courtyard playing badminton with Miles." I try to say it lightly, but even so, she's actively frowning at that news.

"Oh, good," she grumbles. "With any luck he'll arrive from babysitting my kid and find me drunk. He'll have enough ammo for a year."

I'm taken aback by her wrath. He wasn't kidding when he said they had a really long way to go.

"He thinks you're a good mom, Reese," I say gently. "And I don't think he'd judge you for accidentally getting drunk with clients."

She scoffs. "He thinks he knows what it takes to be a parent. Everyone's an expert when they don't actually have to do it themselves."

I'm honestly confused. This is more than just her seeing him in a bad light. This is her literally seeing him *wrong*. "He . . . definitely doesn't think he knows how to be a parent. Seriously, part of the reason why we even hang out together is because he wants to learn how to take care of Ainsley. He's fully aware he's starting at square one."

She turns and really looks at me, brings me into focus. "You like him."

"I do."

"I'd probably like him too," she says low, and tosses her fork back in with her pasta.

I clear my throat. "If . . ."

Either she's been waiting to talk about this or she's too drunk to know where I'm guiding her. "Did you know that Miles is almost exactly nine months younger than I am?" she asks.

I do some quick math. Even to a layperson, nine months younger to a different mother . . . That's not the kind of algebra you want to know about your own dad.

"Ouch."

She laughs humorlessly. "Yeah. I see he told you we're related."

I nod.

"There's this big, famous story about my dad." She's slumped forward, pushing pasta around the bowl. "He had to do this music show. And he got snowed in in Denver when my mom was in labor with me. All the planes were grounded so he went out to the highway and hitched a ride with a truck driver to get back across the country to be with me. He wrote an entire album about the experience. I mean, the drama, the dedication, the *Americana*. It went gold, that album. He won a Grammy for the title track." She pushes the food away, leans back in her chair, and crosses her arms. "Turns out, the whole thing was bullshit."

"Bullshit how? He didn't get snowed in?"

She laughs and drops her head back to look at the ceiling. "No. He did. But apparently he missed the last flight out before the storm because he was with Miles's mom. He missed *my* birth to be with *her*. And then he felt so guilty that he scrambled to find any way back east. And then nine months later Miles was born."

"Ouch," I repeat.

She gets up, walks to the stove, and serves another bowl of pasta. "Reese," I call, "you still have some left over here—" I cut off when she slides the new bowl in front of me.

I eat my pasta and she dissolves toward the table in stages. Her forehead is flat against the place mat and her arms are laced across her belly. "My dad was really sweet, you know. If the only thing you knew about him was that he got some other woman pregnant on the night I was born, you wouldn't understand . . ."

"People are complicated."

"Sure, but my dad didn't *feel* complicated. Like, he was just a genuinely nice guy who made everybody feel good. People loved being around him. He was gentle and thoughtful and . . . I was always so proud that I was the one he loved best in the world."

I'm just reaching a hand across the table to pat her shoulder when she suddenly sits up.

"And I'd probably like Miles too if he weren't such an asshole!" she asserts all at once, fire in her eyes.

Oh. Well, when she started that sentence at the beginning of this conversation, that is not exactly how I thought she was going to end it.

"Miles is—" I start, but she's already swerving back in.

"Not that there's anything wrong with being an asshole." She's gesticulating wildly now. "Plenty of people are assholes and it's charming. But it just bugs me." She pounds one fist, once, against her chest. "It bugs me that he's nothing like my dad at all. And why would he be? My dad wasn't there for him."

"Reese—"

"Do you know what one of the very first conversations I ever had with Miles was?"

"I can only imagine. He doesn't make a great first impression."

"He knocks on my door, and Dad says, *Reese, this is your younger brother you never knew you had.* And then twenty minutes later, Miles is pulling me aside and berating me for how bad Dad's condition was. How could I not see it? he wanted to know. And worse, how could I be letting Dad take care of Ainsley in his condition."

"Oh, boy."

"Yeah." She leans back and drops her head to look at the ceiling. "And the worst part, the part I really can't forgive him for, is that he was right!" She laughs though nothing is funny and props her elbows on the table and her forehead on her hands. "I was too close to really understand just how rough a shape Dad was in. And he insisted to me that he was fine. That he could still help with Ainsley. But then, secretly he's calling Miles in to come be reinforcement. And I'm stuck looking like the woman who didn't even notice that her dad was too sick to take care of her daughter."

"Oh, Reese." I reach across the table to squeeze her hand, but she ends up just giving me a few efficient pats.

"The two people I loved the most in the world and I

couldn't take care of them. And the person who called me out on it is, you know . . ."

"Mr. Personality," I supply, and she laughs.

"Exactly. And now he's got this idea about me. That I can't see what's in front of me. That I can't make the best decisions for Ains. That I wasn't kind to Dad when he was failing."

"Reese, I really, *really* don't think that Miles is judging you like that. I think he's just trying to figure out where he's needed in your life. And he's not . . . graceful."

"Not graceful . . ." she muses. "Every single thing he does reminds me that my wonderful, perfect dad totally hung him out to dry while devoting his life to being a father to me. To helping raise Ainsley. And what am I supposed to do with that?"

The question hangs there. She can't accept Miles for who he is, because it's painful. And the Miles she's created in her head is constantly judging her. This would all be so much easier if she could let herself like him.

The front door bangs open. "Mom!"

"Shit," she murmurs, standing suddenly and swaying a little.

"I'll cover for you," I offer her. "I can stay with Ains."

She blinks at me. "Are you sure? I feel terrible making you stay late just because I—"

"Pay me double, then." I flash her a grin and turn just as Ainsley and Miles enter the kitchen.

"Why was there a tomato in your shoe?" Miles asks me, holding up the offending produce. "Oh. Hey, Reese."

"The bag broke when Reese got home."

"Ah." He walks the tomato over to the fruit basket and then busies himself with putting all the badminton stuff away in the hall closet.

Ainsley is on Reese's lap, eating the pasta from her bowl. I know Reese is drunk because she didn't make her wash her hands first.

"How was badminton?" I ask them.

"Miles can hit the shuttlecock *four* stories into the air," Ainsley informs me, her cheeks flushed and her hair static clinging to the air. "I could only do two. But then he hit it so hard that it banged into Mrs. Greer's window and she leaned out and yelled at us."

Miles, washing his hands at the sink, turns back to Ainsley. "I wouldn't say *yelled*."

Ainsley purses her lips. "She called you a delinquent."

I burst out laughing. "Ah, yes. Badminton. Sure sign of a true delinquent."

"Maybe we learned that badminton is a park sport," Miles says. He dries his hands on a dish towel and fully faces the group and, friends, I'm pretty sure this man is pleased as punch.

He catches my eye. *Badminton worked!* he says to me telepathically.

Badminton totally worked! I agree with my eyes.

Reese yawns loudly, messily, uncharacteristically, and Miles's eyes dart over to her, his head cocking to one side as he studies her.

"Hey, Miles?" I ask, stepping into his eyeline. "Help me with something? Over here?"

He's not getting the hint, his eyes still on Reese, so I take it upon myself to plant two hands on his back and force him out of the room.

"What? What?" he demands, swatting me away when I nearly steer him into the door of Reese's office.

"Okay, so Reese is drunk right now."

His brow furrows. "Too drunk to take care of Ainsley?"

I snap my fingers. "Listen to me! You just had a great afternoon with Ainsley, right?"

He blinks. "Yes."

"So don't get into it with Reese, okay? Don't ruin it. Just get outta here."

"But—"

"Don't worry. I'm staying late to help out." My number one goal right now is getting Miles out of here before he has a run-in with Reese.

His brow furrows. "But you've been on since this morning. You must be exhausted."

His eyes are searching my face.

My heart is squeezing.

Reese is so freaking wrong about Miles.

"That's okay. Ainsley's bedtime is in an hour. I can do another hour. No biggie."

"All right. Well, come upstairs before you go. I'll have some dinner for you."

"Oh, I already—"

"Miles."

The two of us jump six inches in the air when Reese appears at the doorway of the office like an unexpected zombie when you thought it was finally over.

Her eyes narrow while she focuses on him. "Miles," she says again.

"Yeah?"

"Sorry I yelled at you. With the rubber band thing."

"Oh." His hands slide into his pockets. "That's all right. It happens."

A silent moment passes.

"Is your eye okay?" he asks.

"Yeah. It was just a little cut on my eyelid. Healed up after a few days."

More silence.

"Okay," Miles says. "Okay, I'll get going, then."

Reese is blocking the door but she doesn't seem to realize it until Miles walks up and taps the back of one of her hands. Then she jolts backward, tips to one side, and catches herself just in time. Miles looks torn between wanting to shepherd her to safety and getting himself the hell out of Dodge.

I poke him in the back to encourage him in the right direction. It works. He heads down the hall, popping his head into the kitchen to say goodbye to Ainsley.

Reese takes a shower while Ainsley and I clean up dinner. She's a little sobered up by the time Ainsley is practicing her back float in the bathtub. Reese sits on the toilet and chats with her while I get Ainsley's pajamas ready.

I say good night to Ainsley, and then Reese does, tucking her into bed, and the two of us head down the hallway together.

Reese groans and covers her face with her hands. "Something tells me I'm going to be really embarrassed tomorrow."

"You didn't do anything wrong!" I insist.

"I dumped my sordid family business all over you."

I shrug. "I could do the same if it'll make you feel better. My great-uncle Murray fell in love with my great-aunt Lorraine's manicurist. Now all three of them live together in a throuple. Pretty mod if you ask me."

She laughs but then dissolves down into looking completely wiped.

And frankly, I'm about ten seconds from being a cracked egg on the floor.

"Thanks for everything tonight, Lenny. And for everything always."

"You got it."

"I'm serious," she says, drifting after me while I toe into

my now-tomato-less sneakers. "Thanks for staying after that first weekend."

Something occurs to me. "Reese, you know you have Miles to thank for that, right?"

She recoils. "What?"

"Yeah. He came and found me and asked me to stay."

"Oh."

She looks shocked, confused. I'm hoping her worldview on Miles is in a sudden state of radical flux. "See you tomorrow."

I give her a salute and head out.

Chapter Thirteen

I wake up the next morning on Miles's couch. Last night I stopped by his house, let him feed me pizza rolls and cabbage salad even though I'd already had dinner, and then passed out in a heap. Now I'm coming awake in stages, making weak, pleading sounds and signaling to the kitchen by vaguely waving one of my socked feet over the back of the couch.

I hear a heavy sigh and I grin.

There's the scrape of a chair and I hold in a hoot of victory.

A steaming mug of coffee appears over the back of the couch and I just barely resist a fist pump. "Thanks, pal!"

He carefully hands off the coffee and glowers at me. "Is 'Hey, Miles can I have a cup of coffee' too much to ask?"

"If I'd said that, you would have made me get it myself." I take a lava-hot gulp and sink back into the couch, luxuriating.

Miles heads back to the table, dissecting the paper. I finish my coffee, dissecting the celeb gossip section of BuzzFeed on my phone. My mom calls and I immediately decide I am a very busy person who needs to check her email now. So I silence the call and there staring up at me is a reminder email for an event I can't believe I've forgotten.

I roll up so that I'm spooning the back of the couch, peeking over at Miles.

"Hey."

"Hm?" He looks up from the paper and his face relaxes from a heavy squint.

"Thoughts on live music?"

His brow furrows. "Uh. Generally pro?"

I play with an upholstery button. "So, I've got two tickets to this concert . . ."

"Oh." He sets the paper down. "What's the band?"

I roll back so that he can't see me anymore. "Just say yes or no, first."

His chair scrapes and then he's leaning over the edge of the couch again, face-to-face. "Tell me who the band is first."

"Okay. Well. Brace yourself. Because I'm warning you I'm about to completely change your life."

I choose a video and hand it over to him. He comes and plunks down next to me on the couch.

I watch his face as the music starts. He squints, at first I hope in awe, but he only seems to be getting more and more confused as the video goes on. He pauses the video.

"This is the band you want to go see?"

"You stopped it at the best part! Right in the middle of the dance break!"

He studies the still image on the screen. It's five young men in heavy makeup and sequined belts across their chests all splayed out on the stage, thrusting aggressively toward the sky. I love them so much.

"5Night." He reads their name from the bottom of the screen. "That's the name of the group?"

"Yeah."

"Ohhhh." Something clicks for him. He crowds me and his fingers slide against my hip bone. For a short, heart-skipping moment of confusion I'm living in an alternate reality. But no, he's just pincering the laminated list from my pocket. "Number four: go see 5Night," he reads through a squint. "I get it now. I thought 5Night was, like, the new *Fast and the Furious* movie or something. But it's . . . This is K-pop, right? I don't know very much about it."

"I got Lou and me into them. When she was going through a really rough time with chemo, I was looking for something to lift her spirits. I figured . . . endorphins, right? Even if it's brief."

"Totally. Mine was fantasy football. I was pretty obsessive the first few seasons after my mom and Anders died."

"Well, at first I just found a random selection of K-pop videos that were fun to watch. She really liked the choreography and the makeup. But then, it's a slippery slope. We got really into this group in particular. We started watching their livestreams. We joined their fan club. It's a whole thing. Now I'm invested."

"All right . . . so . . ." He gestures back to the screen. "What am I looking at here?"

I tell him each member's name and give him a brief overview of their history as a group. I press play on the rest of the video and he watches it. To my delight he clicks on another one. This one is a ballad with their vocal line all framed on stage in spotlights. The next is a fan edit, shipping two members of the group. The last one is a fancam taken at one of their recent concerts.

"Good lord," he says, then hands the phone back to me. "They've got a lot of fans."

"This is their first stadium tour!" I gush. "I bought the tickets on a whim a few weeks ago."

He scratches the back of his head. "You don't think I'll be out of place there? They won't kick me out for being an old man?"

I shake my head. "People go with their dads and boyfriends all the time. It's mostly women, sure, but I swear you wouldn't be the only dude."

He considers for a long moment. "Okay, listen. I'll go."

I squeal and go to throw my arms around his neck, but he catches me halfway there and holds me back.

"*But*," he continues.

I sag. I knew there was a catch.

"*Only* as your backup."

"Backup? But you're my list buddy! I know it's not your thing, but—"

"It's not that." He waves a hand. "Look, Lenny. From where I'm sitting you are someone who needs friends to be happy. People are your *fuel.* You are never happier than when you're with Ainsley, or flirting with a waiter, or . . ." He tries to come up with another example.

"Pestering you for coffee while you're trying to read the paper?"

"Exactly. I think that you put all your friendship energy into Lou. Which makes sense. She was your soulmate, yeah? But . . . seriously. I think it might be time to make some friends."

I frown and pull my knees up to my chest. "I have friends."

"Name a single person besides me that you've reached out to in the last month."

This is depressing.

"It doesn't have to be a big deal," he says gently. "What about that guy Jericho? His mom is always bragging about him. He seems like good people."

"Oh." Huh.

"Besides, he clearly thought you were cool, and you already bought the tickets, right? He's probably not going to turn down a free concert."

"You did."

He purses his lips. "For your own good."

"You really think he'd go with me? It's not completely random to ask?"

"It's . . . yeah, it's completely random, but *you're* pretty random so it's actually a fairly decent introduction to what being your friend is like."

I laugh despite myself but then sober. "You want me to make friends, huh?"

"It could be good for you."

"Right. Right." I wish I believed him.

Chapter Fourteen

I'm alone with Georgia O'Keeffe.

There are dozens of other people milling around, sure, but I'm parked on this bench, in this museum, and she's showing me what it felt like to leave New York and move to the desert. To have two lives. How to hang a skull in the storm clouds and adorn it with one white flower.

Art museums were Lou's thing. She'd drag me here and spend way too much time standing around quietly. Then I'd drag her to the gift shop and spend way too much time deciding between buying a refrigerator magnet or a coffee mug.

I still have a crayon drawing of my childhood cat that she did for me in third grade. I still have the self-portrait in oil pastels she did during her first round of chemo. I held the mirror for her.

It's on the list. *Go to the Met as often as possible.* I know Miles is my list buddy, but he's made crossing things off look so easy. I thought I might cross this one off on my own.

I'm starting to regret that choice.

She used to come to this museum to be alone with the greats, she'd say. We should have buried her in the Met.

"He wants me to make new friends, Georgia," I tell the painting.

"Oh! That's nice," says the elderly gentleman sitting next to me on the bench.

A pack of middle schoolers on a field trip come to stand in front of the painting and now all that he and I can see are ponytails and snapbacks and headlocks and smiles.

He turns to really study me and I study him back. His eyes start to narrow. "How'd you know my name?"

"Me?" I point at myself and look behind me. "I don't."

"You used it. Just now."

"I said Georgia," I say, pointing toward the painting.

"Oh." His feathers settle back into place. "Well, Georgia can't hear you. But George can." He points to himself.

"Nice to meet you, George." I shake his hand.

"Sorry about the suspicion," he says. "My son is paranoid about people scamming me because of my quote-unquote *advanced age*."

"Probably wise," I say. "People suck."

He eyes me. The kids move away in a clump and I'm back to considering Georgia.

"So, what's the verdict on new friends?" I ask him. "Worth it?"

"At your age? Of course."

"Not at your age, though?"

He bats the idea away. "You live long enough, you're the only one left."

"That . . . sounds like hell."

"That's life," he says matter-of-factly. "And I'm not trying to be a wise old man on a bench. I'm saying life is for those of us among the living, sure, but sometimes you're better off dead."

Well, George is a sour grape. Frankly I'm not sure he's the best one for me to be talking to right now.

"Better off dead? Not really what ya wanna hear, George."

He bats that hand in the air again. "Oh, don't listen to me. Apparently I'm clinically depressed. Go be young. Play baseball or something. Have a couple kids. Have an affair. Read some history books. You'll be fine."

I consider these suggestions. "Being clinically depressed doesn't mean I shouldn't listen to you."

He rolls his eyes. "I'm not depressed. My wife died. I keep trying to tell them it's different."

I decide not to weigh in, leaning back on my palms, eyes on Georgia. "I'm sorry your wife died."

He grunts. "Either she was going to die first, or I was."

"Did she love Georgia O'Keeffe?"

"Huh?" He laughs a little. "Oh no. We don't like art museums. We're Yankees people. My son dragged me here 'for enrichment,' he says. Then I got lost."

I'd been picturing him doing exactly what I'm doing, mourning a loved one, hoping to be closer to them by loving what they loved. But nope.

"Want me to help find your son?"

"No. I'm enjoying the quiet. Actually," he says as he leans back against the wall behind us, situating himself, "I think I'll close my eyes for a few."

"Okay, George. It was really nice to meet you."

He shakes my hand again, crosses his arms over his chest, and closes his eyes.

I stand up from the bench and approach the painting. Storm clouds in dramatic, shadowed grays. The skull of a majestic animal. Horns attached at the bone. Scorched red hills below. And that one silky, rich flower—the only thing left alive—growing from the skull.

You live long enough, you're the only one left.

Either she was going to die first, or I was.

I wipe my tears into the sleeve of my sweatshirt, careful not to alert George. Making my way out of the hall, I feel as lost as he is. Delirious in a maze of paintings.

A man in a faded Yankees sweatshirt rushes through a set of doors in front of me. He's got two hands in his hair and a wild look in his eyes as he turns a full circle.

I approach quickly and tap his shoulder. "George is in the Georgia O'Keeffe exhibit. Sleeping on a bench halfway through," I tell him.

"*Thank you*," he breathes, relief washing over him, and then he sprints in the direction I'm pointing.

Poor George. His nap is over.

Lucky George, he's got someone who loves him so much that he makes him look at art.

I stumble into the vestibule at the head of one of the public restrooms and I just make it into the corner when I slide down the wall. My head is buzzing with tears and I'm sick with grief.

Coming here was a mistake.

"Miss?" a security guard inquires from behind me.

"I'm fine. I'm fine," I say, gaining my feet and jetting toward the stairs. I make it out onto the street.

It's raining today, just enough to make the car tires sing. I dash across the street. There's rain on the back of my neck.

I cast my face toward the sky, and look, there's a mass of Georgia O'Keeffe clouds. But the skull is in my chest, lodged and jagged. No flowers anywhere.

"New friends?" I half shout. "Ha fucking *ha*. The old friend just about killed me."

How come I can't just buy a bouquet of roses and go lay them on her grave when I'm missing her?

No. When I miss Lou I weep at the Met and make passersby cross the street to get away from me.

I shouldn't visit Georgia O'Keeffe and invoke Lou's name. I shouldn't dig her up from the fresh dirt. I should let her rest and just take step after step on this crowded Manhattan avenue.

I want to disappear just like George. Get lost in the world and not tell a soul where I've gone.

Worrying is for the living. George and I, we're caught somewhere in between living and dead.

An hour later, I'm on the Staten Island Ferry, waving at Ellis Island and gasping in the wind.

I want to be good and lost. Forever lost. I want dark night and strangers and oblivion.

I look up from my sleeve in time to make eye contact with Lady Liberty. "Give me Lou or give me death," I whisper to her.

I grip the rail and collapse at the knees, hitting the deck. My eyes are squeezed tight, but even so, the tears find their way out. Then, up from the dark black I'm greeted by one image.

George's son. His hands in his hair, the look in his eyes. Frantic to find the one he loves.

People in sweatshirts who come to collect us when we sleep in public. People who run as fast as they can to keep us earthside.

"Miles," I gasp into the phone when he answers.

"Lenny?" His voice sounds like it's already sliding into shoes, grabbing a coat and his keys off the hook. "What's going on?"

"I'm on the ferry again," I tell him. "I wanna be somewhere else."

Somewhere painless and dark.

"I'm coming," he says. "Don't hang up."

Chapter Fifteen

In the day that's passed since I called him from the ferry, Miles has done something truly despicable: he's made me take up exercise.

"This is *barely* exercise," he asserts, hands on his hips as I drag my ass up a hill.

"I have one little meltdown on the Staten Island Ferry and the punishment is corporal?"

"What's wrong with you?" he asks. "You can walk normally on the street. How come you can't walk normally when it's for your cardiovascular health?"

"Maybe it's the shoes."

"What's wrong with the shoes?" he demands.

"They're for running. They're inherently flawed."

"It's closed-minded to have opinions on something you've never experienced," he informs me.

"Ooh. Burn."

"What do I have to do to make you run?"

"Dance naked around the Empire State Building."

"It can't involve me getting arrested. I'll buy you a new Garfield shirt, how about that?"

"Pass. I don't need two."

"Nutella croissant? Bruce Willis movie marathon? I'll go back to the sporting goods store and see if that married guy will go out on a date with you?"

I come to a full stop and put my hands on my hips. "How do you know me so well? It's creepy."

He laughs and rubs at his eyebrows. "It's not creepy, Lenny. It's called friendship."

"See? Why doesn't *that* count as having a new friend? Why do I have to make even more?"

"You need more than one friend. Trust me."

"How many friends do *you* have?" I demand.

He glowers at me. "Run up this hill right now."

"If I run up this hill . . . I want . . . an afternoon beer. And . . . sunshine. And . . . a basket of fried shrimp. And . . . a view of the ocean."

He blinks at me. And then at the cloudy sky. It's been a full day since my trip to the Met and the clouds haven't let up yet. "Well, I can't promise the sunshine. But I can do everything else."

Three hours later, after an hour of labored feet-moving and a shower apiece, we find ourselves sitting at a picnic table at one of the Russian cafés down the boardwalk from Coney Island.

Yes, there's an extremely cold beer. Yes, there's a basket of shrimp, and apparently he *can* promise sunshine because the old girl has made an appearance, bouncing silver off the ocean.

It's only seventy degrees in the sun, so no one is swimming, but there are plenty of wrinkly late-season sunbathers, men with potbellies and G-strings, beach volleyball enthusiasts, hotties arching their backs for the 'Gram.

I eye his lunch critically.

"What?" he asks, mouth full of sandwich.

"Yours looks better than mine." I pout. "Next time remind me to order whatever you order."

He tears his sandwich in half and puts it in my shrimp basket, stealing some shrimp for himself. "So tell me about the cashier."

"Huh?"

"The cashier. The one you were just lusting after. What makes him your Prince Charming?"

I laugh and take a bite of the sandwich he just gifted me. "He's not a Prince Charming. They're never a Prince Charming. Who wants Prince Charming? I want someone as screwed up as I am so I don't suffer by comparison."

He laughs. "Sounds healthy."

I shrug. "It is what it is."

"So tell me," he prods. "What's your story with the cashier? I'm curious."

"I figure he's an aspiring chef. He's got a TikTok that's got a lot of traction. He'll take me to a ton of restaurants and expos around the city. We'll eventually live in one of those studio apartments right over there and I'll stroll along the boardwalk, even in the winter. He'll get me earmuffs and those badass gloves with the fingers cut off." I'm on a roll and Miles is listening intently. "With him? I bet I get pregnant by accident. We'll get married so my parents don't have a heart attack. And I'll always wonder if he would have married me otherwise. Until one day I join him at an expo he doesn't know I'm coming to. A gorgeous girl is hitting on him but he shows her his wedding ring and tells her he loves me."

Miles eyes me, chewing his food for a long moment. Then he bodily turns around and studies the cashier. The cashier catches Miles's eye and jolts, looking distinctly uncomfortable and busying himself with organizing receipts.

"What you just described *is* a Prince Charming, isn't it?" Miles says, turning back around. "You got your happy ever after."

"Oh." I consider it, and then the cashier again. He catches my eye and starts to look annoyed. "I think the cashier thinks we're about to ask him to spice up our marriage."

Miles chokes, coughs, and then turns around to look at him again. "Whoops. Let's let the poor guy work."

"Maybe you're right about the Prince Charming thing. My fantasies don't always end up happily, though. Sometimes I fantasize about a breakup."

He laughs, balls up his napkin, and tosses it into his empty sandwich basket. "Why would you fantasize about a breakup? Aren't these fantasies supposed to be fun?"

"Hypothetical breakups are totally fun! Come on! They're romantic when they're not actually happening to you."

He eyes me. "You've never had a real breakup, huh?"

"What? How dare you! I've never been so insulted in all my—yeah, not really. I've dated casually. But I've never been heartbroken. Romantically at least."

"Well, it's not something to fantasize about, trust me."

"Well, was your relationship *itself* something to fantasize about?"

"Define fantasy."

"Clothes-tearing, you're-my-other-half, still in love after all these years?"

He gives me a funny little smile, like he just learned a secret about me. "That's what you're looking for?"

"Isn't that what everyone is looking for? High passion? Rose between the teeth?"

"Are you saying you want high passion for the rest of your life? You never want your partner to just be your companion sometimes?"

"It's not that I never want to feel comfortable. It's just . . . It'd be nice to wake up in the morning and *desire*. I'd like to come home from work and be *wanted*. Is that so bad?"

"You want to be having sex in the morning and after work from now until you're dead? . . . That sounds like hell on your joints."

I can't help but burst out laughing. "And what *you* want is . . ." I prod. We've never talked about anything like this and I find myself dangerously close to insatiably curious.

He considers, finishing his beer in one big swallow. I nudge mine across the table and he takes a sip of that too. "I want something that feels . . . natural, even if it's not always sexy. Because relationships change so much while you're in them. And so do the people. Even if you start out wanting one thing, a few years down the road you might want something completely different."

"That's . . . the most depressing thing I've ever heard."

He laughs. "No, it's not. Think of it this way: relationships have phases and they're supposed to. If you're gonna be in a relationship with someone for life, it's like driving from one end of the country to the other. If you do the whole thing in first gear, you're gonna overheat and cook your engine."

"Lifetime New Yorker here. Never even touched a gas pedal in my life."

"Okay, fine. Then think about . . . okay . . . going to the pool. What's the first thing you do when you get there? Maybe you're the type who cannonballs into the pool? But how many cannonballs can one person really do in an afternoon? After a while, you gotta do other stuff. You move to the shade. You read a book. Eat lunch. Take a nap. Whatever. Turns out there's more to do at the pool than just cannonballs."

"And there's more than one thing to do in a relationship than screw each other's brains out?"

"Yes."

"And you don't find that at all disappointing?"

He laughs and takes another drink of my beer. "I mean, everything is vaguely disappointing if you directly compare it to some hypothetical white-hot sex you're not currently having. But yeah. Companionship . . . it's incredible if done right. It's satisfying. And isn't that ultimately what everyone wants? To feel fulfilled?"

"Known."

"Of course."

A teenaged girl on a skateboard comes barreling toward our picnic table. Miles half stands, reaches up, and secures her by the elbow before she takes herself out. "You all right?" he asks.

She jumps back, scoops her skateboard up, and holds it against her chest. "Yes," she breathes, clearly just having fallen disastrously in love with Miles. "Thank you."

He nods and sits back down, turning his attention back toward me. The girl drifts away, looking back over her shoulder as she goes.

My mind is processing what it looks like when someone falls in love with Miles. "So, then, why did you two break up?"

"Hm?" His eyes bounce from the ocean to me.

"Oh, come on. Give me the deets on the ex. When and why and who?"

"It's complicated."

I can't help but notice that's not a *mind your own business.* "Try."

"Why'd we break up? Well, the fight where we actually broke up was because she really, *really* wanted to go to Paris with me."

"Oh, she's one of *those.*"

"One of whats?"

"The kind who wants to go to Paris on a trip with her boyfriend someday. Yuck!"

"I can't tell if you're—"

"She probably wanted to go on dates and wanted you to remember her birthday too, huh? What an asshole. Sounds like you really dodged a bullet. "

"Do you want to hear the story or not?"

"Sorry! Yes. I'm all ears." I fold my fingers under my chin and wait expectantly.

"She wanted to go to Paris. Romantic getaways and stuff. And I don't have anything against any of that. It's just that she wanted to go *there*. And I wanted to come *here*. And get to know Reese and Ainsley."

"Ah. It was right around when your dad had his first stroke."

He nods. "She told me that it wasn't that I chose *them*. It was that I didn't choose *her* . . . I guess she was right."

I sit up straight and my hands come back to the table. "Wait, why was she right?"

"I definitely didn't choose her."

"Maybe she was wrong to make you choose in the first place."

"She wanted to feel like a priority."

"You think maybe she could have done so without setting down an ultimatum between her and the only family you've got left? Might have been beneficial for both of you, not to mention the relationship."

His eyebrows go up, and a small smile kicks up one side of his mouth. "You sound like you're defending me."

"Well, *duh*. Miles, you're my . . ." Grief wingman? List doula? Only companion these days? "Ace."

He blink-blinks and then quickly turns and squints out at the ocean. Takes another sip of my beer.

"Do you miss her a lot?" I ask, trying to read his mood.

"Sometimes," he says with a shrug. "Sometimes not. We were together for five years. But breaking up was the right move. So . . . yeah. It is what it is."

"Five *years?*"

"Yeah."

I'd give anything to juice his memories like an orange. I want the good stuff, no filter. "What's her name? Is she pretty?"

His eyes flick up to mine. "Kira. And yeah."

He laughs at my expression, even though I can't begin to guess what I look like right now. "Well, there's a lot we don't know about each other." He hands the beer back to me and my fingers accidentally overlap with his. "And a lot that we do."

I take a sip of our beer and clear my throat. I haven't made a new friend in so long I forgot that it could feel like this. But Miles isn't just a friend. He's also my version of George's son. He's my handler. My manager. My personal EMT worker. My cook.

I sigh. How am I ever going to repay this debt to him?

"Hey . . ." I clear my throat. "By the way. Thanks for your help yesterday."

His eyes are on the side of my face instead of on the ocean. "Thanks for badminton," he replies easily. And then, "But I'm sorry if I . . . you know . . . triggered your meltdown? When I pushed you toward making friends."

I turn and meet his gaze and it holds for a second longer than I expect it to. "So." I turn back to the sea. "Am I fixed now? Something good for me, something bad for me, and a change of scenery? You drag me off the ferry, make me run a mile in the morning, stuff me full of shrimp and beer, and now I'm all better?"

He doesn't laugh. "That *is* what started it, right?"

I shrug. "Oh, I don't know. Who knows. I'm the dummy who went to the Met by myself. I thought I could cross it off the list."

"You went to the Met before the ferry?"

"Yeah. Now it's on a new list. The list of places I can't go. My apartment. Lou's grave. The Met."

"I didn't realize you hadn't been to her grave."

"Not since we buried her."

He absorbs this. "So . . . you went to the Met and . . ."

"I got overwhelmed. I hadn't been there since she'd died. And she used to take me there all the time. We'd walk around and she'd explain all the art I didn't understand. She was an incredible artist, you know."

"You mentioned Pratt . . ."

"Yeah . . ." I sniffle a little, but it's nothing compared to yesterday's tidal wave. "I just got overwhelmed," I say again. "I went to the ferry, you came and got me, and then you were there for the rest."

His strong grip on my shoulders as he steered me into a cab. Glasses of cold water in his apartment. A heavy blanket. Ibuprofen. The oblivion of sleep. Bananas and coffee and scrambled eggs in the morning. New-to-me workout clothes and a mandatory hill to run up.

"You know," he says, and there's a note in his voice that has me studying him. He's glancing at me and then away. "If *I* had a list, this would be on it." He nods. "The ocean. Or mountains. A view, I guess. Something beautiful and far away."

"Also cardio," I add. "That would be on your list."

"And *The Godfather Part II*." He's finally putting those smile lines to good use.

We watch the water and the foot traffic on the boardwalk for a long time. Those pesky clouds come back and a wind whips up and most everybody starts heading to the train, to their warm houses with warm beds and cups of after-dinner decaf.

I turn to Miles, to suggest we do exactly that, but he's already looking at me. "Lenny. Thank you for calling me," he says in a low voice. His hand slides across the picnic table and lands on mine. We're only touching in four square inches but I'm awash in his warm heat. "For calling when you needed me."

PART TWO

Still After

Chapter Sixteen

"What's wrong?" I ask Ainsley. It's been a week since the ferry, my meltdown, shrimp and beer. I've trod approximately twelve excruciating miles in the park under Miles's watchful eye. It's a battle of wills. He's committed to improving my cardiovascular health. I'm committed to "running" the mile in more than forty minutes, just to spite him.

But I'm not concerned with any of that right now. Right now it's only Ainsley.

Miles looks up sharply and studies her. She's hunched at the kitchen table, snack and juice untouched. Normally she draws loosely, all colors and big shapes. Today is just a dull pencil and she's pressing hard little scribbles into the page.

"*Nothing,*" she says.

"Ains—" I start.

The tip of her pencil breaks. "Ugh!"

Suddenly, she's got bright tears in her eyes. She snaps the pencil clean in two, rearing back and launching one half of it at the wall. It leaves a graphite mark right underneath the big calendar showing all of Reese's work obligations.

"Hey," Miles says, looking back and forth between the wall and Ainsley.

She stands up so fast the kitchen chair falls over backward with a bang. The noise shocks her, makes her jump, and she bursts into tears. She turns and hurries out of the room.

"What was that all about?" Miles asks me, his face slack with shock.

"I have no idea." I'm staring at the door she just disappeared through.

"She was so happy when she got home from school."

"Yeah. She was." I go over and look at her drawing again. It's a mass of angry scribbles. "Okay, let's retrace our steps. When she and I got home from school, she was cheery. And she ran into the kitchen before me. You were already in here, right?"

He nods. "Yeah. I was reading at the table."

"What did she do next?"

He thinks. "She said hi to me and then grabbed the snack you left out and sat down. No, wait. She grabbed the snack and then went and stood over there for a minute. I was distracted with what I was reading . . . Do you think she was mad that I wasn't paying attention to her?"

I shake my head. "No, that's not like her. She stood over there?" I point toward the big calendar that now has the ugly black pencil mark right below it. Like she was aiming for it.

He confirms and I grab my phone. I follow the link to Ainsley's school calendar that updates every month and then stand up and walk over to Reese's calendar.

Sure enough, there is one big conflict. Ainsley's school has their annual dance and talent show. And it sits smack-dab in the middle of a newly blocked off "out of town" work-week for Reese. "Oh, boy."

"What?"

I show Miles the scheduling conflict. "I bet she's really excited about the show and the dance and wanted Reese to come."

"Dang. She must be disappointed." He scratches at the back of his head. "Should we go talk to her?"

"Yes," I say. "You should."

"Me?" He's aghast. "No, no. You know I'd fuck that up. You go in there and put on a wig and make her laugh or something. I'll come in later."

"I'm sorry," Ainsley says in a little voice from the doorway of the kitchen. "I didn't think it would leave a mark."

We both turn to her. She's scrubbing at her eyes and swimming in her T-shirt. She looks bite-sized and miserable.

"Did you hear what we were saying?" I ask her.

She nods.

"Did we guess right about the dance?"

She nods again and then breaks into tears. I rush to her and she lets me pick her up. I hold her close.

"Was there something you were particularly excited about?"

She gulps and talks through her tears. "There's this thing where you dance with your grown-up and it'll be so"—her voice breaks—"*embarrassing* if I don't have a grown-up with me."

"Ohhhh. Like a father/daughter dance?" I ask.

She shrugs. "I guess. They don't call it that, though. It doesn't have to be a father."

"Right. Of course." I clear my throat. "It just has to be a grown-up in your life?"

She nods. "I really wanted it to be Mom."

I kick backward, trying to make contact with Miles. I kick air. So I slowly tilt my body while still hugging Ainsley and bring him into my eyeline.

I make meaningful eyes at him, but he shakes his head.

Do it! I mouth.

No dancing! he mouths back.

I don't care. If you don't offer to dance with this little girl I'm going to kick your ass! I mouth back to him. I'm not sure he got any of it except for the *kick your ass* part because he sighs, pinches the bridge of his nose, and shoves his hands in his pockets.

"Ains . . ."

She lifts her head from my shoulder and looks at him.

"I'll do it with you," he says.

She sits up straight in my arms and frowns. "Oh."

He clears his throat. "I know it's not the same as having your mom do it. But . . . I'm your uncle. I . . . could do it. And, ah, it sounds cool. I'm sure it'll be fun."

She looks at me and then at him. "Really?"

"Sure," he says with a shrug.

She purses her lips and looks him up and down. "Do you even know how to dance?"

"Ainsley!" I can't help but burst out laughing. "I think you meant to say 'Thank you, Miles.'"

She slides down from my arms and walks over to him. "Thank you. Do you know how to dance?"

"I'm rusty," he admits.

She reaches up and takes his hand, tugging him out of the room. "I'll show you."

He looks back at me as she leads him away by the hand and I swear, if there's a word that means shock, elation, and trepidation all at once, it's him, Miles Honey.

Chapter Seventeen

Is hysterical laughter typically the sound one makes while watching *Jeopardy!?* I thought it was more of a civilized show.

Reese called me out of the blue to babysit this morning. I came prepared with all sorts of Saturday activities up my sleeve, but Ainsley and Miles disappeared down to the courtyard for badminton and, as she called it, "dancing boot camp" ("He needs a lot of work, Lenny"). But now they're back upstairs and posted up in front of the TV together.

I balance a bowl of popcorn on one hip and drinks in my other hand, stopping cold when I get to the door of the living room.

Because Ainsley is laughing so hard her face has gone red, her knees pulled into her T-shirt as she overbalances to one side like an Easter egg. Miles, meanwhile, is reclined on the couch, one arm over the back, legs outstretched, and his other hand covering the bottom half of his face as he—and I mean this—howls with laughter.

I have never heard either of them make sounds like these.

I set the food and drinks down and turn to the television. They're watching a man attempt to run across a moving platform ten feet in the air. He jumps, clings like a koala to a gigantic greased-up ball. There's a moment where I think he's achieved the impossible, but then he slides down the side and then belly-flops into what appears to be a pond filled with Jell-O.

I chuckle, but they absolutely explode with laughter.

"Oh, my God," Ainsley gasps weakly. "I can't believe he's trying again."

"This is—" Miles tries to say, but his voice does that high squeaky thing that happens when people try to talk through hysteria. "This is the fifth time he's tried."

I'm bemused and delighted. "I take it *Jeopardy!* reruns were a bust?"

He wipes his eyes and takes a deep, wobbly breath. "We never even made it there. We found this instead."

I'd love to stay and laugh, but it's going so well between them that I decide not to intrude.

I putter around the kitchen and a few minutes later Reese gets home. She puts her bag down on the table and then halts.

"Is that Ainsley making that noise?" Her eyes are wide.

"And Miles. They've been dying laughing at one of those shows where people get greased up and try to complete an obstacle course."

"Wow. I've never heard her laugh that hard." She goes and peeks at them and then comes back looking equal parts befuddled and charmed.

I *knew* she was only about two chess moves away from loving Miles.

An hour later Miles and I leave together, and as soon as the door closes I jump to face him.

"I have to tell you something."

"Okay . . ."

"It's good! I think! But also, when I think about it I might puke!"

"Okay?"

"And also—"

"Tell me, Lenny."

Instead of telling him, I show him. I click into my phone, to a text thread, and hand it over.

He's squinting and scrolling my original text and actually it takes a few swipes because . . . it's long.

"Skip all that!" I demand, and scroll the phone down to the bottom. "The important part is what *he* said!"

Miles stops reading the text, looks up at me, and *grins*. And I'm telling you, this smile is a heart-starter. If I ever go into cardiac arrest, FaceTime Miles and tell him to hit me with *that* smile. "Jericho said yes."

"He really, really said yes!" I clap and jump and it must be because I'm excited even though the idea of a new friend has me a little nauseated.

"Lenny!" And that's all he says. Because then he lifts his hand and, yup, he's going in for the high five. Which, for whatever reason, absolutely cracks me up. But also, *thwack*, we nail that high five.

"Are you busy?" I ask him. "Because there's something I want to do to celebrate this momentous occasion."

"Let me grab a sweatshirt."

Three minutes later Miles jogs down to meet me in the lobby in his faded black hoodie. He looks grumpy and gruff and I'm reminded why I fell momentarily in love with him when we first met. Maybe I'll steal that hoodie someday.

He turns a full circle and then spots me sitting behind the desk with Emil the doorman, watching soccer on a teeny-tiny television with rabbit ears.

"This is the striker," Emil says, pointing aggressively at the grainy image of a man with very tall socks on. "He is best in league."

"He's your hero," I supply.

Emil gives me a look. "I have no hero. I am not child."
Then he dips his head to one side. "But he is very good at
soccer."

I don't tell him this is textbook hero worship.

"Ready?" Miles asks me, leaning one elbow on the desk.

Emil jumps up, not having noticed Miles until now.

"Good afternoon, sir," he says formally, prepared to race
around the desk and swing the door open for us.

"Hi, Emil."

I grab him by the shoulder and force him back onto his
stool. "Your striker is about to score. Don't get up."

I scamper around the desk and outside as fast as I can so
that he doesn't try to beat me there.

Miles jogs after me, pausing to look back at the entryway
as we skid to a stop on the sidewalk. "You're the only person
I've ever seen beat Emil to the door."

"I'm very good," I assure him.

"Apparently." He falls into step as I charge us toward the
train. I won't tell him what our errand is for fear he'll bail.
Luckily he doesn't ask. "So . . . you and Emil are friends?"

"Sure. Buddies. We formed an alliance because we're
both employees of the building, in a way."

"Still fantasizing about him?"

"Huh?" I laugh. "Oh. No. He killed our love a few weeks
ago."

"How?"

"He said, and I quote, 'I see the way you look at me but I
have girlfriend back home.' Now I'm not in love anymore."

"That's all it takes for you to fall out of love? Not very
tenacious."

I shrug. "Falling in love is the fun part. Staying in love is
a chore. You know firsthand, I fell out of love with *you* even
faster than that."

He grunts.

We get to the train, skid down the stairs, and slide through the doors right before they close. It's not too crowded so we sit side by side.

"I don't get you," he says eventually.

"What do you mean?"

"You make googoo eyes at the doorman so obviously that he has to address it with you. You get firmly rejected. And it doesn't even bother you at all. To the extent that you can laugh and chat and watch soccer with him."

I consider this analysis. "You think I should have spent more energy hiding my feelings? Or that I should be too embarrassed to talk to Emil anymore?"

"Not *should*. It's just . . . most people *would*."

"Having a crush isn't embarrassing to me."

He studies me. "And getting rejected? It doesn't hurt? Not even your pride?"

"I mean . . . it was all a fantasy anyways, right? So, kind of, who cares?" Now I'm the one studying him. "How do *you* tell someone you have feelings for them?"

He pushes his lips out and considers. "Michelle Walker in high school, I caught up to her at a football game and said 'let's date.'"

"Amazing. What happened next?"

"We made out in my car."

"So she said yes, I take it?"

"No, actually. But we kept making out for a few weeks after that."

"You dog."

"*She* was the dog. I was the one who wanted commitment."

"And with Kira? How did it all unfold with her?"

"Oh." He extends his feet and thinks back. "She asked me to go to her cousin's christening with her."

"Wow." I'm all eyes. "Heck of a first date."

"Well, it wasn't supposed to be a date. It was just a friend thing."

"Uh-huh." Palpable skepticism on my end.

"But then one of her aunts said, 'Introduce me to your boyfriend.' And she said, 'This is Miles.' And so, that was kind of that."

I laugh and poke his arm. "What do you mean that was that? That's definitely not how people normally decide to be boyfriend and girlfriend!"

"Well, I didn't object and then we slept together that night, so . . ."

"Ah, well." I nod. "*That* is definitely one of the ways people become boyfriend and girlfriend."

"Not the most romantic." He sighs and crosses his ankles in the other direction.

I poke him again. "I'm sure you're plenty romantic when motivated."

He raises his eyebrows but doesn't agree or disagree. "So, what's this errand?"

"Um? Sandwiches? Really good ones?" It's an obvious lie and he just laughs and leaves me to my deception.

I haul him off the train and down one block and then the next. It's perfect sweatshirt weather. The trees on each block shake their green-golden leaves in the breeze. We pull up to a trendy shop with a giant pair of spectacles over the door.

He turns and gapes at me. "For me or for you?" he demands.

"I'm not the one who looks like this when reading." I squint like I'm trying to make out a distant cosmos with the naked eye.

"In order to celebrate Jericho agreeing to go to the concert with you, you want me to get glasses? That doesn't even make sense!"

"Look, you made me invite Jericho, which I didn't originally wanna do, because it was good for me. So now you're gonna do something you don't wanna do because, you guessed it! It's good for you. Tit for tat, baby! You're finally getting a real taste of what it means to be a part of my life!"

He's not impressed with this. "I'm not going in there. You can't make me get glasses."

"Yes, you are. And yes, I can." Actually, turns out I can't. I plant my feet and shove at his back with all my might. The only thing this accomplishes is me eventually sagging, elbows planted on his butt while I breathe for dear life.

"Are you having fun back there?" he asks dryly.

"Miles, we came all the way here! Now go!" I plant my hands and push again.

"I don't need glasses," he asserts, crossing his arms over his chest.

"You can't even read the label on the pickle jar in your fridge, you stubborn arse!"

"Who needs to read that? Pickles. That's what it says. No reading required."

I give up on pushing, because clearly he's made of cement and never thought to tell me. Instead I veer around to the front of him, uncross his arms, and take one of his hands in mine. I expect to have to tug as hard from the front as I had to push from the back, but to my great surprise, he comes easily along in my wake. I pause and blink at our linked hands. Apparently this is the key to getting him to do stuff. Noted.

The bell above the door dings as we go through and a ridiculously hot saleswoman in oversized glasses turns in slow motion, wind tousling her blond hair, cleavage tastefully straining against the buttons of her blouse.

They must sell a shit ton of glasses here.

"Can I help you?"

"Yes. Please," I say. "He needs an eye exam and a pair of glasses. Make it two pairs of glasses. You know what? Let's be on the safe side and say an even twelve."

She laughs. "Let me see if the optometrist has time for an exam."

Miles and I peruse glasses while we wait. Well, I peruse glasses. Miles stands in one spot and glowers at me. A moment later an equally hot woman emerges, also in glasses, though she's wearing a lab coat and has her black hair twisted into a bun at the top of her head.

"I have time to see you now, sir," the hot optometrist says with a friendly smile.

Miles looks back at me plaintively. *Don't make me go*, his puppy of an expression says.

"Go with the nice lady," I tell him.

He doesn't move.

I raise my finger and point at the doorway she's disappeared through. He drops his head and drags his feet as he follows behind her.

The saleslady laughs. She's leaning over a display case, chin resting on her palm. "You two are cute together."

"Thanks," I say. There's no reason to correct her. Miles and I *are* cute together, even though it's not in the way she means. "So." I clap my hands together and rub them up and down. "Let's try on some glasses."

Twenty-five minutes later Miles finds me and Tanya the saleslady laughing our asses off while I try on a truly heinous pair of metal frames. We've eliminated eight different frame shapes for my face. We've yet to find one that looks good. Thank God for Lasik if my vision ever changes.

"You're back!" I grin at him from behind the teeny-tiny frames. He walks up to me and pushes them back up my nose.

"I have 20/20 vision, I'll have you know."

My jaw drops. "You have *got* to be—"

"But I'm ridiculously farsighted and I need reading glasses," he mumbles.

"I knew it!" I slap the counter. "Tanya, let's find this man a pair of cheaters."

"Hmm," Tanya says, surveying him thoughtfully. She dips below the counter and pops back up with a pair of thick black frames. "Let's start with these."

"Aren't these what nerds wear?" Miles asks mildly as he pincers them out of Tanya's hands.

"Hot nerds," I correct him. "If you wear these I think it will greatly increase your chances of being in a porn-style situation where you get to bang a MILF."

"I don't need any help in that department, thanks."

I burst out laughing but abruptly stop when he slides the glasses on and frowns at me. Because wow. Shit. Glasses work for him. Even these ugly ones.

I point over my shoulder at the mirror and he turns his frown on himself. "Pass."

"What?" I screech. "You look incredible in those!"

"I have more options," Tanya insists. And produces just that.

Miles has the opposite problem that I do. He looks good in every pair of glasses he tries on. Which is actually a problem for *me*. Because at some point I stop being able to look at him for any length of time. Unfortunately, he demands I study him in every pair Tanya makes him try on.

I'm looking at my nails, my shoes, glossy ads of celebs in glasses with their mouths open. He's drumming his fingers on the counter, watching me avoiding his eyeline.

"Lenny."

I brush at my T-shirt.

"Lenny."

"Hm?" I spin a rack of sunglasses.

"*Lenny.*"

I turn and glance at him over one shoulder. "Yes?"

"Choose a pair."

I resent the fact that this makes a little flutter happen in my stomach. Rude. "Why should I choose a pair? They're your glasses."

"You're the one who made me come here. Choose a pair. Any pair. Preferably one that you can actually make eye contact with me in."

That earns him a glare, he glowers back, and I feel the world right itself. There's the grouch I've come to tolerate. "How about . . ." I face away from him and choose a pair of heart-shaped cheetah-print sunglasses and slide them on my face. "These!" I jump back around and face him.

He squints at me. "Perfect for reading the pickle jar."

I saunter back over to him, confidence restored by these ridiculous sunglasses. "Oh, these." I point to the pair on the counter that look the most comfortable. "You won't mind wearing them and they looked good."

"Great." He digs in his pocket for his wallet and I make myself scarce while he pays for everything and arranges to have his glasses sent to his house when they're all ready. I wave goodbye to Tanya and go wait for him on the sidewalk in a patch of sun that is almost warm.

I'm eyes closed, chin tipped toward the sky when he walks up next to me and kicks his toes lightly against mine. Something is being slid into my hand. I blink down at the glasses case.

I glance at him and then back at the case, snapping it open and laughing. "You bought them?" The cheetah-print heart-shaped glasses smile back at me.

"They're perfect for you." He shrugs and then nods to a shop across the street. "Sandwiches. Let's go. You're buying."

Chapter Eighteen

Ainsley and I stand outside Miles's apartment door, laden with groceries and about to knock, when I hear the distant strains of a vaguely familiar song. I can almost place it. I put my ear to the door but then Ainsley rings the doorbell and the music abruptly cuts off.

Miles answers the door, sliding his phone into his pocket. He's wearing his new reading glasses, and I almost reflexively slap them off his face. He's not supposed to be hot. That's not part of our deal.

"We need your kitchen!" I power through the hotness.

He blinks at me and Ainsley. "Sure? Hey, Ains."

She salutes and we bustle past him, kicking our shoes off and hauling our groceries.

"Not complaining," he says, drifting after us into his kitchen. "But there's a kitchen downstairs."

"Mom's working down there and I really, really wanted to make her a birthday cake. As a surprise," Ainsley says.

"Secret mission," I add.

"Ah. Okay." He's hands in his pockets, watching us unload a bunch of stuff and open and close his cabinet doors looking for everything we need.

"We're good," I tell him over my shoulder. "Feel free to go back to brooding. Ainsley, reach that mixing bowl up there." I lift her up to stand on the counter so she can grab the thing I can't reach.

Miles strides over, lifts her off the counter in one hand, and reaches up to grab the bowl with the other. "I'll stay and help," he decides.

Half an hour later I open the oven door and Miles carefully slides three layers of sheet cake in there. One chocolate, one vanilla, and one Funfetti.

"I still don't understand what Funfetti is," Miles says as I close the door on the cakes.

"It can't be explained," I tell him. "Only *intuited.*"

Miles is already piling dishes in the sink. "I'm just amazed you two managed to make a baked good without adding cocktail onions."

"That's only for cupcakes," Ainsley informs him. "And it doesn't have to be onions. Sometimes it's lunch meat."

He turns around in horror, and Ainsley and I crack up laughing.

I steer her by the shoulders to the bathroom. "Wash hands, please. We can watch a movie or something while the cake bakes, but I don't want you getting cake batter on Miles's couch."

While she washes up I go back to the kitchen and start wiping the counters down.

"You really know how to trash a place," Miles says, picking up the bowl of chocolate cake batter and swiping his finger through the remains.

"It's part of my charm."

He waggles his batter-y finger in my direction. "Speaking of your charms, I really think you need a unibrow."

He's threatening to draw one on with cake mix, so I lunge forward and lick the batter clean off his finger. "Problem solved."

His jaw drops open. He tries to say something and fails, his finger still extended. His eyes land on my mouth and then go back to his finger. I watch while his system reboots. And then finally, "There was raw egg in that."

"Are we gonna watch *Ghostbusters* or what?" Ainsley asks, back from the bathroom and hands on her hips.

"I'm in! Miles?"

"If you can figure out how to pull it up on my TV, we can watch it."

She scrambles to the couch and roughly twelve seconds later she's shouting back to us, "It's three ninety-nine to rent, can I do it?"

"Knock yourself out," Miles calls.

She starts it and Miles and I finish cleaning up his kitchen. As he's wiping down the last countertop, I raid his fridge and make a plate of veggies and cheese and crackers for Ainsley to snack on.

We go plop on the couch next to her right as the old lady screams in the library. Ainsley eats her snack for a bit and then leaves the rest.

I realize then that he's got his eyes closed, one arm along the back of the couch behind me, his feet crossed at the ankles in front of him.

I'm not sure if he's dozing or what. His glasses are off and with his eyes closed he's not distracting. Actually, he looks sort of . . . soft. His hair is getting longer these days and as I study him I realize that it grows in a natural cowlick on the left side of his hairline.

So strange, when his eyes are open, he's fierce and *almost* handsome. When his eyes are closed he's not handsome at all and much more huggable. I find myself wanting very much to lean into the negative space created by his open arm along the back of the couch. It looks very warm there, next to his chest.

Ainsley laughs and it brings me back to the movie. When

I glance back at Miles, his eyes are open again, but he's looking at me, not at the screen.

The timer on the oven dings and I scramble up, away from the couch. My heart seems to be running up a hill inside my chest. I wonder what's at the top.

AN HOUR LATER Miles is holding a plate stacked with frosted cake and we're making a game plan outside Reese's apartment.

"Ains, we don't want to spoil it at the last second. So you go in and distract her. If she's in the kitchen, bring her to your room to show her something. Miles and I will get the cake set up on the kitchen table."

"Okay." She nods solemnly and then lifts her watch and beep-beeps it. "In exactly five minutes I'll bring her to the kitchen, so have the candles lit."

I lift my matching watch and set the same alarm. "Deal."

She uses her key and slips in through the door.

"She's so excited," I whisper up to Miles. "I love seeing her like this. Sometimes she seems almost too mature for her—"

"Catch the door!" Miles hisses.

Too late. The door clicks closed behind Ainsley and locks us out.

"Shit." Now we'll have to ring the doorbell to get inside and we'll ruin the surprise. "What do we do? Clock's ticking!"

"I have keys," he says.

"Really? Then why are you always ringing the doorbell?"

"You're the nosiest person I've ever met, so you might not realize, but it's not actually polite to enter someone else's home without permission."

"Well, birthday cake surprise wins over manners today."

"The keys are in my left front pocket."

"Oh." I blink. "Let me take the plate—whoa."

We iced the cake when it was way too warm, and the three layers may have been a little ambitious. The whole thing is slippery and tenuous. Miles carried it down here like a wire walker at the circus. When I try to take the cake now, the whole thing slides an inch to one side.

"Too risky," he says, then lifts the cake plate to eye level, clearing the way for me to retrieve the keys.

Okay. So. No big deal. Just have to put my hand in Miles's pocket. Cool. Easy as pie.

If I dither, this'll get weird fast, so I just step forward and go in for the kill. I plunge my hand wrist deep into his front pocket. It's very warm in there.

He grunts and clears his throat.

"Good lord, how deep is this pocket?" I have to go up on my tiptoes to get the right angle and I still have no contact with keys. "Men have all the luck. Girl pockets are like the size of a pack of Tic Tacs. Meanwhile you could hide a dictionary in here."

He clears his throat again as I'm forced to fish around. My fingers close around something. "Wallet." I push it to one side and his hips kick accordingly away.

"Careful," he says menacingly, eyes narrowing on me.

"Right, right, sorry. There's good stuff in there, I forgot. I'll keep it at the forefront of my mind."

"Keys, Lenny. Focus."

"Right." I keep fishing. "Unidentified piece of paper."

I swerve around it and his hips kick to the side again and this time it's accompanied by a—surely involuntary—chuckle.

"Oh, my God." I still. "Tell me—did I just learn—are you ticklish?"

My delight must be as palpable as our clear power imbalance.

"Lenny, I swear to God, if you make me drop this cake . . ."

"Right, right." I'm scuba-diver deep in this man's pocket right now and finally, there at the bottom, my fingers close around the keys. "Got 'em."

Is it just me or does it take an absurdly long time to extract my hand from his pocket?

Finally, I'm free and I jingle the keys, grinning up at him.

He glances at me and then away. And yes. Those are pink cheeks.

He blushes and he's ticklish. I literally can't wait to ponder this later.

For now, we've got a mission.

We sneak into the apartment and set up the cake, wincing when the lighter seems suspiciously loud. But all goes off without a hitch and Reese gasps and laughs when she comes into a dark kitchen, lit only by the candles on her birthday cake.

"Happy birthday, Mommy!" Ainsley shouts, launching herself bodily at Reese.

Reese scoops her up and then sits right down on the kitchen floor. "*Thank you*, baby! I love my cake so much."

It's the best cake in the world. Sloppy and sliding off the plate, candles tilting wretchedly this way and that. Hot pink icing mixed with sort of a gray icing that was meant to be purple.

Miles has his hands in his pockets and he's standing a few feet back, like he doesn't want to get in the way of this beautiful moment.

How silly. Doesn't he know that he's one quarter of this beautiful moment? I elbow him forward.

"Happy birthday, Reese," he says low. I realize then that Reese's birthday might actually be a bit of a sensitive moment for the two of them, given their family history. But if it is, Reese chooses to breeze past it. She stands up with Ainsley and then comes over to give Miles a brief one-armed hug. It's casual and it delights me. I hope he realizes that that kind of hug is not the polite and obligatory kind. That's a *thanks, bro* hug.

And so the four of us eat terrible cake before dinner.

Chapter Nineteen

I'm nervous, pacing outside Madison Square Garden. I have a friend-date with a near stranger to go scream for barely legal boy banders while they shake their asses in glittery BDSM gear. What could go wrong?

Everything. Absolutely everything. This night ends with me writing an apology letter to Jericho's mother, I just know it.

The only thing that lifts my spirits are all my fellow fans as they excitedly laugh and shout their way into the venue. They're dressed in band merch, toting handmade signs. Some of them are dressed up like members of the group, some in costume as inside jokes that only the most die-hard members of the fandom would understand. I love them all. I hope Jericho isn't scared off.

I'm still pacing when I spot the best costume yet. It's a full bodysuit, glitter lightning, OMG, this guy has re-created the killer lightning monster from their most recent music video. Amazing. I must speak to this die-hard fan—

"Oh. My. God." My jaw drops, my finger points, I'm stock-still. "*Jericho?*"

He glares at me. "This is your fault. I looked them up yesterday just to learn their names and one thing led to another!"

"That's how it always starts!" I shout, clapping and jumping up and down. "*Are you stanning with me?*"

He loops his arm with mine and we start clomping toward the venue. "Let's go. I'm not missing a second of this show."

We spend the next three hours alternating between screaming, laughing, and dancing. I've sent approximately fifty selfies and blurry distant stage pics to Miles. Half of me is smeared with Jericho's silver glitter from where we've been smashing faces together to take pics.

When the lights in the venue finally turn back on, we stumble outside and he tugs me through the crowd and to the other side of the street.

"Hey," he says, glancing around for a nearby metro station. "My friends are at a bar a few stops away. Wanna join?"

I'm sure I'm technically exhausted. It's one A.M., after all, and I've been nonstop dancing and screaming and emoting for hours. But I'm buzzing with adrenaline and something else . . . I think it might be . . . friendship?

"Besides Miles and you, I haven't made a new friend in years," I tell him.

"You should call Miles!"

"Why?"

He shrugs, a prism of color under the streetlight. "It'll be fun!"

So I do just that. It rings twice before Miles answers. "How was the concert?"

"I'm making friends, you tyrant!"

"That's great. Where are you?"

"We're headed to a bar in the West Village. Get off your ass and come down here!"

He says nothing and I remember my lesson outside the glasses store. Take him by the hand.

"Hey, Miles."

"Yeah?"

"Will you come join us? Please?"

"Oh. Yeah. Okay. Send me the address."

I hang up and text him the address, looking up at Jericho.

"Let's go!" He tugs me on and off the train and then into the bar and it's crowded, but the fun kind, not the bad kind.

Thirty minutes later I feel a dark presence at my shoulder and I jerk around. Miles is standing there, hands in pockets.

"Hi!" I tug him forward into the group. "This is Miles. You already know Jericho, of course. And this is Rica and Jeffy."

Rica is Dominican, with light brown skin, over six feet tall, and she has the kind of makeup that makes a person look real-life photo-filtered. She's got earrings the size of my face and a sleek black braid down her back. High heels so tall I could crouch underneath them in an unexpected rain. Her voice is devilishly soft and her smile is devastating.

Jeffy is small and wiry, his blond hair in a bun on top of his head and his eyes suspicious over the top of his beer. My guess is that Jericho brings newcomers more often than he'd like.

Jericho is drunkenly pontificating on Chris Evans's brilliance as an actor.

Jeffy's eyes are so narrowed he's going to see the inside of his own skull soon. "Chris Evans is an absolute *zero*," he asserts.

Rica is bored.

"It seems like they've had this argument before?" I ask her.

She points. "Jeffy gets personally affronted when anyone conflates good acting with good writing." She points again. "And Jericho conflates talent with hotness." She pauses. "Only when they're drunk, of course."

I turn back to the group. "But don't you think being super hot *is* a talent?"

Now *I'm* the recipient of Rica's pointer finger. "Interesting. Continue."

"It's not a talent!" Jeffy insists. "It's a trait."

I consider this. "Maybe for a lucky few. But most people expend a lot of energy and know-how to be hot."

"Facts." Rica points at herself now. "This makeup represents . . . six years of YouTube videos? My outfit is . . . what, twenty years of fashion mags and fashion blogs and dating insufferable FIT students. You're looking at some serious sweat equity right here."

"Okay, fine," Jeffy concedes. "It takes effort to be hot. But the point of him on the screen is not that he's unbelievably hot. We're supposed to be moved by his actual acting, no?"

"I think you're supposed to *think* you're moved by his acting," I say. "But really you just want to lick whipped cream off his collarbones. It's a switcheroo."

"Wait a second," Jericho shouts, throwing his hands out like he's stopping an oncoming train, reality bearing down on him. "Are we saying that . . . effortless hotness doesn't *exist*? It's a *myth*?"

"Calm down." Rica pats Jericho's shoulder. "It obviously exists." She gestures in Miles's direction.

He turns and looks behind him, turns back, and then, in a state of clear dismay and disbelief, points to his own chest. "Me?"

"No offense," Rica says. "But there's an obvious lack of effort here."

He scratches at the back of his neck and looks down at his faded sweatshirt and, yup, cargo pants. "I . . . showered."

"Be still my beating heart." Rica is fluttering long eyelashes at him.

"So I should have worn . . . a sweater?" he guesses.

"Oh, God bless him for trying," I say as the group bursts out laughing.

Miles is still looking completely stymied when a harried waitress weed-whacks her way through the crowd with our tray of food and next round of drinks held high over her head. "Fries, fries, fries." She slides each basket onto the table. "Beer, beer, Manhattan, martini."

She forgot my beer but she's already gone. Miles takes my empty glass and tips half of his fresh beer into it. He says something, but a group shouts with laughter behind us and I shake my head to show I didn't hear him.

He leans down, pulls back, pushes my hair over my shoulder, and then leans back down. "I asked if you had fun tonight."

His breath tickles my ear and I fight the urge to shiver. "I did. I can't believe I got to see them perform live!"

"You're happy?"

"Yes!"

He nods and pulls away, facing toward whatever Jeffy is saying, but there's one slice of a second that I catch sight of the expression on his face. A briefly incandescent smile. And then it's gone.

Before I stuff my face with fries I excuse myself and head to the bathroom to wash my hands. On my way out I bump into Rica waiting in line at the single-stall bathroom.

"Hi!" I say brightly.

She cocks her head and eyes me. "How did you say you met Jericho, again?"

I pause. "I was there when his bike got wrecked."

"Right." She's still eyeing me.

"I take it Jericho brings a lot of newcomers around and it's up to you and Jeffy to weed out the losers?"

She laughs and it surprises her. "There's not *that* many losers. But yeah. He's an easy mark."

I raise two fingers. "I promise I don't want anything from him but a concert buddy."

She nods, casts a glance over her shoulder, and then sighs.

Whoever is in the bathroom is clearly setting up shop. Rica shifts from side to side on her heels. She unzips her leather bomber and underneath is a shirt advertising Dad's Books and Wisdom.

"Oh, I like your T-shirt. That shop is so great. One of the best bookstores in the city. It's a shame more people don't know about it."

"It's the *best* bookstore in the city. My family runs it."

"Oh, really? Wow. Wait . . . are you saying that Dad of Dad's Books and Wisdom is your actual dad?"

She softens. "Yeah."

"Wow. Your dad is everybody's dad. Surrogate father to everybody who stops in. What's that like?"

She shrugs. "I liked growing up there."

"All the books and wisdom you could ever need."

A lifted eyebrow: "The wisdom gets a little stale after a while."

We both can't help but laugh.

"So, what's the deal with you and Miles?" she asks.

I stop laughing. "You interested in him?"

She shrugs. "Sure."

"Oh. Well, there's no deal to speak of between us."

"Friends?" she asks.

"Yeah . . ." Why doesn't that seem like the right word? "More like . . . Dr. Frankenstein and Frankenstein's monster." I point to him and then to myself.

She laughs in confusion. "Explain."

"Well . . . He's sort of taken it upon himself to . . . bring me back to life. Any day now he's going to hook me up to electricity. *It's alive!*" I do the accent and everything.

"You're not alive?" she asks, one eyebrow raised.

"My best friend died this year. It's been . . . pretty hard." I scrub two palms into my eyes, suddenly exhausted. "Miles is helping me do this, like, bucket list thing? It's supposed to bring me back to life, I guess. That's why Miles pushed Jericho and me to go to the concert together. He thinks I should try to make some friends."

I look up at her and it's hard to interpret her expression. "I'm sorry."

"Thanks. Anyways, yeah, you've got the green light from me. Pursue away." I gesture toward Miles.

"No." She shakes her head discerningly. "No, I don't think I will. Bringing someone to life seems like a delicate operation. I better not get mixed up in it."

My shoulders lower an inch and I'm suddenly much less exhausted. "Hey, what do you think they're doing in there? A crossword puzzle?" I lean forward and knock loudly on the bathroom door. No answer. "Are you sure it's not just locked from the inside?"

"I saw somebody go in." She shifts from one foot to the other again.

"Hold on." I duck into the ladies' room and back out. "No presh. But it's empty."

She pauses.

"I'm happy to block the door for you if you want," I offer.

Rica blinks, considers me, and then nods. I stand outside the door. Two minutes later, Rica emerges. We head back to the table, lively with conversation. They seem to be having a heated argument about dog breeds. I think debate might be Jeffy's love language.

"Hey, so," Miles says, his cheeks going a little pink when he gets everyone's attention. "Does anybody like camping? Because, um, Lenny and I were thinking of going on a camping trip."

My eyes grow round at this non sequitur. *Number five on the list!* I mouth to him. And inviting new friends while he's at it!

Rica looks between Miles and me and then slings an arm around Jeffy's neck.

"Jeffy's obsessed with camping, you know."

"What?" He laughs. "When did I ever say that?"

"Oh, come on. Aren't you dying to smell the campfire smoke? Watch the embers mingle with the stars? Fall asleep to the sound of frogs? Think of all the poetry you could write."

"Um," he says, nonplussed.

"Wait, Rica," Jericho says. "Are you saying that *you'd* go camping?"

She nods semicommittedly. "I'd wander into an REI if I had to."

"Yes!" Jericho claps his hands once, twice. Then he turns to Jeffy, anticipating. "Come on, Jeffy. It'll be so fun. Let's do it!"

I'm open-mouthed, marveling at what Miles has just manifested.

"Oh, fine," Jeffy grouches, smiling into his beer. "I'll go camping."

I'm laughing while Rica and Jericho cheer and pull a clearly happy Jeffy back and forth between them. There's a tug on my T-shirt and I turn to Miles.

"Should have asked," he whispers.

"No, it's great," I assert. "You just pulled a camping trip out of thin air!"

"Well."

"Miles," I say with a grin. "We're, like, *totally socializing*."

He grimaces, but there's happiness in it.

Chapter Twenty

Two hours later the two of us collapse onto Miles's couch.

"You are filthy," I inform him.

"Excuse me?"

"You've got paint from Jericho's costume all over you."

He laughs with his eyes closed. "So do you."

"Don't sleep yet."

"I'm not sleeping."

I'm pretty sure he's sleeping. I jump up from the couch and come back from the bathroom with a wet washcloth. His eyes don't come open even when I plop onto the couch next to him.

"Hold still."

He does the exact opposite. Reflexively, his eyes burst open and he lunges away from me. I lunge after him on a laugh, stretching across him to swipe at the silver paint on his cheek and neck.

"Ah!" He's stiff-arming me away from him. "That's cold!"

"You," I pant, batting his hand away, and stretching across him, "have paint inside your ear."

He's squirming and yelping and sliding off the couch while I scrub at the paint. Eventually we're a heap on the floor and I'm making good progress on the paint on his neck. I think he's succumbed to his reality. He's gone still, watching my eyes while I thoroughly rub down every inch of his face. I'm warm and happy and it strikes me that I should probably feel awkward sitting mostly on top of him, putting my hands just inside the collar of his shirt, but I don't. I feel . . . invited.

When he's all scrubbed clean I sit back on my heels and grin at him. "My work here is done. You're brand spankin' new."

He just sits up and shoots me a dry look. "Come on." He tugs me into the bathroom and gets a new washcloth, slapping it into my hand. "Make sure you get the inside of your own ears."

"Hey!" I shout after him as he leaves. "You're not going to wash me?"

"Pass," he calls tonelessly. I can hear him open the fridge door.

"Come on! You're Mr. First Aid Kit. This is totally in your wheelhouse."

"If you can't clean your own ears, I quit."

I laugh and start scrubbing.

I quit, Miles joked. And I laughed because I knew he was joking. *Ha ha ha* because that's the last thing he's ever going to do.

When I emerge back into the living room, he's feet up on the coffee table and a bowl of ice cream in his lap, flipping channels.

"Hey!" I put my hands on my hips. "Can I have some of that?" I point to the ice cream.

He points to the bowl of ice cream on the coffee table that he already brought for me. We sit side by side and watch infomercials and eat ice cream while the sun comes up behind us.

We wake up late morning. I'm rested, because five hours of sleep is a boon for me. Miles wakes up wrecked, because he's a solid-nine-or-bust type of guy.

I brush in his bathroom with the toothbrush I keep in his cup and flip his toilet paper because he's put it on wrong again. When I'm done I fully intend to make him coffee and pancakes, because, come on, he did not need to schlep across the city to help me make friends last night, but by the time I'm out, there's already a steaming cup of coffee waiting for me and two bowls of cereal.

"You're disgustingly self-sufficient," I inform him as I pull up a chair at his table.

"Totally," he agrees absently, thumbing through yesterday's paper and then picking up today's, his reading glasses in place. "People who pour their own cereal are so high and mighty."

"Thanks for breakfast, by the way."

"Mm-hmm."

"And for coming to the bar."

"Mm-hmm."

"And for buying me a car, really top-notch stuff."

"What would you even do with a car?" he asks over the top of his newspaper. "Besides sit behind the wheel and make vroom-vroom noises."

"Dang, I thought for sure you weren't listening. I'd sell it, obviously. And use the money to buy a pair of roller skates. Roller skates are more my speed. "

"Expensive pair of roller skates."

"They'd be made of NFTs."

"You have no idea what NFTs are, do you?"

"Does anyone? No! Don't attempt to explain it." I stare into nothing as I start in on my cereal and coffee. "Hey, I went to a 5Night concert last night."

"Was it everything you dreamed it would be?" he asks as he sips coffee. It's a lighthearted question, but his eyes are carefully trained to my face. He's sensing that this is a mine-field.

The truth is, the concert was amazing, Jericho is the best, I'd do it again in a heartbeat . . . but. But there's a pit in my stomach this morning. Because I went to a 5Night concert and there's only one person in the whole universe who I'd like to tell about it. And I can't.

"Hey, Miles?" I've finished my cereal, so I get up with my coffee and walk around to the couch and plunk down.

"Hm?"

"Do you ever get used to not being able to give updates on your life?"

He pauses. I can feel his eyes on the back of my head. "You mean to my mom and Anders?"

"Yeah."

He pauses again and I hear him scooch his chair back a few inches from the table. "No. No, that part has always been hard for me. *Hey, Mom. Dad finally told Reese about me. I'm moving to New York City to try to help raise Ainsley* . . . so weird that I couldn't tell her that. I mean . . . this is the woman who used to ask me what I'd had for lunch that day because she was genuinely curious. She loved knowing the details of my life. Every little boring nothing, she wanted to know. And now . . . literally every aspect of my life is different and I can't tell her."

"Hey, Lou," I try, dropping my head to the back of the couch and looking at the ceiling. "I made a friend last night. Maybe three friends. I went to a 5Night concert and Eunho poured water on himself and gave a lap dance to a folding chair. You would have loved it."

"Sounds enriching." Miles walks over and places an apple in my hand and comes around to sit on the couch, news-paper in hand.

I laugh and take a bite of the apple. "Hey, Lou. You ruined me for friends. I don't know how to be casual friends with anyone. You were my soulmate. How do I settle for less?"

He turns a page of the newspaper. "It's not a contest. There's no reason to rank friendships."

"Hey, Lou. Miles is taking me and some new friends camping. Can you even imagine me camping? I'm going to get lost in the mountains and airlifted out. I'll be on the local news."

"I'll attach you to me with a leash. You won't get lost."

"Hey, Lou. Miles is taking care of everything. He's going to make sure I don't get arrested for weeping at the grocery store."

"You can weep at the grocery store. That's not illegal." He turns another page.

"Hey, Lou. Miles says when you left, you took my heart with you. He says it was like a heart transplant. Only . . ." I lean forward and thump my chest. My hair falls in a tent around me, blocking out the light. "I don't know what this new heart is supposed to be living for."

I hear the paper rustling as he sets it down. My hair gets swept to one side and the light gets in. Miles peeks through the door to the outside world. "That's okay," he says in a quiet voice. "You don't have to know yet."

The light catches on something sparkly in my hair and I realize there's a whole swath of silver paint still smeared there.

Paint from a friend, a new friend. From a concert, one I should have seen with Lou. How come we never got to see them in person together? We fell in love with 5Night while we were crammed side by side in a hospital bed, staring at the five-inch screen of my cell phone. How could that possibly have been it? That's really all we got?

I tug at the silvery section of my hair and toss it over my back. I'm up and striding toward the bathroom. I open the medicine cabinet, searching. I don't find what I'm looking for so I march back out into the living room, right toward the small desk under the window. Miles is watching me from the couch. I wrench open the desk drawer and find what I need, striding back to the bathroom.

I'm breathing hard in the mirror, lifting the hank of silvery hair, Miles's scissors opening wide, ready to take a bite out of this fresh pain.

And then he's there. In the mirror, standing behind me. He reaches around with two hands. One hand on the silver section of my hair and one hand on the scissors, his chest pressing against my back. "Don't cut your hair, Lenny."

"I can't stand to look at it anymore," I gasp. Tears fill my eyes and he's just a blur of color and light in the mirror now. "I grew it out because she asked me to, but I'm the one who has to haul it everywhere."

"Don't hack it off like this. You wanna do something big? Great. Wonderful. But I can't let you do this."

I sag and the scissors are removed from my hand, neatly set aside. The sink starts running and Miles dunks me. I splutter under the water and cough and sob. "You asshole," I curse him, but there's no bite. I'm sagging against the porcelain sink, watching the water run silver down the drain. "You keep saying it's for my own good, you *pushing me*. Through the list, to make friends. And *still* I end up like this! Hyperventilating and sick to my stomach. Guess what! None of this is making me miss her less! I'm sick of trying so hard to do this right. So just . . . just let me do something I'll regret. I can't be healthy for you. That's not fair. It's too hard."

He's quiet. I hear the *snick* of his shampoo bottle and then he rubs at my hair, my scalp, scouring the silvery part between two hands. When the shampoo is gone, there's conditioner and I don't even have the energy to comment on the fact that he's upgraded from 2-in-1. He deposits me onto the edge of the bathtub and wraps a towel around my shoulders. He carefully combs out my hair and it takes ages. There are knots galore and I shut my eyes and endure it all, both the snaps of pain when he tugs and the delicious buzz of gentle fingers.

I finally open my eyes when I feel him gather my hair back, twisting it carefully into a wet bun at the top of my head. He's concentrating so hard his tongue is sticking out. He just barely gets a ponytail holder around it all and miraculously it stays. Because my hair is feet long and wet, the bun weighs about five pounds, but I don't adjust it.

He's wet from shoulders to belt buckle. The shampoo and conditioner are open and sitting on the edge of the sink, the scissors cast aside on the toilet. I'm just about to apologize for calling him an asshole, but then he speaks.

"You're right," he says quietly. "It's not fair."

I furrow my brow. "What?"

"I don't want you to be healthy for me. I want you to be healthy for *you*. So . . . if you need to do something you'll regret . . . let's do it. I'm in. Just not your hair."

"Are you serious?"

"Yes."

I'm breathing hard, standing up, energy back. "Let's go get a tattoo."

Chapter Twenty-One

Forty-five minutes later and thirty blocks from the apartment, Miles and I stand out front of our destination.

"Okay," he says. "Just checking one last time. There's really nothing else you want to do? Anything at all? Maybe something that doesn't involve eternity? Why don't we do something on the list?"

"I'm pretty sure all that's left on the list are sex positions." (Not true and he knows it.) "And besides, I want to do this because it's *not* on the list. I'm sick of trying to Live Again TM. Today we're doing Bad Stuff TM and we're doing it in style."

I tug him into the tattoo parlor.

"Are you taking walk-ins?" I ask the kid behind the register.

He looks up from his phone. "Lemme go check."

He disappears into the back of the shop and Miles and I stare wide-eyed at the wall of photographs of other people's tattoos.

"I'm so scared!" I laugh, clapping my hands to my cheeks.

"We can always leave," Miles mumbles.

"*Or* we can stay and get a tattoo."

He leans forward and studies a photograph of a tattoo on someone's asscheek. "Do they have to match?" he asks, sighing deeply.

I blink at him. "Does what have to match?"

"Our tattoos."

Sound fades as I momentarily stop processing information. "I'm sorry . . . are you telling me . . . that you're getting one too?"

He scratches his head. "Isn't that why you dragged us here? To do something we'll regret?" He shrugs. "I told you I was in."

I'm still staring at him, trying to catch up, when the kid reemerges. "Yup. We've actually got two chairs open now. As long as you're not getting something too complicated it should be fine. They've got about two hours."

He leads Miles and me to the back of the shop. I was expecting a sort of dungeonlike situation with ghoulishly repurposed dentist chairs or something? But this is more like a fancy massage place. Padded tables, wide windows to a small back patio, and flowers in jars on a far countertop. Two tattoo artists are leaning against a counter and chatting, but they straighten up when we come in.

"Hey there!" one of them chirps. She's short, my height, with a shaved head and everything from her collarbones to her chin tattooed in intricate florals. "I'm Iris."

"Hakim," the other artist says, introducing himself. He's wearing long sleeves and I can't see any tattoos, but he has a bar through his nose and in both eyebrows, and there's pretty much no available real estate on his ears. He comes over to me and leans down, inspecting my eyebrow piercing. "I like your hardware."

"Thanks!" He's so handsome I lose a little time. Maybe Hakim and I will hike the Appalachian Trail together one day. We'll stop to nap in the sun and soak our feet in a river and he'll feed me granola bars.

Miles sighs and takes me by the shoulders, leading me to one of the padded tables and tapping it until I hop up.

"So what're you thinking? Did you bring any pictures or drawings?" Hakim asks Miles as he follows him back to the other side of the room.

"She's gonna decide," Miles says, pointing with his thumb over his shoulder at me. "Whatever she wants."

Hakim and Iris glance at one another but don't say anything else. Iris and I spend about ten minutes chatting about the design while she sketches and shows me some examples. We talk about placement and then make a few amendments to the design. When I happily hold up the paper to show to Miles across the room, he gives me a closed-mouth smile and two thumbs up.

"Miles," I say, and lower the paper. "You really don't need to get one too. Just come stand by me while I get mine."

He sighs and pulls the back of his shirt up over his head, stopping when it gets down to his elbows. My eyes get stuck on his stomach, the bit of chest hair I can see. This is probably obvious by now, but there's a lot of man on that man. He looks up at me, all bare shoulders and tousled hair, a wry expression on his face. "We came for matching tattoos."

I shrug and lie down on the table. He's a big boy and I gave him ample opportunity to back out.

The tattoo artists fiddle around for a bit, printing out the design, drawing, planning, sterilizing.

I'm getting my tattoo on my side and he's getting his on his back. We're lying on parallel tables; I'm facing him and he's got his head tipped toward me, so we're actually face to face. He's lying there, eyes closed as usual.

When the buzzing starts, his eyes pop open. We catch one another's eyes and start laughing. But the laugh dissolves when Iris starts working on me. I slam my eyes closed and get used to the feeling. It's not unbearable, and after a while, the scratchy-prickling sensation sort of dissolves into a cloud of general discomfort. I don't mind it.

As I finally open my eyes, I realize that Miles has been studying me. When my eyes catch his, I expect him to glance away, but he doesn't. The eye contact stretches out and there's a moment when it becomes uncomfortable and I almost look away, but then we're past that moment and it feels weirdly . . . lovely. We stare into one another's eyes absently, almost the same way that two people hold hands as they stroll along. I can see that he's lost in thought and so am I. Time rolls and gathers and picks up speed. Iris hits a tender spot and I wince, wrinkling my nose, and Miles unconsciously mirrors my expression. I smile and so does he.

"How long have you two been together?" Iris asks.

The spell is broken and I look away, my eyes tracking down to where Hakim is working on Miles. "We're not," I explain.

My words seem to awkwardly echo and I can almost feel the question that no one is asking. *Why not?*

To dispel the awkwardness, I roll my head to look at Iris. "You must hear all sorts of wild stuff from people who walk in for tattoos."

She raises her eyebrows. "I honestly don't think I'm capable of being surprised anymore."

Iris and I start chatting and don't stop until the tattoo is done. Hakim is faster than Iris, so Miles is all bandaged up and clothed, standing next to my head, when Iris finally turns off the tattoo gun. They take us through the aftercare instructions and send us on our way, and I elbow Miles away from the register to pay.

"You should've let me pay for mine," Miles grumbles as

we emerge back onto the street into the afternoon sunlight. "That was expensive."

"Miles, you just involuntarily got a tattoo of a wolf howling at the moon. There's no way in hell I would have let you pay for it."

"I need lunch," he says. "A lot of it. Let's find a buffet."

We stroll, apparently in the direction of a buffet, and I glance up at him. "I would have thought you'd have called me out on the tattoo choice," I say, attempting casual.

His eyebrows furrow. "Why?"

"Well, you know, lone wolf howling at the moon? Pretty lonely. I thought you'd make me go for something happier."

He frowns. "They're not lonely." He gestures between our two bandages. "There's two of them."

My throat instantly clogs up and I sniffle. I've cried from grief so much over the last few months that it's disorienting and startling to cry *happy* tears.

He glances down at me and then pushes at the heavy bun that's begun sliding sideways down my head. It mushes back down as soon as he takes his hand away. "You know, Lenny," he says. "When a wolf is howling at the moon, it's not actually because it's lonely."

"Really?"

"Yeah." He nods. "It's sort of a location technique, for when members of the pack get separated and they need to find one another."

"Oh." I brush the happy tears away.

"So when you hear a wolf call, and then in the distance, you hear another wolf call back, do you know what that can be roughly translated as?"

"What's that?"

"The first one saying, *I'm here! I'm here!* And then the other one says, *Me too! Me too!*"

I reach up and pull the ponytail holder out of my hair, let it all tumble, still damp, all around. Then I begin the process of packing it all away into my hood as I tuck myself into my hoodie. The scent of Miles's shampoo surrounds me and our tattoo stings at my side.

"Thanks," I whisper to him. "Thank you."

Chapter Twenty-Two

"Hmmm hm hmmm," I hum to myself as I hold up a T-shirt from the dollar bin and discard it due to collar stretching.

"Hmmmmmm hmm," Ainsley chimes in, resolving the melody of the decade-old pop song that's been stuck in my head. She tosses aside a purple T-shirt in lieu of a yellow one.

"I really didn't think you were going to be so picky," Miles says with a frown. He's been standing with his hands in his pockets for twenty minutes while Ainsley and I make a determined effort to visually scan every single T-shirt in this resale shop.

"Rude! I am extremely picky about what I wear," I lie.

His brow furrows. "You have a T-shirt that claims you're a part of a Frisbee golf league in St. Paul."

"You need a hobby," I decide, turning around to scan him from head to toe. "You pay too much attention to me."

"I think I'm ready to try on," Ainsley says from behind a pile of T-shirts so tall I can only see the static'd pieces of her hair.

"Excellent." I hand over my bag and phone to Miles and cart a truly ridiculous number of T-shirts back to the changing area.

We make a deal to show each other every shirt, no matter how heinous. I whittle my pile down to two, an orange baby tee with an inexplicable cob of corn on it, and a gigantic dark blue T-shirt featuring Schroeder tickling the ivories. Ainsley is far more discerning than I am and chooses only one: a gray long-sleeve with Baby Spice on it.

She whips back the curtain of the dressing room to reveal Miles standing ten feet away, my bag over his shoulder, looking down at his phone.

"Look!" Ainsley holds up her prize.

"Are you familiar with the Spice Girls?" he asks in surprise.

"Are *you* familiar with the Spice Girls?" I ask in even more surprise.

"I was alive in the nineties. So, yes."

"PopPop left me his record collection," Ainsley says by way of explanation. "Should we return these to the dollar bin?"

I signal to the bored employee scrolling TikTok behind the register and he shoots me a thumbs-up. We cart the piles of unselected shirts back to the bin.

"So, your pop-pop was into the Spice Girls?" I ask Ainsley.

"He was into all kinds of music," she says.

"I didn't know that," Miles says. He hands over a five-dollar bill and it covers our three T-shirts and a horrific green thermal hoodie thing that he hands to me on the way out.

"What's this?"

"You need more coats."

My stomach swoops and I stop to watch while he and Ainsley walk on ahead of me, my backpack still slung over one of his shoulders. Upon further inspection, I actually love this ugly hoodie.

We walk Ainsley home and she disappears with a book. Miles and I left kind of a mess from our after-school snack, so he washes the dishes and I dry them.

"Is that your phone?" I ask. There's been an off-and-on buzzing for the last few minutes.

"Hm? No, mine's set to ring."

"Well, then what the hell is vibrating in your pants?"

"What? Oh, I forgot you handed me your phone in the store." He digs into his back pocket, which he apparently can't feel, and hands over my phone.

My stomach drops. I missed another call from my mom. And then she left a voicemail. And sent a text.

I fear that my *Everything's fine, I'm just really busy, I swear!* excuse is wearing thin. She smells a rat. Her assertion that I need to come over and submit to a motherly inspection is growing more and more insistent.

"It's gonna be warm this weekend," Miles says. "For the camping trip."

"Hm?" I pull myself out of my phone and focus on him. "Oh. Really? How warm?"

"It'll hit eighty on Friday."

"Wow, I thought fall was gonna stick this time."

"One last heat wave, I guess."

It's been two weeks since we got our tattoos. Two weeks since we promised a camping trip to our new friends.

Here's our text thread from last week:

Jericho: *When are we camping?? Next weekend work for everybody?*

Miles: *Yeah, perfect. I was thinking Blue Creek Campground. It's only three hours from the city and there's a river where we can swim if it's warm enough. I saw their best campsite is open Friday around lunch until Saturday afternoon. Does that work for everyone?*

Lenny: *Hey, Miles, can you check and see if there are any*

axe murderers at that campsite? Because if there are, then I'm gonna change my rsvp to maybe.

Rica: I can handle axe murderers but I'm a hard no on skunks. Miles, check for skunks.

Jeffy: Ignoring these two. Miles, do we need any of these things? (list attached)

Jericho: Good lord, Jeffy. I've been scrolling for two and a half minutes and I'm still not to the bottom of that list.

Miles: Good list, Jeffy! You obviously did some research. I have all the camping equipment we'll need for cooking and relaxing. You will need to get your hands on a tent and sleeping bags.

Jericho: I can borrow a tent for us. It fits three in a pinch.

Miles: I've got a two-man. So someone can share with me.

Lenny: What do people eat in the wilderness? I'm thinking wings. Let's bring buffalo wings.

Jericho: Ooh! And donuts for dessert. And we should have quiche for breakfast in the morning.

Rica: Isn't camping food made when you add hot water to powder and call it scrambled eggs?

Jeffy: They definitely sell that at REI.

Miles: Just double checking here: have any of you ever actually been camping?

Lenny: Nope.

Jericho: Nah.

Jeffy: No.

Rica: What part of this conversation makes you think I have?

Miles: Cool. I'll take care of food.

It only deteriorated from there, but Miles has since somehow cobbled together a camping trip for us. Jeffy is driving him and Rica from Queens, and Miles is driving Jericho and me from uptown.

"You can drive this?" I demand when he walks me to the long-term parking lot where he rents a space and reveals a ten-year-old Jeep.

"Yes, Lenny."

"*What?*"

"It's just a car."

"Jeeps are a *lifestyle*. For people who ford rivers, et cetera! You should know this! You own one!"

Jericho and I flip a coin, ensuring him the front seat. Setting off at nine A.M., we play Twenty Questions and listen to 5Night for three hours straight. I would have assumed Miles would have demanded we play the silent game by now, but there's a little smile in his eyes when our gazes clash in the rearview mirror.

He pulls up to the campsite and five minutes later, Jeffy and Rica arrive as well. We all stand outside the cars, absorbing our surroundings.

"Haaaaaaaaaaaaaahhhhhhhhhh. Smell that nature?" I ask, throwing my arms wide.

"Haaaaaaaaaaaaahhhhhhh." Jericho immediately imitates both my stance and my smelling vigor. "Smells like an Old Spice commercial out here."

"Oh, you poor deprived city kid." Rica pats Jericho on one shoulder. "But yeah. Dang. These trees are really tree-ing."

"Cardinal! Cardinal, right, Miles? Ooh! Squirrel!" Jeffy is frenetically snapping photos on his iPhone and has been since the second we got out of the car. He's wearing a beanie, dungarees, and a button-down flannel, even though it's seventy-five degrees outside. As jaded as he seems when he's in the city, put this kid in the wilderness and suddenly he's wholeheartedly eager.

"We have squirrels in the city, Jeffy," Jericho says with a laugh, watching his friend pat a tree with awe.

Jeffy doesn't care. He's just discovered the river through the trees and he's already down the path, shucking his shoes off, rolling up his pants legs, knee deep in the water, hooting at the cold and snapping pictures of the riverbed.

Miles, meanwhile, sets up camp with the tenacity of a Marine. Two tents, camp chairs around a firepit, and a picnic table set up with a cooler and drinks and sandwiches. And . . .

"A hammock!" I sprint to the far side of the campsite and gracelessly attempt to hoist myself into the hammock. My face presses fabric, my feet dangle, the world tips, but then—phew—I'm flat on my back and watching the green-red-golden canopy open its hands toward the sky.

A sparrow flits between two leaves, pauses on a branch, and then a second one arrives. They both launch themselves into the unknown, one after the other.

My view is eclipsed by a big, frowning forehead.

"I had thought you might like this amenity."

"You're wrong. I hate it." It's the kind of hammock that the fabric sort of wraps around you, so I'm a lying, grinning cannoli. "I think my blood pressure has dropped about seventy points."

"That sounds like a major health emergency. Here. Sit up." I follow his directions and then there's room for two if we sit perpendicular to the hammock. It dips considerably and I tumble into Miles's space as we recline like an easy chair, legs over the side. He hands me a sandwich. I try to get back into my own space but just end up rolling into his gravity. I give up and settle into him. Head on his shoulder and sort of spooning into his side. For a moment he's stiff, clearing his throat, and then he takes a bite of his sandwich and relaxes. I do the same.

"PB&J. Perfection."

"Good camping food," he agrees. Apparently his legs are long enough to push us gently against the ground.

The sandwiches are gone, the sun is warm, I'm floating above the earth. There's a big warm noisemaker under my cheek and it tells me over and over, bump-bump we're here. Bump-bump we exist. Bump-bump we're alive.

"Hey. Wake up, children." I flutter my eyes open to see Rica blocking out the sun. "Let's go do something!"

Miles stretches a little and clears his throat. "There's a swimming hole about a fifteen-minute hike from here. Wanna check it out?"

She points at him. "Yes. Let's do it."

I've dimly heard the conversation about the swimming hole, but I'm still slowly coming to terms with the fact that I've somehow ended up completely on top of Miles. He's on his back, legs over the side of the hammock, and I'm curled like a snail against him. Head on his chest, arm across his middle, one leg over top of his. We're lucky I didn't unbutton his shirt and crawl inside. My heart is beating uncomfortably fast.

I freeze, unsure how to extricate myself from this without touching him even more. His hand lands on top of mine, over his ribs, warm and firm, and I feel his fingers in between mine. He lifts my hand. Wait, is he about to kiss my palm? I'm sweating.

He lifts up halfway so that I'm on my back now and he's three quarters over me. I can't see his face against the sun; my heart is beating all the way out to my toes, my lips, my scalp.

And then he tosses my hand to the side, hoists my leg away from him, and stands all at once. The hammock re-bounds and the fabric cocoons around me.

By the time I extricate myself from the hammock, the

others are in various states of dress and undress around the campsite. Miles has already changed into swimming trunks and a T-shirt. Jericho is shirt off and hopping his feet back into hiking boots, a towel slung around his shoulders. Jeffy's changing underneath a gigantic towel, and Rica unzips from the tent and emerges in a bright yellow sundress and sneakers with big white socks.

I grab my bag from the car, unzip my towel, and then toss everything else into the tent.

"You're not changing?" Miles asks me.

I shrug. "No bathing suit. I'll swim in my skivvies."

"Swimming!" Jericho is confidently leading us in the wrong direction.

Miles turns us around and leads the way toward the swimming hole. Jeffy and I take turns schlepping the gigantic backpack he's packed with chips and drinks and sunscreen and bug spray and Mad Libs. He is taking this extremely seriously.

We're surrounded by layers of gray-green rock and stately, swaying trees. The shallow river slides swiftly over sheet rock as smooth as a dance floor. The water gathers and swells at a great blue hole that seems to have no bottom. Jericho wades directly into it and dunks himself, Jeffy tests the water, and Rica has set up a bed of towels and lounges like a cat, eating chips.

Miles motions me up the side of a rocky outcropping. We get to the top, fifteen feet above everyone else. "If I had a list," he says, "this would be on it."

"What?"

He nods toward the little cliff. "Cannonball."

"Me? Now?" I look down at the seven-thousand-foot drop, the hole in the water that clearly opens up into the underworld. "I respectfully, eternally, decline."

He shrugs and shucks his shirt off. Our wolf howls from his back and I get the momentary urge to wrap my arms around his sturdy rib cage, to keep him from doing what I know he's about to do. But then his feet are at the edge of the mini cliff, turning to face me. He bends, and his arms go up-around and carry the rest with him. He spins into the air, hangs there, rotates cleanly, and *whoosh* the splash reaches the canopy.

And Rica.

"Show-off!" she calls in a friendly way, sloughing water off her toned legs.

"I *told* you Jeep was a lifestyle!" I shout down to him again as he treads water and grins.

I grab his shirt, climb down the sane way, and go about stripping myself nude. Well, not nude. But bra and undies. Good thing I wore a sports bra today. Good thing my undies are black. I hobble into the water and ascend gorgeously into a transcendent doggie paddle.

Jeffy and Jericho are laughing hysterically at me, and Miles is shaking his head. "How you've managed to survive the last three decades is a real mystery to me."

"What?" I demand, my mouth and eyebrows pretty much the only part of me managing to stay afloat.

"You call this swimming? This is called slowly perishing." He swims fiercely across the swimming hole and plants a knee under my butt, his palm between my shoulder blades. "At least back float, okay?"

I follow directions while he treads next to me, his brow furrowed. When I'm tired, I reach out to him and he plants my two hands onto his two shoulders, swimming me to the edge of the drop-off. His shoulder muscles whisper secret things to the palms of my hands. I try very hard not to listen.

"Stay on shore," he instructs me.

The afternoon tumbles on. There's more swimming, a little bit of drinking, kayakers who slice down the river with a shout and a wave. The boys engage in water games. It devolves quickly into Jericho and Jeffy doing everything they can to dunk Miles, and Miles finally succumbing gruesomely. Later, Jericho, Rica, and I amble down the shoreline and back, finding pretty rocks and shells and talking about nothing at all. When we get back, Miles is lying on his back, two arms behind his head. I like his armpit hair, but that's not really something you mention aloud. I plunk down next to him. "Are you sleeping?" I stage-whisper.

"Not anymore," he stage-whispers back, and opens one eye.

"Oh! Great!" I cock my head and warily eye his naked chest. Water droplets and chest hair and shadows and ribs and flushed skin and—

"You know, you're pretty hot without clothes on."

He's got his head tipped up toward the sun. He answers without opening his eyes. "Thanks."

"Hey, here's an idea." I fold up my legs and turn to him. "How about we have a super passionate affair for like two years. And then a really horrific breakup. Oooh! I know, we'll make our friends and family choose sides!"

He still hasn't opened his eyes. "Sure. Sounds good."

"What? Why would you agree to that?"

He finally opens his eyes. "Why would you suggest it?"

"Because I just discovered how hot you look with no clothes on. Duh."

He yawns. "I need a nap."

"How about some of that ice cream from the cooler instead? I'll smear it in my cleavage and you can forgo the cone."

He laughs. "My abs broke you, huh?"

My eyes drop down against my will. "It's the happy trail for me, actually."

He snaps his fingers up near his eyeline and I reluctantly return to the world of eye contact. "One of these days I'm going to take you at your word for one of the utterly absurd things that you say."

"And then what?"

"Then I'll just be someone who's eaten ice cream from between your boobs."

"What are you two chatting about?" Rica asks, sauntering over and wagging two beers in our direction.

"Abs," I say. We gratefully take the beers and they pop and foam, briefly catapulting us into a Coors Light commercial circa 1998.

"A favored topic of mine, that's for sure." Rica sits down on Miles's other side with a sigh. She tips her head back and her long black hair starts drying in beachy waves. "No sirens, no horns, no garbage trucks."

"Just axe murderers and skunks," I agree with a luxurious sigh.

"So," Rica says with a smile for both of us. "Matching tattoos, huh?"

Miles rolls, trying to see his own back. "I keep forgetting it's back there."

"They were a whim," I admit. "I wanted to do something reckless. That I'd regret." I frown and run a hand over the wolf on my side. "It didn't work, though."

"What?" Miles is furrowing his brow at me, like, *Are you telling me I got this damn tattoo for nothing?*

"Yeah," I say with a shrug. "I don't regret it. So it didn't serve its purpose."

"Was it part of the bring-you-back-to-life bucket list?" Rica asks.

Miles's eyes shoot over to me. "You two talked about the list?"

"A little," I admit. "When I told her about Lou."

"What sort of things are on the list?" Rica asks.

"Oh," I sigh. "The usual. Acting out romantic scenes from movies. K-pop concerts. Finding a firefighter and having gold-medal sex."

"I believe it says 'firefighter or something,'" Miles corrects.

"Quite a list," Rica observes.

"Lou was quite a gal."

Rica is exceptionally intelligent because she immediately senses my mood change and jumps to distract me.

"Well, if you don't regret the tattoo, then I guess you'll have to do something else you'll regret," Rica decides. "Let's brainstorm."

"I could invest in real estate. I'd probably regret that."

"What about unprotected sex with a stranger? That one's sure-fire."

"Please don't give her ideas," Miles growls.

"Miles would like to keep my regrets family friendly," I say.

"You could always sell everything you own and go live on a boat," Rica suggests.

"Veto," Miles grumbles. He hates this game. "I get seasick."

This answer makes Rica catch my eye with a grin. "Dr. Frankenstein does Nantucket."

I burst out laughing. Miles is still frowning. "Am I Dr. Frankenstein in this scenario?"

Before she can answer, Rica's attention snags on Jericho, who's sitting on top of the mini cliff and badly botching some sunscreen application. "These boys wouldn't last a day with-out me." She waves to us and goes to rescue her friend.

Miles watches her go and then turns his head to me, bringing me into focus. I can see the clouds and blue sky re-flected in the clear of his eye. "You talked about Lou to Rica. You talked about the list. Casually." He reaches up and brushes sand from my cheek. "And you didn't cry."

"Believe it or not, historically I'm not a crier." I say it dryly, but internally I'm quaking. It's equal parts lovely and terrible, this revelation. Lou is not a topic of conversation. She's the love of my life, goddammit.

"It's good to bring her up. People like to hear about the things other people love."

I drop my chin. "Nobody wants to hear about dead friends."

He takes me by that very same chin. "Don't talk about your grief like that." He lets my chin free and softens it with a tug at my hair. "Have a little respect."

I'm shook but covering it all. Covering everything. "I don't respect anything. Except that which elicits genuine awe. Then I'm nothing but respect. I bow down in the face of genuine awe."

"What elicits genuine awe for you?" He's one hundred percent skepticism.

"Mmmm." I consider the question thoroughly. Just to win. Just to vex him. "Waterfalls? Shooting stars? Men shed-ding the bonds of masculinity? A truly killer sax solo? Pants that actually fit? Tulips! Croissants! Fresh cherries! Mmph!"

He covers my mouth with two fingers. "I get it. Enough. Let's be quiet now."

Producing a book from nowhere, he reclines and is im-mediately the picture of someone who can entertain themself with nothing but their own intellect. It's irritating. In an attractive way.

I toss my head back and absorb the sunshine. The leaves shimmy and talk to one another and don't give a fuck that winter is the grim reaper around the corner. The river babbles and smooths out every pebble. New friends shriek. Everyone loves one another in a new and special way. I'm falling but for the first time in a long time I'm not terrified of the concrete. Maybe there is no concrete. Maybe there's just all this brilliant color in messy strokes. Leaves and sky and air and water water water, rushing by. Maybe I've been wrong this whole time and the entire world is not through my eyes. Maybe I've been trapped in a painting all along. Smeared and brilliantly applied. Every color is from the eye of someone who knows exactly what the hell they're doing.

I'm uncontainable. I've just cracked the code. How to live a perfect existence: just embrace it all, every lovely/excruciating color. I'm so glad Miles is here.

I throw my arms out to the sides. "Let's be oil paintings, you beautiful bitch!"

He lowers his book and eyes me over top of it. "It must be truly exhausting to live in your brain."

"You have no idea." I turn and collapse onto him and throw his book as far as I can. It lands with a *thock* on a nearby boulder.

"Hey!"

"I'll buy you another!" I shout. "A million, if you want!"

"A million copies of the same book? Pass." He eyes me, splayed across his bare chest, my heart racing hard against his. "What the hell is happening to you down there?"

"I talked about Lou without crying," I say into his chest hair.

I feel his shoulders rotate; a shadow crosses my eyes and

pauses. And then, there are his arms around me. He's holding me tight. Too tight. His arms pulse against me. One, two, three tight squeezes.

"You're doing great," he says. I draw every single nutrient out of that statement. "But try not to be too weird in front of our new friends."

It makes me burst out laughing. Because he's right. You have to teaspoon out the weirdness.

"Point taken."

"You know what you need?" he asks, his arms still tight around me and the sunlight kissing all our skin.

"What's that?"

"Campfire," he lists. "Hot dinner. Stars. Sleeping bag. Hard ground. Night sounds. Cool air. Everyone sleeping at once."

"Oh." My eyes grow round. "Yeah. *Yeah.* That sounds like exactly the ticket."

He untangles us and stands up, stretching, reaching a hand down to me. "Let's go get it."

Chapter Twenty-Three

Jeffy and I cannot be stopped. We're annihilating. We were born to play Hearts as a team. Miles and Rica, our opposing team, went through the following stages: mild surprise they weren't trouncing us, alarm when they continued getting walloped, resolve to serve up an ass-kicking, which led swiftly into broken and dejected spirits, and finally acceptance that they can never beat Jeffy and me. And never shall.

Jericho is the picture of elation. He can't believe that anyone can ever beat Rica in cards. He's been topping off everyone's drinks and doing the Macarena.

We put the final nail in the coffin and Jeffy and I allow ourselves to give their team a proper funeral. He even sings "Amazing Grace" in their honor. I'm on the bagpipes, of course. Jericho jumps in and performs a stunning eulogy.

Rica puts Jeffy in a headlock. Miles, quiet and calculating, silently gestures me over to him. *Come here*, he mouths.

I shake my head.

One finger crooks at me. *Come here.*

I shake my head and back up.

He's beckoning with his whole hand. *Lenny*, he mouths. *Come here.*

Yeah, right. I can spot a wolf in Grandma's clothes from ten miles away.

He takes one tiny step toward me and I'm off like a shot. But I've run in the wrong direction like an absolute fool. A strong arm catches me around the waist as I'm halfway down the path toward the river. I'm a rag doll over the barrel of a shoulder and there's a very familiar ass in my face.

"No! Sore loser! You can't manhandle me just because you're bad at Hearts!"

He grunts and speeds up toward the river. "Bad at Hearts?"

Considering we're only fifteen feet from a racing band of ice-cold water, I have a sudden change of heart. "Never mind! Forget I said that! You're gifted at Hearts. You were robbed!"

"You can't take it back now," he growls.

The docile babble of the river threatens me.

It's getting closer and closer with every step. "No!" I beg and wiggle. "No! Miles, don't do it! I'll quit teasing you, I swear!"

We're ten steps away. "Oh, now you're remorseful?" he asks, striding with purpose toward my punishment.

"Yes! So remorseful! Don't do it!" I'm full-body wiggling now, kicking my feet and stiff-arming his back. Anything to not get tossed in the river.

There's no way he'll do it, right? He wouldn't toss me into a dark, fast river after sunset—he ignores the riverbank and steps directly into the water, wading in to his knees.

Shit. He's gonna dunk me, there's no stopping him. "No! NOooooooo!" I shriek, and now instead of trying to get away from him, my strategy changes to clinging bodily to him.

He peels me off his back and holds me princess style, readying himself for retribution.

"Don't do it, Miles," I beg. I've got my arms around his neck, my forehead pressed to his throat. I'm even gripping one of his arms with the backs of my knees. "I'm sorry!" I shout.

He pauses. "You're sorry for teasing me?"

"I'm so sorry! You're the king of Hearts! The best Hearts

player. I should never have teased you." I tip my head back and make big doe eyes at him, my bottom lip caught in my teeth. I make my voice extra breathy. "Nobody plays Hearts like you." His muscles are still tense; he's holding me away from him.

He's about to do it. I go for broke.

I give myself Bambi eyes and fold my hands under my chin. "Please?"

If this doesn't work, I'm going to have to pull my very last card and call him Daddy. Chips fall where they may.

He's either very beguiled or very disturbed by me, at his mercy, begging, because he sighs and shakes his head, eyes pinched closed.

Then he turns back toward the shore.

When he steps back onto the riverbank, our three friends all boo from the trail. "Come on! Dunk her!" Jericho pouts.

"Traitor!" I shout, and point. Now that I'm not going to get dunked, I'm kind of enjoying my placement in Miles's arms. I rest my head on his shoulder. "To the campsite!"

"She's about to get dunked and instead she gets carried back to the campsite?" Jeffy gripes. "How'd that happen?"

"Is it really such a mystery?" Rica asks.

We arrive back at the campsite and Miles dumps me into a camp chair. "Who wants dinner?"

Half an hour later there's a crackling campfire and a hot dog in my hands. He also produces a big potato salad and slices up some fruit. It might be the best meal I've ever eaten. I wiggle my toes at the fire and reposition Miles's upside-down sneakers, drying out in the heat.

"We all need gorgeous lovers," Jericho decides, leaning back on his hands and looking up through the canopy at the stars. "There's too much natural beauty here to waste it on *friends*."

I cock my head. "Did none of you ever date each other?" I ask curiously.

Rica shakes her head and stretches like a cat. "Everyone falls in love with Jericho at least once in their life, but he just won't date us."

"Oh, my God!" Jericho is squirming uncomfortably. "That is so not true."

"Actually it is," Jeffy asserts with a nod.

Jericho is eager to change the subject, I can tell. "What about you two?" he asks. "I saw the way you ran across the street to protect Lenny when my bike got hit."

Miles purses his lips. "We barely knew each other then."

Which, by the way, does not actually answer the question at hand.

"Don't stir the pot." Rica chastises Jericho. "Or, if you must, at least do it *secretly*."

Jeffy and I laugh, thinking she's being cheeky, but Jericho seems to take her at her word. He leans his camping chair over to Miles and ostentatiously whispers in his ear.

Miles's eyebrows rise at whatever Jericho's just said to him. His eyes drop to the ground. He doesn't look at anything or anyone.

"Yes."

That's all he says. Clear and strong. One word.

My world flips upside down for a moment. *Yes.* I hear it again in my head. There's no clear reason for me to think that *yes* was about me. But one moment passes and then two. When I look up, everyone is looking at me but Miles.

THE NIGHT BECOMES tipsy and fuzzy and cools down. Before long, the fire is just embers and an occasional snap to remind us it's alive. Jeffy and Rica head for the big tent and, when

Miles heads to the bathroom, I shove Jericho into Miles's tent in punishment for being a pot-stirrer. I think everyone assumed Miles and I would share, but I can't sleep in a tent with Miles and that *yes* banging around in my head.

I zip Jericho in and dust my hands. There!

The regret is almost instantaneous.

When Miles comes back from the shared bathroom after washing up, he finds me still standing at the dying fire.

"What's wrong?" he asks as soon as he sees my face.

"I . . . made a miscalculation," I whisper.

"What's that?"

"Well, first of all, camping trip! Yay!" I dig the laminated list out of my pocket and cross off number five with my finger-tip. And then I look at the list for a long time, the dying fire flickering between light and shadow. Eat something famous you can only get in New York. Go to the Met as often as possible. Find a big boat and do *The Godfather* thing. Go see 5Night in concert. Go camping. So many of them are crossed off now, and yet . . . "I forgot that when you go camping with people, you sleep next to them. And my nights are . . . you know . . . still terrible and private and I cry the whole time."

"Do you want to sleep in my tent?"

"I just sent Jericho in there."

His head cocks to one side and he studies me for a long beat. "Okay."

He's looking for an answer in my expression but I don't think he's gonna find one.

"Wait here," he says. He zips in and then out of his tent, his sleeping bag over one arm.

The air is fresh and cold and lonely. Miles is lit by the moon, which must mean that I am too.

He wordlessly motions me to follow him down the path

toward the river. On the shore, out of the cover of the trees, everything is cast in silver.

We sit on the riverbank and he unzips the sleeping bag, putting it around our shoulders like a giant blanket. I'm cocooned against him.

"I'm so tired," I whisper, dropping my forehead down to my knees.

He gives my back a firm hand, the kind of pressure you use to flatten a grilled cheese in a pan. "Just give it up," he says. "Don't hold it in."

So I cry. Good and hard for a long time. New friends are exhilarating, but they're also exhausting. I've spent the entire day pretending I'm not bleeding on the inside. The emotion fights its way out of me in waves. I lean forward, dunk my hands in the icy river, and scrub at my tears and snot. I take a deep breath and stick my tongue all the way out. "Ahhhhhhh. That's better."

"Good."

"I think that's all I needed to cry. For now."

We lie back on the ground and drape the sleeping bag over ourselves, eyes on the unfathomable expanse of black distance and burning stars.

"You know," I say eventually, my eyes glued to the cosmos, "in my normal life, when I'm not grieving, I think I'm a really simple bitch."

He laughs. "Meaning?"

"Meaning I think I'm used to feeling one feeling at a time. If I'm happy, I'm happy. If I'm lonely, I'm totally lonely. If I'm bored, well, you get it. I get one feeling and just feel the absolute crap out of it . . . But these days . . ."

He nods. "All the feelings?"

"At once! I didn't know anyone could ever be this confused. How do other people handle feeling so many things at the same time?"

He considers this. "Well. Usually poorly. And with very little functionality."

"What do you mean?"

He takes a deep breath. "I mean that when people are feeling a thousand things at once, that's when the wheels come off. They start messing up at work or in their marriages or whatever. Nobody lives *skillfully* when they're experiencing this sort of thing."

"Miles, you are, like, freakishly insightful."

"I'm really not sure about that."

"Come on. There's no way you haven't heard that from other people."

He shakes his head. "You've seen me with other people. You just think I'm insightful because you're currently experiencing the one thing I'm an expert at."

"You really think grief is so singular that you can't apply some of the rules to other situations?"

He shrugs. "I'm not that close with very many people, so I guess I haven't tried very hard to do that."

"Why aren't you close with very many people?" I demand. "You're charming the pants off Rica and Jericho and Jeffy."

"Honestly, Lenny? I think they like me because *you* like me. Not that I'm not . . . I just mean that the Miles who engineered this whole camping trip, fed everybody, that guy exists *because* you're in my life."

"Well, that's mutual, okay?! I wouldn't be here if you weren't here." I try to say it forcefully, firmly, like there's absolutely no weirdness about saying it. But also my stomach has nearly dropped into the river and my heart has started racing. I need to get this conversation back on track and fast. "What about your friends back home? Do you keep in touch?"

"Well, most of my friends were Kira's friends. And I moved away. So . . . no. I have a few old friends I check in with now and then, but . . . I drove a lot of people away after my mom and Anders died." His hand scrape-scrapes across his stubble. "Well . . . maybe I drove *some* of them away. Some of them ran away." He turns and smirks at me. "Grieving people are scary."

"Tell me about it," I say with a laugh. "There's no telling what we might say or do."

"Even Kira was freaked out sometimes. She said I had a dark place where she couldn't get to me. Once I realized that that was separating me from, you know, the world, I tried to stop showing it. But when you don't show your whole self . . . it's harder to be close with people and . . . yeah. Here I am."

I look at him for a long while. Long enough that he finally tears his eyes away from the stars and tips his head to look at me too.

"Is that why you have such a hard time connecting with Reese and Ainsley?" I ask. "You . . . don't show them your whole self?"

His lips purse and he turns back to the stars. "Yeah. That and probably because the stakes are so high. They're my only family left. I can't help but choke."

I mull this over for a bit. "You're so natural with me. Which must mean that the stakes aren't high with me?"

"No," he says in a low voice. "They're not."

My gut tightens. This was not the answer I wanted. "Because you aren't expecting anything from me?"

He quirks his face and turns to look at me again. "No."

I hold his gaze, not yielding, and he gently kicks his shin

into my foot. "Lenny, the stakes are low with you because you're the most loyal person I've ever met. You're fully on my team. Now that you're here, I think there's very little I could do to kick you out . . . I don't have to worry about losing you. I can just . . . relax."

"Oh." I was braced for a letdown, but instead I got to hear one of the best things ever said. "That's good," I whisper, pillowing my hands under my cheek and continuing to watch him.

He nods. His eyes on the stars.

Chapter Twenty-Four

It's sad to see the campsite packed and tidy.

"Let's stay," I say.

"Forever," Jeffy says, and lays his head on Rica's shoulder.

"Let's go home and shower," Rica asserts.

"I like Rica's plan better. Shotgun!" Jericho races toward Jeffy's car.

Rica takes a step toward Jeffy's car too, and I'm involuntarily seized with the possible reality of being alone with Miles in his car, windows down and racing south.

"Hey." Miles comes over. He's screwing a baseball cap onto his head so I can barely see his eyes. "I'm . . . actually not going home tonight."

"Oh. Really?" My windows-down fantasy dries up, leaving a thin cast of disappointment behind.

He adjusts his cap. "Yeah, so if you're anxious to get back to the city you should ride with them. But . . . if you . . . Uh. I'm actually headed to my house up here. To check things out, turn off the water for the winter. If you . . . wanted to see it, we could stay the night there."

"Oh!"

"It's nothing fancy. But it's nice and—"

"I'm in. Super curious to see your log cabin."

He laughs. "It's not a log cabin."

"Nothing you can say will ever convince me it's not. You obviously have a butter churn."

"You're probably going to be devastated when you see the vinyl siding, aren't you?"

"You kids riding together?" Rica calls.

"Yeah," Miles says. He doesn't mention the pending overnight and neither do I. Jeffy and Jericho round the car and it's hugs all around. And then they're all piled into Jeffy's Honda. Miles double-taps the hood like a dad.

"Dinner next week?" he asks through the open passenger window.

"Oh!" Jericho checks his calendar. "I'm free on Friday."

"Me too!"

"Sure, I'll be there."

And then, magically, we have friends and plans with those friends. Miles and I watch as they drive away.

"So . . ." He clears his throat. "Let's go."

We drive for an hour in almost complete silence. I'm tired and contemplative and happy for the quiet. He, on the other hand, seems to be chewing the kind of thoughts that get stuck in your teeth. His brow is deeply furrowed and one of his thumbs drums on the steering wheel when we stop at stoplights.

"Rhonda's." I read aloud the name of a little roadside café and my sudden voice makes him jump. "Pull over, I wanna go in there. It looks so cute!"

He steps on the gas. "No way."

"Why?"

"My former fourth-grade teacher runs the place," he says. "She'll wanna hear every single detail of my life. Actually she'll wanna hear every single detail of *your* life, too. You really want to go through that?"

I crane backward to look at the café. "Are you kidding me? Of course I want to meet your fourth-grade teacher. I want to hear what you were like in fourth grade!"

"Bigger than all the other kids, shy, and bad at reading. There. You're caught up."

"Bad at reading? Really? But you're always reading now."

He shrugs. "I stuck with it. We're here."

Our car takes a right turn directly into a forest. If we weren't driving down it, I never would have known there was a gravel road here. It's overgrown, and leaves slide against the windows of the car.

"Is this your driveway?" I ask in awe. "It's like that scene in *Beauty and the Beast*."

He frowns. "I gotta talk to Burt about trimming down these trees."

I'm beyond charmed. I've never lived somewhere that even had grass to mow, let alone the necessity for Burt the tree trimmer.

We round a bend and there's a little blue house. Big, boisterous bushes seem to throw their arms out to us under the front windows.

It's obviously been a while since anyone was here, but it's a handsome sort of disheveled.

"Well, this is it," Miles says. "The only place I lived before Manhattan."

"You went from here to the studio where I'm staying?"

"Yeah."

"Culture shock."

"Yeah."

We grab our bags and Miles leads the way up the front walk, onto the porch and clickety clack, through the front door.

We push into the entryway. On the wood-paneled wall there's a photo of young Miles getting tickled to pieces by a woman who must be his mother. They don't look that much alike, but the love on her face . . . yeah, this kid is her whole world. As Miles walks past, long-worn habit has him absent-mindedly lifting his fingers to the frame to give it a quick tap-tap. *Hi, Mom.*

I stand there and watch him disappear into the house, looking back and forth between him and the photo. Does it get that natural for everyone? To be reminded of the hole torn through your heart and be able to just tap the picture frame on the way past?

I catch up to him in the living room. The house is dark but he does a big circuit, opening all the blinds. Dusty shafts of light illuminate the furniture. His apartment in Manhattan is minimal and stylish. This home is floral prints and plaids, a ginormous rug, and a wall of knickknacks. It's a little dusty but otherwise well cared for. Friendly and dated, and I can picture giant, shy, fourth-grade Miles lying in front of that very fireplace practicing reading with all his heart.

I turn to him, hands clasped under my chin. "I love it so much here."

He lets out a breath and adjusts his ball cap again. "Really?"

"What should we do tonight?" I ask, inspecting a bookshelf filled to the gills with paperback thrillers. "Let's play cards and eat hot dogs again, that was fun last night." I gasp at an exciting discovery. "You can show me all your yearbooks."

He comes up behind me and firmly pushes the yearbooks back onto the shelf. When I turn to him, he looks distinctly uncomfortable. "About tonight . . ."

"Hm?"

"I . . . didn't tell you all of it. About why I needed to come here."

"Oh?"

"Yeah . . . actually, there's this thing I need to go to tonight. And . . . if you want, you can totally just stay here. I can build a fire for you. You can relax. I won't be too long, I don't think . . ."

I blink.

He blinks.

"Or . . ." I prompt him.

"Or . . ." He takes a breath. "You could come with me."

"I'll come with you."

"You don't even know what the event is!" He's all relieved exasperation.

"Well, what is it?"

"It's . . . it's this wedding thing."

I drop my chin and survey him over imaginary reading glasses. "Miles. Is it a wedding thing or a wedding?"

He clears his throat. "It's a wedding."

"Whose?"

"Cody Ketterman. An old friend. He's, uh, Kira's older brother. So, yeah. She and her family are gonna be there. Obviously."

I gape at him. "Your ex-girlfriend's brother is getting married, invited you, and you want to take . . ." I look down at myself. Mud-streaked, hanks of unwashed hair, overalls with a truly nonsensical number of shells in the pockets, dirt under my fingernails, a stretched-out NASA T-shirt. "A *swamp thing* as your plus one?"

His eyes drop to my toes and back up to my hair. The corner of his mouth quirks up into a microscopic smile. "Yeah."

"Am I even invited? You can't just spring an extra guest on them last minute."

"It's really casual. More of a barbecue than anything.

There weren't even invitations. Cody just sent a mass text about it. We wouldn't be crashing." His hands have found their way into his pockets.

"Are you wearing that?" I point to his creased jeans and flannel shirt.

"No. I've got some clothes here."

I uncross my arms. "Well, I would be wearing *this*. So."

He laughs but then considers. "I think there's still a box of my mom's dresses in one of the closets. How about this. You shower and I'll find the dresses. If you don't find something you want to wear, you can skip the wedding. If you find something you want to wear . . ."

Now my hands are on my hips and I pin him with a stare. "If there's nothing here for me to wear, we'll hit up a second-hand store on the way. I'm sure I could find something. Which way to the shower? Trust me, this is gonna take a while. Do you have a hair dryer? What's wrong with your face?"

He quickly wipes away the look he was giving me. Halfway stuck between nerves and gratitude, I think.

"Nothing. Over there. Second door. Grab a towel from the closet on your way in. There might be a hair dryer under the sink."

I clap my hands and scrub them together. "How much time do we have?"

"Three hours?"

"All right," I say, cracking my neck and rolling my shoulders. "Prepare yourself. Because you're really about to see something special."

THE SHOWER IS everything I need it to be. Scouring and peaceful. The water's starting to go cold by the time I get out.

I spend forty-five straight minutes blow-drying my mane, and by the time I'm done I can no longer feel my arms. Even washed and blow-dried, my raggedly long hair does not look good. I have just enough strength left to French braid two plaits in my hair, but it's giving Heidi (and not Klum), so I open the door and shout out to Miles. "Little help!"

He emerges down the hall, snacking on pretzels, but pauses ten feet away when he gets his first glimpse of me. He turns halfway and faces the wall. "Um, now?" he calls.

I glance down at myself. I've got the towel firmly pinned over me but from his point of view, peeking out from the door, yeah, I probably looked naked. "Yeah. C'mere."

He shuffles to the bathroom door, his eyes on the wall behind me. He's embarrassed. Cute.

"I want to twist these braids up, but my arms are noodles. Will you do it for me?"

He clears his throat. "Yeah."

Miles stands behind me and takes directions well. He only gouges my scalp with a bobby pin once. I cement my hands to the towel and the very second the final bobby pin is in place he jets out of the bathroom.

"I found the dresses," he calls over his shoulder. "I'll grab them."

There's an old tube of mascara and some eye shadow and lipstick in my bathroom bag, by some miracle, so I use muscle memory from my former life and apply it all. He comes back and hangs four dresses on the doorknob.

"I'm gonna shower and get dressed," he says.

"I used all the hot water like a total asshole."

Finally, his normal smile is back. "Well, I probably deserve it, considering I sprang this whole thing on you. If you hear someone screaming like a baby, that'll just be me."

He disappears back toward his end of the house. I survey the dresses.

Her taste was simple and sweet. I like all four dresses but nix two of them right away. One has shoulder pads and I just don't have the swag for that. The other is jean, which seems rude to wear to a wedding, even if it's casual. One is sky blue and lovely, but it drags on the floor when I try it on so I reluctantly put it back on the hanger. The last one is light pink and short and shapeless. I try it on and step out to the big mirror in the hallway. I almost make myself blush. In braids and pink I look so girly and fun!

I lean closer to the hallway mirror and give myself a thorough inspection. My face is rounder than it was last month. The blue smudges under my eyes are receding. I've got pink cheeks and lips.

I look lively.

Another word for lively: alive.

I take a step back and really survey myself: bare toes, everything scrubbed raw in the shower, pink dress, and hair in an actual style.

Alive.

I hear footsteps at the end of the hallway and turn toward Miles, about to throw my arms out and make some joke about Dr. Frankenstein's success.

But then all the jokes take one look at Miles in a suit and promptly pass out.

Hello, shoulders.

They say a good suit does for a man what expensive lingerie does for a woman.

And I finally understand the sentiment because I can barely make eye contact with that tie he's currently straightening while he walks. He glances up at me and—thank you very much—does a double take.

"Good?" I ask, saving him the trouble of coming up with something to say.

He arrives at my end of the hallway. "You look," he tries anyway. "Yeah."

"*Nice* is the word you're looking for," I inform him. "You look . . ." I step back and survey him, hand on my chin.

He braces for impact.

"Like a businessman who spanks his secretary with the door unlocked," I decide.

He lets out a chuff of incredulity. He steps forward and puts one finger lightly on the bottom of my chin, tipping my head up. "*Nice* is the word you're looking for."

But he doesn't look nice. He looks like the kind of man you cheat on your inattentive husband with.

He glances at my bare feet, my neckline, my lipstick. I reach up and properly straighten the tie he's given up fiddling with. The moment grows thick and my fingers tingle with warm fabric. One of his hands moves infinitesimally and then settles back at his side.

There's only one way out of this kind of tension.

"I think somebody needs to check to see if that belt buckle is real gold," I tell him, tracing a finger over it and chomping my teeth meaningfully.

"Quit compulsively flirting," he scowls and slaps my hand away. "I'm nervous enough already."

"Compulsively flirting?" I'm the picture of outrage. "How dare you!"

He presses one finger into my forehead and moves me to the side so he can pass. "We should get going."

"Miles." I pinch the back of his suit coat and he stops immediately. "Are you sure it's okay for me to wear this? It's not . . . weird for you?"

He shakes his head. "I only chose the dresses that I

couldn't really remember. It's fine. She didn't dress up very often. Now, if you were in her bowling league jacket, that might be weird."

I smile. "She sounds so awesome."

He nods. "She was." And then he frowns, his eyes on my short sleeves. "Won't you be cold?"

"I'm more concerned about the lack of footwear."

"I scrubbed down your boots while you were showering."

"Oh. Thanks! You think combat boots will . . . work?"

He shrugs. "There's extra coats in the closet at the end of the hall." He motions with his head. "Grab one and meet me in the car."

He leaves and I double back to the coat closet. But when I swing open the door, I come face to face with a dim bedroom. Golden afternoon light juts through the cracks in the shutters and my heart promptly stops beating. This is a teenager's room. There's a signed Buffalo Bills jersey framed on the wall and a twin bed under the window. A desk with calculus textbooks stacked on the corner and a pair of gigantic sneakers lined up underneath the chair.

I blink back the tears that sting my eyes and immediately feel like such a bad friend.

Miles never talks about Anders. His cousin who died in the same crash as his mother. His cousin who lived with them. The cousin whose room Miles has clearly not touched.

I think of his mother as the hole torn in Miles's heart, but he pats her picture when he walks past and has moved and packed and downsized her things to just a box of dresses that he can tear open and lend out.

I quietly close the bedroom door and go to the opposite wall. It's the coat closet I was supposed to find. I grope through it and pull out a jacket and go join my friend in the car.

Chapter Twenty-Five

Miles is silent on the drive. We drive down a long country road with fields on either side. We round a curve in the road and there's a picturesque barn in the distance. I can see the twinkle lights and a line of cars from here. Miles's knuckles turn white on the steering wheel.

"Nervous?" I ask.

"Hm?" His fingers quickly drum the steering wheel. "Yeah."

I frown. "Is it just seeing Kira again? Or is there something else to be nervous about?"

He clears his throat and sort of shrugs.

I hazard a guess. "You're worried that . . . you'll see her and feel . . . regret? For breaking up with her?"

His eyebrows rise and he glances at me. "No. Not worried about that."

I purse my lips. "What is this? Twenty Questions? Spill, Miles! You engineered an entire camping trip just to get me to be your backup at this shindig but you won't let me help you, for shit's sake!"

He scowls at me. "The camping trip was for the list!"

"Uh-huh."

He parks at the very end of the line of cars. And just sits there.

"Miles—"

"Okay, okay. Look. In a town this small . . . if you're the

guy whose entire family dies in a car crash . . . you're sort of famous? In a terrible way? Right after they died I had some . . . outbursts." He gives me a wry look.

"I'm familiar with the concept." Worst inside joke ever.

"Well, it felt like everyone was sort of afraid of what I might do or say after that." I wince at how painful that must have been, and he lets out a long sigh. "Kira's the town sweetheart. When we started dating, everyone seemed to sort of . . . accept me again."

"But then you broke up."

"And she was very mad and very hurt and she stayed here and I left. So . . . yeah. I have no idea what we're about to walk into. With Kira or with everyone else."

I consider this. "Okay, yes. That sounds scary."

And now I see why he brought me here.

"You love Cody, right?" I ask him. "You *definitely* want to show up for his big day?"

Miles nods.

"Great! Let's go eat barbecue and do the Cupid Shuffle. If anyone judges you or treats you weird they can take it up with me. Today, I'm your enforcer."

I slam out of the car and he follows suit. "That simple, huh?"

The ceremony is taking place along the side of the barn, and luckily we can sidle up and stand in the back behind the folding chairs. Miles gets a few nods, a few smiles, and I get a few wide eyes and up-and-downs. But then the music starts and a redheaded man with a cane starts down the aisle. The groom, I assume. He makes his way to the altar (a plume of willow branches), turns around, and breaks into an absolutely soul-melting smile.

I crane my neck to see the bride and I'm extremely beguiled by the woman in black leather pants, Louboutins, and a black button-down charging down the aisle. She only has eyes for Cody. When she makes it to his side, she rests one hand on top of the hand he's resting on his cane. It stands between them and they lean in toward one another for a quick pre-ceremony kiss.

"Oh, my God." I swoon and quickly grab the nearest man. Luckily it's Miles. He looks down at me. "I want to be them," I whisper.

He smiles, searching my eyes, and looks back up at his pal at the altar.

The ceremony is brief and sincere and they just can't stop kissing each other.

Next up is barbecue and dancing. Miles and I stand at the outskirts. He hasn't said hello to anyone yet. I bump his shoulder with mine. "Should we go say congrats to Cody and Tasha, was it?"

He clears his throat and scans the crowd.

"And by should we," I continue, "I mean we should."

"Right. Yeah. Okay, let's go. Oh shit." He's taken one step and stalled. "It's Kira. She's coming over here. I can't tell if she's mad." His eyes are boring into mine, his hands jammed into his pockets. "What should I do?"

"Say hello, be sweet. If you think she's open to it, a light hug. Tell her she looks lovely, if you think she does."

There's no substance to my advice, but he's wholly latched to it. "Okay." He nods resolutely and then turns to face the woman inching her way toward us. She's got strawberry blond hair and is absurdly pretty. She's wearing a lilac dress and a nervous smile.

"Hi," she says shyly, one hand behind her back and the other doing a little wave.

"Hello," Miles says sweetly, quoting me verbatim. "How are you?" He goes in for a quick hug. "You look nice."

"I'm good. Thanks." After their hug, her eyes dart to me. "Hi, I'm Kira."

"Lenny," I say with a hand gesture that starts as a shake and ends as a wave. Kira's a waver, not a shaker. "Nice to meet you."

"You too." She pauses, stares at Miles's shoes for a moment, and then perks up a little. "I'm so glad you came, Miles. Cody will be so happy."

"Yeah." Miles clears his throat. "I'm really happy for him."

"Well . . ." She clears her throat too.

"Is that your dad manning the grill?" I ask her, throwing all three of us a topic.

"Yes!" She jumps onto the lifeboat. "Barbecue was his idea. My mom wanted something fancier."

"Like manicotti?" Miles asks, and it's clearly an inside joke between the two of them because they're suddenly grinning at each other.

"I think it's still too soon to tease her about that."

They continue grinning and then they realize they're grinning at each other. The moment swells and deflates. She's nervous again. "Well, I just wanted to say hi."

She starts backing away but then stops cold, both hands grabbing her skirt. "Miles . . . I came with Sean."

There's a distinct pause.

"I mean . . . I mean that I'm *with* Sean. I came with him and I'm with him." She looks very much like she'd like the earth to open wide and end things mercifully.

Miles clears his throat again. "That's great, Kira. That's really great."

"Oh! Okay. Right." She does one more little wave and then scampers back to the party.

I turn to him and cock my head, studying him. "Okay?"

"Yeah."

"Who is Sean?"

"Sean Vogel." Like that answers my question.

"And he is . . . ?"

He's still watching her walk away. "She cheated on me with Sean a few years ago. I took her back. Nobody ever knew but the three of us."

Ice spears through my chest. *Kira's the town sweetheart. When we started dating, everyone seemed to sort of . . . accept me again.* I'm aching for the younger version of Miles who didn't want to be the outcast anymore. Who couldn't pack up Anders's room but stayed with Kira to prove he was all better. Who wanted happiness at any cost.

"Are you really okay?" I ask.

He takes a deep breath and drops his head back, letting all the air out in a thin stream toward the sky.

"You know? Yeah. I'm glad she found someone. And I'm really glad she's not mad anymore. Mostly it's a relief that the saying hi part is over with. Should we eat?"

He's already walking toward the buffet line, but I'm stuck ten feet back.

Instinctually I know that he doesn't need soft sympathy right now. I scramble to catch up to him. "We should have given me a major makeover. I'm talking, like, lip fillers and a boob job. I should be wearing a Jessica Rabbit dress."

He stops walking and frowns at me. "You're not my revenge date. You're my . . . copilot."

His words fill me with helium. I explode into a grin.

"Miles!" We turn and there's a high school buddy: toothy grin, receding hairline, two arms thrown around Miles. "My guy! So happy to see you!"

We've attracted some attention, and a small crowd gathers around Miles. There's some backslapping and some high fives and some kisses on the cheek.

Finally we get food and we sit down and watch white people dance. Always a treat.

"So. There's 'Purple Rain.'"

He looks up from his beer.

"Any interest in dancing cheek to cheek?" I ask him.

That gets a laugh. He turns to watch all the couples holding one another. Some loosely, friendly, chatting with other couples as they twirl past. Some have hands in each other's hair, their eyes locked. Some look like this is the one time of year they put their arms around each other, at someone else's wedding. Some look shy, elated, tentative. Like finally there's an excuse to feel body heat through a dress shirt.

He hasn't said no yet.

"I'm a good dance partner, Miles," I prod. He doesn't turn back to me, so I knock my knuckles against his. He looks at our hands lying next to each other on the tablecloth. Then he knocks my knuckles back, only this time it's more of a brush.

"I know you are, Lenny."

I cock my head. "How would you know that?"

And now I've got his whole attention. His gaze starts at my eyes and then it draws a slow, sinuous line down my nose, my earring against my cheek, the gloss on my lips.

By the time his eyes make it back to mine, my heart has started beating very fast. He hasn't answered my question and I don't think he's going to.

WE STILL HAVEN'T made it across the barn to where Tasha and Cody are eating ribs with giant rubber bibs on. There have been too many people to either greet or avoid. Right now, Miles is patiently enduring a headlock from a man who's braying like Ray Liotta in *Goodfellas*. I'm five feet away and enjoying the spectacle but decide to take the moment to use the bathroom.

As I'm washing up I notice that this bathroom is accessible through a door to the outside as well. And that door is flapping open in the wind. I go to secure it when I glance through the crack and see a person crouching out there.

Kira is gloomily scrolling sports highlights and sighing. It strikes me that being the town sweetheart might be a real drag. Like a performance you're never allowed to retire from. She springs to a stand when she sees me.

"Oh, hi," I say. "Sorry to interrupt."

I'm about to head back inside when she takes a quick step toward me.

"Wait?" she requests. She's got her hands behind her back again and her eyes on the ground. Either she's mastered demure or she could really use a confidence boost.

"What's up?" I step out into the night. The wind has started to pick up a little, and she and I both reflexively grab the bottom hems of our skirts.

"It's not my business," she says.

And whatever she's referring to, no, it isn't, but I'm curious, so I give her a nod.

"But Miles is a really great guy and he's been through so much . . . I swore to myself that no matter who he ended up with . . . I'd make sure she knew . . ."

Her eyes are glossy with tears.

"He doesn't know he's doing it—he doesn't mean to—but he hides." She taps her chest. "In here."

I blink at her. This doesn't quite compute.

"And it might be hard to deal with at times. But . . . he needs a really gentle touch. He seems like a tough guy, but he needs someone really gentle."

Gentle? Miles?

They dated for five years, so I've been assuming that Kira knew Miles inside and out but—

Somebody comes around the corner behind Kira.

"Baby?" he calls.

"Hi." She turns to smile at the man who, I assume, is the infamous Sean Vogel. All her artifice drops. Her hands come out from behind her back, her lip suddenly unbitten. She's reaching out for him, grabbing on to what clearly lives in her heart.

He's happy to see her, one arm around her neck and his nose against her temple. Then he spots me and stiffens. "Oh. Hey."

"Hello. Sean? I'm guessing?" I smile at them and it's genuine. There's love here and I'm glad they've found it with each other. "Good to talk with you, Kira. I'll get going." I give them a wave and slide back through the door and the bathroom and back to where Miles is waiting for me in the hallway.

The event rolls on and I laugh at the right places during the toasts, snag Miles a slice of cake so he doesn't have to run into anyone else on the way, and, in perhaps my most brilliant moment, drag him outside the barn when Kira, laughing and bashful, lines up to try to catch the bouquet. "Hey," I tell him as he turns to look back over his shoulder. "I have a great idea."

He's still looking back, so I take a leaf from his book and put one finger on his chin. He obediently turns to look down at me.

"Let's leave," I tell him.

He squints and runs a hand over the back of his neck. "I haven't talked to Cody yet." Then he looks back into the party and we are treated to a high-definition clip of Kira jumping into the air and clamping her hands around the hot-pink bouquet. The crowd cheers.

"Yeah," I say. "I think Cody will understand."

Miles turns back to me and laughs, dragging a hand down his face and over his stubble. "Let's get out of here."

We start at a normal pace, catch one another's eye, and start speedwalking. By the time we're halfway to the car, we're laughing and all-out running.

I plant my palms against the hood of his car and fight to stay alive.

"I can't believe," he pants, "that all it took to get you to run was to make you come to this god-awful wedding."

We slam into the car. "The ceremony itself was lovely," I say with an assertive finger pointed in his direction. "Tasha and Cody seem awesome."

He nods, then basically does a donut on the dirt road to get us the hell out of Dodge. "Everything else, though . . ."

"Was kind of a mixed bag."

"Thanks for coming with me. Jesus. What would I have possibly done without you?"

I ruminate on that. "Yeah, what *would* you have done without me?"

"Probably knocked over the barbecue pit by accident and set the barn on fire."

The lighting goes screwy and there's a crack of lightning to our left. It's the kind that shows you how tall the sky actually is, ten skyscrapers high, and followed quickly by a BOOM that cracks the world in two.

I scream with panicked laughter, flinging myself across the center console and squeezing the blood out of Miles's bicep. "*WHERE THE HELL DID THAT COME FROM?*"

Miles is shockingly stoic. He leans over the steering wheel

to peer out at the sky. "I didn't know there was supposed to be weather tonight."

"That wasn't *weather*. That was God asserting her masculinity!"

"We'll be fine. Let's just get home before—"

Raindrops the size of grapes start splatting on our windshield.

"Lenny, I need this arm to drive." He peels my fingers off his bicep and attaches them to the console. Luckily, it isn't until we're in his driveway that the heavens truly open up.

He parks. "Ready?" The rain is so loud I have to lip-read that.

"Let's do this."

Turns out I wasn't ready. It's like walking through a waterfall.

Just running from the driveway into the house has us completely drenched. He's cursing at the door while he jiggles the lock. We fall across the threshold and slam the door behind us. Miles's suit is toast. We stand in the front entryway making puddles and shivering. We're two inches from one another in the cold dark. Miles's hand brushes my shoulder on the way to the light switch. I shiver.

Click. Click. Clickety clickety clickety clickety. Nothing.

He groans and plants his forehead into the wood-paneled wall. "Perfect ending to the perfect night. I'll go flip the breakers."

"Don't leave me here! Are you joking?"

"Are you going to come with me into the basement, then?"

"Yeah, right! Obviously where the murderer is."

"Oh, great. Just a little something for me to meditate on while I fix the power."

Thunder earthquakes the house and we both jolt. Miles sighs. "Come on. Let's get you settled."

I don't know the house well, so I stumble and grope into the dark for Miles's back. I get a face full of sopping wet suit.

"Sorry," I mumble, and feel for the wall.

I jump when his hand lands on the top of my head. "There you are. Here, take my hand."

I reach up and peel his hand off my hair and wrap all ten of my fingers around his warm palm.

He leads us down the hall and swings a door open. A fluffy towel lands on my head. "Where's your bag?"

"In the bathroom where I showered earlier. But all my clothes are muddy."

"Right. Okay." He closes the closet door and leads me out of the hallway and across the living room. We go into what must be his bedroom.

Lightning—scream—thunder and I get one vivid flash of a giant comfy bed and another fireplace.

He opens some drawers. "I don't know what clothes these are, but here. They're not muddy."

It's a pile of soft cotton and I'm overjoyed. I carefully turn toward the bed and set the warm clothes down for safe-keeping.

I strip the wet dress up over my head and it thwacks onto the ground. I hear him rustling around next to me. Lightning, thunder, a flash of Miles standing next to me, next to a bed, in nothing but tight boxer briefs.

Lightning, thunder, tattoo.

Lightning, thunder, his head turned halfway toward me.

My wet bra is off, the clean shirt in my hands, my back is to him, lightning, thunder. I feel the flash of light over my entire body, touching me everywhere. I've got goosebumps.

I turn back toward him, the lightning flashes, and his bare chest is suddenly within kissing distance and the thunder shakes me down to my bones. Then it's ferociously dark again and there's a wash of warm exhale over my upturned face.

I hear him move and the towel is pressed into my hands again. "Your hair is wet." His voice is low and calm. "I'm gonna get a fire going in the living room to keep you company while I'm in the basement."

I barely get hold of the back of his shirt and then we're carefully picking our way through the dark out to the living room. I sit on the floor, knees tented underneath the giant shirt, and listen while he muscle-memories a crackling fire. The light is sudden, friendly and welcome and warm. We're awash in gold.

Just then, an alert on our phones, the power is out county-wide. So much for trying the breakers. I make a nest of pillows and blankets in front of the fire, and Miles joins me with a groan.

"Longest day ever," he says, yawning. He's on his belly, head toward the fire, chin resting on the backs of his stacked hands.

"You did great."

He laughs. "I did decidedly okay."

"Okay is great in this scenario. You were brave and kind. What more could you ask for?"

He tips his head and studies me. I study him back.

He hides. In here. He needs a really gentle touch.

"Miles?"

"Yeah?"

"Are you still devastated over Anders?" I ask bluntly.

He blinks. His eyes narrow. "You saw the bedroom, didn't you?"

I shrug and nod.

He lets out a long sigh. "I should have warned you. I know what that looks like."

"It looks like a shrine."

He considers this and then nods reluctantly. "I had to face the rest of the house because I *lived* in it, you know? And I moved into the large bedroom. So I eventually went through all my mom's stuff. But that room? I don't know."

I consider this for a while. "You don't really talk about Anders."

Miles closes his eyes and when he opens them, he's looking straight through the fire, seeing a different life. "Anders was . . ."

"Your Lou?"

His smile is quick and gone. "No. Sort of. We weren't best friends. I was five years older than him. When he came to live with us I became . . . the big brother."

His voice goes hoarse on the last two words and Miles drops his forehead to his arm and silently cries. Just like that. Open wide.

He hides.

No, he doesn't.

He needs a gentle touch.

No, he doesn't.

I crawl over to him and plop my head onto his back, right over our wolf, ear to his ribs. I listen to his crying through the drum of his chest. It doesn't last for too long. He scrubs a hand over his face and takes deep breaths that balloon my head toward heaven and then back to earth.

"He was so young. Just eighteen. It's so fucking fucked up that he died," Miles says simply.

"It tore your heart out."

"It was hard to know what the point of living was without them. But . . . I wanted to. Keep living. So I did."

I give his back some pats and then sit up and do a very comprehensive two-hand back scratch. He grumbles low in his chest and drops his head to one side. His eyes are closed and his eyelashes are wet.

"I like hearing about them, Miles. When you're thinking about them, you can tell me."

His eyes flutter open and land on my bare feet next to his shoulder. He unfolds one hand and flicks my big toe. "Okay."

It's a one-word promise that he's just made.

We sit like that for a long time.

Miles gets up and fiddles with the fire. "You must be exhausted after all that too."

I yawn and stretch and then curl up tight. "It's definitely been a social few days."

He smirks over his shoulder at me. "You love a social day. You're a butterfly."

I scowl. "Am not."

"Oh, please. You're incredibly socially gifted."

"Oh, fine. Maybe you're right. But it's all so much more exhausting than it used to be. Plus, these days I get nervous. I didn't use to get nervous all the time."

He considers that and then wordlessly stands up and goes to his room. He comes back with his two hands cupped around something, like he's caught a butterfly in there.

He sits next to me and holds his hands out. "You did a good job making friends, Lenny. And thank you for coming with me to the wedding." He clears his throat. "If you're feeling nervous about social stuff, I got you something that might help."

I look at him and then at his hands and he waggles them when I don't hop to.

I drag myself up to a sit. Instead of holding my hands out for the gift, I pry open a crack between his fingers and peer inside. The firelight flickers and I get a flash of silver. I reach into the cave between his palms and come up with a slightly tarnished silver locket. The initials WG are engraved in stylized cursive. I look at Miles quizzically.

"I got it secondhand, so the initials are from some random person," he says with a shrug. "But I actually thought you'd like that more than new." He nudges me with his foot. "Open it."

I slot a fingernail in between the two halves and it comes apart with a satisfying click. I gape for half a second before my eyes fill with tears. I recognize the photo immediately. It's one of me and Lou when we're about eighteen. It was her first attempt at giving us full faces of makeup and we were laughing so hard we couldn't breathe, falling all over one another. Crooked falsies and lipstick on our teeth. Queen Fuglies.

I laugh and swipe at my trembly tears.

"It's not an eight-by-ten, like you wanted . . ." He clears his throat. "But I figured this would be a good way to carry a photo of her with you wherever you went. If she's with you . . . then maybe you won't feel so nervous."

Studying it, I realize that he's gone to the trouble to print the photo quarter size. It's asymmetrically cut, slightly choppy on one side from where his scissors slipped. I'd bet my life there's a careful dot of Elmer's glue on the back of this photo.

The opposite side of the locket is grubby and empty. "What photo should I put in this side?" I ask him in a scratchy voice I barely recognize.

He cocks his head to one side and shrugs, a satisfied look on his face at my reaction to his gift. "You get to decide."

There's a distant roll of thunder from the storm that's passed us. One last stab of lightning changes the room momentarily from a flickering gold to bright platinum. It's like a camera flash.

I get one still of Miles's face—dark eyes, dark hair—familiar and . . . beloved.

This lightning-photo of him embeds itself sharply in my heart.

I grip the locket so hard it creates heat.

I know exactly what goes in the other half.

PART THREE

Forever After

I am laughing with my hands over my face so that Lou doesn't know I'm actually crying. Shaving my head was a piece of cake. Honestly, it feels light and cool and lovely to have no more hair. But Lou? I can't watch as the hairstylist hacks her gorgeous red hair to the ground.

But I've underestimated her. Because when I pull my hands down, her eyes are on me in the mirror, and she knows I've been crying. And she's crying, too. And now we're both bald and five feet apart and the world is rushing at us top speed.

She swivels in the chair to face me.

"We look . . ." She drops her chin. "Terrible."

And that's when the real laughter starts.

I FINISH FOLDING MY and Lou's laundry right as the oven dings. I pull the lasagna out to cool. It's about time for her to get home from work and I'm so excited to hear all about it. It's her first real job since her recovery and it means that Lou gets to be in the world, the real world, and will hopefully go days, weeks, months, or years without thinking about cancer.

When she comes in through our apartment door, she kicks off one high heel and then the other, dumps her bag in a heap.

"I did it," she says, doing the disco man pose. "I conquered corporate America."

"In one day? Wow, I hope it came with a raise."

"Nope, still broke. Is that lasagna? OMG! Should we get you a frilly apron? I'll be so sad when you get married and you're someone else's actual wife."

"God, I can't wait for that. Get me out of this hellhole."

"Totally. It's terrible here. Must be the lemon verbena candles and the perpetually full cookie jar."

I turn to her, pulling oven mitts off. "It was good, though? Work?"

She's glowing. "It was perfect."

LOU IS SITTING next to me in a wheelchair. She's got a big fleece hat on and an Aladdin blanket over her lap. The wind is blowing where we're sitting on the deck of the ferry and it gives me an excuse to slide closer to her. She lifts the blanket and I pull it over my legs too.

"You think other people take public transportation to hospice?" she asks, drawn and exhausted.

"You said no limos," I say with a shrug.

"Yeah, would have been overkill." She glances at me. "I won't say thanks this time. I know you hate that."

"You're welcome, Lou."

We huddle under the blanket and wait.

Chapter Twenty-Six

A word about my general love life: shriveled.

I *have* dated.

Here's a brief overview: virginity (fictional, contrived, social construct but I digress) mutually lost at seventeen with a sort-of boyfriend at his dad's house. No technique or skill. We conked heads and laughed hysterically. He made me pizza bites afterward.

Then followed a series of unserious hookups with randoms that occasionally culminated in some underwhelming penetration.

At twenty-four I was pretty firmly swept away by one guy, Tony. His best friend, Mario, was head over heels for Lou and the four of us used to go on double dates, which was probably a large part of the appeal. It was very fun until Mario started sucking and everybody broke up with everybody. I slept with Tony a few more times over the years, which was generally a thumbs-up. He came to Lou's funeral in a suit but I couldn't even look at him. And now you're up to date.

Which brings us to now. This moment, where I'm peeking out from a crack in the blankets in the dusty dawn light and trying not to scream every time Miles's chest rises and falls with his breath.

He's asleep on his back, face turned toward me, and why have I never noticed before that you could brush those eyelashes with a hairbrush they're so long?

The locket is clutched in my hand. It feels like a wedding ring he doesn't realize he's given me.

Do some people slowly fall in love and not realize it? Have I been in denial? Or did he hand me a locket with my best friend's face glued into it and *bam* just like that two hundred gallons of *feelings* upturned onto my head?

Does it matter when it started? I don't know. All I know is that I've never felt like this before and I'm not handling it well.

I slide out of the living room and track down my bag. I've never moved more quietly in my life. I change back into muddy camping clothes and don't care. I can't wear Miles's gigantic white T-shirt anymore or I'm going to go out there and crawl under the blanket with him.

I'm completely packed, bag in the car, his mother's dress laid out and all the towels already in the dryer by the time he wakes up.

I may or may not be sitting on the back porch in an Adirondack chair tapping my foot at sixty miles an hour.

"You're up already?" he asks, sliding open the glass door. His breath makes clouds and he's in boxer briefs and a T-shirt. I think. I can't look at him directly.

"Yup. All packed."

"It's only seven." He's flabbergasted.

"Ready to get back to the city." *Or at least away from this place where I can't catch my breath and have absolutely no idea what to say to you.*

"Oh. All right." He slides the door closed and comes back five minutes later with a steaming cup of coffee. When I take it from him, I bow my head to him in thanks. You know. Nice and natural. Like I'm the queen of England.

He scratches his head and looks down at me. "You good?"

"Yup."

He waits for me to say more. But I can't. So he heads back inside and I wait on the porch for him to do whatever he needs to do to prepare his house for winter.

I drink my coffee and try not to think too hard about the man who delivered it. Because Miles? Miles is? Miles is my list shepherd. My constant companion. My ace. Miles is my *pal.*

Friends to lovers is not, like, groundbreaking, I know. But I'm having a lot of trouble imagining changing literally anything about my relationship with him. He's seen me unkempt, unwashed, crying on sidewalks, shouting at strangers. He's dragged me off dance floors. I've shamelessly gotten crumbs on his couch.

Impertinent, teasy, bratty, goofy, unbothered . . . this is my wheelhouse. But suddenly, none of that seems even remotely reachable. I've broken a boundary between us. Our entire house of cards is built on the fact that we're *friends.*

And aren't feelings like *this* supposed to feel good?

Because this doesn't feel good. This feels . . . uncomfortable. There's a certain high-flying euphoria with every inhale, sure, but on every exhale, there's a corresponding emotion. One that pierces my gut and almost makes me gasp. Why am I feeling like total shit right now?

This isn't, like, *Oh, I'm so scared of what the future might hold with Miles,* this is a *bad* feeling. Almost overwhelming. It's creeping up from my gut, into my throat, stealing my words, battling for control.

I grasp the locket in one fist and fight to breathe. The coffee, for once, is not helping. I set it aside and try to focus on the trees in his backyard, the blue sky, the icy-damp air.

"You're shivering," Miles says behind me. I hadn't even heard him open the glass door.

"Yeah. Should we get going?" I hop up and force myself to

look at his face. My euphoria blooms and so does this name-less awful feeling. I'm being torn in two.

ON THE DRIVE back to the city I sit on my hands and look out the side window. Miles has noticed my silent anxiety and can't stop worrying himself. "Seriously, what the hell is hap-pening right now?" he asks approximately eighteen times.

"Autumn's here," I observe, because I have to say some-thing. And indeed. The weather's finally turned. There were spiderwebs of frost on the Jeep windshield this morning. There are comets of red and yellow and orange on every tree. The world is on fire with change.

When he pulls up outside the studio apartment, I grab my bag from my feet and scramble out of the car. His door slams and then he's in front of me on the sidewalk.

He's got one hand tugging on his short hair. "Lenny, are you sure you're okay? Is this . . . a Staten Island Ferry sort of thing?" he asks.

"I'm okay," I say, trying to reassure him. I see the worry etched in stone. "This isn't that kind of problem."

His hands slide into his jeans pockets and he suddenly looks so bewildered that I just want to koala-bear-hug him.

"Oh. Okay . . ." He clears his throat and then bounces on his heels. "Obviously you don't want to talk about it but . . . could you tell me what *genre* this problem is?"

I laugh, because cute. But then I get serious. Because what genre problem *is* this? This is a love-life problem. An ache-in-my-heart problem. A hysterical terror at the thought of loving someone wholeheartedly. And maybe it's also me realizing that I simply *can't* love someone wholeheartedly. The love-maker in my chest is too injured. When it creates love, it creates dread in equal measure.

"It's . . . out of your jurisdiction," I eventually say.

He recoils like I've slapped him. I almost take it back. He's the man who helps me. That's his job and he's proud of it. I've just stripped him of the Superman S on his onesie.

"Just . . . I'm fine," I say. "It's okay. I think this weekend was a lot and I just need some time on my own to get my head on straight."

"Okay." His eyes narrow and he cocks his head to one side. I think he's gotten over the shock of my rejection and has moved back into problem-solving mode. "I'll . . . give you a little space."

My heart skitters with panic. He's turning away from me toward the car and I drop my bag on the ground and leap forward, pinching his sleeve. "Just a *little* space."

He's paused, turned back toward me, his eyes on my hands white-knuckling his sleeve. When our eyes meet, there's a softness there that's almost immediately wiped away by resolve. "Just a little," he agrees.

I don't watch him go. I gather my bag and run upstairs. I slam the door of the studio behind me and collapse onto the tiny bed, trying to take a catalog of my emotions.

Giddiness, disbelief, sadness, panic, happiness, fear, excitement, confusion. It's a wall of white noise bearing down on me and turns out, I didn't want to be upstate and I don't want to be in this tiny apartment either! There's so much adrenaline in my system that when a plan pops into my head, I just barrel toward it, advisable or not. It's a bandage that I've been needing to rip off anyhow; might as well do it now, when everything already feels intense.

After a quick shower, I open the old wooden dresser and there, look, my Big Bird sweatshirt is holding hands with an old red hoodie of Miles's. My knees hit the floor and I try my best not to hyperventilate. If this were two days ago I would've worn Miles's sweatshirt in a heartbeat. Cozy, pre-loved, over-sized men's wear? I mean, come on.

But today, right now, with the locket pressed against my heart, the thought of wearing Miles's clothes makes me feel like I just did cocaine.

I slide into leggings, the Big Bird sweatshirt, and my jean jacket. I have to go.

AFTER A BRIEF stop at a bodega and a long train ride, I'm standing outside wrought-iron gates I can't pass through.

Greenwood Cemetery is a beautiful, peaceful place. A pond is in there. Flocks of migratory birds. Blue skies and a patchwork quilt of rolling hills.

Lou is in there, too.

I've wanted Lou, mourned Lou, grieved her.

But this is the first time since she's died that I've actually *needed* her. These feelings for Miles . . . it's the first time in my life I've felt this way. I'm aching, panicking, and promptly rethinking every single leap in logic I just took to get myself here.

Why did I think coming here was going to help clear my head?

My stomach is churning, my heart burning. I put one hand on the wrought-iron threshold that I cannot make my body cross.

My hands shake and I jam them into the pockets of my jean jacket.

What will I say when I get to her grave?

Sorry I don't come visit you? Are you taking care of the part of me that died along with you? Are you warm enough? Are you happy?

"Oh, Lou." I drop down to a three-point stance, right

there in the entrance of the cemetery. I can't be the only person who couldn't make their legs take another step inside these gates.

If I weren't feeling so confused about Miles I'd call him and gripe. *The change of scenery didn't work,* I'd tell him. I reach into my pocket and pull out the Snickers bar I bought at the bodega on the way here. I take half of it down in one bite. *The something bad for me didn't work either, you know-it-all* is what I'd say to him.

But then I realize I've likely left out the most important component of his recipe for feeling better.

I pull out my phone and pull up a contact.

Something good for me.

Oh, this is going to hurt.

I swallow the rest of the Snickers bar and I can't tell if my heart is racing from what I'm about to do or because I'm the closest I've been to Lou in months.

On a deep breath, I press call. The phone barely makes it through the first ring before it's answered. I gasp words, reveal my location.

"I'll be there in twenty." The words come through the line, clear as a bell. "Wait for me."

I'm grateful for the instruction. I lean against the iron fence around the cemetery and wait.

Twenty minutes later on the dot, I lift my head and look up toward the hill that Lou is buried on the other side of. The sun is off-kilter beside it and a woman atop it is backlit and distant. I push to a stand and now the woman walking down the hill is twenty yards from me.

When I called, I didn't expect her to walk through the cemetery to get to me.

"Mom," I shout, my voice like a frog.

She stops in her tracks, scanning for me. The wind must

have carried my voice because she looks back over her shoulder, in Lou's direction.

"Mom!" I call again, this time my voice stronger.

She whips around, locates me, pauses, and then breaks into a flat-out run. She's a marathon runner, so this is not shocking. Her peacoat flaps open around her hips; her long dyed-dark ponytail sails behind her. As soon as she's upon me I'm in her arms, inside her coat, my hands gripping her sweater and hanging on like I've been lost in a grocery store and she's just found me.

"Baby," she gasps into my hair. She takes me by the shoulders and pushes me back to look at me. "Where have you *been*."

Her tears are like glass spears down her cheeks. Her fingers turn into talons on my shoulders and she repeats her question. "*Where have you been?*"

"I'm okay, Mom. I'm okay."

"A few texts here and there. A voice message or two. *Months*, Helen. Months!"

No one but Mom calls me by my full name. "I'm sorry," I whisper to the ground.

"You haven't been going home," she accuses. "I know because I did a goddamn *stakeout*."

"I've been working uptown," I offer. But from the way her eyes are burning I can tell that I'm going to have to give up a lot more than that. "I haven't been able . . . to . . ."

She reads the months of misery in my expression and her own softens accordingly. "I was about half a week away from hiring a private investigator."

"I really am okay," I assert again. "I'm . . ." Alive. Surviving. Learning to wake up in the mornings like the happy people do.

These are all accurate descriptions, but it's different

words that bubble up inside me. I can't make myself walk through the gate to get to Lou's grave, but everything I came to tell her is scratching to get out.

"I'm . . ." I try again and the words just tumble. "*I think I might be falling in love with someone, Mom.* With someone who has *saved me* these last few months." I cover my face with my hands. "I don't know where I'd *be* without him. And I mean that literally. He's kept me earthbound, Mom. The only reason I'm standing here right now is him. And I'm feeling so much and it *hurts*—" I drop back into the three-point stance. "It hurts and no one ever tells you that when you want someone this hard, you risk *everything* you built with them. And I came here to tell Lou, because I've never felt like this before and I had to tell her. But I couldn't even go in."

Mom tugs me up to a stand by the scruff of my jacket and takes me by the shoulders again. She's got a look like she's about to say something profound and illuminating. Then her face scrunches up like a paper ball. "*What?*"

I can't help it. I laugh. "It's really good to see you, Mom."

"Don't change the subject. Did you just tell me you're in love with someone? Who is this person?"

I scrub my hands over my face again. "His name is Miles. He's . . . new."

"Miles . . . I heard something about him from Marzia."

"Ah, God. Don't get me started on that. Whatever she told you is patently false."

She puts her hands on her hips. "He treats you well?"

"Mom, he walked into hell and dragged me back out."

Her face cracks into alarm. The months since I've seen her in person splat between us. "Baby, how bad was it?"

"I wasn't okay for a while. But I am now." I try for a reassuring tone, but the alarm has not receded from her face.

"Well, how can I believe you? You were lying to me for

months!" She scrambles her phone out of her pocket and pulls up our text thread. I wince when I see all the lying, cheating exclamation points I've been sending her. The phone goes black and she shoves it away. "Not that I bought any of it."

There are more tears in her eyes, and these ones are angry.

"You want to talk about hell, Helen?" She points up the hill toward Lou. "I feel like I'm down *two* daughters."

Her words pierce me, but they're also overdramatic and said with a flair for theater. Just enough to keep me from spinning off into her world. "Mom."

"Texts are *not enough*." She steps into my space. "One call is not enough. You don't want to live in your apartment? That's fine. Come home and live with me and Dad."

I hold my ground. "I'm not moving home."

Her eyes narrow. She wants me where she can keep an eye on me. "Fine. Then I want a weekly dinner. A rain-or-shine dinner. And if you don't come to Bay Ridge, then I'm coming uptown. Wherever you are. Once a week."

I roll my eyes like a teenager and unlock a flood of lovely chemicals. How wonderful to be casually annoyed at my mother. How wonderful for my mother to boss me around and threaten me with her overbearing presence. How wonderful to word-vomit my thoughts and fears to her in one big gob and have her say the wrong things.

"Okay." I agree to her terms. "Once a week."

And then I'm back in her arms, inside her coat. She trembles as we grip each other and I realize something awful. That at some point I'm going to have to deal with the fallout of my complete disappearance from my former life.

It occurs to me for the first time that people have been . . . missing me.

"Oh, Lenny-girl." Mom grips me so tight it hurts and then releases me all at once. "Give me your phone."

I do as she says because when she's in this mood, it's way easier to just succumb. She's scrolling my contacts. I know who she's looking for.

I watch in suspended animation while she texts herself his contact info from my phone.

She tips her phone away from me and texts him something.

I cover my face with my hands again. "You just invited him to dinner, didn't you."

"I need to befriend him if he's going to keep tabs on you for me."

"Mom. Come on—please don't—things between us are weird right now and I—"

"Why are they weird? Oh, he just texted back. He asked what he could bring. That's sweet. Doesn't seem weird to me."

The flood of emotions from earlier is receding and I'm left with some good old-fashioned sheepishness. "I don't know." I play with my sleeve. "I, like, *just* realized how I feel about him. So, now I . . . don't know how to act . . . or if I should tell him . . . and I know that he cares about me, but that could be so different than how *I* feel about him and wait, yeah, how do I know if he likes me?"

Mom's pretty green eyes grow wide. *"You're not together?* I thought—Oh, Helen. You *do* need Lou, don't you?" She says this on a laugh and I'm smiling in spite of the stab of pain that comes with it. "Regardless. Bring him to dinner. Bring the after-dinner fruit. Tomorrow night. We'll do Sunday dinner on a Monday. Just for you. He already agreed to come, so don't try to get out of it."

I hold up my hands in surrender. She loops her arm

through mine and I think I'm walking her to the train until she stops next to a dinosaur of a Subaru. I blink, my eyes widening. "You got it out of long-term parking?"

"You think my long-lost daughter finally calls me and I'm going to fool around with the subway? Get in."

"Mom, you're not going to drive me all the way to the Upper West Side."

Her eyes widen a little at my mention of the neighborhood she didn't know I was staying in. But apparently, that's exactly where she's driving me, because she stuffs me into the car. We spend the next hour and ten minutes fighting traffic and mildly arguing. When we stop in front of the studio apartment, Mom puts on her hazards and gets out to take a picture of my front door. She even drops a pin on her Google Maps. She's got my location and she's holding on with two hands. I hug her goodbye on the sidewalk but she follows me up the stoop.

"Should I come up? We could order in."

Now that we're separating, her alarm lines are creasing her face again.

"I'll be there tomorrow, Mom. I promise."

"You promise."

"I promise."

A UPS truck lays on its horn and makes us both jump. It can't get past Mom's idling car. "Okay. I'll go." She gives me one last hug and then I stand on the stoop and watch her drive away.

It's chilly. And I'm hungry. And I should really go inside now. But instead I just sit there and think about how tightly she held on to me.

Chapter Twenty-Seven

"This fruit is wrong," I tell Miles. We're standing in a ludicrously expensive Italian market. T minus one hour until we're due on my parents' doorstep.

He blinks at me and then at the assortment in his grocery basket. "How could fruit be wrong? It's fruit."

"She didn't mean apples and oranges. She meant fancy fruit."

"Fancy fruit?" He pulls out his phone and squints at the text my mother sent to him. "She said to bring after-dinner fruit. That means fancy fruit?"

"Where are your glasses?" I don't let him answer because I can't actually chat about his super hot glasses right now. I'm doing a barely passable job of not acting like a panicky, lovestruck fool and I don't want to blow it. "My mom was raised proper Italian. Well, the Brooklyn kind. We're doing the full-course menu tonight, my friend. And that's not a euphemism. The fruit course is after the main course but before the cookie course."

He's gaping at me. I take pity on him and bodily turn him back toward the produce section. "Go ask somebody what's in season and buy the prettiest ones," I advise.

He toddles off and I wander the store, rubbing my palms on my pants and trying to forget the warm-soft of his shirt under my hands. I make accidental eye contact with an obviously DTF cheesemonger behind the counter, and he and I engage in a brief and intense affair. But he turns quickly back to the wheels of cheese when Miles appears at my shoulder.

"The apples *are* in season," he tells me. "So I kept them, but she also recommended . . ." He holds them up one at a time. "Plums, persimmons, and pomegranate."

"That's a lot of Ps."

He frowns. "I didn't get any peas. Should I get some—oh. Ps. Right. Hey, are you sure I don't look stupid? I feel stupid. These pants are way too tight."

He's wearing freshly creased jeans and a dark blue flannel button-down. He holds his hands out to his sides, basket of fruit and all.

"You look nice," I assure him. Trying very hard to play it cool. "Fresh out of a J. Crew catalog."

"Oh." He frowns down at himself. "That's exactly what happened."

"Huh?"

"I went to J. Crew and bought this outfit this morning so that I'd have something to wear."

This news is literally painful for me. My chest is tight and achy. I've never had anyone dress up to meet my parents before.

"Well, you look nice," I eventually say again.

Miles cocks his head to one side and studies me. "Lenny, should we talk about why you're—"

"We're gonna be late!" I chirp, pretending to study the time on my phone but actually seeing nothing at all.

We make it out to Brooklyn in record time, not even close to being late. The two of us stand outside my parents' apartment door.

My mom, a recovering Roman Catholic, has given up almost all of her family's Sunday traditions except for the gigantic, sprawling meal starting at about four P.M. I've tried to warn Miles about what he's set to endure.

I still don't think he's prepared.

Miles and I are barely through the threshold before my mom is yanking our coats off and bustling us toward the living room. There are already aperitifs sweating on coasters on the coffee table.

"Sit. Sit!" she commands. Then she sprints off to the kitchen.

"Your mom is . . ." Miles blinks.

"Energetic," I supply.

"This apartment is . . ." He slowly looks around at the potted herbs spilling off the top of the never-used piano, the gilded map of Italy, the red velvet couch we're sitting on, the framed needlepoints of our deceased Siamese cats, my dad's corner of the room with its two years of half-read newspapers and two-decades-old television.

"Unique," I offer.

"This drink is . . ." He holds up the bright red concoction.

"Campari and soda with an orange peel," I inform him. "The only—"

"—suitable drink for the cocktail hour," my mom finishes, bustling back in with a platter of olives.

"Where's Dad?"

"Picking up the cookies from the bakery."

I blink at my mom. It's not like her to outsource the baking. Is she trying to impress?

"So." My mom has finally settled herself on the armchair across from us. She reaches across to Miles with one hand out. "Eva. And you're Miles."

"Yes, hello." Miles shakes her hand, and then, in a moment of brilliance, quickly picks up his drink and holds it out to cheers my mother.

Her eyes flicker with approval and she takes a hearty swig. So does Miles. I watch him carefully for reaction to the flavor of the drink. I love Campari, but he's a lifelong beer drinker. He does nothing but lick his lips and set the cup back down.

Just then we hear the front door opening and my typically quiet father absolutely shouts down the hall. "Elena? Elena!"

He charges into the living room, shoves the box of cookies toward my mother, and then yanks me off the couch and into his hug. I press my face into his familiar brown cardigan. He hugs me so tight I can't breathe and then pulls me back just far enough to kiss my cheek. His eyes are red and glossy with tears. "Oh, sweetheart," he murmurs.

Yeah. I'm the worst.

My parents have been missing me so much that all they can do is hug me and cry and meanwhile I've been sleeping on the Q train and sending their calls to voicemail.

My dad glances down at Miles and, without unhanding me, shakes his hand. "Kevin. I'm Lenny's dad," he explains unnecessarily.

My mom is crying now too, just watching our reunion, and it's all a big soggy mess. "Kev, will you help me with the—"

"Yes," he says, wiping at his eyes and immediately following her to the kitchen to compose himself.

I plunk back down on the couch in a heap. I don't know if I can even remember the last time I saw my dad cry at something that wasn't *Field of Dreams*.

"Elena?" Miles asks, looking fully confused.

"Oh. Right. My full name is Helen Elena. My dad wanted to name me after *his* mom, Helen. And my mom wanted to name me after *her* mom, Elena. So they gave me both names, only now my mom usually calls me Helen and my dad calls me Elena. Go figure."

He considers this. "And Lou only called you Lenny."

I nod with a little smile. "Yeah. I guess the people who love me the most all have unique names for me."

"All of them?" His brow immediately furrows as he stares into nothing. I have the distinct impression he's racking his brain.

"Eat up!" My mom is back from composing herself in the kitchen and she's realized that the olive plate has gone untouched.

"Miles," my dad says, reemerging as well. "Do you play Hearts?"

I snicker and Miles barely restrains himself from glaring at me.

"Yes. I do." He clears his throat and takes another sip of his drink.

"The last time we played Hearts, he almost threw me in a river."

"Dunked," he quickly corrects. "I almost *dunked* her in a river."

My parents are delighted with this information. "Oh, Lenny is the absolute worst sport when it comes to Hearts," my mom says.

My dad is digging in the desk drawer. "Losing to her in *anything* has always been miserable. Who raised you?" he demands as he turns back around with the cards in hand. "They did a terrible job."

"I really like that everyone here has already agreed they'll be losing to me."

Miles is ignoring me and scrubbing his hands together, mentally preparing for battle.

"What should the teams be?" I ask the group. "Girls v. boys? Geminis against the world?" I gesture to myself and my dad.

My mom cracks her knuckles. "Let's show 'em how it's done, Kev."

"Ah," I say. "Good call. Youngs v. olds. If we're on the same team then he's far less likely to throw me in a river."

"*Dunk*," Miles asserts again. "I would have gone in with you."

Of course he would have. This makes me chest-tight and achy and I gulp at my aperitif to soothe the burn.

We eat olives and play Hearts and my parents wheedle bits of information about Miles between hands of cards.

My parents absolutely spank us at Hearts, and Miles is stunned. I try to yank him to a stand but he just sits there in a pile. "I win at Hearts," he insists. "In my normal life."

"Welcome to your new reality."

"Come eat!" my mom shouts from the kitchen, and Miles finally resurrects.

There are goblets of wine and garlic bread and a trough of spaghetti, homemade, in marinara sauce, also homemade.

"Serve yourself!" Mom calls, her head in the fridge, hunting down the Parmesan.

Miles takes a humongous scoop of pasta and I quickly reach over and scoop half of it back into the bowl. "Pace yourself," I warn out of the corner of my mouth.

He sort of follows directions, but agrees to another serving when my mom offers it to him. He's just scraping the last of the sauce with the side of his fork when my mom stands up with an evil grin and dons her apron. She opens the oven he hadn't realized was warming the actual main course.

She turns with the baking dish between two oven mitts and his fork squeaks against his plate.

"That's . . ." he says dimly. "That's an entire duck."

And it is. Complete with roasted potatoes and olive gremolata.

This one is not a "serve yourself" dish. Mom piles Miles's plate with food. I've learned the hard way to yank my plate away from her the second I've gotten the amount I want to eat. My dad has passively come to accept reality and just takes it upon himself to top off our wineglasses while my mom tortures us with ancestral cooking.

We eat and chat and eat and chat. Miles clears his plate, but I detect a bead of sweat running down the side of his face. The remains of the duck are cleared away, and Miles pats his stomach and sits back.

My mom stands and with the flair of a magician pulls a kitchen towel off the top of an enormous vat of salad. "To help you digest," she explains when Miles catches some of the salad in one hand as she overfills his plate.

"You don't have to eat it all," I say out of the side of my mouth a few minutes later. He's three quarters of the way through and is chewing like a cow on cud.

The salad and salad plates are cleared away and Miles gets up to help with the dishes. "Sit down, sit down," Mom says, waving him away. "You can help when we're done eating."

He turns to me, eyes wide with horror. *When we're done eating?* he mouths.

"There's two more courses," I whisper.

He clunks into his chair, hands flat on the table. Mom plates the fruit that Miles brought and hands out the tiny dessert forks for us all to eat from the plate at once. Dad goes to the cabinet and emerges with half skinny/half bulbous cordial glasses.

"Dad. No."

"It's a digestif," he explains to Miles. "Would you like some?"

"Oh. Sure."

"Just say no!" I whisper to him. I try out this tactic myself. "Dad! No!"

He ignores me and sits back at the table, handing out the glasses to everyone but me. "Miles, are you Italian by chance?"

Miles shakes his head.

"Well," my dad says. "You will be by the end of this meal."

He and my mom laugh heartily, as if my dad hasn't been making that joke for thirty years.

"Dad's not Italian either," I explain to Miles. "But he's a big fan of grappa."

Dad pours the clear liquid for each of them.

"Seriously," I whisper to Miles, "You don't have to—"

But he shoots it back in one go. He does not (1) grimace, (2) gasp, or (3) cough. But I'm pretty sure he's not breathing and his eyes have gone glassy. He might be having a brief tête-à-tête with God.

Mom and Dad drink their own grappa and eat fruit and gab. Dad fills Miles's grappa glass twice more before I'm surreptitiously able to swipe the grappa bottle and restore it to the cabinet before a fourth round can be dispensed.

By the time the cookies course (final one, I swear) comes out, I'm the only one who's not drunk as a skunk. We move the party back to the living room.

"So, you've been keeping an eye our Lenny-girl, huh?" Mom asks, plunking down in between Miles and me on the couch.

Dad emerges balancing a tray of piping hot espressos and passes them around. I immediately set mine aside. Miles tries to figure out how to hold the tiny cup without burning his fingerprints off and settles on taking the coffee down in one scalding swallow. He's looking a little woozy over there.

"So . . ." Mom nudges Miles to answer her question.

"Hm? Oh." He's fanning his tongue and sort of sliding to one side of the couch. "She keeps an eye on me too."

I get up to retrieve a glass of ice water in order to save his life so I miss the next few moments of conversation, but when I return Miles is glancing at me, a blush on his cheeks.

"Quit interrogating him," I say, handing him the ice water and reclaiming my seat.

Mom ignores me completely. "She's a total and complete mess but there's no one else like her."

Miles's brow furrows. He's drunk, but not so drunk he'll stand for that. "She's not a mess," he says in a low voice. "She's perfect."

Mom scowls right back at him and leans across the couch to throw an arm around my neck, pressing our temples together. "Of *course* she's perfect. Who says she isn't?"

"She means it as a compliment," I assure Miles. "They think I'm charmingly free-spirited."

He's still frowning at my mom and she's still frowning back.

"Messy," he concedes. "But not a mess."

Mom turns to me—I'm still in a headlock, by the way. "I like him." She turns back to him. "Do you know how to turn on the GPS in someone's phone? Will you turn on Lenny's and make it so that I can see it on my phone?"

She's picked my pocket and is handing my phone over to Miles.

"Oh! Good idea." Dad is handing his own phone over to Miles as well. "Hook her up to mine, too."

I'm yoinking phones and handing them back to their owners. "You don't need to surveil me! I swear I'll start calling more often."

"If you can't catch Lenny you can always call or text me," Miles offers, and my mom's face immediately slinks into a knowing smile. This was what she was hoping for all along.

"Wonderful."

Chapter Twenty-Eight

By the time we make it back to Miles's apartment, it feels like a year has passed, but it's only eight-thirty. We took a cab because I didn't think Miles was physically capable of managing the stairs down to the train. Luckily Emil met us at the cab door and helped me drag Miles into the elevator.

Right now his body has the same basic structural integrity as a bag of hot soup. I lodge my shoulder into his armpit and scrabble at the lock on his front door. I can't help but notice that every second the door stays locked we sink about six inches toward the floor. By the time the door handle finally turns, I'm eye-level with it and we pretty much crawl inside on all fours. He drags his ass over to the couch and collapses.

"I think . . ." he says. "I think grappa hits in stages."

"Grappa is basically rubbing alcohol."

"Am I Italian yet?"

I laugh and go into the kitchen to collect him a glass of water.

"Your parents do that every week?"

"Only when they have company. And there's not usually quite so much grappa."

He groans. "Don't say grappa."

"You were saying it like five seconds ago!"

He groans again. "The tides have turned."

"You need to sleep."

"Yes. Let's go to bed."

I ignore the lurch in my gut at the idea of going to bed with Miles. It's ridiculous to feel this way. Miles and I have slept beside each other a handful of times and it's never made me giddy-sick before.

He slumps sideways onto the couch and closes his eyes. And then he abruptly rolls off the couch and lands on the floor in a shocking heap.

"Are you okay?" I rush over to him.

"That was a preemptive strike," he grumbles into the floor. "I figured if I was sleeping on the couch and you were sleeping on the floor, I'd roll off and crush you in the night. So I did it first."

"Good point." It's not a good point, but he's too drunk to argue with right now. I'm calmer now that I fully realize he meant "let's go to bed" on the couch and floor. Of course he did.

I help him onto a floor bed I've just made and take his pre-warmed spot on the couch. His head is on his pillow and his eyes are closed, so I guess we're going to sleep now. But then there's a poke-poke on my shoulder.

"Hm?" I lean over the edge of the couch and peek at him.

"Are you going to tell me?"

"Tell you what?"

His eyes come open. "What's been going on with you."

"Oh." I shift and the locket falls out of the collar of my shirt, hanging suspended between us. Miles lifts one big finger and taps it, makes it swing.

"Should I not have given that to you?"

"What? No! I love it." I tuck it back into my shirt and roll back onto the couch where he can't see me.

"So, what is it?"

How can I explain this to him without actually explaining it?

I'm racking my brain, trying to think of a way, when there's a long, low rumble coming from the floor and I realize the poor sucker's already snoring.

Which is a good thing because what would I have said? *I just realized I have feelings for you and for some reason it's making me feel like a humongous bag of trash?*

Yeah, that's probably something one should keep to oneself.

I get up off the couch, because it's only nine P.M. and I'm not tired. I make my way to his desk under the window and look out at the silvery moonlight. I can't get close enough to the sky, so I crawl on top of the desk and lean against the glass. From this vantage point I can see a sliver of the Hudson, the hulking stalagmites of the buildings, the glowing orange squares of everyone's unique and common lives.

I'm still curled in that position, knees to my chin, head against the glass when, a few hours later, Miles stirs, groans, and goes to the bathroom.

He washes his hands and emerges, heading toward the darkened kitchen, probably for water.

"Hungover yet?" I ask from my dark corner.

"Whoa!" He spins to face me. "I thought you went home!"

He pours a glass of water and pads over to me, free hand in his pocket.

"I was just about to call you to make sure you made it all right," he says.

"I won't leave without telling you."

He stops in his tracks at my words, as if I've just said something very important, and even though I'm still looking out the window, I can feel his eyes all over my face. He clears his throat. "The hangover hurts like hell. I'm never going to your parents' house again."

I laugh but then pause. "Wait. Really?"

He gives me a friendly smirk. "Of course not really."

"So you'll come with me if I ask?"

His eyes pierce me in the shadows of the kitchen. "Lenny, I'll do anything you ask me to."

I've never had anyone say anything even a tenth this passionate to me and I don't know how to handle it.

His words have softened whatever gate I've been putting up. I can't hide it anymore. The truth pours out of me.

"Miles, have you ever felt terrible about something you should be happy about?"

He blinks. "Well. Sure."

He approaches slowly and pulls the desk chair out to sit below me. When I don't say more, he hands the rest of his glass of water over to me and I polish it off.

"You gave me this . . ." I pull the locket out of the collar of my T-shirt, and his eyes fall to the glint of silver. "And Miles . . . I felt joy." And love. "Real joy. And I didn't know I was capable of that feeling anymore. But there it was."

His eyes are soft and sympathetic. I think he might already know where I'm going with this. Which is amazing because I don't even know where I'm going with this.

"But along with that joy," I try to explain, "came a horrible feeling. Something so . . ."

"Guilt," he whispers.

All the air leaves my lungs. "Guilt?"

"I wonder if . . . you felt guilt because Lou is gone but you were still able to feel joy in spite of it."

My wheels are spinning viciously as I try to understand. "You think I'm beating myself up for—" *Falling in love?*

He lets out a long, slow breath. "Sometimes, when grief recedes, even momentarily, there can be a kind of disorientation or, yeah, guilt that comes along."

I understand all at once and it makes me panicky. "Re-cedes? No. Ha. No. Miles. Grieving . . . that's the only thing that I can . . . I can't just *get over* her death, Miles. I can't . . . I *have* to feel the grief. How could I ever get used to her being gone? It makes me *sick*. How could I do that to her?"

I hear my own words in my own ears and I didn't even know, until this second, that I've been *protecting* this unten-able pain, because it's all I have left of her.

I'm gasping and reaching out for a handhold, anything to keep me from plummeting. I find his hands and then his shoulders. He leans forward in his chair, and with a strong grip he circles his arms around my hips.

"Grief," he says in a low voice, pinning me to him, hold-ing me in place against him, "becomes your companion, Lenny. As awful as it is, it's your constant. And so when it starts to leave . . . when you start to heal—"

"I can't *heal*, Miles!" I'm gripping him with claws, incon-solable. What a horrific concept. So sickeningly backward. Lou wouldn't have wanted this for me, but . . . "Grieving her . . . it's the only connection . . . it's how I hold on to her. It's—" I break off and fight for breath.

"It's not," he says, and holds me even tighter. "I swear it's not. Listen to me, Lenny. This does not mean you are forget-ting her or losing her all over again."

My choppy breaths dissolve into tears. I sob and cling to him and he clings to me right back.

"Grief is a relationship," he continues. "It's the way we figure out how to keep loving them even though they're gone. And in order to do that we have to keep on going. And going and going." His hold is tighter and tighter and mine is tighter and tighter and I've slid off the desk and into his lap. "You are not betraying her by healing," he whispers directly into my ear. "You are honoring her. You are learning to love

her exactly as she is. As someone who isn't here anymore . . .
That's who she is now. And this journey through grief . . . It's
what we *do* for the great loves of our lives."

The fact that he knows me well enough to call Lou a
great love of my life has me clinging to him while I shudder
through this new and terrible idea. It'll take years to process.
I'm so tired and so tired of being awake in the middle of the
night. I want cool sheets and huge pajamas. I can't take much
more of this.

I'm about to slide off him when his arms tighten so slightly
around me I think I might have imagined it. It's the softest
resistance imaginable, but it's enough to still me, to keep me
from going anywhere.

Some things are okay because it's nighttime. Because one
of us has recently been sobbing. Because he and I . . . we
haven't found the limits to what he will or won't do for me.

So it feels *natural*—admittedly new—when he reaches up
and presses one palm to my cheek. I don't blink or move. His
hand shifts and his movements become light as an eyelash.
Long moments pass while he methodically brushes my hair
back from my face. I tip toward him to make it easier. He's
calm and fond.

He's both with me and not. I can see in his eyes that he's
reflecting, mulling, going over the night we've just had.
There's a sudden flash of white from his quick smile. "So the
locket made you feel joy, huh?"

I give a watery laugh. "Miles, the locket made me feel . . ."
The buttons on his new fancy flannel catch my eye. I reach
down and fix one that's gone crooked through its brave attempts at doubling as pajamas. "You giving me that locket . . ."
I try again and then huff with frustration when I can't gener-
ate the words.

"You don't have to figure it all out right now," he says in a low voice.

My body informs me that I'm about to do something really risky, because suddenly I'm all adrenaline, shaky with nerves and ecstatic promise. "I think I already *do* have it all figured out."

I glance at his dark, patient gaze and then away. It's too much to look in his eyes right now. "You've been . . . these last few months . . . there's been nothing I can't talk to you about."

His hand leaves my face now and clasps his other at my back, encircling me again. "And it feels *weird*," I say in almost a whisper, "to have had this gigantic thing happen to me that I can't tell you."

His brow furrows. "Gigantic thing?"

"You've probably noticed that I'm not good at holding my feelings in."

He laughs a little but doesn't agree or disagree. I pluck at his now-familiar button. He slouches down some to get back in my eyeline.

"I have no experience with this," I whisper.

"With what?"

"It's never happened to me before—I mean, I've never told anybody that I—" I put a hand flat over the locket and realize belatedly that that hand is also flat over my heart.

This time my eyes get stuck on his and I just can't say any more. But maybe I've already said enough because his face, just a foot from mine, goes from attentive listening to surprised understanding. His eyes bounce-bounce between mine. His eyebrows raise.

We're both stock-still. I'm suddenly extremely aware of the fact that we're tangled together and he's warm and strong and I'm definitely staring at his mouth, which I realize because he licks his lips and it makes me lick mine too.

My heart is hollow, tripping down an incline. I've got one hand on his collar. My thumb traces a circle against hot skin and I feel him swallow. I'm pulled into his gaze. There are no words, just a buzzing cloud of adrenaline and warmth.

I'm suddenly two inches away from his mouth and I'm not sure how I got there. I've got a hand on either side of his face and it's just so dark and lovely in this room. So quiet except for our breaths. His hand comes up to grip my wrist.

"Lenny."

"Hm?" I'm stuck in his eyes, awash in his warm breath, melting into his lap, leaning close. Now I'm an inch away. I can almost taste him.

Clop. His hand shoots up between us and claps over my mouth.

"Mmfff!" My gaze flings to his.

"Lenny," he says with a little smile on his face. "Wait."

I struggle back from his hand. "If you don't want to kiss me, that's fine, but you don't have to muzzle me!"

He strong-arms me from wiggling off his lap and puts one light finger under my chin, holding me in place.

"I didn't say no," he says, and I've never heard his voice rumble low quite like that before. His eyes drop to my mouth. Then his hand slides back up and his palm covers my lips again. He leans in slow, eyes on mine, and presses a soft kiss to the back of his own hand, directly over where my lips are. "I said *wait*."

He pushes the chair back, sets me on my feet, and then leans forward, elbows on knees. He lets out a long breath. I must breathe it directly in because I'm gasping for air.

I grip the locket with both hands and stare at him as he

unfolds himself from the chair and comes to a stand in front of me.

"Wait for what?" I ask in a hoarse voice. "Is this about the list? You want to wait until it's finished or something?"

"No." He clears his throat. "No, not exactly."

"Then what are we waiting for?"

He takes a skein of my hair; he traces it all the way down to the ends before he lets it fall. Then he slides his hands into his pockets, his face tipped down first to the floor and then back to me. "We'll know it when we see it."

"*What?*" But he's already gone to gather our shoes and coats.

"I'll walk you home."

"Hey." I'm scrambling to intercept him at the front door.

He pulls on his black sweatshirt and tosses me my coat so that it lands on my head. My shoes arrive in a heap at my feet.

"Hey!" I say again as we toe into our shoes simultaneously. "Miles!"

He pauses at his front door and turns back to me, one hand on the doorknob.

I stalk over to him and bat his hand off the doorknob because he's rushing me. "You're saying you're not ready for—you're not ready to—you're not ready?"

He laughs and I think I detect a touch of exasperation, but it melts into something soft. "No. I'm not saying that."

I translate this with fierce and aggressive vim. "Wait. You think *I'm* not ready? I was the one who made the move! That's the definition of ready!"

"Sure." He's got me by the shoulders and is steering me out into the hallway.

I jump around and point a finger at him. "But you wanted to, right? I'm not . . . the only one . . ."

I'm suddenly swamped with embarrassment. I cover my face with two hands and crouch down like a frog. "Oh, my *God.*"

His knees bump into my knees as he crouches down in front of me. "Lenny, you gotta listen to me, okay? I . . . I have a grand plan and I think it's a good one."

A grand plan? About . . . me? Him and me and kissing and waiting? My blood is pure fizz.

"But you won't tell me what the plan is?"

"The plan is we wait."

"For something you won't tell me what it is."

He sighs again. "If I tell you then it won't count when it happens. I mean it from the bottom of my heart. Just *wait.*"

For what? I'd really like to shout again, but it didn't get me anywhere the first time.

I unfold from the floor and follow him to the elevator. We make it out of the lobby and into the fresh night. We walk toward the studio apartment in charged silence.

When we get to my stoop I walk up to the door and he stays on the sidewalk below. I turn to him, ornery and determined.

"Answer me this."

"Yeah?" His voice is gravelly and expectant as he looks up at me. I'm nearly sidetracked by the set of his shoulders, his black sweatshirt pooled against the strong line of his neck. But no. I need answers. If not just to save my pride.

"You've thought about kissing me? Before that moment just now, I mean?"

He goes still. It doesn't matter that there's eight feet of free fall between us, my blood is racing like he's inches away and leaning in.

"Yes."

My hands in my coat pockets reflexively tighten. That

single word instantly reminds me of sitting around the camp-fire, Jericho whispering a mystery question to Miles. His one-word answer, clear and concise and certain. And now he's handing me that same *yes*.

I should take it for an answer and just go to bed happy. But I'm anxious and trembly and elated and nervous. I know that I won't sleep unless there's nothing left for me to panic over. So I push just a little harder.

"And when you were thinking about it . . . it's because . . . you've been wanting it?"

There's a long pause, his dark eyes staring up at me.

"Yes."

"Okay, cool!" I chirp. His answer has snapped me like a fishing line and I scamper through the door, barely making eye contact with him. "Have a good night!" Slam.

I wait twenty seconds and slide the door open a crack.

He's walking back down the sidewalk, laughing and shaking his head like *WTF, Lenny*.

I watch him until I can't see him anymore.

Chapter Twenty-Nine

So, yeah. Here I am, playing it cool, super cool.

I like a guy and that guy likes me.

No big.

Lots to just sort of casually ponder in a totally relaxed and contemplative way.

My next few days are complete crap. Miles is leaving Tupperwares of food for me after work and checking in by text, but I've yet to lay eyes on him again since I watched him walk down the sidewalk.

How does one interpret this? He's avoiding me because . . . he thinks I'll take him unawares with my prodigious seduction technique?

He's providing space after a really intense and emotional change in our relationship?

He's spending his free time hyperventilating into a pillow at the mere thought of my silky lips?

He assumes that I'm stumped over this *waiting* idea and will likely badger him relentlessly to tell me what he means? I mean, correct, but . . .

Ainsley is lounging next to me on the couch and singing a song she's had stuck in her head for days. I'm prickly and sensitized to everything. Especially with this load of staticky laundry that I'm attempting to fold. It's attracted every bit of lint known to man and there are socks hiding in all the shirt sleeves.

I chase down a rogue undershirt three quarters of the way inside a bedsheet and yelp when I get about fifty static shocks in a row. "Ow! No! Why?"

The sheet gets lifted off me all at once and my hair goes with it.

"This is a good look for you," Miles says, standing over me.

"Hopefully irresistible?" I say with a half glower/half grin. Because I like him and he likes me and he just made my heart skip and I don't understand why we he won't kiss me.

Lots to feel while folding laundry.

He just raises his eyebrows and glances over at Ainsley. "You ready?"

"Sure!" She scrambles up and leaps off the back of the couch. Miles catches her reflexively and sets her on her feet.

"Where are you going?" I ask, on my feet, hands on my hips. The unsaid part of that sentence is: *without me?* I, too, would like to jump off the back of this couch into Miles's waiting arms.

"Practicing dancing," Ainsley says.

"Why are you folding their laundry?" Miles asks. "Reese doesn't ask you to do that, does she?"

"No, I just needed something to do. To occupy my brain." I playfully glare at him.

He nods and then backs away from me.

"Hey!" I say, and step toward him.

He reaches down and picks up Ainsley by the armpits, holding her in between us. "Protect me," he tells her.

She cranes around to look at him. "From what? Lenny?"

"Yeah. She's frustrated with me."

She turns and looks at me. "What'd he do?"

Made me want to kiss him.

"Nothing. I'm being a butthead."

"Oh, okay, then. I'll protect you, Miles." She, still in his grip, lifts two little boxer fists. "Don't make me do this, Lenny."

Miles and I burst out laughing and Ainsley looks mighty pleased with herself. Miles sets her back on her feet. "It's cold out today," he tells her, and she scampers to go get her coat and boots.

And then the two of us are standing alone, the dregs of laughter subsiding, with almost nowhere to look.

I kick my socked foot at the carpet. "Where have you been? I haven't seen you these last few days. I know nothing is settled but . . . You don't have to *avoid* me, okay?"

There's a long pause and then, "Okay."

And that's all I get.

"What's going on, guys?" Reese asks, leaning against the living room entry and eyeing the two of us. I have no idea how long she's been standing there.

"I'm rea-dy!" Ainsley sing-shouts from the front hall, once again saving the day.

"Be back in an hour or so," Miles says with a lightning-quick wave, and disappears.

Reese comes in and picks up the now-discarded sheet. "You really *don't* have to fold laundry," she says. "I'd never ask you to do that. No matter what Miles thinks."

"I don't mind," I say. "And he was just . . . being Miles."

She eyes me and then tosses the sheet down. "All right. Come clean. What's happening between you two?"

"Me?" I point at myself. "And him?" I point at the direction he's gone.

She laughs at my clearly over-the-top acting but then sobers. "I hope . . . It's not my business, like at all, but I don't want Ainsley to . . ."

"Get caught in the middle of a whirlwind love affair between her babysitter and her uncle?"

Reese raises her eyebrows. "Your words, not mine."

I start pairing socks.

"First of all, there's no love affair to speak of," I say. "And second of all, most importantly, we *both* really care about Ainsley and her well-being."

Reese purses her lips and folds a top sheet.

"Reese."

She finally looks up at me.

"Miles is never going to do something to intentionally hurt her. She's one half of the entire reason he's even in New York City." *And you're the other half,* I don't say. But her eyes darken. She understands, even if she wishes she didn't.

IT'S THE GROUP chat that breaks the stalemate.

I'd forgotten the tentative plans we'd put in place, but Rica hasn't.

Rica: *Still on for tonight, everybody?*

I text immediately: *I'm in. How's 8?*

Jericho texts next: *Perfect.*

Jeffy is next: *K.*

Rica: *Don't sound so excited Jeffy.*

And then Miles swoops in and makes everything wonderful: *What about we meet at the disco bar.*

There's a very long pause where I think all of us are processing the fact that Miles has suggested we go to a disco bar.

But then Jericho chimes in: *You mean Sacha's?*

Yeah.

Jericho again, *What do you know about Sacha's???*

Miles sends a shrugging emoji. *It's not too far of a hike from Queens for Rica and Jeffy.*

Jeffy up next: *I hate Sacha's but Miles suggested it so I'm in.*

Rica: *Literally can't wait to see Miles disco.*

I didn't think this through, Miles texts.

Too late! Jericho says. *Attn: everyone. The dress code tonight is no pockets.*

What? Miles texts. *Dress code? No pockets??* I can taste the panic. *What am I supposed to wear for pants? And where do I put my wallet?*

After the plans are set, and Miles has insisted to me over text that he can handle his own outfit, I hit a thrift store. I'm torn between two lovers. One of them is a sweater dress so red and soft that you could bake it in a pie. The other is a metallic purple jumpsuit that's skintight everywhere except the cowl-neck collar. It's horrific and uncomfortable. Of course I choose that one. We're going to a disco bar, after all.

Miles texts that he's late due to dress code requirements, and we all wait outside the bar for him.

"I'm surprised you didn't come together!" Jericho says to me.

I shrug. Exactly how much do I tell them? "I'm pretty sure I'm falling in love with him, but he says we need to slow things down so now we're giving each other space or something?" Apparently, I just err on the side of telling them everything.

I turn to see all three of them gaping at me. I laugh at their identical expressions.

"This . . ." Jeffy says dimly. "All happened since we saw you on Saturday?"

I shake my head at myself. "Oh, God. I guess so?"

Rica's viciously frowning. "He said you need to slow things down . . . Like he's not ready for commitment?"

"Oh. No." I realize now what that sounded like. "I think he thinks *I* need more time."

This is apparently just as confusing to them as it is to me. But at that second the man of the hour comes jogging around the corner, his breath puffing into frigid clouds and his cheeks pink with cold. He screeches to a stop in front of the group.

All of us give him an epic up-and-down. He's in blue sneakers, pale green pleated suit pants (no pockets, of course), and a white long-sleeve waffle tee.

"Where's your coat?" Jeffy demands.

"You said no pockets! All my coats have pockets!" And then he digests the fact that all of us are wearing coats with pockets. "Wait, what the fuck!"

We burst out laughing and Rica and Jericho both promptly unzip their coats and envelop him inside a coatful hug.

"Sorry," Jericho says sincerely. "I should have clarified that weather-necessary clothing is an exemption."

"Wow, you really didn't want to get disqualified on a technicality," Jeffy muses.

"Let's go inside before Miles gets pneumonia," Rica suggests.

Miles and Jericho go first, followed by Jeffy, but Rica tugs at my hand and we fall back. "Tell me exactly what happened between you two. Leave no stone unturned."

Miles is glancing back at me and I'm glancing at him, but I tell her the whole story out of the corner of my mouth. By the end of it she looks like she gets what I clearly don't.

She pats my shoulder. "You got yourself a good one, Lenny. Don't worry about it too much. Enjoy the ride."

I open my mouth to further inquire, but she narrows her eyes and I find myself at the receiving end of a perfectly gorgeous nail with a gemstone glued on. "That's an order," she says.

I'm really good at taking orders, turns out. "Enjoy the ride," I repeat with a shrug. "Okay."

We sweep inside and it's got the lights, the mirrors, a long curving bar with upholstered barstools, and—I squint—

a motorcycle suspended from the ceiling of the dance floor, neon-style flames spewing from the exhaust pipe.

Jeffy secures a high-top table for us and we divest ourselves of our coats (except for Miles). Jeffy's in sweats (no pockets, of course), and this earns him a frown from Jericho. Rica's in what can only be described as an Oscars dress the color of Ariel's tail, and this earns her a thumbs-up from Jericho. I pull off my coat and get a "You've got to be kidding me!" He strips off his coat and, oh, boy, we're both in purple jumpsuits. He laughs and we hug and Rica takes a bunch of photos of us.

Miles leaves and comes back with a tray of prescribed drinks and then quickly agrees to pilot the table while we test-drive the dance floor.

I've barely spoken to him tonight but I can feel his eyes all over me and by all over me, I mean that I think he might like the jumpsuit.

I saw Jericho's confident dance moves at the concert, so they don't surprise me. He melts toward the middle of the dance floor. Jeffy's dance moves consist of jumping up and down and a halfway committed air guitar. Rica, however, takes one step onto the dance floor and is immediately confronted by a man with two long French braids down his back and a Yankees cap on. "You," he says, taking off the cap and holding it over his heart. "You are the one I've been waiting for."

She's gaping at him, clearly never having met him before, but then she does a long, lazy appraisal and shrugs. "Sure," she says. "Why not?"

She holds out one hand and he twirls her away.

"Aaaand," Jeffy says, "that's the last we'll see of Jericho or Rica tonight."

"Really?" I ask, accidentally bumping him.

"Oh, yeah." He offers his hand as a slower song comes on and I immediately take it. "She and Jericho tend to get swept away by suitors pretty early on."

"Got it. And you?" I ask, clasping my hands around his neck and feeling very charmed by his extremely light touch against my waist as we step to one side and back, one side and back.

"Oh, I've learned to make friends with bartenders."

We chuckle. "You can always call me when you're lonely," I promise. "I keep odd hours. I'll swoop in and save you from drinking beer by yourself."

He cocks his head and smiles, a real smile. I feel, for a moment, almost overwhelmed with luck. Then he glances to the side and does a double take. "Should we go sit with Miles?"

I glance over as well and burst out laughing at the expression on Miles's face as he watches Jeffy and me dance.

We make our way over to him and take a stool on either side of him. "Why were you laughing at me?" he asks.

"Your glower," I say, still laughing. "You look like Satan's hot little brother."

He immediately frowns. "I can never tell if you're flirting with me or heckling me."

"*I* can tell," Jeffy says, and leans in and clinks Miles's beer glass on the table. "And on that note, I'm going to go see what the bartender's favorite Marvel movie is."

He's gone before I can insist he stay behind, and Miles and I sit and watch the dance floor. "So."

He turns to me. "Hm?"

I take a hand and gesture to my boobs, point at my ass, sweep up and down my entire visage. "So, eat your heart out."

He stifles a grin, shakes his head, and casts his gaze back to the dance floor, taking a sip of beer. "Lenny, I'm eating my heart out even when you're in your Morty's Car Wash T-shirt."

I nearly inhale half my drink up nose and he gives me a few helpful thwacks.

"Miles, for the love of God, can we go into that hallway over there and make out?"

He gives me a disapproving frown. "By the bathrooms? Gross."

"Fine! Then take me home and do me!"

Now he's the one inhaling his drink through his nose and I'm the one thwacking him. Gotta say, much more fun to be the thwacker.

His Satan glower is back. "You want me to take you home and do you."

"Sure!"

He leans back, crosses his arms over his chest, and eyes me. And I mean, this is a thorough appraisal. "Nah. My way is better."

"We haven't even tried my way!" I poke his shoulder. "My way you get to put your hand inside this jumpsuit."

A few hairline cracks seem to spiderweb their way up his resolve. His eyes drop from my face down to my body before they skitter away back to the dance floor.

I'm encouraged by this reaction. I pull my hair out of my ponytail and flip the whole mess of it over to one side, looking up at him through a pout. "Miles," I purr, drawing a circle over the back of one of his hands. "Have I waited long enough?"

He groan-laughs and scrubs his hands over his face. "You're torturing me."

"Well, that makes two of us!" I drop the sexpot act and sit up straight. "You're the one who's obsessed with waiting!"

He crosses his arms again and watches me. "You know,

you acclimated to this change a lot quicker than I thought you would."

"What change? Oh, from friends to lov-ahs?"

He icks at my use of that word but carries on. "It would be . . . a big change."

I consider this solemnly. "Well, obviously I freaked out upstate when I realized how I felt."

"But that was more about Lou than about . . . you and me, right?"

"Right. And in terms of you and me . . . maybe it *isn't* such a big change."

"What do you mean?"

"I mean . . . I can't say how long I've been feeling exactly like *this*. But I've been wanting to crawl inside your sweatshirts for a while now." I shift a little bit closer to him and play with the pushed-up fabric at the bend of his elbow. "And you've been feeding me and washing my hair and herding me around town."

His eyes are on my hand, and when I brush my fingers down to his exposed forearm, the muscle goes tense. He takes a big swallow of beer and forces himself to look at anything that isn't me touching him.

I tug-tug at his shirt and he looks back at me. "My mom asked me if you treat me well, Miles. You know what I said to her?"

"What's that?" he says in a low, husky voice.

"I said that you walked into hell and dragged me back out."

Something crosses his face, I'm not sure what, and he turns away from me, covering the bottom half of his expression with his free hand. "Lenny."

"Why should I be scared of kissing you, Miles? I'd just be getting even closer to the safest place in the whole world."

He slams his eyes closed for a moment and when they come open, he's burning with determination. "I'm gonna go."

"What? Why?"

He laughs, exasperated. "I'm not obsessed with *waiting*, Len. I'm obsessed with . . . Look, I really want to get this right. It's important. There are signs that'll tell me that you're . . . But if we rush . . . So . . . when the timing is right . . . it won't just be because you're looking hot as fuck in . . . that thing." He gestures to my jumpsuit. "It's not about that for me. You're not an itch. You're . . . You're . . ."

Perhaps the most important thing in his life.

He doesn't say the words but they rise up between us, and some of my confusion about his reticence vapors away.

"Dance with Jeffy," he says instead of finishing his thought. "Text me when you wanna go home? I'll call you a cab so I know you're safe." He's standing up, really readying himself to leave. I twirl on the stool and grab him by the shoulders. But he won't be stopped. "Have *fun*, okay?" He says it like he really means it, takes my hands off his shoulders and, for a moment, just holds them. He gives them a quick squeeze and then drops them.

He waves goodbye to Jeffy at the bar and is gone.

What happened? Jeffy mouths to me with big, illustrative movements. I shrug and shake my head. Hell if I know.

BREAKING: A MAN *can* resist the bend and snap.

I know this because I performed one in front of Miles and he only expressed mild concern that I'd just slipped a disc.

Now that I know he eats his heart out when I'm in an oversized tee and torn jeans, I'm curious about stretching the bounds of my power. He claims our connection is not contingent on sex appeal. But I'm interested in speeding this myth-ical "timing" along a bit.

He's not avoiding me nearly as much as before, but neither is he accepting my advances. Of which there are many.

I eat a peanut butter and jelly sandwich with porno-graphic enthusiasm. He rolls his eyes and checks his email.

I spread my legs à la *Basic Instinct,* but I'm wearing granny panties and cargo pants besides and all it accomplishes is Miles telling me to get my feet off his kitchen table.

I pretend to fall asleep on his couch and he pokes me and tells me to hit the road.

A week of this bullshit and I'm about ready to give up the whole endeavor.

"He can't be seduced!" I shout into the phone.

"I don't think other daughters say this kind of thing to their mothers," my mom placidly replies.

"Well, you asked!"

She did, indeed, ask how things were going with Miles when she called and I answered.

"I'm thrilled you answered the phone, Lenny, but I don't think I'm going to be much help here. I'm not an expert."

"You've been with Dad for thirty years."

"Exactly. Which means I haven't tried to get something started with someone in thirty years. But how hard could it really be? He's obviously gaga for you."

"Are you sure? Like, really sure?"

"No one comes to Sunday dinner and lets a man force-feed him grappa unless he's hoping that man will be his father-in-law someday."

"I see you've conveniently excluded the duck from the list of things Miles was force-fed."

"See? He clearly loves you. The duck just proves my point."

Mom signs off with me because she's standing out in front of her pottery class and she doesn't want to be late. I continue my long walk through Central Park, stopping only to stand with a big group of birders and pretending to see what they see when one lady repeatedly points it out to me.

I keep on going, winding my way through the twisting paths. It strikes me that I feel at home here. As a lifelong Brooklynite, I've settled into the Upper West Side over the last few months. It's disorienting to not be lost up here.

It strikes me that all the hardest stuff in my life—spiraling out from grief, abandonment of my former loved ones, retreat from my entire life—that somewhere along the line the hardest stuff might have become . . . the easiest thing to do.

And now the hardest stuff in my life is no longer the plummet into despair. Now it's trying to pull myself up out of it.

I've unintentionally started speedwalking, and by the time I make it back to the studio apartment I'm breathing hard and have broken out in a sweat. I'd like to change clothes, but I don't really have any clean ones so I take this energy and I haul everything to the laundromat and back. I put all my clean and folded clothes away. But now that the dirty clothes are clean, all the other clutter is bothering me.

I straighten everything up, wipe down all the counters, take out the trash and recycling, and dig Miles's tiny little dust buster out of the tiny little closet. When everything is neat as a pin, I call it a good job and go take a shower. The sun's gone down in the meantime so I deem pajamas necessary.

Finally I'm a heap on the bed and watching shadows on the ceiling. My mom's thrilled voice when I answered the phone today washes over me.

Bang-bang-BANG. I jolt out of a dream and scramble to my feet. The room is layered with shadows and soft with sleep. Someone is banging on my door at the witching hour and I suddenly have . . . a Converse in my hands? Where did that come from? Terrible weapon.

"Lenny?"

Oh. "Miles?"

I *ca-klunk* open the door, rubbing at my eyes and tossing the shoe aside.

"What's going on?" I ask, sleep still tugging at all my edges, making everything, including him, wobble.

He's stepping inside, glancing around. "Oh. Were you sleeping?"

"I was having a dream that I invented a new recipe with figs and cheddar and it was so good they brought me on *Live with Regis and Kathie Lee* to talk about it."

I close the door behind him and go back to collapse on the bed. "What's going on?" I ask again through a yawn, fluffing my pillow. "Is everything all right?"

"Yeah," he says, still standing by the door, taking in everything.

"Well," I prompt him. "Why are you banging on my door in the middle of the night?"

He blinks at me. "It's nine-forty-five."

"Oh."

"And you weren't answering my calls or texts so I got worried. But . . . you were just sleeping." He blinks. "At a normal hour. In pajamas."

I shrug and snuggle against the pillow. "I was sleepy."

There's nowhere for him to sit in the tiny apartment, so he toes off his shoes and comes to sit at the foot of the bed. "Still are, from the looks of it."

"Mm-hmm." My eyes pop open. "But you interrupted my REM so I'll probably never be able to sleep now. Thanks a lot."

He crinkles his nose. "Sorry."

"You assumed I'd be wandering the streets, looking for traffic violators to accost?"

"Or hungry in Queens with nowhere to go and nothing to eat."

"Or drunkenly dancing with strangers whilst wearing my entire life in a backpack."

"Hey," he says, looking around the apartment with a frown on his face. "It's clean in here."

"Yeah," I agree with a cracking yawn.

He slides off the bed to the floor and comes to sit by my head. We're eye-level this way. "Why?"

"Why did I clean?"

He nods. I didn't bother to turn on any lights, so he's richly shadowed and inscrutable. His cinnamon eyes have gone coffee.

"I was aggravated by the mess. And amped up from all the *waiting*," I say with a scowl.

He briefly smiles, his eyes all over my face. I'm taking long blinks and snuggling further into the pillow.

"And then," I continue, "I got tired from all the cleaning so I went to bed. You know, you're extremely interested in the details of what is turning out to be a very boring story."

To my surprise, and contrary to all the arms-length-ing he's been doing recently, he actually comes *closer* to me.

He puts his head on the bed next to my pillow, stacking his hands under his chin. "*Live with Regis and Kathie Lee,* huh?"

I laugh. "That's how you know you've hit the big time."

"I once had a dream that I got to meet the queen of England but when I got to the front of the line, I handed her a burrito instead. And then I took it back and ate it."

I'm laughing more. "That actually explains a lot about you."

We're inches away from each other's smiles and I'm just happy to be here. He reaches down and untwists the blankets, pulling them up over my shoulder. When he's done tucking me in, his hand gets heavy and just rests against me.

"When did you get this?" he asks. His hand leaves my shoulder and migrates upward, his thumb gently tracing my eyebrow piercing. It makes my stomach swoop, this casual exploration, this confident line-crossing, like he knows he's welcome on the other side.

"A couple years ago," I say on a whisper, because if I talk at a normal volume, he'll hear the tremble. "No big story there. I just thought my face was too boring without it."

He gives me a laughing frown. "Boring? Come on."

I shrug, affecting nonchalance, even though he's still tracing my eyebrow and my heart is racing so hard I can no longer feel my fingertips. "Too ordinary, then."

He gets a knowing look. "You're fishing for compliments."

"Well." I dislodge one finger from under the pillow and poke at his shoulder. "Oblige me."

"Not boring," he says, and traces that thumb down my nose. He gets to my lips and hesitates. His eyes meet mine. "Not ordinary." His thumb sweeps across my lower lip.

And just like that, "not ordinary" becomes perhaps the highest compliment of my life. How sad. I should probably have higher expectations, but how could I when he's looking at me like *that*. As if he's made of honey and he'd like to give it all to me.

"Yes, yes." I rush to make a joke so he can't see my aching heart. "Moderately attractive. That's me."

His nostrils flare with a silent laugh. "Whatever you say."

"Mediocre at best, but you can't win 'em all."

He raises an eyebrow.

"Not *hot* as much as tepid, but then again, some people like that."

He rolls his eyes.

"Let's just call me passably adequate—mmmf."

He pinches my lips closed. "Lenny, when I look at your face, I feel like I'm finally home after a really long day at work."

I immediately turn my face into my pillow and attempt to withstand rapture. Because making someone feel like they're home is so much better than being told I'm pretty. I come up for air. "I hear that ages well."

"Hm." He's laid his head down on his arm now, so it's almost like we're lying in this bed together.

"You'll age well too, I think." I reach forward and trace the line between his eyebrows. His crow's feet. His eyes fall closed and I skim the fringe of his lashes.

"I should go," he murmurs, not seeming like he actually wants to leave at all.

My eyes are drifting closed, the world blurs, and when I blink them open Miles is looking at me. When I blink them open again a few minutes later he's not looking at me. He's got his little Nancy Drew notebook out and he's making a line in it.

"What's that?" I ask.

He jolts. "Thought you were sleeping."

"What were you writing?" I reach for it but he flips it closed and quickly slides it into his back pocket.

"Not important."

But actually, now that I think about it, he wasn't writing in the notebook. He was making a motion I've become very familiar with over the last few months.

"You were crossing something out, weren't you!" I scramble up to a sit.

"Oh, great. Now you'll never sleep."

He's trying to get away, but I lunge forward and catch him by the shirt. "Miles, you called it a grand plan . . . but is it actually that you have your own list? You weren't kidding when you mentioned the ocean? Mountains? The cannonball? Do you actually have a list of things that might need to happen before you think I'm ready to be with you? Do you have a Kiss Lenny list?"

He's squeezing his eyes shut.

"You said there were things that wouldn't count if you told me what they are. Things I have to do for myself." He's opened his eyes and I'm searching them. "Was me cleaning the apartment, or getting my stuff in order, one of the things?"

He sighs and turns to get his shoes on. "I think you might be pathologically incapable of patience."

"I'm right!" I crow.

"Lists happen to be a really useful way to keep your thoughts organized," he says grumpily.

"Now I just have to guess what else is on the list."

"You think you're besting me, but that would actually make me extremely happy."

"Mark my words, we're gonna be making out within a week."

He's laughing and rolling his eyes. "G'night, Len."

He pushes out the door and I'm alone with all my thoughts and for the very first time since Lou died, that's not a bad thing at all.

Chapter Thirty

"Hi, wow, what's happening?" Miles says as he opens his door, his eyes big when he sees that I pretty much can't see over top of these grocery bags I've filled with supplies from the grocery store.

"Hi. Go about your business. Just here to cross an obvious one off your list."

He's frowning at me. "Obvious?"

"Food. You're obsessed with feeding me. I'm going to prove I know how to feed myself. And feed you for once." I push past him and kick my shoes off. And then I get the literal shock of a literal lifetime.

There is a man sitting on Miles's couch.

I nearly drop the groceries on the floor. "Miles," I say stiltedly. "You. Have. A friend."

Both he and the man start laughing.

"Hello." The man stands up and attempts to shake my hand around the grocery bags. He ends up just taking one of the bags from me. "I'm Ethan."

He's got copper hair and a wolfish smile. Handsome like a brand-new shined-up pickup truck. I'm immediately skydiving into love. Ethan and I will become a singer-songwriter husband-and-wife duo, we'll—Miles lifts the other grocery bag away from my hands and then proceeds to put his own hands *inside* my coat. I nearly swallow my tongue. Yes, he's technically just helping me take my coat off, but did he have to touch my entire rib cage like that? By the time he's slid it carefully down my arms and assertively straightened my fuzzy sweater that's just gone askew, this guy Ethan is basically just man-shaped fog, and everything in my life is fuzzy except for Miles. Based on the semi-smug look on his face, I think that might have been his intention.

"This is Lenny. Ethan is a friend from back home. A few years younger than I am."

"Oh! Are you visiting the city?"

He shakes his head. "Actually I live in Brooklyn. We haven't gotten to see each other much since Miles moved here, though. I've got an eighteen-month-old and I run a bar, so things are pretty jam-packed for me."

He pulls his phone out of his pocket and shows me his lock screen. He's cheek to chubby cheek with a grinning red-headed baby. I can't tell which one of them is happier.

"Wow," I say, grinning myself. "Your kid is happiness in human form."

"Miriam." He supplies her name. "She really is." His smile turns thoughtful and affectionate. "Unless you have to get her into rain boots. Then she's rage in human form."

We all laugh, but then I suddenly feel bad. "I didn't mean to crash. I'll let you two catch up."

"Well, wait a second. What were you gonna make?" Miles asks. He's back from dropping one of my grocery bags on the kitchen counter and now he's divesting Ethan of the other one.

"Oh. Well, I thought I'd make guac."

Ethan glances between us. "I'd eat some guac."

"Oh! Great. Okay!"

"Do you want some help?" Miles asks.

"No, no! That defeats the point of me making you food. You sit. Visit. I'll be done soon."

I go to the kitchen and quickly unload my perishables to bring home later. Then I set about washing and dicing and mixing.

Miles and Ethan are looking at some photos on Ethan's phone, and there's such affection in Ethan's voice that I think for sure they're still talking about Miriam, but then Miles says something about the brickwork and I realize they must be talking about Ethan's bar.

I mostly tune them out, but every time I hear Miles's rich laughter, my stomach flips. Ethan's phone rings with a video call and I have to stop everything and watch as his entire demeanor turns into banana pudding. "Hi, sweetie!"

I hear a *Dada!* And then a long string of gurgle-babble that, shockingly, Ethan is able to answer cogently. "It's in your bedroom, sweetie. That's where we keep it."

He disappears into Miles's bedroom to take the rest of the phone call. I grab a chip and am just about to test the guac when there's heat and pressure and Miles sliding up behind me. He bends down and rests his chin on my shoulder.

"You came over to make guac for me," he rumbles in a low tone.

"Mm-hmm." I can barely talk because he's voluntarily pressing his body up against mine.

"You got hungry and went out and bought groceries and then came over to cook."

"It's not *cooking*. It's a snack."

"I want a bite." He opens his mouth, chin still resting on my shoulder.

So I dip the chip and reach back to put it in his mouth. "Mmm," he groans, chewing in my ear, and I hate that I think that's cute.

"Is it good?"

"It's the best guac I've ever had," he says. And then

he simultaneously slides one arm over my belly, resting his palm on my opposite hip, and lifts the other hand to the cabinet overhead. He grabs a salt shaker and adds some to the guac.

I can't believe he's got an arm wrapped firmly around my middle but also I'm laughing at this smooth operator. "The best guac you ever had needed salt?" I ask dryly.

"It's the best I ever had because you made it for me." Then he reaches over to the half-juiced lime and squeezes more into the bowl.

"Well, so much for wowing you with my culinary skills."

"I'm so wowed." He mixes and then dips a chip for me.

I crunch on it thoughtfully. "It'll do."

He dips another chip and this is getting absurd but I guess this one's for me too. But before I can claim it, Ethan's head pops out from behind Miles. "Save some for me."

We both laugh and Miles hands him the chip. I expect him to step out of my space and back into friend distance, but to my surprise, he just curls us back from the chip bowl, to clear space for Ethan, and continues to stand *directly* behind me. He's not hugging me anymore, though. His big hand is now resting on the counter next to my hip.

As the two of them talk, I study Miles's hand. Strong, very still, dry skin at the knuckles and other signs of being a lifelong craftsman. There's a bit of chip dust on his pointer finger so I brush it off. He moves in another quarter inch behind me and I feel dozy with the sheer heat of him. I get the impression that if I leaned into that hand even a millimeter, he'd place it on my hip, skate it over my belly, pull me back into him, and keep on talking to Ethan like nothing was happening at all.

"Well, the designer wants to paint it black," Ethan says about something (to which I've barely listened).

"Jesus, no. Bad idea," Miles says (and now he has my full attention).

"Why?" Ethan asks.

"I mean, aesthetically, painting brick . . ." Miles says.

"Is a *choice,*" Ethan confirms. "But that's why I hired a designer. So that I don't have to make choices on my own."

"Okay, fine. But painting fireplaces is usually a bad idea. Most paint is flammable at certain temperatures. So if you ever wanted to use the fireplace for its intended purpose, then you've basically put a trail of kindling out into your living room."

"Oh." Ethan looks stymied. "Well . . . yeah. Okay, then it is a bad idea."

"I can help you choose the right paint, if you're in love with the aesthetic. But if you're not . . ."

"Yeah, whatever. I'm not. I just want my place to be nice for Mimi."

"Is that your nickname for Miriam?" I ask, lips sucked into my mouth as I try to gird my loins for such cuteness.

He laughs and shakes his head at himself. "Yeah. I just bought my place and I really want to make it a home. Mimi's mom's place is so nice and . . . I just want my place to compare, you know? Does that sound petty? I don't mean to be petty."

It doesn't sound petty at all. A father who's hired an interior designer so that his daughter will feel just as comfortable at his house as she does at her mom's? Swoon. I tip my head back and make aggressive eye contact with Miles. "You *must* help this man paint his fireplace."

Miles smiles. "Apparently I have marching orders," he says to Ethan.

"Thanks," Ethan says to me.

"Do you have any pictures of it?" Miles asks, and they are back to chatting and planning and looking at Ethan's phone.

Apparently they already had plans to head out to dinner at some place Ethan knows in Harlem, and even though both of them insist I'm invited, I'm not *that* much of a party crasher.

They do walk me home, though, each of them carrying one of my bags of groceries. And then I head upstairs and start a viciously determined Google search. I'm delighted with my findings.

I wait until I'm certain there's no way I'll be interrupting Miles's friend-date and I snuggle into the twin bed, cup of tea clutched in one hand and phone clutched in the other.

Are you good at bricklaying? I text Miles.

What kind of question is that? His reply is almost immediate.

Ah, you've gone with evasion, I see. So you're bad at bricklaying, huh?

I'm good at it, Lenny.

How good?

What are you actually asking me?

I send him a link to the Google page for bricklayers in NYC. There are, seriously, not very many.

This skill is hot, I inform him.

Hot in what way?

You could be a hot fucking commodity, Miles Honey.

There's silence, so, of course, I fill it.

You could wear a tool belt and go impress sad, rich women. Charge exorbitant prices. Custom design brickwork for their renovations. You'll be the hottest shit on the Upper West Side.

What brought this on?

You seemed really happy and interested and knowledgeable when you were talking to Ethan today. I think you need a job.

I have a job.

You need a job that ISN'T chasing me around the city with oven mitts on.

I like to take care of you.

I go hot and cold, melty and shivery; how does one just carry on texting after a comment like that? I get too impatient and call him. When he answers, he doesn't even bother with a hi.

"The truth is, I've considered it before."

"Well, what's stopping you?" I demand.

"It's not exactly a nine-to-five. There's the job itself and then there's everything that comes with starting your own business. I'd basically be MIA for a couple years while I tried to get everything off the ground."

I understand right away, because, I'm proud to note, I'm starting to understand Miles's heart. "You're worried you wouldn't be there for Reese and Ainsley." I pause, and because I'm not dense or currently fishing for compliments, I add one more person to the list. "And me, I assume."

He hums in agreement but then sighs. "It's not just about being there in case they needed me . . . It's about being there at all. I mean, things are going pretty well with Ainsley right now, mostly thanks to you. But still, the main thing I've got going for me is that I'm just reliably always around. I'm Old Trusty, remember? I can't be Old Trusty if I'm out of the house fourteen hours a day."

I pause, momentarily thwarted by this line of logic. But then, "I call bullshit."

"Okay?" he says on a laugh.

"Miles, the main thing you've got going for you is that you're *you*. I mean, sure, a lot of being Old Trusty is being there. But that doesn't mean just being there aimlessly. It means being there when it really matters. And people do that in lots of ways other than sitting around in one anoth-er's houses."

"Okay . . ." He seems partially convinced.

"You are doggedly devoted and there's nothing you wouldn't do for your people. That's super clear. But you need a job for *you*. Part of taking care of the people you love is tak-ing care of yourself, right?"

As soon as I say it, the lightbulb goes off.

The Live Again list. The Kiss Lenny list. Very different at first glance. But they have something in common. At their core.

Both of these lists are about me taking care of myself again.

I finally understand what Miles is waiting for. Because, sure, who would want to date me if I can't even take care of myself. But mostly, why would *I* want to date anyone if I can't even take care of myself.

He's been my lifeboat for months. And that comes with a very specific job description. I wonder if he's reluctant to change his position in my life until he's sure I can float on my own.

Determination pops open like a can of Coke. I'm fizzing and energized. Because once upon a time, I was the person who scrubbed my apartment down once a week. When Lou was going through chemo, I did her laundry and mine, shopped and cooked. I used to take long, winding walks around my neighborhood and call my mom when I got sad. I used to wear mascara and go to dentist appointments.

Miles might be my lifeboat, but he doesn't have to be my lifelong Coast Guard. And I'm going to prove it to him.

AND SO . . . I officially stop trying to seduce Miles. And I stop trying to guess at what's on the Kiss Lenny list.

Here are some places I redirect that energy:

I ask Reese if we can put a contract in place, outlining my hours, wage, and vacation time. She is so thrilled she collapses down and rests her forehead on her hands and I finally understand how uncomfortable our arrangement has been making her. All she wants for Ainsley is constancy and she's been taking a huge risk on me, hoping I'll continue to show up to work.

I call Rica and beg her to force me to go to a yoga class with her. To my complete and utter horror, not only is it a hot yoga class but she's signed me up for ten straight weeks. I leave the class looking like a thirty-year-old Barbie that someone left in a hot car, but I'm determined to persevere.

To my utter delight, Jeffy actually takes me up on my offer to call me when he's lonely. I'm working, but no problem. I put Ainsley on the train and meet Jeffy at Dad's Books and Wisdom, where she, Jeffy, and Dad have a very long conversation about the Isley Brothers. Jeffy gives her a recommendation of a series of novels from the nineties about a scuba-diving detective who solves mysteries in shipwrecks. She leaves with a stack of used copies courtesy of Dad.

I spare Miles the hangover and bring Jericho to my parents' house for Sunday dinner instead. He brings a selection of baked goods from his bakery that are so gorgeous it literally brings a tear to my mother's eye. When my dad breaks out the grappa, Jericho turns his cup upside down and crosses his arms in an X over his chest. Mom laughs in genuine delight. "See?" she says. "*He* doesn't want to marry you."

I stuff some of the extra cookies in my purse and an hour later I'm about to walk into Miles's building when he comes jogging out, zipping up his coat.

"Hi!" I step so close to him I have to tip my head back to

see his face. "Are you heading out? I was just coming to see you."

His face brightens. "I was gonna drop by your place, actually. I wanted to see how dinner went with Jericho."

"I think he fared better than you did."

His face falls. "Well, he's charming."

I quickly course-correct. "My mom said to tell you that she wants you to come next week."

He perks up. "Okay." There's not much space but he steps a little closer. "I missed you."

"I missed you too."

I've been racing around town trying to figure out how to feed and water myself, and it hasn't left a lot of time for pestering Miles.

"I've been trying this thing where I take care of myself. And I'm actually doing a pretty good job."

I give in to what every single molecule of my being is screaming for me to do. I press my face against his chest, my arms banding around his rib cage. He doesn't even pause before he matches my hold. This is the kind of hug that would keep our front halves dry in a rainstorm.

At this very second I'm elated and warm and I don't care if we're supposed to be waiting or I'm supposed to be wowing him with my self-sufficiency. He bends a little and rests his cheek on the top of my head.

"And how's that been going?"

I tip back and catch him by surprise, his head still bent down. If I went up on my tiptoes, I could take a bite out of his smile. "Nothing's gone disastrously wrong. Actually, everything went right. And every day I still end up sad," I say with a little shrug. "Go figure."

"You are blocking foot traffic," Emil says from the doorway of the building.

Miles and I loosen our grip to glance around the basically deserted block. "What foot traffic?" I ask. "That lady down on the corner? I think she'll be able to manage."

"Move along," he says, shooing us inside, a little smile on his face.

Miles and I board the elevator and the very second the doors close, I resume our hug. "Hey, I'm hungry," I tell him. "Will you feed me these cookies from my purse while I tell you about my day?"

I can physically feel his smile. "Of course."

Chapter Thirty-One

*E*mil is holding two palms up for Ainsley to shadowbox against. "One. Two. One. Two," he says in complete deadpan.

She stops boxing and puts her hands on her hips. "You gotta pump me up, I said!"

"I believe that is job for Lenny," Emil says, and honestly, I might have agreed with him if I hadn't also failed at the task.

We've got half an hour until we're due at her school for the big dance, and we already stomped around the living room, fist-pumping and kicking couch pillows into the wall while we listened to the entirety of *Jock Jams*. I expected Miles to complain, but, shockingly, he had his eyes closed on the couch mouthing the words to "Whoomp! (There It Is)."

When that wasn't enough for Ainsley, she dragged us all down to the lobby. "Don't you know any soccer chants or something you could do?" she demands of Emil.

These nerves seem out of proportion to me for a school dance, but Reese has been gone for two and a half days already and I want to keep Ainsley's mind off it.

"Come on, tiger," I tell her, pulling her away from Emil. "We don't want to be late."

It's funny to be heading to a dance with the birds still chirping, but this is elementary school, so the shindig starts at five.

When Ainsley sees her school down the block, she removes her hand from mine and pushes her hair back from her eyes. Her chin comes up, her shoulders go back, and she starts strutting. She takes off her purple glasses and from her pocket, materializes my cheetah-print heart-shaped sunglasses that Miles gave me.

"Where'd you get those?" I ask in shock.

"You left them on the counter a couple weeks ago," she says. "And tonight they're *mine*."

I can't argue because she's channeling rock star and it's a good look for her. Apparently she's going to sit with her class, so we wave goodbye in the lobby on the way in to the talent show that's going to happen before the dance.

Miles and I take our seats in the auditorium and I have a fun time watching him try to figure out what to do with his legs in child-sized seating. The lights dim and the theater teacher comes out to introduce the talent show.

Then the real fun begins.

We watch two successive kids rock from foot to foot while self-consciously lip-syncing the same Taylor Swift song. One girl does eight cartwheels in a row (pretty neat, if you ask me). Another kid bounces a tennis ball on a racket 468 times before the theater teacher comes back out and basically shepherd-hooks him off stage. That's when I notice that one of Miles's knees is doing a darn fine impression of a jackrabbit. And is he . . . is he biting his fingernails?

"Hey." I poke him in the side and lean in to whisper, "What's wrong?"

He immediately stills his knee and takes his fingernail out of his mouth. "Nothing."

Apparently he's riveted by the girl who's guessing which card the principal is holding. I shrug and scan the audience for Ainsley, but I don't spot her. Then that fingernail goes back into that mouth and his knee is really making a break for it.

"Are you really that nervous about the father/daughter dance?" I lean in and ask him.

He doesn't even glance at me. His elbows hit his knees and he slowly rubs his palms together. I'm reminded of NBA players right before they play in the championship game.

"Miles."

He ignores me.

"*Miles.*" I tug his shirt until he's forced to look at me. "No one is even going to pay attention to you! You just have to sway back and forth while she stands on your sneakers. No big."

His expression instantly becomes so *Can it, Lenny* that I recoil and hold up two hands.

A few more acts pass and then Miles stands all at once. "Excuse me," he whispers to the person next to him.

I grab his arm. "Where are you going?"

"I'll be back."

I watch him go, wondering if I should chase after him. If he has to go publicly vomit over an eventual slow dance with his niece, then he hates dancing more than I even imagined. Maybe he grew up in some sort of *Footloose* situation where dancing was punishable by eternal burning in hell.

But then the theater teacher is back out and really jazz-handing that mic. "And now!" they say. "It's time for a new tradition here at Attain Academy. It's the family portion of the talent show. Where some of our ambitious students have worked with a family member to put together an act."

All the hairs on my arms rise up in unison.

"Please put your hands together for our inaugural family act, Ainsley Hollis and her uncle Miles!"

I always thought *Knock me over with a feather* was just a saying, but right now a light wind would literally face-plant me.

I've got two hands over everything but my eyes as the lights on the stage come up and Ainsley and Miles are dramatically lit. They've got their backs to us and they are *both* wearing matching black pants and ruffled gray shirts. Which doesn't make sense to me until music starts playing.

"Oh, my God."

The opening strain of Robyn's "Dancing on My Own" is blaring from the auditorium's speakers and Miles and Ainsley are wearing versions of what she wore in the music video.

"Oh, my *God.*" I can't say anything else. I'm frozen in a rictus of ecstasy, burning every last second of this into my brain.

They turn in unison and hit the choreo *hard.* Hands are tick-tocking like a clock. There are hips. There are shoulder bounces. There are—and I can't stress this enough—body rolls.

Ainsley is an utter rock star. Maybe she inherited some stage swag from her pop-pop or maybe it's all her, but she is rocking it. Clearly singing her heart out even though we can't hear her over the track.

Miles, on the other hand, God bless him, has not lost himself to the moment. He's concentrating with all his heart. His careful, technically correct movements speak to exactly how much practice he's put into this.

I've had this song stuck in my head a thousand times recently. I realize now it's because *they've* had this song stuck in *their* heads.

He must have practiced every day. For Ains.

"What am I seeing?" someone asks beside me as she plunks into Miles's vacated seat.

I do a double take. "Reese!"

"I came home early," she says dimly, one finger vaguely pointed in the direction of the stage. "Did you . . ."

"I did not."

They're really bringing it home now. Ainsley is half his size, her blond hair gelled into a Robyn coif, and her outfit really does suit her. Miles's outfit makes him look like he's doing a pretty bad *Interview with a Vampire* cosplay.

My feelings for him double-triple-quadruple and it is honestly painful to confine it all to my chest. I would very much like to lay him out like a linebacker. To kiss him into oblivion. Propose marriage, et cetera.

I finally register the fact that the audience is really responding to this performance. People are hooting and shouting, clapping along. A small contingent near the front are standing and dancing.

"This is not a very appropriate song for an elementary school," the lady next to me mutters to her companion.

Finally, the song ends, the stage lights go black, and Ainsley and Miles get a very pleased round of applause.

"How the hell did she get him to do that?" Reese asks, looking fully shell-shocked.

It must be willful that she doesn't already know this about him. "Reese, he wanted to."

She blinks at me, processing this.

"If you push him," I explain patiently, holding my hands out as an example. "Then he pushes back. But if you take him by the hand, he follows you anywhere." She's still blinking at me. "He'd do *anything* for you and Ains."

Reese sits back and chews on this. The talent show continues on and Miles doesn't return. The second it's over, Reese and I bolt to the lobby.

All the talent show participants stream out of a set of

double doors, the kids racing into the arms of their grown-ups and the few adult participants looking equal parts cha-grined and proud. Regrettably, Miles and Ainsley have changed back into their street clothes. What a shame. I'd give a pinky toe for a photo of Miles in that shirt.

Ainsley, thinking her mom was coming home tomorrow, sees Reese and all-out sprints across the hall, launching into her arms. And yeah, that's just what the doctor ordered.

I ready myself to jump into Miles's arms. To tell him, in no uncertain terms, exactly how I feel about him. To ascend with him.

I am exploding with euphoria and . . . I watch as he regis-ters Reese in surprise. He slides his hands into his pockets and eyes her for her reaction to the big show.

Oh. Right.

This moment is absolutely not about me and my feelings at all.

I step back into the crowd as Miles crosses the hall to Reese's side. She says something to him and he laughs self-consciously, raising a hand to the back of his head and clearly groaning.

He straightens and cranes around, scanning the crowd. He catches my eye and I give him a strong-power thumbs-up. One step toward me but then Ainsley, from her perch in Reese's arms, reaches out to Miles and he's suddenly got a koala bear for a niece. I get a perfect frame of Miles smiling with his whole heart, his eyes closed as he hugs her, saying something to her and then setting her down on the ground.

Reese is grinning now too. The three of them. Happy and family and finally, at least for a moment, on the same page.

I sneak out onto the street and then Miles's call starts buzzing in my pocket.

"Where'd you go?" he asks.

"Take them out to dinner!" I shout gleefully into the phone. "Seriously . . . Reese . . . stick a fork in her, she's done."

"Come with us!" he insists.

"Miles, you can do this. It's what you do best. You think you need me there, but you really don't. You made this moment with Ainsley all on your own. Feed them, listen to them, laugh when they make jokes, carry Ainsley home when she gets too tired to walk."

He's quiet for a moment. "Are you heading home?"

"Call me later," I say by way of answer, because I'm not sure if I'm headed home or not. "When you're done with your family."

He's quiet again but this time I think I sense a pulse of joy coming off him. His *family*. "Okay. I will."

THE TALENT SHOW ended early, so it's only six P.M. I decide to take myself on a date. There's a Thai food place in the East Village I used to love, so I take a chance and head there.

I'm on the train, sandwiched between strangers, hands over my face and awash in unadulterated joy. As long as I live, I'll never forget the look on his face as he diligently executed a body roll on stage. In a ruffled shirt.

This man doesn't even two-step and yet . . .

He did that for Ainsley. To show up for her. To be her uncle.

I think of him yanking me out of that dance party this summer. How nervous he was, how uncomfortable he was to be asking for my help, to offer his. And then he demanded I wake him up in the night if I needed him. He schlepped himself to Cody's wedding and endured the awkwardness. He forced himself to learn an entire choreo just to make his niece feel supported. Does this man ever take the easy way out? No. Not ever.

The only way out is through.

Miles survived his own hell and learned that lesson. It's the hard way or bust for him. There's no discomfort he won't push through to just keep on living and living well.

I glance up to check which stop the train is pulling into, and I get an idea. I'm one stop ahead of the Thai restaurant, but I dash off the train anyhow, coming aboveground among cocktail bars with outdoor seating and gargantuan heaters.

I run a block and skid to a stop in front of the giant window with stick-figure people painted in a big pile on the glass.

I laugh because it's still here, because it hasn't changed at all, because it's open at six-thirty P.M.

The only other time I've ever been here, I was twenty. Lou and I chose this spot out of all the other hair salons in the city solely because of its name. I step forward and trace the lettering with my finger, the pile of stick figure people tumbling out into cursive. Spaghetti Head, it reads. Perfectly ridiculous. Perfectly wonderful.

I duck into the small shop. There's no one there at first, but a woman sticks her head out of the back at the sound of the bell.

"Sorry, but I was just about to—" She steps out fully from the back and puts her hands on her hips. "Hey. I've cut your hair before, haven't I?"

Her shop hasn't changed, but she sure has. The last time I saw her she had straight blue mermaid hair. Today she's got a curly brown shag and enormous hoop earrings.

"Good memory," I say. "A long time ago. My friend and I came in to shave our heads together."

Her eyes narrow in thought, and then widen in recognition. "That's right. She had gorgeous hair. Red."

"Yes," I say with a nod. "She did."

"Cancer, right?"

I nod again. "We came in when she started losing her hair from chemo."

She walks toward me thoughtfully and purposefully. She gently picks up a hank of my hair and studies the ends. "You haven't cut your hair in . . ."

I clear my throat. "About five years. When her cancer came back, she shaved her head again. But she asked me to keep mine. To let it grow."

Her eyes track up to mine. "And now you're here to cut it off."

"I can't just let it keep growing forever," I say quietly.

She gives me a laborious sigh, meant to make me laugh, and bustles me toward one of the chairs. "I hope you tip well, I'm skipping dinner for you."

"You got it."

The bell dings, and a man ducks into the shop.

"No," the hairdresser says simply. "I'm busy."

He cowers back out to the street.

If I wanted a gentle touch for this, I've come to the wrong place. But who wants gentle? Hard way or bust, Lenny. *The only way out is through.*

She puts the poncho thingy on me and magically any modicum of attractiveness I've ever possessed is immediately gone. I suddenly look like a rodent that's just gotten over the flu.

She's studying my hair again. "Your ends are egregious but actually the rest is very healthy. How short are we going?"

I shrug. "I don't care."

She sucks her teeth at me. "*I don't care* is how I end up with lousy Google reviews."

"No, seriously, I'd love a bad haircut. Any haircut. I need to take the plunge."

She considers this with an unimpressed look. "I don't give

bad haircuts. But if you're not worried about going too short, then do you want to donate it?"

"My hair?" I haven't considered this before.

"You've got more than enough for a donation to Locks of Love. They use the donations to make wigs for kids with cancer. I can cut it off as a ponytail and send it in."

My stomach jumps. "Yes! Let's do that."

"Okay. Then, how about chin length? Just long enough to pull it back into a stubby ponytail if you want? That length will suit your bone structure and it'll look cute under a winter hat."

"Perfect."

She ties my hair up and pulls out a pair of shears. I lean forward all of a sudden, out of her reach, and grab my ponytail, running my hands over it. Feeling the weight of it, the smooth parts in the middle, the familiar roughness of the ends. It's just hair. But it was with me through everything. The chemo, the hospital, the hospice, the funeral, those lost and wandering months before Miles found me.

I pat the hair at the top of my head, all my new hair. The pat turns into a pet and I'm telling myself *Good job, Lenny. You're doing so well.*

I sit back up, tears in my eyes, and nod at the hairdresser through the mirror.

"Are you *sure* you wanna do this, love?"

"Absolutely not!" I chirp resolutely. "I'll probably be a total wreck. Let's do it."

She holds up the shears and gives them a snip-snip in the air. "Yeah?"

I point one finger to the sky. "Onward."

HE CALLS ME later because of course he does.

Instead of saying hello, he says, "Current location."

The wind almost carries his voice away, out to sea. I tighten my hood under my chin. "Staten Island Ferry."

"Really?" There was something light in his tone but it immediately tightens down. "I'll be right there."

"Miles."

"Yeah?"

"Everything is okay! I'm okay!"

"What? I can't hear over the wind! I'm on my way!"

Forty minutes later, the ferry I'm riding lands in Manhattan and a sweaty, panting Miles collapses against the railing beside me. The gorgeous, glittering, underworld version of Manhattan sparkles up from the black water. Wind takes the hood off Miles's head.

"Hi."

"Hey . . ." He squints at me. "You look okay."

"I told you I was okay!"

"Yeah . . . but you *actually* look okay."

I laugh and shake my head at this conversation. "I really am. Hey."

"Yeah?"

He's leaning elbows on the railing the same way that I am, so when the ferry kicks forward, away from the dock, I use the momentum to lift one of his arms and slide into his negative space. We're nested together, both looking out toward the water now. "You learned an entire choreo for Ainsley."

He hums a low, vaguely proud, vaguely humiliated noise. "Yeah."

"And Reese saw it."

"Yeah."

"Miles, this is huge!"

"Yeah."

I tip my head to the side to see him. "Hey. Be excited."

"Okay."

I shake my head at him and we both laugh. His hands slide over each other on the railing, enclosing me, and I'm in the safest place on earth. His stubbly chin grazes my cheek. "I *am* excited," he says low as we watch Ellis Island slide past. He gives me a squeeze. "When we got back to the apartment Reese asked me to take the trash out."

My eyebrows fly upward. "She asked you for help?"

"Yup." He gives one happy nod.

"Wow."

"Wow," he agrees.

A tanker, dinosaurian and dimly lit, cuts a path toward the ocean and we watch it in silence.

"Hey, Lenny?"

"Hm?"

"Why are you on the Staten Island Ferry if you're okay?"

I consider this. How much of my personality is grief and how much is me?

I am who I am because of Lou, but am I also who I am because Lou died?

Is it possible that I'm here *both* because I'm grieving *and* experiencing a near-perfect happiness?

"You know, I never mentioned this, but when it was time to move Lou to hospice, we picked a facility out on Staten Island."

"Oh," he says, surprised.

"I stayed there with her as much as I could, but sometimes I'd go home and shower and sleep and what not. So . . . now whenever I'm on the ferry, I guess part of me feels like I'm headed toward her."

His arms tighten even more. "I didn't know that."

"Hey . . . you wanna see something cool?"

"Yes." No hesitation.

I turn in the circle of his arms and pull my hood back.

The wind kicks up and tosses my chin-length hairdo into the sky as far as it'll go. I'm laughing, messy, framed by monumental change.

Miles grips the railing and leans back to see me better. He is in *shock*.

"Len!" he gasps. And then he unhands the railing to press me into it, put two hands on my face, and just look. "*Lenny*."

My name is the only thing he can call this moment.

"I donated it," I say, happily sobbing because life is so fucking hard and sometimes, every once in a while, you get a win.

His eyes are as glossy and dark as the water underneath the ferry. I'm reflected back to myself as Miles sees me, wonderfully human, trying my absolute hardest, dubious haircut and an honest attempt at living.

"*You look so cute*," he says, and his face scrunches down in the kind of pain that feels good. He drops his forehead to my shoulder for a long moment. When he surfaces, his lips land on my cheeks, my nose, my forehead and chin. "I always thought I'd kiss you and your long hair would be everywhere," he says, and my heart soars. "I guess I waited too long."

"Not too long," I say. "The right amount."

"I guess this means I'll have to stick around for a really long time to live out that fantasy, huh? How many years until you can grow it out again?"

"Only five years," I scowl, and he throws his head back and *laughs*, not because this is funny, but because he's overflowing with the kind of elation that comes with someone you love doing something so, so right.

"Well, there's no way only five years will be enough time for us," he decides.

I've got him by the strings of his hoodie. I tug him gently toward me. "Not a chance."

He lands in a hug against me. His hands find their way to my hair and don't stop touching the ends. It's a blunt cut. It's never been more clear where I end and the world begins. For the first time in a very long time I don't feel in danger of fading away.

"Miles," I say, and he pulls up from our hug, bent so that our noses are just an inch apart. "I'm here to stay."

His eyes warm; I feel a current from his heart and it vibrates all the way out to where his fingertips meet my jawbone. "I've always known that," he says.

I go tiptoes and he leans down. Our lips meet and it's that lightning storm all over again. I can feel this kiss down to my toes in white-hot streaks that form the general shape of my nervous system. His mouth is smooth and stubble-rough, and the nonsense of a kiss—why do people put their lips together when they're in love?—has never made more sense. Because him. Because this moment. Because Miles would turn his life inside out just to make me okay. And if he gets to be the man who kisses me, well, what wouldn't he do? And I'll never have to know the answer to that.

He bands an arm around my back and the boat lurches and we tip our heads with the inertia. I gasp his warmth. Welcome him into my softest places. Our tongues touch and oh my God *he's shy*, but not for long. His fingers have found their way clear down to my scalp as he holds me in place, because he knows me, and he knows that he has to pin me down to accept what's good for me.

I've got arms around his neck, only big toes on the ground as I strain upward; he's bracing us against the railing, tasting me, pulling back to show me his eyes and then leaning forward for further tasting.

The boat rises, slams down on a wave, and we get dappled with bright-dark water. It feels like rice tossed at a wedding.

It feels like the world's blessing. He holds me even tighter. Our tongues slide and I wish I had the strength to pull back from him, just long enough to tell him exactly how I feel.

The boat rises again and this time, when it lands on a wave, we get a proper dousing. It's a wet slap of water across our faces and jackets.

We don't stop kissing but we do start laughing. He softens the kiss and it becomes an offering; he walks backward, taking me with him by the mouth, and the third smack of water lands in the spot we've just vacated.

"Hell of a night!" a man shouts beside us.

We roll our faces cheek to cheek, thereby ending our first kiss, and bringing this man into view. He's wearing a wool bowler and a clear poncho.

We say nothing and he doesn't seem to realize he's interrupted one of the most important moments of my life.

"Didn't expect the storm!" He gestures out, distantly, beyond, to a nest of glowing clouds, lit by lightning.

I take Miles by the hoodie strings again, bringing his attention back to me and only me. "Every time I fall in love with you there's lightning."

He closes his eyes, opens them and there's his brilliant love. "There's only you, Lenny. Every time . . . it's just you," he says, muffled as he kisses me. "And you." He kisses me again. "And you."

I cry, of course. I laugh, of course. I hold him desperately close, of course.

We take the ferry all the way there. And then all the way back.

Chapter Thirty-Two

We come aboveground in our neighborhood uptown. It's chilly and we're still a little damp with the Hudson.

"So!" I clap my hands together. "What do we do now?"

"I honestly have no idea."

I'm utterly baffled by this. "What? You always know what to do."

"Are you hungry?"

I shake my head. "No. I ate Thai food after I got my haircut."

I was definitely right about this feeding-myself thing being a part of the Kissing Lenny list because, right there on the sidewalk, he slides his arms around me and kisses me deeply.

Hot tongue and strong arms and I'm breathless when we pull back and people are eyeing us as they walk past.

"You're very easy to make happy, you know," I tell him.

"Yes," he agrees. "I am."

"Let's go." I grab his sleeve and start in the direction of the studio apartment. He breaks the hold just to grab for my hand, lacing our fingers and creating a world of warmth between our palms.

I lift those hands and study them as we walk. We hold hands now. It's wild to me how someone who makes me feel more safe than anyone else in the world can also make me so unbelievably nervous.

We get to my stoop and he hesitates. I don't take this for an answer, tugging him inside and up the stairs. He isn't saying anything, so I don't say anything either. I kick off my shoes and grab pajamas from the drawers, disappearing into the bathroom.

My short-haired reflection shocks me in the mirror. The hairstylist cut off so much hair, so much weight, that my roots are physically sore. Which feels apt. It should ache when you change this much.

I brush and change into the pajamas and when I re-emerge, Miles is sitting on the foot of the bed. He took his shoes off but not his coat.

I don't like this at all.

I yawn hugely, theatrically, rubbing one hand into my eyes. "I'm so beat."

"Oh, yeah?"

"Yeah." I plop down next to him on the bed. "I just want to curl up in bed and get a solid eight hours, you know?"

He gets a sly, understanding smile. "You're playing me."

"Hey, you get flirty when I'm responsible. I can't be blamed if I use this to my advantage."

His eyes drop to my thermal pajamas, his smile soft. "You want me to stay and get flirty?"

"Yes."

He stands and shoulders out of his coat, hanging it over the top of mine. He walks to the dresser and opens the bottom drawer where he's still got some clothes, digging out some sweatpants and a T-shirt.

"Dang," I say. "I thought you'd have no choice but to go full monty."

He laughs and disappears into the bathroom. A few minutes later he comes out looking full boyfriend. His hairline is wet from where he washed his face. I find this so cute I can barely hold in my excited scream.

I'm already under the covers and he joins me, lifting the blanket and sliding in. His body forces mine up against the wall. I'd be shocked if he had more than a centimeter of clearance on his other side.

"Ugh," he groans happily. "We should have gone to my house. Where the beds are the size of two people."

"You have a bed at your house?" I'm very skeptical.

He laughs. "What do you think I sleep on?"

"Well, I've never seen your bedroom."

He quirks his face in disbelief. "You're kidding."

"You always keep your door closed! And contrary to pop- ular belief I do understand *some* social boundaries. Okay, let me guess. Waterbed? Black silk sheets? Strobe light and techno music for when you're feeling amorous?"

"It's crazy how well you know me."

"Oh, I know! There's no bed at all. Just a bearskin rug. You sleep in the nude and snack on beef jerky."

He laughs and shakes his head at me. "Hey, while we're on the subject of scenarios your brain creates . . ." He rolls up on one side and props his head on his hand. "When we first met, what was your love-at-first-sight fantasy about me?"

His hand comes to rest on my rib cage. I follow his lead and trace a hand over his body. It's meant as a power move, to seduce and tantalize him, but I find myself immediately drawn in by his heat, the firm pushback of his muscles, the hardened tracks of his bones. His hand starts to wander me, gliding down from my ribs, over my ass, down my thigh until he finds the back of my knee. He effortlessly, easily, lifts my leg so that it rests on top of his.

I gasp a little, my eyes finding his. His eyebrows lift, like *Go on with what you were saying.*

I try to remember what we were even talking about. "Oh, the fantasy? Well, remember that the whole thing took place in, like, the very first second I saw you. Right when Reese opened the door for you and you were arguing with her. So I got this kind of intense version of you right off the bat."

"And . . ."

"Well, the fantasy was that you were kind of hardcore. Punk rock or something? And we were sort of fuck buddies but you were cheating on me a ton and treating me bad. So one day I got super fed up with you and broke it off and then you finally realized that you were in love with me and came crawling back, totally devoted to me. And then I guess we got married or something?"

He's bodily aghast. "What? Are you serious?"

I shrug.

"What kind of fantasy is that? It sounds more like a cautionary tale."

"They're not predictions! They don't mean anything. Who even knows why I do it."

His face makes a face.

"What?" I prod. "Oh, you think *you* know why I do it?"

"I think . . . you are indomitable."

"Thanks. But why would that have anything to do with compulsive romantic fantasies?"

"I think that even in all your worst moments of grief, you've wished for companionship. I think you're always, secretly, hoping for happy endings, even when they don't seem possible. You say *compulsive* but I think they're actually kind of just . . . tenacious. Like daisies popping up out of the snow. Grief has been sort of, I don't know, it sounds sappy, but like *winter* for you. And I think that the part of you that can't help but manufacture happiness, because that's who you are, it's been sending up these little flowers to pop up and keep you company."

I'm gaping at him. There are no words. I knew he paid attention to me, but this is like . . . *knowing* me.

Luckily he saves me from having to respond to this by serving me a light insult. "But this whole time I kind of thought that you generally got a good read on people right away with these fantasies. But come to find out you're just *so* wrong."

"I know," I say with a sigh, collapsing down onto my back and looking up at him. In this position, he's the wall between me and the world and it's so lovely I could cry. "I'm pretty much wrong about everything. Honestly, it's one of my favorite parts of life. It turns everything into a surprise."

He smiles and tucks me against him. "You surprised me too."

"Because your first impression of me was so bad?"

"No. Well, yeah. But I meant that you surprised me because . . . I feel corny saying it, but . . . I've never felt like this before."

"Oh, come on. You've been in love before."

"That's not quite what I mean. Yes, I've been in love before. And it was real and I'm grateful for it and I wouldn't change it. But with you, Len, when I met you . . . I sort of feel like I met *myself*." I tip my face up but he's watching the ceiling. "Not that I didn't know myself before . . . it's more like, after my mom and Anders died I was just so injured that I couldn't do anything but survive. It got better little by little, but I was still the guy with the tragic backstory. Everyone was always very *careful*. And then I moved here and met you. And you . . . let me help you. I got to remember what it feels like to *give*. And you're not in the least bit careful with me. Which . . . yeah. Feels good. You helped me remember how to feel strong. Healthy. Needed. I didn't know I could feel like that anymore."

There is nothing he could have said that could have possibly made me feel better about myself. "Thank you," I whisper, holding him so tight. "I'm so, so grateful that we met each other."

He holds me tight. "Yeah. It really worked out well."

We laugh and even as I'm wondering how we're ever gonna last a whole night crammed on this minuscule bed, I'm starting to drift. My pajamas tangle with his pajamas and his breaths get long and everything is so warm and fuzzy. I dip easily down into the kind of lazy, loopy sleep that I used to beg the universe for not three months ago. I cannot believe how much has changed.

"NO! IT'S MORE like *yah!*" Ainsley does a karate kick so high that even Emil looks impressed.

He turns to me. "Get her lessons. She should train."

"What about me?"

Emil has been showing Ainsley and me how to dribble a soccer ball on the sidewalk in front the building. That devolved into a how-high-can-you-kick contest, at which Ainsley has just bested us both.

"No. You are hopeless," he says. It's not even an insult. To him it's just fact.

"She's not hopeless!" Ainsley insists, looping her warm hand around mine and staring indignantly at Emil.

"I mean at karate."

"Oh." Ainsley nods matter-of-factly. "Yeah, she's hopeless at that."

"Couple of karate experts we've got here."

"Hey, let's give him the . . ." Ainsley says, waggling her eyebrows meaningfully.

"Oh! Right."

Ainsley and I engaged in a little something we dubbed "the victory lap" today. We wanted to celebrate her absolutely stellar stage debut, so we went in a big circle around her neighborhood and ate all the good food and drank all the good drinks and bought all the good books and even watched a (pretty good) movie. Now we're home and we have extra muffins from Jericho's bakery.

I hand her one of the bags and she proudly holds it out to Emil. "Do you like lemon muffins?"

He's got a yuck face on.

She waits expectantly, her face a bright, hopeful moon. He can't withstand her charm.

"Oh, did you say lemon muffins? Yes, I eat those." He takes the bag. "Thank you."

"We got one for Mom, too. We're celebrating!"

"Your birthday?" he asks.

"No. The performance! Lenny, show him the video!"

In what was simultaneously the worst moment of Miles's life and the best moment of mine, Ainsley's theater teacher sent out a link this morning to the recording of the entire talent show. Ainsley and I have shown the clip of her dance performance to three separate shop owners (and Jericho twice) already this afternoon.

I queue it up and hand my phone to Emil. He is completely straight-faced through the entire performance. He hands the phone back to me and then immediately walks inside without saying anything.

Ainsley and I shrug at each other and follow him inside. He's just coming back around from the desk with a pen and paper in his hand.

"I want an autograph," he says. "You'll be famous."

She's lit up with effervescent joy as she kneels on the ground and painstakingly writes out:

This is my first autograph—Ainsley Hollis.

She changes the O in her last name to a star and I swear, Emil is right, because that is some serious gonna-be-famous mojo.

He takes the paper from her and carefully pins it to the bulletin board behind the desk.

We head up and tumble into the apartment, chatting, and skid to a halt in Reese's kitchen.

"Mom!" Ainsley launches herself into her mother's lap.

Reese was supposed to be working until late tonight to make up for cutting out early on the conference yesterday. But there she sits at the kitchen table with Miles. We've clearly just interrupted an important moment; they're both serious. But not tense. Actually, Miles looks downright relaxed.

"Hi," I say to him, and it takes every modicum of strength I have not to draw a little heart on the ground with my big toe.

"Hi."

"Oh, my *God*. Get out of here, you two," Reese says playfully. "Spare me."

Miles stands up and stretches. "Shall we?"

"Oh." I glance between them. "I thought I was supposed to be staying until bedtime?" It's only four o'clock right now.

"Go, go," Reese says. "I'm taking off work. I thought Ainsley and I might do something fun."

Ainsley jolts up in Reese's lap and puts a hand on either shoulder. "What is it?" she asks too loudly, three inches from Reese's face.

"Harper invited us to her cabin for the weekend."

"Oh." Ainsley deflates a little.

"And her cabin just happens to be next to an indoor water park."

"Oh!" *And she's back!* "We're going right now? Should I go pack?"

"I already packed for you."

"You can eat the muffin in the car!"

Reese is laughing and hugging Ainsley; she looks lighter and happier than I've ever seen her. "What muffin?"

I hand over the muffin and wave as Miles tugs me out of the kitchen and all the way up to his apartment.

"Was everything all right with you and Reese?" I ask as we toe off our shoes. "It seemed serious."

"Yeah." He heads to the kitchen and comes back to join me on the couch; he's got two little bowls of mixed nuts.

"What'd you talk about?"

"A lot. Let's see . . . well, for starters she's thinking she might take a leave of absence at work."

"Really? Whoa."

"Yeah. She mentioned that she'd definitely keep you on, though."

I wave a hand through the air. "I love working for them, but I can always find another family to work with. That's the nature of nannying work. They need you until they don't."

"Mary Poppins. OG commitment-phobe."

I smile. "Reese was just feeling overworked?"

"No. I think she actually really enjoys the pace of her work. But it gives Ains the short end of the stick. When she saw the dance last night"—he valiantly makes an effort not to bodily wince at the memory—"I think it made her sad. Not because I was the one dancing with Ainsley. But because *she* wasn't. So her plan is to use up the vacation she's accrued and see how it feels. If she wants more time, she might take the leave of absence."

"Wow. That would really change their lives."

He nods. "Hey," he observes, peering into our almost empty bowls. "We both left the almonds till last."

"Uch, I hate almonds," I say, dutifully eating one so it doesn't go to waste.

"You're kidding." He eats a small handful. "I love them." He watches me retch my way through another. "If you hate them so much, then why do you save them for last?"

"You gotta eat the best ones first, obviously!"

"No, Len. You gotta save the best for *last!*" He brings our empty bowls back to the kitchen.

"We're doomed," I say on a sigh, leaning over the back of the couch and watching him wash his hands. "Our worldviews are way too divergent. We should probably just break up now and get it over with."

"Totally," he agrees. "If we ever get a divorce, instead of irreconcilable differences, we'll just cite almonds."

I'm outraged. "Don't say 'divorce' to me!"

He's grinning. "It's not *Beetlejuice*, Lenny. You can say the word without bringing it upon yourself."

He's on his way back over, so I tug him down and install him back on the couch.

"Miles." I put my hands over my face. "I really don't know anything about relationships. What if I'm so bad at it and everything gets screwed up and we have no choice but to . . . break up! I get sick just thinking about it! That can never happen!"

His hands slide up my arms and to my wrists, he gently pulls my hands away from my face and kisses one palm and then the other. "Lenny." His voice is coal-black and there's steel in his eyes. I start to melt. When he's like this, all I have to do is listen to him. "No breakups."

I nod obediently. He sits up all at once, scooping me into

his lap. We're nose to nose. He puts one finger under my chin and takes an indulgent sip from my lips. "No," he says, and I get a kiss. "Divorces." I get another kiss.

I'm liquid in his arms and all I have to do is open wide for his kiss. When he pulls back this time I sigh. "How'd you possibly make divorce so sexy?"

He chuckles and it makes me bounce lightly against his lap. "I was going for romantic."

"Well, then, you majorly failed," I say, tipping my head to one side when he starts to kiss his way down my neck.

"Should I try again?"

"Definitely."

He's kissing at the hinge of my jaw and I can't help but wiggle against him. Thank God for his jeans because that's good friction right there. "You don't have to worry about marriage. I'm going to go slow, Lenny. And I'll take a good, long time getting you ready." I'm gasping and grasping his T-shirt when he starts to lay me back on the couch. "And when it's time, you won't be scared anymore. You're just going to want it so badly."

"Is this . . ." I gasp. "Matrimonial dirty talk?"

He chuckles darkly, nuzzling my sternum through my T-shirt. "Is it working?"

"Depends. Are you trying to get me to marry you or fuck you?"

"Sure," he says with a shrug and I laugh, just generally thrilled.

He leans up and returns to my mouth. He's teasing me, preventing the kiss from deepening. He slides one big hand just under my shirt, thumb on my bare hip. He's mostly got me pinned, but even so, my legs reflexively push open and I taste his smile. He likes that.

He takes himself on a little tour. His fingers press over my ribs and lodge, a quarter inch, under the elastic of my bra. "Hey . . . what do you like?" His head is cocked to one side and he's studying my whole face.

"Sex," I say, attempting to lever up and keep kissing.

He laughs. "Okay, great."

He's pulling the collar of my T-shirt from one side to the other, kissing as low as he can while his hand works its way higher. He opens his mouth over my chest, slipping the fabric, leaving wet heat in his wake, stroking any skin he can find.

I've got hands in his short hair, clenched in his T-shirt, grabbing his arms, his shoulders, everything I can reach. His mouth is on mine again and he does the impossible: he undoes the button on my jeans without breaking the kiss.

And then he waits. "Thoughts?"

I kick my legs, scrambling to get my pants down and out of the way. He chuckles, leans to one side to make room, and then *thwump!* We overbalance and topple off the couch. He's on his back and I'm slapped over top of him, my pants around my knees.

We burst into laughter. "Where's this alleged bed?" I demand, hauling myself up to my knees.

"Yeah. Good idea." We help each other stand and he leads the way toward one of the mysterious doors I've never been through before. I rip my pants and socks off on the way, toss my shirt on the ground.

He opens the door of the bedroom and steps aside to let me through first.

There's an enormous framed photo of the full moon over a big wooden bed frame. I wonder vaguely if he got it before or after I made him get a howling wolf tattooed on his back. He's got a gray-blue bedspread, an off-white knitted blanket tossed over the foot of the bed. The walls are a darker gray-blue and there's a dark leather armchair under the window. A brass lamp leans over the chair, a stack of books on the floor underneath. His black hoodie hangs out of a semi-open dresser drawer and I'd like to hug it for being the only thing I recognize.

He comes up behind me and kisses my shoulder, my neck. His hands land on my belly and he pulls me back against him. He's taken his shirt off apparently because all I can feel is skin-heat and chest hair. I make an involuntary noise and push back against him. Reaching back, I get two thumbs into the waistband of his jeans and underwear. I push down but don't get very far.

He pulls his hips away, undoes his jeans, and this time when I push, his clothes fall down. I feel something very interesting and very domineering pressing into my lower back and when I turn, into my belly.

His hands trace from my back to my ass and when I jump up he catches me. My legs go around his waist and he walks backward to the armchair in the corner, sitting down with me on his lap.

We're separated only by my underwear and holy smokes this is *Miles* who I'm naked with and more than that, this is someone who I *love* that I'm naked with. I turn my head away from our kiss and he goes automatically to my neck.

I'm about to have sex for the first time in two years. No, wait. I'm about to *make love* for the first time in my *life*. A hysterical bubble of laughter rises in my throat and I swallow it down.

What is this room? Seriously? I feel like I'm in a stranger's house. Like I'm one-night-standing Miles, which makes this even weirder.

All at once, I scramble off his lap and turn away, taking deep breaths and trying not to completely freak out.

"You okay?"

Slowly, I turn back to him. He's legs spread, elbows on the arms of the chair, one temple resting on his fist and staring at me.

My eyes finally drop to his crotch and I come face to face with the very interesting, very domineering part of him, but unfortunately for everyone involved the hysteria wins, and I explode into laughter.

He shakes his head and raises his eyes to God.

"Oh no," I say on a gasp for air. "I'm completely ruining this."

His chin drops. "Well, yeah. Raucous laughter isn't what you hope for when you show someone your dick for the first time."

"Your dick is wonderful! I love your dick. Miles, how are you so calm over there? We're *naked*."

His temple goes back to his fist. "*We* are not naked."

I glance down at my bra and panties. "Oh. Right. Sorry." I quickly and gracelessly strip out of my bra and hop on one foot to get out of my undies, kicking everything to the side.

And then I'm completely naked in front of Miles.

I put my hands out to the sides in a T. "Ta-da?"

Now he's the one laughing.

"How do we make this less weird?" I ask, shaking my hands out and starting to pace.

"For starters you could come over here."

"Not yet. I think we need to get super horned up first. I wish this were a porn, then the sex would just happen like bam!" An idea strikes and I freeze halfway through one lap of his bedroom. "Should I pretend you're my stepbrother? They do that in porn."

"Oh, my God."

"Or I could be your high school teacher?"

Heavy sigh.

"Ooh! I know, I'll just get on all fours and you can do me from the back. Then we wouldn't even have to look at each other."

"If you don't even want to look at me, then I don't think we should be sleeping together."

I pace past him with a scowl. "Hey! I love looking at you. Looking at you is one of my favorite things to do in the world."

"Well, that's a relief."

"Is this how you pictured this going?"

"Well, I definitely didn't anticipate a naked soliloquy but—" He pauses and considers. "I probably should have. Yeah, that's on me. Hey, Lenny. Come sit on my lap. Right now."

As soon as he's offered an instruction, I immediately comply. I walk over and flop onto his lap. That was easy.

I'm treated to a warm, firm hug, complete with wiry chest and leg hair. I try to stiffen up and say more stuff, but his arms tighten and my forehead is pressed into his neck.

His hands are on a lot of places. He gives my back a vigorous rub. Not the kind you halfheartedly do to suggest some boning, the really good kind. When he's finished with that he lifts one of my hands and laces our fingers. I hide my thumb between our palms and he kisses my haircut.

"Here's an idea," he says.

"What's that?"

"Let's not have sex." He lifts me off his lap and plunks me onto the floor. He's already back into his underwear and tossing mine to me before I can catch up.

"Hey! No! Terrible idea!" I'm chasing him back out to the living room.

He waves a hand toward me. "It was too much at once.

The bedroom reveal. My dick. You need a slow rollout, I think."

He drops onto the couch and turns to see that I've put my underwear back on but not my bra. This is met with obvious approval but no comment.

He reaches for the remote. "Let's watch TV and try again later."

He thinks he's the boss of me? No. I'm the boss of him. And I'm going to take charge and do the sex!

He must read it in my eyes because he raises an eyebrow when he sees me coming and then defensively rolls onto his stomach. He pillows his hands under his cheek, stretched out completely.

"Hey." I put my hands on my hips and loom over him. "I'm wearing nothing but underwear and a frown and this couch is getting more action than I am."

"Look, *Speed* is on."

I begrudgingly give up the sex fight and condescend to lie atop Miles the way he's lying atop the couch. I'm fully stretched out along his body, boobs pressed to his back and my toes tucked between his calves.

At first I think he's unaffected and impervious, but then I realize that I can hear his heartbeat where my ear is against his back and every time I wiggle it starts to beat like wild.

I prop up a little and start to fiddle with his hair. His ears are big and cute and I can't help but lean down and kiss his earlobe. He clears his throat. I walk my fingers from shoulder to bicep, poking at each muscle as I go. He resituates himself under me and I think I might be creating a problem for him down there. Yay.

I'm certain that any moment now he's going to flip over and ravage me but after I return from an adventure with the inside of his elbow I realize his eyes are closed.

"Hey," I say.

He grunts.

"No sleeping."

His lips kick up into a smile. "I'm not sleeping."

"You always say that when I catch you sleeping."

"I'm never sleeping when I close my eyes like this with you."

"Then what are you doing?"

He pauses and I think he might not answer. But then he says, "I'm committing the moment to memory."

I freeze and melt at the same time. There's a quick flipbook of moments that skim past. Miles with his eyes closed on this very couch, on the tattoo table, beside the swimming hole, on the floor at his mother's house. Never sleeping, just savoring. Committing it all to memory. Committing *me* to memory.

I still haven't replied and his eyes come open. He tries to lift his head to better see me but I stop him with an open mouth at his neck. I kiss his throat slowly, letting heat bloom against his skin, tasting him.

I make it to his shoulder and test his rounded muscle with my teeth. He grunts and when I check, his eyes are closed again. Now that I know he's burning me into his brain, I couldn't love it more. I scoot up and kiss one of his closed eyes and he pounces. Landing his mouth on mine.

It's gotta be a bad angle for him so I slide off his back and land my knees on the floor, next to the couch, kissing him with all I'm worth. He's draping an arm over me, leaning off the couch to get closer to me, and I'm drawing him backward, down to the floor. He comes willingly, immediately. I lie out on my back and he crawls over top of me. One glance down shows me that his pal is poking out of the top band of his underwear, desperate to get to me.

Desperate is a wonderful thing.

I touch his hips, his stomach, lock my legs around his back, and to my utter delight, I note that his hands have turned into fists on either side of my head.

I take one of those fists and put it on my chest and it immediately transforms into a warm, open palm, an attentive thumb. He tests and presses and has to stop everything to watch his own hand touch me.

"Bed, take two," I request on a gasp.

He looks up, takes a long pull at my mouth, and then shakes his head. "Not tonight."

"What?"

"Remember the panicking like ten minutes ago? Let's go slow."

I'm not sure what his definition of slow is, considering he's kissing his way down my throat and sucking my nipple into his mouth. I arch off the floor and an idea occurs to me.

I sit up and he goes immediately backward, giving me space.

I want, very badly, to see him crawl toward me again. I scoot back, spread my legs, bite my lip. It has the intended effect. Miles is all shoulders, collarbone, and pecs, crawling toward me and then there's stubble at my neck. Wet heat on my breasts, firm hands at my ass, yanking me toward him. Again, I pull back from him, scooting backward. Again, he crawls toward me. This time, a glint in his eye.

He finally gets my intention when we get to the doorframe of the bedroom. He looks up from where he's been tongue-kissing my rib cage and realizes where I've dragged us. He said *no bed*, I said *why not*.

I go for the kill stroke, sitting on my heels—the picture of obedience. "Please."

He's a strong man, maybe the strongest I've ever met. But he's not strong enough to withstand that.

I'm lifted up and tossed bodily onto the bed, laughing and turned on and delighted.

He joins me there, crawling over me again, his eyes are horny as hell and everywhere, he likes what he sees and he can't kiss me as many places as he'd like to all at once. There are teeth at my hip. He tongues my thigh, then he's back up to my mouth, my neck. A big hand draws a map from my sternum down to my belly button and down to the waistband of my underwear. I take initiative and do the same to the beautiful body in front of me.

We read each other's eyes and cross each other's waistbands at the same moment, breaking eye contact when sensation takes the wheel. Miles is smooth and firm in my hand. He's got teeth against my collarbone and two fingers between my legs.

We're banded together by his arm at my back, holding me in place. He's breathing through his teeth and suffering against pleasure. All at once, I have to stop my explorations of him and grab the bed behind my head. Because he's pressing those fingers inside. I say his name and see nothing but his dark, promising smile. He watches my face and patiently pushes me closer and closer. I think I'm giving instructions, I think I'm asking for something, I think I'm begging. He takes it all and turns it into magic. I cling to him and go stiff as lightning, arching toward the afterlife, held to earth by Miles, brought all the way there and all the way back by the man saying my name into my hair.

I fall back to the bed, laughing into my hands, curling onto my side, dimly aware that the world still turns. Miles is sitting on his heels, breathing like he's been running and studying me. The second I start working my underwear down my legs, he strips them off me. He's pulling my knees open, situating his shoulders.

"Look at me."

I follow directions immediately, up on my elbows.

"I'll always take care of you, Lenny." He kisses my thigh. "Tell me you know that."

"I know it. I swear I know it."

He open-mouth kisses me between my legs and I'm a goner. I writhe and plead and tell him everything I want. He's got me so close again, with that persistent, patient mouth. But this time . . .

"Miles."

He lifts up. He looks heavily drugged.

"I want *that*," I say, pointing between his legs. "Here or here." I point to my top half and then my bottom half. "Take your pick."

He looks seriously torn but then he's lying out over top of me to reach the bedside drawer. He produces a condom and we momentarily battle for it.

"Please." I say the magic word and he closes his eyes in pain. He hands me the condom and leans up, bracing two hands on the wall behind me while I shimmy his underwear down and carefully, lovingly sheathe him.

I'm coming back for you, buddy, I silently promise his dick, but then I get distracted because he's laying me down, guiding my legs around his back so that I can hold him with my entire body.

He kisses my mouth open, uses one hand to guide himself to the right place between my legs. He holds my eyes. *Please.* He pushes in and it's everything, everything, everything.

I stretch and slide and open to make way for him and he doesn't stop pushing his way in. His eyes are reading me, his body powerful and gentle, demanding and giving. Our temples press together. When I think he's fully seated I gasp and let my head fall back to the pillow. And then he sinks in the final inch.

"That's right," Miles groans against my throat. His praise has me flushing, proud, I want more of everything. I tell him so and am rewarded with a slicing smile, his eyes on mine, one strong arm scooping my hips even closer.

Thump goes Miles's body against mine.

Thump goes the headboard against the wall.

Thump goes my heart in my chest.

His style of sex is slow and steady and thorough and patient and *of course* this is how he has sex.

Some people are Ferraris. Miles is a Mack truck. He seems to want to restrain himself and he almost can, until his body forces him to thrust and he gives me everything he can't hold back. I hold him as tight as I can, I ask for more, I grab the headboard when he gives it to me.

He's methodically working me up the bed and finally, his protective hand is the only thing between my skull and hardwood and I'll bet his knuckles will end up bruised because he can't stop giving. Giving in. Giving it up. Giving it all to me.

I climb with him and reach between us to use my own hand, free-falling before he does. He pulls back from my shoulder to watch me and then goes rigid against me, still pumping, volcanic, inexorable.

Chapter Thirty-Three

An hour later we're in the shower and I finally get to see 2-in-1 as God intended it. Miles is wearing a crown of suds that's only getting bigger the more he scrubs.

"Your poor hair."

He frowns at me, still scrubbing. "What's wrong with my hair?"

"You might as well just use nail polish remover."

"Huh?"

"First order of business as your lov-ah," I say, and grin when he grimaces, "is to get you on the conditioner train."

"There's conditioner in 2-in-1! It's half of the 2."

"Why don't you use those?" I ask, pointing to the bottles of shampoo and conditioner he once used on my hair after dunking me in the sink.

"They're yours."

I blink at him. "They're mine? You bought shampoo for me, like, two months ago? How'd you know I'd be showering with you, you pervert?"

He laughs and elbows me out from under the water to rinse the suds off his head. "I wasn't plotting to get you to shower *with me*. But you already had a toothbrush in my cup. You were already switching my toilet paper to your preferred setting. You were sleeping on my couch and eating my food. I thought a shower was highly probable. Get back under the water, you look freezing."

He snicks open the shampoo bottle and hands it to me. I wince getting my haircut wet and gently massage my aching hair.

"What's wrong?" he asks, eyeing me carefully.

"My scalp is getting used to its new reality."

He gives me a naked, soapy hug. "*I'm* still getting used to the new reality."

I rinse and he hands me the conditioner next.

"So . . ." he says, glancing at me. "Was your reaction to my room because my room is weird?"

I laugh. "No! There's nothing wrong with your room. It's really lovely. My reaction was because I'm me. And anything new is weird."

He sighs, hugging in next to me under the spray to rinse. "Len, I don't think I'm gonna keep this apartment."

"Wait, what? Your bedroom is not weird! Seriously! I'm sorry I panicked. Don't take it to heart!"

He turns the shower off and distributes towels. "It's not that . . . Actually, it's part of what Reese and I were talking about earlier."

I scramble to catch up. "She *asked* you to *leave?*"

Miles mentioned a long time ago that he keeps the studio apartment because even though he owns this place, if Reese asked him to leave, he'd go. But I always thought that was overprecautionary.

"No! No, but we talked about how our relationship might . . . thrive . . . if I weren't looming ominously over them. Her words, not mine." He laughs. "She mentioned that it might feel good to call me up when she wanted me around, rather than just assume I'm always there whether she wants me or not."

"How do you feel about that?"

"Well, I think . . . I think she's really gonna try. To include me in her life, I mean. Things have changed a lot. Mostly thanks to you. So, that feels good. And forcing my way in . . . hasn't worked, so if she's telling me this will work for her, then I'll listen."

I'm momentarily distracted by his toweling style. Dripping feet on the bath mat, first his face, then he scrubs his head, arms, back, then ties the towel around his waist. He doesn't even notice how rough he is with himself. Meanwhile I'm wrapped like a newborn.

"But you live here, Miles. Your dad left you this apartment."

He heads to the bedroom and I drift after him. "It's never really felt like mine. It was Reese's first and I think, given our situation, that doesn't feel right." He pulls clothes out of his drawers. "There's a reason this room feels so different than the rest of the house. It's the only room I had anything to do with. The rest is all Reese. Besides, I've got this place and some of my stuff here, the studio and some of my stuff there, and my house upstate with stuff there too."

"Yeah, wow. Three places. Now that you mention it, I'm kind of dating, like, a mogul."

He laughs and shakes his head. "It's more like you're dating someone who's been incapable of setting up a real life. But I wanna really settle in somewhere."

"So . . . what would your plan be?"

"Well." He glances at me, stepping into underwear. "I'm not going to kick you out of the studio. But we can't both fit there. So I'll have to find someplace. Hopefully close to you and Reese and Ains. And I was thinking . . . that I'd sell this place."

"That makes sense. So you could buy a new place?"

"Or." He sits down on the bed next to me. "Or I'd have some capital to get a business off the ground."

"Oh, Miles, *really*?" I toss my arms around his neck and get him wet with my hair. He laughs and squeezes me tight, rearranging the towel over me so I don't get chilly. "It's *such* a good idea. All of it."

"It's time. Both feet in."

"Cannonball, right?"

He nods. "I'll wanna keep my place upstate, of course, but yeah. It's time to . . . work on Anders's room. Anyways. Lots to think about." He looks grumpy and pleased at the same time.

"Don't worry," I tell him with a pat. "I'll help you get your life on track. I'm very organized and put together."

For that, he tugs me back onto the bed.

ALL THE LEAVES DROP, we get a few flurries, and I take to carrying a hot cup of tea with me around Miles's apartment. Miles drives upstate for a day to meet with his old bricklayer mentor and returns home with a plan of action for his business. And with Anders's framed football jersey.

I wear Miles's old black hoodie every single second that I can, but Miles's only rule is that I have to be naked underneath it. I think this is because he knows if he lets me wear it out of the house, it'll be mine forever. He puts his head underneath that hoodie while we watch TV. Puts his hands underneath it while I attempt to pour a bowl of cereal. Strips it off me and pushes me down on his bed. We easily cross all three sex positions off the list. I beg him to get a fireman costume so we can finally live out number one on the list but he claims that the *or something* has already fulfilled it.

We spend three weeks only peeling ourselves off one another so that I can shower and go take care of Ainsley.

He's stopped tagging along with me and Ainsley for the most part. When he wants to hang out with Ains, he texts Reese and sets a time. Reese excitedly informs him that an apartment opened up in Harper's walk-up a few blocks away.

He becomes a staple at Sunday dinner and my dad has—thankfully—stopped punishing him with grappa.

He signs a lease for the new apartment and starts putting his things in boxes. It aggravates me so much that I start hiding in his bed and regularly get him off-task by unzipping his pants.

"Lenny, I have to get this done!" he asserts, love-drunkenly sagging down to his own knees to meet me on the floor. He's panting, I'm panting. For all his bossy words, he's tenderly nuzzling my neck and rubbing his hands over my back. Blowjobs make him extremely affectionate and I bask in his afterglow. "I really do," he tries again.

"I hate your new apartment. It's different."

"You haven't even seen it yet," he says firmly. And then much more gently, "What are you so scared of?"

"I don't want to say goodbye to anything else in my life, ever. I love this apartment. I fell in love with you in this apartment."

"Trust me, Len. The thing you think you love about this apartment is actually *me*."

Well, he's right, of course.

Then he's all packed up and moved out. We hand over the keys to the new owners, and then we begin unpacking him in his new place. There's a lot more pants-unzipping but now that the moving part is over, Miles doesn't protest it in the least.

It takes time to get everything set up the way he wants it. His new place is far smaller and older. There's creaky, original hardwood flooring and tin ceilings. He's taken approximately two hundred photos of the tiny stained-glass window in the kitchen. He's adamant that it looks different in all lighting.

He's moved completely out of the studio, which has left more space for me, but honestly, I rarely stay there anymore.

Finally when we're just careening into winter, he and I lie in his new bedroom, in his old bed, and enjoy a lazy Sunday. He's reading and I'm laid across him, looking out the window at the chilly blue.

"Miles?"

"Hm?" He doesn't look up from his book.

"Can you promise me something."

"Maybe."

"Can I die first?"

He turns a page in his book. "Sure."

"Hey." I lunge up and attempt to yank the book from him, but he must have been expecting the sneak attack because his grip is like iron. "That was a very emotional question I just asked. And that's all you have to say?"

"Was I supposed to argue with you?" He pries my fingers off his book and smooths out one of the wrinkled pages.

"You're supposed to take it seriously at least! I'm talking about dying over here. Isn't that a pretty serious cry for help?"

"Cry for help? No." He snaps the book closed. "For attention? Definitely." He puts the book on the nightstand and gets out of bed and opens the top drawer of his dresser. The one with the workout clothes. "Come on, then."

"What? What's this?" My plan has gone south very quickly.

"You want attention, you're getting it. Get your running shoes on."

"I don't want attention anymore. Now I want a divorce."

"You said we can't joke about divorce. Besides, we're not even married yet."

"I know you're trying to distract me with marriage talk, you wily fox! Hey! Get off me!"

He's attempting to squeeze me into a sports bra.

"Jesus Christ, these things are like a torture device!" He's just snapped himself with the elastic.

"I prefer it when you take the bra *off* me."

"Me too," he says on a grunt.

"You're not going to give up on my cardiovascular health, are you."

"Never."

I glare at him, push him aside, and put on my own work-out clothes. "It's terrible to be loved! Who wants to jog!"

"Yes. A true burden, all."

"I'll run, but I'm not happy about it."

"I can accept that."

"And you better put out tonight," I grumble.

"Understood," he says with a grin. But then the smile falls and he steps back. Studying me. "Cry for attention or not . . . you weren't serious, were you?"

I'm digging through my drawer for the matching athletic sock. "I mean . . . obviously one person can't promise that to another."

My unsaid *but* hangs in the air between us: But how could I ever go on without him?

He studies me again for a long moment and then leaves the room. He's back just as I'm tying my hair up into a stubby little bun. He has something in his hands that he holds out to me.

"Your Nancy Drew notebook?"

He recoils. "What makes this a Nancy Drew notebook? The fact that it's a notebook at all?"

"Obviously."

"Here." He wags it at me until I take it. "I actually thought this issue might come up at some point."

I open the notebook and see pages and pages of his scribbled notes about babysitting. My heart skips when I get to his list, untitled, that has almost everything crossed off. The Kiss Lenny list.

He hands me a pen. "There's plenty of space for more."

"But you've already kissed me! Like every single part of me!"

"You're the only one who thinks that list is about kissing. That list is about making sure you're okay." He takes a step toward me. "And I'll never stop adding to it. And if I died first . . . then *you* should never stop adding to it."

"WHAT'RE YOU LOOKING AT?"

"Nothing."

We're drinking an afternoon coffee on his new (used) couch. He's watching a sport (that I don't even bother to identify) and I'm scrolling on my phone.

There's a pause where I think I've thrown him off the trail.

But then he lunges out of nowhere and snags the phone halfway out of my hand, tipping it so that he can see. "Are you staring at pictures of me?"

"No! Who cares!"

"*Why?*"

"I'm not mooning over you. I'm trying to decide which photo of you to print out and put in my locket."

He pauses and this time I can't take the silence. His expression is inscrutable, his eyes bouncing between mine. "Really?"

"You're *obviously* the other half of my locket."

He clicks off the TV.

I crawled away from him during the scuffle, so he firmly grabs my ankle and pulls me back under him. He kisses me deeply, slowly.

When he comes up for air his eyes are serious and kind. He points at himself. "Lenny, the other half of your locket has something to tell you."

"Hm?"

He holds me tenderly, softly, firmly. His eyes darken. This must be serious. I come to attention.

"It's time," he says.

I instantly know exactly what he's talking about and I start shaking my head. "No."

"It is."

"No. No no no." Tears are pricking my eyes.

"Shhh." He kisses me long and slow until I'm calm again, and then he pulls back. "I was waiting for you to get there on your own, but . . . but I think you need me to take charge on this one."

"I can't do it, Miles." I'm instantly crying again. "I can't move out of that apartment. I can't go back there. I can't pack up all her stuff. Give it away or throw it away? How can I do that?"

"I'll help you."

"Miles, I *can't.*" But I know he's right. That apartment has sucked almost my entire savings away. And it's an artifact of a former life. I don't just mean the life I used to have with Lou. I mean that having my belongings and residences be scattered, abandoned, messy, and something to cringe away from . . . that's who I was before I met Miles. He and I, we're moving past that. It's not who I am anymore. Clinging to that apartment is clinging to a moment in time that's gone. If

I want to step into this life with Miles, fully into it, I need to follow his lead and step fully *out* of the pieces of a past life I'll never have back.

"You can."

"It's gonna be *so* bad," I sob, hands over my face.

He hugs me tightly, because I've just agreed that it's necessary. So terribly necessary. *The only way out is through.* He gently kisses the backs of my hands and when I peek up at him, all I can see is how proud he is of me.

"You know," he says cautiously, "I think cleaning out the apartment will go faster with more people."

"Okay," I whisper. "I'll ask my parents to help. And Jericho."

He's blinking at me in complete surprise. He thought that was going to be a battle. There's been no one but him who's been allowed to see me disintegrate. And surely I will disintegrate when tasked with sorting Lou's belongings.

But maybe it won't bring everyone down with me. Maybe instead it'll be the other way around. Maybe they'll bring me up, where the light is.

I WAKE UP at the studio the next morning. I roll onto my side and the locket falls out of my shirt and onto the pillow. Clicking it open, I can't help but grin at the screengrab of Miles in a ruffled gray blouse that I glued in there yesterday. Me and Lou and Miles, all in one place.

Something occurs to me.

I text Miles one sentence: *I want you to meet Lou.*

He texts back immediately: *When and where.*

Forty minutes later, we're holding hands next to a hot dog cart, both of us staring up the foreboding steps of the Met.

He squeezes my hand and I turn to look at him. His head is cocked to one side, *Are you sure?* written in his eyes.

I sigh and tug him after me.

I ignore the first floor and take the elevator up. I hope she's still there. We find our way through the maze of paintings that George and I hid our pain inside a few months ago. And finally, there we are. The gray clouds and the skull in the sky. The single, living flower.

"'Go to the Met as often as possible,'" Miles quotes as we stand in front of Georgia O'Keeffe. "I guess it's one we'll have to cross off over and over."

I frown a little. "I thought it would feel a certain way. To cross everything off the list. To get it all done. But . . . in reality. In the world that doesn't have an actual plan . . . I still haven't been to Lou's grave. Not since her funeral. And there's a lot of other things to do still. I guess it all feels a little arbitrary. The things I actually wrote on the list."

Miles cocks his head to one side, his brows drawn. "The things *you* wrote on the list? I thought . . . I thought Lou wrote that list for you. Things for you to do to live again after she . . ."

"No." I shake my head. "I wrote that list for *her.* A long time ago. For after her hysterectomy. When . . . going on with her life didn't feel possible for her anymore." My eyes mist. "She carried it with her for a long time. That's why the paper is so raggedy. Right before she died she had it laminated and gave it back to me."

I take it out of my pocket and hand it to him. He holds it up and studies it. It spends so much time in my pocket, under my fingers, it's weird to see it out in the daylight, in the world.

"What's the last thing on the list?" Miles asks, handing it back to me.

"What do you mean? We checked everything off."

He shakes his head. "The paper is folded there, see? If you hold it up to the light, there's something written."

I still.

Heart racing, I slide my fingernail between the curling lamination and peel it slowly open, careful not to tear the paper.

And there, written in her artsy handwriting, with a pencil she'd surely just been sketching with, are Lou's last words to me.

Get over it already, loser.

And her best gift to me, always, is that there is genuine laughter mixed in with the jagged, heart-torn tears. I clutch her handwriting to my chest and bury my face in Miles's sweatshirt.

"She knew, Miles," I say when I come up for air. "She knew that there isn't actually a checklist for learning to live again. She knew that some days you do it and some days you don't."

Today, all I can do is bring Miles to a place where I feel Lou. And the rest is for another tomorrow.

I take a deep, watery breath and gesture to the painting. "Miles, meet Lou Merritt. The love of my life. Lou, meet Miles Honey, the other love of my life."

He waves at the painting. "Hi." He looks down at me. "Was this one her favorite?"

I laugh. "I have no idea. Actually, maybe this one is *my* favorite." It's a striking idea, considering I've never had an opinion on fine art in my life. But maybe I osmosed a love of art just from loving Lou. "I feel Lou in the Met. Every time we used to come here together, she always wanted to stay longer. So if her spirit is somewhere still . . . I hope it's here. And now she can spend as long as she wants."

Miles nods and we fall thoughtful.

"I'm taking good care of her," Miles assures the painting. "I feel like I know you. I see you in Lenny every day." He squeezes me while tears fall. "I love you."

For a moment, I think he's telling Lou that he loves her, but when I look up, his eyes are on me. It occurs to me that he *does* love Lou. *Because* he loves me.

We study the painting until other people come, and then we mosey through the museum. We look at the art, but it's mostly just an excuse to hold hands. When we circle back down to the gift shop I get lost in the section with all the silk scarves. Miles finds me ten minutes later and he has two books in his hands. "You think Lou would have liked this one on Louise Bourgeois or this one on Monet better?"

"Oh, that one, I think."

"Great."

I follow him curiously and watch as he purchases it. "You're going to read a book that Lou would have liked?" I ask with wide, brimming eyes.

He hands me the bag. "No. You are."

"Me?" I blink and peek inside the bag.

"Yeah. It'll be good for you. Think of it like taking vitamins."

I scowl and try to put the book back in his hand. "I hate doing things that are good for me."

"No, you don't."

We're both smiling because he's right.

We button our coats and step outside, back atop those sweeping steps. To our shock, while we were inside, the world has been completely iced over. Everywhere we look, rain is freezing in drippy stalactites. Off the bumpers of cars, from the spokes of parked bicycles, from the drooping umbrella spires over the hot dog carts on the corner. The words *steaming hot* have a crown of ice.

The world is fresh and frozen, and Miles and I turn a full circle to appreciate the spectacle, the rare beauty of it. The cars migrate slowly from one intersection to the next; the people grip one another and take baby steps.

I've been gifted with this day. Frozen in time. A day where everyone moves slowly and carefully. Where the world is cast in diamond. Where the sunshine, never promised, is achingly bright and cold and there's nowhere to hide.

I thought it would be immeasurably painful for me to walk this familiar museum again, to know that the closest Miles and Lou will ever get to actually meeting is in my own heart. But instead, I get to see the world—this whole life—in a sparkling and miraculous light.

Miles is smiling and shaking his head at the unexpected gorgeousness of the world and so am I. What a perfect day to have torn some of this pain out of my heart. I shiver and clutch him and we hobble down the block toward the park.

We slip and slide and walk like ducks, white-knuckling each other's coats. We are side by side, sweating and freezing at the same time, laughing and yelping, both terrified of falling and exhilarated with every step we take toward home. Toward whatever comes next. And if that isn't living, then I don't know what is.

Acknowledgments

Remember that morning you woke up and realized that you were completely professionally fulfilled and your daily life was punctuated with explosions of creative freedom and lined with intellectually stimulating thought-homework and also, whenever you interacted with the people who read your work they were all so incredibly supportive and joyful? Oh, wait, that was me? (Laughs nervously.)

Reader. I would not have been able to write that sentence without you and your role in my life. Reading a book is intensely personal. You are allowing my words into your brain. I have just had a 100k-word conversation with myself inside your head. Reading a book is a precious, precious gift to that author and I do not take it lightly. You could have watched a K-drama. You could have conducted extensive research on the new hairdryer you want to buy. You could have saved the universe with your videogame controller. But instead (or maybe in addition), you read my book! I cannot thank you enough. I want to talk to you! I'm bad at the internet! Please email me.

Let's keep the gratitude going, shall we? Tara Gelsomino, my agent and biggest advocate, I learn something new about our relationship with every book. This book taught me this: Tara wants me to be happy and healthy regardless of (perceived) professional consequences. Thank you for towing my professional life, as always, and thank you for guarding my mental health too.

Emma Caruso, my brilliant editor, my pal . . . maybe in some universe our brains were born as one and that person is just absolutely churning out flawless content. But in this universe, it sure does take two! Okay, reader, picture this. You're hungry for a new book. You'd like a meal. I, the writer, have gone to the grocery store in my brain and selected some very fine ingredients. Emma, the editor, is the reason you're not eating those ingredients out of the grocery bag on the kitchen floor. Emma *sure* knows how to set a dang table. I bring the (copious) similes, the flavor, the make-outs. Emma gently reminds me of such trivial things as plot, structure, pacing. Thank you, Emma! I'm so grateful to learn from you and problem solve with you. It is seriously fun. Also, credit where credit is due, she wrote the ever-hilarious "it's laminated" line.

To the entire team at Dial . . . my God, you work hard. Brianna Kusilek, Madison Dettlinger, Talia Cieslinksi, all of you have created my dream-work scenario. It is a true honor of my life to work with you. Whitney Frick, I live in gratitude to you for reading my work and thinking we'd be a good fit. You sure know how to support your authors!

Hannah Sloane, Camille Kellogg, Georgia Clark, Claudia Craven, Justine Champine, Kerry Winfrey, Amy Ewing, Jess Verdi, Ruby Lang, your work continues to inspire me, your support continues to humble me. Let's write books together forever!

Bennett and Libby, the staycation at your house is the reason this book got a final draft. To the Melingers, all the sweet moments between Reese and Ainsley (and Emil!) were written because I was allowed to be a part of your family for those years. I hope you see a few tender glimpses of what a special time that was for me.

Lauren Whitehead, there are no words for what your support has meant to me. You created the bridge between my professional and personal life. I feel like one whole person now. *Thank you.* Mahogany Browne and Adam Falkner, I can't wait to celebrate your big moments the way you so tenderly celebrated mine. Thank you.

Noah Arhm Choi, we're now, officially, in our third decade of friendship. Your hard work, intellect, and heart made this book better. Thank you for doing the authenticity read. Having you in my corner is equal parts exhilarating and reassuring.

To my family, I have never felt more cheered on in my life than I have by all of you this past year. Yes, I know I'm a grownup with kids and a job, blah blah blah. But having my family celebrate me so clearly and loudly . . . it made me feel like a kid again. Like I was winning my very first rec and ed basketball game and you all showed up to cheer. I am achingly proud of myself and you made it that way. I love you.

Jon, Frank, and Sonny. Well, I literally teared up just typing your names, so that should tell you a little bit about how grateful I am to come home to you. You support me, shelter me, grow me, push me, test me, open me, defend me, humor me, and share your lives with me. My life's work is returning that gift. I love you infinity.

And last, WRB, PM, and BS. I wrote this book in the before. But of course, it will live forever in the after. Thank you for living there with me.

Promise Me Sunshine

Cara Bastone

Dial Delights

*Love Stories
for the
Open-Hearted*

Promise Me Sunshine
"Mad Libs"

Hi! If you're like me, you never learn. You just keep expecting that life will someday be a little bit easier. Shocker! It really never is.

After her hard time, Lenny has a Live Again List that helps her figure out how to . . . well, live again, and I wanted to include ideas for anyone who wants one of their own.

Life has a way of KOing us sometimes. Here are some ideas for getting back up.

1.   Buy the (dress, socks, fedora, lederhosen) you never thought you could pull off and wear it to your next (dentist appointment, PTA meeting, dog-grooming appointment, date).

2.   Go to (location in your town filled with all the cool people) and buy a stranger a (drink, cupcake, pay their library fines).

3.   Gut it out through your older brother's favorite movie. (I'm sure it'll be a terrible experience, but you'll surely *learn* something, right?) If not an older brother . . . then mail-delivery person. Yes, ask your mail-delivery person.

4.   Take a (figure drawing, opera writing, croquet) work-

shop from your local library. Choose at random! The only requirement is that you must already be bad at it!

5. Eat (pistachio eclairs, pepperoni pizza, tteokbokki, ceviche). Feed yourself, baby!

6. Learn a (Spice girls, Irish step dance, Black Swan, Madonna) choreo. This one is mandatory. Learn a choreo.

7. Show the choreo to someone who will laugh their ass off with joy and delight.

8. Yeah, yeah, Miles is right. Cleaning your house works. Or, alternatively, changing up your space. So go buy some (veridian, vermilion, puce) paint and slap a crappy (or stunning) mural on your (wall, freshly dusted bookshelf, bathroom mirror).

9. Here's the worst one. I know, I hate it too. Sit down, right now, and reply to that email. Whichever email. You know the email. Okay, good job, now's the time to return to #5 and the aforementioned pistachio eclair.

10. Finally, one of Lenny's hardest lessons: the phone call. No one can be your Miles if you don't call them when you need them. So call up (your mom, your old next-door neighbor, your pickleball buddy, your snarky cousin, the object of your fervent desire) and talk, talk, talk.

HERE'S A SNEAK PEEK FROM

THE NAKED EYE

BY CARA BASTONE

There's a pair of brown velvet trousers with a matching top in a vintage shop on 23rd Street that I'm ninety-nine percent sure would turn my life around.

They sound hideous, yes, but with a few well-placed safety pins, I'd be chic and unique.

I got this bob for a reason, you know. So that I could wear pants like that and look like I know what I'm doing.

Cigarettes are out, so how to signal to the masses that you're effortlessly cool, couldn't care less, and have cultural value and relevance?

Brown velvet trousers, of course!

Is now a good time to mention my husband is leaving me in increments (first the far side of the bed, then the guest room, and now, apparently, his own apartment) and I'm not taking it well?

I've been seized with the unshakeable certainty that I need a new selection of matte lipsticks on hand. I need, probably, a complete re-envisioning of my eyebrows. Pilates. Green juice.

And a lot more money.

Oh, I know, I know. Tale as old as time. Happiness is just one more purchase away! (Perpetually.) But seriously, maybe it's time for some Mary Janes.

It's not, of course. What it's actually time for is cooking. And self-reflection. And a recommitment to personal values.

Well, let's start with the one I was going to do anyway because I get paid to do it.

Cooking!

So. When my world is crumbling, I feed people.

Actually, when my world is gorgeous and peachy and shining with the light of a thousand Instagram filters, I feed people.

Can you guess the pattern?

I feed people!

So, now, join me here in my kitchen, with this glass of wine that's somehow found its way into my trembling hand, staring at this sheaf of paper that he's pinned to the kitchen counter with a 28-ounce can of diced tomatoes.

Lease start date August 15.

So.

He's moving out.

What the fuck do we do with this? If you're like me, you might be asking yourself this very question.

Well, what the fuck *do* I do with it?

The fact that he's chosen a 28-ounce can of diced tomatoes to pin that note to the counter suddenly feels a bit like a gauntlet. He could have chosen a 12-ounce can. He could have used a centimeter of scotch tape.

He could have not left it for me to find and relayed this information with words and eye contact, but no, who am I kidding, this is Vin we're talking about here.

Twenty-eight ounces? Game on.

I don my second favorite striped apron. The one that makes me feel like Queen Martha Stewart. I've never diced onions into neater squares. Never once peeled garlic with such speed. When they hit the hot oil in the pot, they sear with such a satisfying hiss I grin like the devil.

And now. For the fun part. I grab the diced tomatoes off the counter. The note immediately skates a foot to the side in the breeze from our open kitchen window. The can pops open, and I feel I've done something almost naughty. Every crank of the opener feels like another inch of skin I'm not supposed to expose to someone. I'm supposed to be crying over these tomatoes, right? Surely not simmering them.

I watch until they bubble on the stove.

Holding the immersion blender in one hand, I rev it in the air, yes, like that one murderer with the chainsaw in those movies I've never actually seen. And then the sauce gets it. I'm turning those tomatoes to velvet in that pot. My hand slips on the immersion blender and tomato sauce paints a zebra stripe across the counter. And the lease.

A splash of red across the murder weapon.

I season and simmer and stir. When the scent grows heady and rich and layered, when there's nothing left to do but clean up the kitchen, when the wine is gone but the tremble in my hand is not, I pick up the note from the counter and fasten it to the fridge door like all of our to-do lists. Step one: Get a divorce. Step two: Buy mushrooms.

There's the unmistakable scrunch of keys in our apartment door but I refuse to stiffen. I reach out and swipe the stripe of sauce off the lease with one finger. It leaves a stain behind.

Vin steps into our apartment. I turn to him, just a normal woman in an apron.

He's got an intensely determined, did-she-see-it-yet look on his face, he's breathing hard. His endlessly green eyes dart from the empty kitchen counter to the fridge door and then to my face.

I lick the sauce off my finger.

"Sauce is on the stove if you're hungry."

One hand still on the doorknob, he looks again from the lease to me. I wait, interminably, for him to say anything.

And then he turns and he walks back out, closing the door behind him, like he'd never even been there.

~~She was pretty.~~

~~She had a flower on her sweater. I don't know what kind. Not a real one. Part of the fabric. Actually it might have just been a shirt. Not a sweater.~~ Why am I so bad at this?

She was pretty. Her smile. Her mouth. But mostly her eyes. When she smiled. Dark eyes. Friendly. That's what I remember. About the first time I ever saw her.

OKAY, SO THERE'S an imaginary world. And in that imaginary world, you just happen to know the address of the apartment your husband is moving into on August 15.

And look, you're you. You're not me, but I imagine, some of you, in your version of this imaginary world, *don't* Google Maps that apartment building and imagine him arriving there after work, with those tired eyes he gets and some of you, probably, would be like, screw him! and fair, that's fair, but *I* am a tiny bit like, well, what's he going to eat after that long day of work? Ramen? Fried chicken from down the block? Cold cuts on sandwich bread with not even a slice of tomato?

I understand this reaction of mine is just depressing. But I swear I don't mean it in a repressed/oppressed 1950s housewife sort of way. I don't consider it my mission in life to service my husband.

I'm just, like, actually wondering this. The same way I'm also wondering who in God's name is going to drop my compost off at the drop-off point on Sunday mornings. Because one of the best parts of forming a partnership with someone is divvying up all the crap you didn't want to do in the first place.

And now he wants to undivvy? We already divvied! You can't take back a divvy!

Just to paint the picture, I'm currently standing in the kitchen, fridge door open, buried in a ten-year-old sweatshirt with socks up to my knees, contemplating my fridge and saying the word *divvy* to myself over and over.

Times are good!

I'm saved from myself—and this moment, and getting lost in a perpetual loop of trying to make the word *divvy* sound like an actual word again (am I crazy or would that make a really cute baby name? For someone else's baby, of course)—by a text from my erratic but brilliant custom-framing guy.

Frame is ready. Leaving for Montreaux in half an hour. You can get it next week if you can't make it.

His name is, I kid you not, St. Michel, and he does extremely fine, shockingly cheap work, but his shop does not keep regular hours and occasionally he'll keep your project hostage for a year. And I need this framed portrait *tonight.*

On my way!

I shove my feet into running shoes (because I'll need them) and jog out the door. I skid from one bus to another, and then sprint the last two blocks to the shop. I'm forty feet away when I see him step out onto the sidewalk with a rolly bag.

"St. Michel! I'm here!"

He turns, his silver hair hidden under a stocking cap, even though it's seventy degrees outside. I make it to his side and sag against the bricks of his building, panting, melting, trying very hard not to puke on his, surely, cobbled shoes.

"Darling," he says with a frown. "What is this look?"

Look, I'm not high fashion, but normally I can throw a silhouette together. I'm on the shorter side, with dark hair I keep in bangs straight down to my eyebrows and a pair of gigantic, colorful glasses for every occasion. I have—if not style—*a* style. And let's just say it doesn't normally include bike shorts, knee socks, a sweatshirt, running shoes, and my hair in a pile on my head.

"Well, I didn't have much warning before I left the house!" I have my hands on my hips and a scowl on my face. St. Michel responds positively to light derision.

"Right, right. Your project. Let's go." He keys us into his darkened shop, and we walk straight back to the work area. It smells like freshly sawn wood and polyurethane. He doesn't bother flipping on the lights.

He hands me a brown paper package, 16" x 20", and when my fingers close around it, they start to tingle.

"Open, open!" he demands. "I have a flight."

Normally I'd be peeling back the tape and inspecting his work. The first time I ever did this was to make sure I'd gotten what I'd paid for. Every time since then has simply been to make him preen with compliments because his work is just *that* good. But now, the weight of the frame in my hands, I'm suddenly remembering which photo he's framed and I just can't do it. I can't look at that right now.

"I don't want to make you late!" I say instead and head back out through the shop. "What's in Montreaux?" I ask as he relocks the shop and drags his bag to the curb, his hand already in the air for a cab.

"Montreaux," he responds, as if I'm absurd for even asking.

"Just going to sightsee?"

A cab pulls up and St. Michel walks around to the back

and pulls open the trunk door. He tosses his bag in and turns to look at me, hands on his hips. "What is going on with you?" His eyes are narrowed.

I don't usually make small talk in knee socks while I wait to wave goodbye to him on the street. It's possible I'm coming off a little wrecked.

And he's just such a *handsome* older man. With his one silver tooth and vintage pea coat. I once ran into him on a Tuesday morning drinking an aperitif at an outdoor café and eating oysters. On a Tuesday morning! He's a man of the world with a sharp and realistic view on life and maybe that's why I clutch the package to my chest and say my worst fear. "My husband is moving out. I think I might be getting a divorce."

My eyes fill and he disappears into a blur of light and color.

Something cold touches my face and then again. I dash my tears away and realize that a light drizzle has started up.

The cab driver calls something terse out the passenger-side window, and St. Michel waves a dismissive hand toward him. And then he's there, right in front of me. He puts one finger under my chin, a light, friendly touch.

"Darling," he says.

I'm rapt.

He's about to say something medicinal and necessary, I can feel it.

"Divorce is *fine*," he finishes.

"Oh."

And then he kisses me brusquely on the cheek and waves his hand over his head as he walks back to the cab and slides away down the street.

"Okay," I say to myself. "So . . ."

The bus stop is two blocks away, and the brown paper

around my package is already starting to dampen from the drizzle.

Mad dash home is the logical train of thought, probably.

But . . . here's the thing about having memorized the address of the apartment that your husband is moving into on August 15 . . . here's the thing about having put it into Google Maps . . . and having pinned it on the map . . . it beats like a blinking cursor on the map in your head.

Which is what is happening to me. Right this very second.

The rain is increasing from a drizzle to a more insistent pitter patter, enough that I see a drip form at the end of my bangs. This package is not going to survive if I keep standing on the curb in front of St. Michel's shop. I can't keep standing still. I have to move.

So, I shove the package under my sweatshirt as best as I can and start to run. In the direction of the bus stop, and home. Within moments my socks and shoes are soaked. It's dumping rain now, and a buffet of wind tosses a sheet of water onto me from the side. There's the bus stop at the end of the block!

Here it is!

There it goes!

I keep running right on past.

In front of me, cars slice a gigantic puddle in half. The light changes, I jump the puddle, scamper across the street, there's rain down my back. This is such a bad idea that the universe is attempting to stop me in my tracks with bodily discomfort. But I've chosen belligerence. I press on.

There's a yellow awning up ahead and I sprint.

I make it there just in time to huddle up onto the single stair, out of the worst of the downpour.

NINE FIVE FOUR. The enormous metal numbers leer

down at me. It's a brick building, this new address of Vin's, which I immediately hate because I've always wanted to live in a brick building in New York. I can't see, because the rain has turned the world gray and opaque, but I bet there are flowers on the windowsills. Probably someone upstairs plays a grand piano with their window open on the sunny days. There is probably a band of plucky and precocious children who knock on the doors of their neighbors to deliver the kugel their mothers have just made too much of.

This is clearly the most charming apartment building in all five boroughs and I hate it.

I'm just about finished cursing it, about to drag my soggy ass back into the pouring rain, when the foggy glass door behind me comes open an inch and shunts me back onto the street, out of the cover of the awning.

"Honey, come in! Come in!" a voice says behind me.

There's rain dripping down the back of my neck, wetting my eyelashes, dripping off my ears.

Come in? As in enter the premises? Of 954?

Unthinkable.

"Come in!" she says again, and this time she grips my wrist and tugs. All my aforementioned belligerence ashes away into meek obedience. Maybe I'm too soaked? Maybe she's just the right amount bossy? I stumble through the door and gasp with relief when I step into a warm, dry hallway. The door slams shut behind me.

"Are you Miri?" she asks.

I wipe at my glasses and turn to see my savior. She's white, with big brown eyes, probably sixty years old, with a long gray braid spiraled into a crown on her head. She's wearing a cashmere sweater set and New Balance sneakers.

"Oh. No, I'm Roz."

"Ah. Well. We're waiting on Miri." She cracks the door

and sticks her head out, peering through the torrential rain. She ducks back in and shrugs. "They sent me to wait here for participants because the buzzer broke, but I doubt she's coming in this rain. We always lose a few on the first day anyhow. People sign up but don't end up showing. Come on, then."

Her voice is full of authority so I almost take a step after her. "Sorry, I . . . I'm not signed up." I actually don't know what this is.

This is an apartment building, no?

She stops and beckons me. "It's raining. At least come sit. I think there are towels in the classroom."

As I follow her down the hallway (hardwood floors and a mop bucket off to one side, a cheerily flickering line of lights along the wall, rows of doors with nameplates instead of numbers), I see that this is a mixed-use building. We pass a dermatologist's office, a therapist, a door that just says "MR GREG" in all caps and then, finally, on to the only open doorway in the hallway.

She disappears through and I peek in after her. It's bright and merry in there. Ten or so people chatting and milling. Ah. I see. It's a figure-drawing class. They're setting up their easels in a circle, sharpening pencils, flipping gigantic sheets of paper to the clean side. In the middle of the circle is a mid-twenties Asian man in a terrycloth robe to his knees. He's sitting on a wooden platform, leaning on his palms and yawning hugely.

"Miri? Hi, I'm David. The instructor," a man says from next to me in the doorway. He's middle-aged, trim brown beard and friendly eyes, just an inch or two taller than I am.

"No. This is Roz," calls the older woman as she digs through a big set of drawers in the corner. "I'm calling Miri as a no-show."

The man smiles fondly at her. "Esther is our registrar."

"Ah."

Esther pads back to me, hand towel in hand. "Here you go, love."

After a moment's consideration, I pull the packaged frame out from under my sweatshirt, which makes both Esther and the man laugh in surprise. Then I gratefully take the towel and scrunch at my hair, wipe off my soaking wet legs.

"If you wanted to stay and warm up," David, the instructor, says, "you could take the class. We're not at capacity, you know."

"Oh." I'm completely befuddled by this suggestion.

Doesn't he know I'm a cook? That I haven't picked up a pencil to draw since middle school? Doesn't he see that I'm soaking wet and need to go home and change into my fuzzy slippers that go almost up to my knees? And most important, doesn't he know that I'm only here because I'm creeping on my husband's new address and under no circumstances was I actually supposed to *enter* this building?!

He's looking at me expectantly and all I've said is "Oh."

I try again. "Um . . ."

His eyebrows rise in a friendly way. "Lots of beginners in the class."

"Right."

"'Scuse me," says a deep voice at my back.

I jump to the side and a man who, I shit you not, looks exactly like Aladdin, is grinning, dripping wet, peering down at me from under a raincoat.

"Sorry!"

"No worries." He gives me a lingering, seashell-white smile, friendly eyes, and floppy black hair. As he walks past me, he pulls his hood down and I get a whiff of his scent. He smells like Louis Vuitton's rich Gen Z grandson.

"Lauro!"

"Laur-OH!"

"It's my man."

The class has perked up immensely at this man's presence and he makes his rounds, bussing cheeks, giving daps, and finally one enormous hug to the model who doesn't seem to mind embracing a sopping wet raincoat even though he's clearly completely naked underneath his ratty robe.

"So, Roz." David checks his watch and then looks down at my feet, neatly lined up in the hallway, while my head peeks around the doorway. "In or out. Class is about to start, and we keep the door closed during session out of respect for our model."

"I'm not signed up . . ." I say again, uselessly, as if it will stop time and prevent any sort of decision from needing to be made. And I could just drip on this doorstep into infinity, enjoying the vibes and risking nothing.

"First one's free." He winks but then furrows his brow. "I mean, not literally. But if you decide to sign up you can pay later."

"I don't have any supplies . . ."

"We have plenty extra lying around."

"I'm soaking wet . . ."

"Live with it?" he suggests and I laugh.

It looks so warm and bright in there. The people, each very different from the next, seem to know one another well. The air is rich with charcoal and wax and paper. This is how some people spend an early Friday evening in May.

My toe hits one wet corner of the packaged frame resting on the floor and it tips, jabbing into my shin. I wince and gather it up, clutching it against my chest.

"I really have to go," I whisper.

"Sure," the man says easily. "In that case . . ." He steps back into the room, grips the door, and closes it most of the way. At the last second, he pokes his head back out and catches my eye. "I'm closing this, but door's always open. I mean, again, not literally, because like I said we keep it closed during class. But if you want to come back. Come back. Okay. Home safe."

And then the door is closed in my face and the hallway dims accordingly.

And then I walk back down the hallway toward the rain. Because the framed photo is beating like a heart on its last few pumps. Because I really don't think I can try something new when everything old in my life is dying.

I waited a week before I asked Raff about her. ~~No, wait, I should tell about the night I first saw her. But we weren't together yet. So maybe that part doesn't matter. Whatever.~~ I waited a week. That's probably what she would say was the important part.

(What do you think is the most important part?)

I really, honestly, don't know how to tell this story. It's supposed to be the story of how we met, right? That's the assignment.

(Start at the beginning.)

Which beginning? She's my wife. The story of who I am to her, the story of what kind of husband I am, all that starts decades before I even met her.

(Start anywhere!) (Just start!) (There's no wrong answer!)

Okay. Anywhere. Okay. Well. Have you ever met someone for the first time and it seems like you've already known them for a really long time?

I spent a week trying to figure out where I knew her from. And then I figured it out.

(Where?) (Where was it?!)

Nowhere. I didn't know her from anywhere. I just . . . I just recognized her. Remember that sweater I talked about last week? The one I couldn't describe? Flower or whatever? Well, she walked in, wearing that sweater, and her hair and that smile and I just . . . recognized her. That's the best I can describe it.

I saw her and thought, here comes my wife.

COURTESY OF AUTUMN LAYNE PHOTOGRAPHY

CARA BASTONE, the author of *Ready or Not,* lives and writes in Brooklyn with her husband, kids, and an almost-goldendoodle. Her goal with her work is to find the swoon in ordinary love stories. She's been a fan of the romance genre since she found a grocery bag filled with her grandmother's old Harlequin romances when she was in high school. She's a fangirl for pretzel sticks, long walks through Prospect Park, and love stories featuring men who aren't hobbled by their own masculinity.

Instagram: @carabastone

ABOUT THE TYPE

This book was set in Goudy Old Style, a typeface designed by Frederic William Goudy (1865–1947). Goudy began his career as a bookkeeper, but devoted the rest of his life to the pursuit of "recognized quality" in a printing type.

Goudy Old Style was produced in 1914 and was an instant bestseller for the foundry. It has generous curves and smooth, even color. It is regarded as one of Goudy's finest achievements.

Books Driven by the Heart

Sign up for our newsletter
and find more you'll love:

thedialpress.com

⊙ @THEDIALPRESS

▶ @THEDIALPRESS

Penguin Random House collects and processes your
personal information. See our Notice at Collection
and Privacy Policy at prh.com/notice.